PEG KEHRET

THRILL-OGY

HORROR
AT THE
HAUNTED
HOUSE

DANGER
AT THE
FAIR

TERROR
AT THE
ZOO

SCHOLASTIC INC.

TERROR
AT THE
ZOO

*This book is dedicated, with love and gratitude,
to the women who gave birth to my children.*

Omnibus Edition ISBN 978-0-545-78469-6

12 11 10 9 8 7 6 5 4 3 2 1   14 15 16 17 18 19/0

Printed in the U.S.A.   40

First Scholastic printing, September 2014

Special thanks to
Elaine Bowers, Carol Raitt, Katharyn Gerlich,
Ira and Delaney Gerlich, Carrie Rhodes and Alex Alvord,
and the Woodland Park Zoological Society, Seattle, WA.

1

ELLEN STREATER looked across the yard at Prince, her German shepherd. Silently, she directed her thoughts to him: *Come, Prince. Come to me.* She didn't call his name aloud, or whistle, or clap her hands. She only sent her thoughts.

Prince quit sniffing the grass and turned to look at Ellen.

Come, Prince, she thought again. Then she closed her eyes and imagined Prince walking across the grass toward her.

When she opened her eyes, Prince stood in front of her, wagging his tail.

"Good dog," Ellen said. "What a fine dog." She patted Prince's head for a few moments and then wrote the date, time, her command, and Prince's response in her notebook.

Her experiment was turning out far better than she had expected. The last six times she had called him silently, Prince had responded. Once he even came when he was sitting under the big maple tree, waiting for a squirrel to come down. Prince had been trying all his life to catch a squirrel and was not easily distracted when he saw one. But when Ellen directed him, in her mind, to come, Prince took his eyes from the squirrel and walked straight to Ellen.

Ellen planned to enter her animal communication experiment in the annual All-City Science Fair. Her science teacher had suggested the subject last spring and loaned Ellen a book on animal communication.

Ellen had been skeptical of success, despite the claims in the book, but she had worked on her project all summer, carefully recording her efforts with Prince.

With summer nearly over, Prince frequently obeyed her nonverbal commands to come. Now she wondered if he might be able to understand other thoughts, as well.

She closed her eyes again, focusing all her attention on Prince. *Get your ball*, she thought. *Get your ball.*

"Hey, Ellen!"

Ellen's eyes flew open, startled by her younger brother's loud call.

Corey yelled again. "Mom says to tell you it's time to quit playing with Prince and get ready for dinner."

Ellen glared across the yard at him, her concentration shattered.

From the back porch, she heard her mother scold, "Corey! I could have shouted at Ellen myself. Next time, go out and speak to her quietly."

Prince loped toward the porch, hoping, no doubt, that he was going to get dinner, too. Ellen sighed and started toward the house. She didn't know which irritated her more—Corey's yelling or the fact that her mother had instructed her to quit "playing" with Prince.

Mrs. Streater knew about Ellen's science fair experiment in animal communication. Why did her mother insist on calling it play, as if Ellen were still a little kid talking to her Barbie?

Today, of all days, Ellen thought, I should think Mom would realize that I'm finally mature.

Mature. She liked that word. As she washed her hands for dinner, she decided that this birthday was a turning point. Now that she was twelve years old, she would always act mature.

Maybe after tonight's birthday dinner, her parents would realize that Ellen was no longer their baby girl. Maybe they would treat her like a grown-up, for a change. Maybe they would quit lumping her together with Corey, as if she and her brother were Siamese twins, when he was a mere infant compared to Ellen.

The kids. That's how Ellen's parents always referred to her and Corey. "Let's take the kids to a movie." "Would you kids please clean up your rooms?" "Dinner's ready, kids."

Now that she was twelve (and Corey wouldn't be eight for two more weeks) surely her parents would realize she was no longer one of the kids. She was one of the adults.

"Hello! Where's our birthday girl?"

Ellen smiled as she heard her grandparents arrive. She was certain that Grandma and Grandpa would acknowledge her new mature status by giving her an appropriately adult birthday present. Grandma and Grandpa always seemed to know exactly what Ellen wanted, even when she didn't know herself.

Maybe they would give her a makeup kit or one of those big scarves that were so fashionable now. At least she could count on Grandma and Grandpa not to buy her a doll or some kiddie game, like the stupid one Corey wanted for his birthday.

Ellen hugged her grandparents. She noticed that they didn't carry a wrapped package. They put a large white envelope on the table where the other birthday presents were.

It's a gift certificate, Ellen thought. Maybe they bought me a make-over at a fashionable beauty salon. I'll get my hair styled and my nails manicured and I'll be able to pass for fourteen, if I want to.

The more she thought about it, the more she was positive that's what the envelope contained. She had been trying to grow her brown hair long enough to wear it in a French braid but meanwhile, it just flapped around her ears, like fringe on a blanket. A good styling salon would change that. She would be gorgeous. Well, maybe not gorgeous—even the best salons can't work miracles—but anything was bound to be better than her hair the way it was.

She decided to open the envelope last, to save Grandma and Grandpa's surprise for the very end. The grand finale.

After dinner and the birthday cake, and after she had opened a gift from her parents and one from Corey, she finally reached for the envelope from Grandma and Grandpa.

As she did, Grandma said, "Before you open that, we need to tell you that it is a joint birthday gift for you and Corey."

"You mean," Corey said, "what's in the envelope is half mine?"

"That's right."

Ellen could not believe her ears. A joint present with Corey? That infant? How could this be? If her present was something Corey would like, it would be way too babyish for her. Especially now that she was mature. And what about her hair? She tried to hide her disappointment.

"Do I get to see it today, too?" Corey asked. "Even though my birthday is still two weeks away?"

"Yes. We didn't want to make Ellen wait, so you get your gift early this year, Corey."

Ellen forced a smile as she opened the envelope. She didn't want to seem ungrateful, no matter how much she wished they had given her a present of her own instead of something to share with Corey.

There was a certificate inside the envelope. "What's it say?" Corey cried. "Hurry up and read it!"

THIS CERTIFICATE IS GOOD FOR AN
OVERNIGHT CAMP-OUT
AT THE WOODLAND PARK ZOO

Corey, who was leaning over her shoulder, read the words out loud and then let out a whoop.

"No kidding?" Ellen said. "We get to stay overnight at the zoo?"

Ellen loved the zoo. Grandma and Grandpa had given

her some good presents before but never anything like this. She forgot all about her hair.

"The zoo is closed at night," Corey said. "How will we get in? Are you sure they'll let us camp there? What if the zoo people call the police and have us arrested for trespassing on private property and what if we get taken to jail and locked up with the drug addicts and . . ."

"Whoa," Grandpa said, holding up his hand to silence Corey. Ellen knew Grandpa wasn't being rude. Sometimes you have to interrupt Corey when he gets started on one of his what-if stories. Otherwise he'd babble on all night.

"The camp-out was one of the auction items this year," Grandma explained.

Ellen knew which auction she meant. It was a charity auction, an annual event which benefited several community organizations. Grandma and Grandpa went to the auction every year and they always bought some unusual item donated by the zoological society.

Once they paid four hundred dollars for the chance to give an elephant a bath. With the elephant's trainer supervising, Ellen and Corey got to help Grandpa and Grandma wash Hugo, a gentle old African elephant. Another time, Grandma and Grandpa went fishing in the moat inside the lion exhibit. They were on the other side of the moat from the lions but still, it was pretty exciting.

Last year they bought a portrait with a python. Ellen thought that purchase was gross but Grandma and Grandpa had their picture taken with a humongous python draped around their shoulders, and sent prints to all their friends.

"We're going with you," Grandpa said. "The camp-out is for four people."

"When is it?" Ellen asked. "When do we go?"

"September tenth. Since your folks will be in San Francisco that week and we were going to stay with you anyway, we thought it would be the perfect time to do the camp-out."

"September tenth is Friday," Mrs. Streater said. "Dad and I will get in late that night. We'll come to the zoo in the morning to take pictures."

Corey scratched himself under both arms and made chattering sounds. "I want to sleep in the monkey house," he said.

Where he belongs, thought Ellen.

"The zoological society will decide where we sleep," Grandpa said. "Wherever it is, I'm sure we will have quite an adventure."

"Thanks, Grandpa and Grandma," Ellen said, as she gave them each a hug. Her smile was genuine now. Even though it wasn't a salon make-over, it certainly wasn't a babyish gift, either. Her parents still liked to go to the zoo. Lots of adults do. An overnight camp-out at the zoo would be wonderful, even if Corey was there, too. She went to the calendar and drew a big red circle around September tenth.

2

Tony HAYMES waited until a woman with two small children entered the secondhand store; then he went in, too. Kids would distract the clerk. Tony didn't know if the story of his escape from prison was on the news yet but the last thing he needed was for someone to recognize him.

He went straight to the housewares section and examined several trays of kitchen utensils before he spotted what he wanted: a sturdy butcher knife. Tony felt the six-inch blade with his thumb. Good. It was sharp and strong.

While the salesclerk helped the woman shopper find shoes that would fit her children, Tony slipped the knife up the sleeve of his jacket and left the store.

Too bad he'd lost the first knife, the one he stole from the prison kitchen, when he jumped. The rest of his plan had worked perfectly. He had crawled through the secret hole he'd cut in the roof of his cell, then slithered across the rafters in the attic and out onto the roof.

The jump from the roof to the top of the prison wall had been the big gamble. For weeks, Tony worried that he would miss, that he would fall and break a leg and be carried back inside the prison walls on a stretcher.

But September tenth was his lucky day. He had planned the escape for his birthday, thinking it would bring him good fortune and it did.

He didn't fall. All of the knee bends and push-ups in his cell, night after night, had resulted in a lean body with powerful muscles. When his hands hit the top of the wall he had swung easily over the top. Except for losing the knife, it was a perfect leap.

He dropped to the ground, landed running, and didn't quit until his breath came in such painful gasps that he thought his chest would burst if he didn't stop.

After that, everything went his way.

The clothesline was an incredible piece of luck. He had planned to look for a do-it-yourself laundromat near one of the motels on the outskirts of town. People often put their clothes in the machines and leave them unattended while they go somewhere to eat or shop. He could help himself from one of the clothes dryers.

But as he walked toward the city, staying in the ditch of the old, seldom-used road that had long since been made obsolete by a freeway, he saw a white farmhouse. In the yard, rows of clothes fluttered dry in the breeze.

He circled the house and approached it from behind. A shaggy yellow dog barked once from the back porch; Tony flattened himself in the grass.

The dog came closer, its ears back.

"Go away," Tony hissed. "Scram! Get out of here."

The dog gave a low growl. Tony hated animals and they always seemed to sense his feelings and return them. In the grass, his finger closed around a small stone. Tony flung the stone at the dog. It hit the top of the dog's head and bounced off. The dog yelped. It turned, put its tail between its legs, and slunk back to the porch.

Tony stayed low in the grass a few minutes, in case someone came to see why the dog had barked. His ears strained to hear possible footsteps.

Nothing.

Slowly, he raised his head and looked in all directions. The dog was curled up beside the back door; it appeared to be asleep. Tony saw no one and heard nothing. He stood and walked quickly to the clothesline. He jerked the clothespins loose with one hand and grabbed the clothes with the other. A faded pair of overalls. A bright red shirt. A khaki jacket.

Later, when he was safely away from the house, he hid in a clump of bushes and changed into his new clothes. The sleeves of the red shirt were an inch too long, so he rolled them partway up. The overalls were a bit big, too, but overalls are always loose fitting. The length was just right. Whoever owned those overalls must be very close to Tony's height of six feet one inch.

He found a large rock, dug a hole in the dirt beside it, and put his prison clothes in the hole. Then he sat on the ground and, using his feet, pushed the rock over the hole.

Dressed in his red shirt and overalls, with the khaki jacket tied around his waist, Tony returned to the road.

This time he didn't stay low. He hiked in plain sight along the shoulder and when he heard a vehicle approach, he boldly put out his thumb.

An old pickup whizzed past, then slammed on its brakes and backed up. A young man, seventeen or eighteen years old, was driving; two girls of about the same age were with him. The girls giggled as they looked at Tony.

"How far are you going?" Tony asked.

"Seattle," the driver said. "If you don't mind riding in the back end, hop in." The girls giggled again.

Tony put one foot on the back bumper and swung his leg over the tailgate. It was perfect. He could lie down, where nobody could see him. And he didn't have to talk to anyone, didn't have to make up a story about who he was or where he came from or where he was going. By tomorrow, the kids in the pickup wouldn't even remember what he looked like.

The truck roared off again. Tony cushioned his head on his arms and tried to brace himself when the truck hit rough spots. Soon the bumpiness ended and, peering over the top of the truck bed, Tony saw they had reached the freeway on-ramp. It was smooth riding all the way to Seattle.

At the first red light after the truck had left the freeway, Tony hopped out. The three people in the pickup were putting a new tape in the tape deck. They didn't notice when he left.

Two hours later, Tony slipped the knife up the sleeve of his jacket and walked out of the secondhand store.

He had dreamed of this day for months, ever since he was convicted of armed robbery. No way was Tony

Haymes going to stay locked in prison. Forget it. Old Tony had plans for his life and they didn't include years behind bars. No way.

This time, the cops wouldn't find him. This time, luck was with him. First the clothes. Then those kids in the pickup. And now the knife. Everything was going exactly the way he had hoped. Even better. September tenth was definitely his lucky day.

He walked briskly away from the secondhand store. Next he needed to find a safe place to spend the night. Not a room. Even if he had money to rent a room, he didn't want to talk to any room clerk.

A park bench would do, or a tree to lie under. The weather was mild for September and it wouldn't be the first time Tony had slept all night on the ground. But it had to be someplace where he could be sure no cop would come nosing around. The last thing he needed was for a cop to think he was a drunken wino and try to take him in.

Tony sauntered up the street, sizing up doorways, watching for back alleys.

Ahead, a large sign said, WOODLAND PARK ZOO. Bingo.

That's where he would spend the night. A zoo would have dozens of hiding places and no people around at night.

He crossed the zoo parking lot and watched the entrance. Three elderly women bought tickets and went in.

Tony frowned. The ticket booths were the only entrances and he didn't have any money. Brick walls extended on either side of the booths and when the wall ended, chain link fence began.

A group of schoolchildren and their teacher came out of the zoo through an exit turnstile. The turnstile was like a revolving door and the kids laughed and hollered as they tried to see how fast they could push it.

Rowdy little monsters, Tony thought. They reminded him of the kid who had tipped off the cops and got Tony arrested. Who would have guessed that a ten-year-old boy, watching out his bedroom window, would get the license plate number of Tony's car and turn him in? If it hadn't been for that lousy kid, Tony would never have done time. Tony hated kids even more than he hated animals.

Well, his time in prison was finished now and they'd never catch Tony Haymes again. Never.

A bus pulled up and forty or fifty people got off. On the side of the bus large green letters spelled out, CLASS ACT TOURS. The people all wore round green buttons. A man in a green jacket headed straight for the ticket booth. The other people milled around, talking and reading colorful brochures.

"This way, please," the man in the green jacket called. "The zoo closes in just two hours, so we need to hurry." He went through the gate and the people in the group trailed after him.

And that's when Tony saw it, lying right on the curb beside the tour bus: one of the round green buttons. Trying to look casual, he strolled toward the bus, picked up the button, and walked away. The button said, Class

Act Tours. As he hurried toward the gate, he pinned the button on the front of his overalls.

The woman in the ticket booth didn't pay any attention to him as he followed the rest of the group into the zoo. She only looked at his Class Act Tours button.

Once inside, it was easy to leave the group. They were busy consulting their maps of the zoo and deciding which way to go first. No one noticed Tony, as he slipped away.

The Indian summer sun glowed golden through the leaves as Tony walked past the Elephant Forest, the Feline House, and the African Savanna.

I did it, he thought triumphantly. I'm free. There wasn't a cop in the world who would look for him in the zoo.

3

ELLEN looked at the clock again. "Where *are* they?" she said, as she walked to the window for the third time in five minutes. "Even if traffic was bad, they should have been here by now."

"What if their plane crashed?" Corey said. "Or maybe it was hijacked." He began to talk fast, the way he always did when he was excited by some story he was making up. "What if the plane took off on time and then a band of terrorists threatened to blow everyone up if the pilot didn't fly them all to—" Corey hesitated, trying to decide the worst possible place.

"Stop it," said Ellen. "You sound like you want Mom and Dad to get hijacked."

"I would have them escape," Corey said. "I would have them trick the hijackers and save all the people and get their pictures in the paper. Besides, it was just a story."

Ellen sighed. Her brother was always making up stories; the least little thing set him off. Her parents were sure he was going to be a famous writer some day.

She snapped on the television. That was the trouble with Corey's stories. They always seemed plausible. There was just enough truth in them to make people think that the events he described might really have happened.

She flipped from channel to channel. If an airplane headed for Seattle had been hijacked, the TV stations would be covering the story. Reporters would be broadcasting from the airport. Instead, there were the usual talk shows. Relieved, she turned the TV off.

"I'm going to call the airport and see if the plane landed on time," she said. She took her parents' itinerary off the kitchen bulletin board and read which airline and flight number.

"I'm sorry," she was told, "that flight has been delayed. I'm not sure what time it will arrive."

Ellen hung up. "Their plane isn't in yet," she said.

"But what about the zoo?" Corey cried. "Mrs. Caruthers will be waiting for us." He plopped down on the sofa and socked one of the pillows. "Mom and Dad should have come home sooner," he said. "Grandpa shouldn't have taken Grandma to the doctor today."

"It isn't Mom and Dad's fault if their plane doesn't arrive on time," Ellen said, "and Grandma can't help it that her leg hurt."

Corey punched the pillow again.

Two weeks ago, Grandma broke her leg; she was in a cast. Grandma and Grandpa had still come to stay while Mr. and Mrs. Streater were in San Francisco, but they couldn't do the camp-out. It was hard for Grandma to get around on her crutches and sleeping in a tent was out of the question.

Since Grandpa didn't want to do the camp-out without Grandma, Ellen's parents had rearranged their schedule to catch an earlier flight. They were supposed to be home in time to pick up Ellen and Corey and get to the zoo by five.

That's when they were supposed to meet Mrs. Caruthers, the representative of the zoological society. She would have their picnic supper and would show them the tent where they were going to sleep.

Ellen looked at the clock again. It was almost 4:30. She wondered what her parents would want them to do.

Corey's bottom lip trembled. "We're going to miss the camp-out," he said.

I'm the adult, Ellen thought. I have to be mature, to take charge. "We'll go to the zoo," she said. "Mom and Dad know what time we're supposed to be there. They'll probably assume that Grandpa will drive us to the zoo and they'll go straight to the zoo from the airport. We'll take their sleeping bags with us and meet them there."

"How are we going to get there? It's too late to take a bus."

"Maybe Mr. Zither will drive us." Mr. Zither was the Streaters' next-door neighbor.

"Mr. Zither isn't home. I saw him leave."

Ellen dialed Mr. Zither's number, just in case he had returned. There was no answer.

"I told you he wasn't home," Corey said, as Ellen hung

up the phone. "How come nobody ever believes me?"

Because you're always telling stories, Ellen thought. But all she said was, "I'm going to call a cab."

Corey hopped off the sofa and threw the pillow in the air. "Get one of the limousine cabs," he said. "A white one. They're about a hundred feet long. When we drive up, everyone will stare and think we're TV actors. Maybe someone will ask me for my autograph."

"Limos are too expensive," Ellen said.

After she called the cab, she took money, to pay the cab driver, from the "emergency envelope" that her mother kept in a kitchen drawer. She had never taken money from it before but she felt sure she was doing the right thing. Grandma and Grandpa had spent several hundred dollars for the zoo camp-out, and Mrs. Caruthers was waiting for them. It would be terrible not to show up.

She hoped she was guessing correctly that her parents would go straight to the zoo. What if they didn't? They might think that Grandpa would go on the camp-out, in which case they would come home to be with Grandma, instead of going to the zoo.

Prince whined and sat by the door.

"Take Prince out, while I leave a note," Ellen said. "Grandma and Grandpa will probably eat dinner out after they see the doctor. They might not get back until late."

While Corey took Prince outside, Ellen wrote a note, just in case her parents came home instead of going directly to the zoo.

Dear Mom and Dad:

We are waiting for you at the zoo. We have your sleeping bags. We took a cab because Grandma had trouble with her cast and Grandpa took her to the doctor to have it checked. Grandma says to have fun on the camp-out and not to worry about her.

Love,
Ellen

She placed the note on top of the telephone answering machine. Her parents always checked the answering machine as soon as they got home, to see if there were any messages. Ellen believed her parents would go straight to the zoo from the airport, but if they didn't, they would find her note and go to the zoo then.

As Corey and Prince came in the back door, the cab honked in front of the house. Corey dashed outside. Ellen gathered sleeping bags in her arms, locked the front door, and left.

Mrs. Caruthers was pacing outside the zoo's south gate, where they were supposed to meet her, when the cab pulled up. "Thank heaven you're here," she cried. "Just before I left home to come to meet you, I had a call from my son-in-law. My daughter has gone to the hospital to have her baby."

Ellen paid the driver and he helped them unload their sleeping bags.

"Where are your parents?" Mrs. Caruthers asked.

"They'll meet us here," Ellen said. "Their flight from San Francisco was late."

"Oh," Mrs. Caruthers said. "Oh, dear." She bit her bottom lip. "The tent is all set up for you, in the North Meadow. I was hoping . . ."

"You don't need to stay with us," Ellen said. "We'll wait inside the gate for Mom and Dad and we know where the North Meadow is. We've been to the zoo lots of times."

"I can't leave you here alone," Mrs. Caruthers said.

"Mom and Dad will be here any minute," Ellen said.

"Maybe your daughter will have twins," Corey said. Mrs. Caruthers's eyes widened. "Maybe even triplets! If she has triplets, she'll win lots of prizes, like diaper service and cases of baby food. She might even get her picture in the paper, with all her babies."

"This is my first grandchild," Mrs. Caruthers said. She sounded a trifle breathless.

"Then you should hurry along to the hospital," Ellen said. "We don't want you to miss the birth of your grandchild—"

"Or grandchildren," Corey interjected.

"Because of us," Ellen finished.

"I'll have someone else wait with you until your parents arrive." Mrs. Caruthers led the way to the ticket booth. "Your tent is on the far side of the North Meadow," she said. "I'll get a map for you from the ticket booth."

"We don't need a map," Corey said. "The North Meadow's that way." He pointed. "The monkeys are that way, and . . ."

"There are flashlights in the tent, and a first-aid kit and an ice chest containing your picnic supper."

"I hope there's plenty of dessert," said Corey.

Ellen poked him in the ribs with her elbow and said, "Shh."

"The night security guard will pass the North Meadow around midnight and again at three. If you need anything, he'll help." She stopped at the ticket booth. "These are the campers," she said to the woman in the booth, as Ellen and Corey proceeded into the zoo. The ticket seller nodded without looking up from the novel she was reading. "They're going to wait here with you until their parents arrive."

Mrs. Caruthers stepped inside the ticket booth and picked up the telephone. "I'll call the zoo office," she said to Ellen and Corey, "so they know what's happened."

"Here come Mom and Dad!" cried Corey.

"Thank goodness," said Mrs. Caruthers, as she hung up the phone.

"Where?" said Ellen.

"There," said Corey, as he pointed to the far left side of the parking lot. "They just drove in. They're parking the car over there, behind that bus."

"In that case," said Mrs. Caruthers, "I'll be on my way. Tell your parents I'm sorry I had to rush off." She patted the ticket person's shoulder. "We don't need your help, after all," she said.

"We'll read the paper tomorrow," Corey said, "in case it's twins. Or triplets."

Mrs. Caruthers gulped. "Have a wonderful time tonight," she said, as she turned and dashed toward the right end of the parking lot. Seconds later, she drove out of the lot.

"You shouldn't have upset Mrs. Caruthers like that,"

Ellen said. "She's probably worried enough about her daughter, without you cackling about twins."

Corey looked innocent. "Maybe her daughter *will* have twins," he said. "Or triplets."

"People who are going to have more than one baby know it ahead of time," Ellen said.

"Always?"

"Almost always." Ellen peered across the rows of cars in the parking lot. "I don't see Mom and Dad," she said.

Corey looked at his shoes and didn't answer.

Ellen scowled at her brother. "Corey Streater! Did you make that up, about seeing them?"

Corey put his finger to his lips. He took Ellen's arm and led her away from the ticket booth. "Mrs. Caruthers was going to put that dopey ticket lady in charge of us," he whispered.

"You lied to Mrs. Caruthers."

"She really wanted to go," Corey said. "I just made it so she wouldn't feel bad about leaving us. And Mom and Dad will get here any minute. You said so yourself."

"Still, it was wrong to pretend you saw them."

Corey hung his head. "I guess it was," he admitted. "I'm sorry."

"You should be."

Straight ahead was a partially enclosed viewing area where the zoo visitors could watch the African animals. Ellen and Corey carried their gear to a wooden bench and sat down. "We might as well watch the animals while we wait for Mom and Dad," Ellen said. "We can take turns going back to the gate, so we don't miss them."

"Let's look through the telescopes," Corey said, pointing at one of the coin-operated metal telescopes that were mounted on each side of the enclosure.

"They cost a quarter and I don't have any money."

"Didn't you get change from the cab?"

"I let the driver keep it. You're supposed to tip the cab driver."

"Look," Corey cried. "Giraffes! Maybe the giraffes sprout wings at night and fly all around the zoo and we'll jump on their backs and ride them."

For once Corey's wild imagination didn't irritate her. She was too excited about spending the night at the zoo to be bothered by her brother. Except for his storytelling, he wasn't so bad, for an eight year old. By the time he was mature, like her, maybe he would learn to control his tall tales.

A small child began crying and Ellen went back to the entrance area to see what was wrong. It was a little girl who didn't want to leave the zoo. Her parents kept telling her they'd come again another day but the child sobbed as they carried her through the exit turnstile.

Quite a few people were leaving. Three old women. A young couple. A whole group of people wearing green buttons that said, Class Act Tours. A man in a green jacket hurried the tour group along, calling, "The zoo is closed! The bus leaves in five minutes."

Ellen glanced at the entry again. The ticket booth was empty. She looked out toward the parking area. There was no sign of her parents.

"Maybe they won't show," Corey said. "Maybe their plane crashed and . . ."

"Stop it!"

" . . . and they were the only survivors who weren't hurt and they can't call us because they're busy helping the injured. Mom and Dad will be heroes and get their pictures in the paper."

Ellen had noticed that Corey's stories often ended with the person getting his or her picture in the newspaper.

She wondered whether to wait where they were or go to the North Meadow where they were supposed to camp. She decided to wait awhile longer. Surely her parents would arrive at any moment.

A giraffe nibbled hay that hung from a strap, high in a tree. It always astonished her that such large animals were so graceful. She gazed up at the long, slender neck. *How beautiful you are*, she thought.

The giraffe quit eating and looked down at Ellen. Was it possible that the giraffe had received her message? Without planning to, had she communicated with an animal besides Prince? Maybe she could experiment with the zoo animals while she was here. That would add a new dimension to her science project.

She looked up, directly into the giraffe's big brown eyes. *How beautiful you are.*

"Ellen! Come quick!" Corey's excited cry came from around the corner, out of sight.

She left the enclosed viewing area and hurried along the path toward the sound of his voice. She found him standing on a big rock, pointing in delight. "The zebras," he said, "are doing the hula."

Ellen looked. Two zebras stood in the field, swishing their tails and moving their rear ends back and forth. Probably trying to get rid of flies, Ellen thought.

"At night," Corey said, "all the animals dance. When there are no people watching, all the zebras do the hula. And the bears boogie."

Ellen giggled. Maybe her parents were right; maybe Corey would be a writer some day.

While Ellen watched the zebras wiggle their rear ends, Corey jumped off the rock and disappeared again. Soon he came dashing back. "I found Hugo," he said. "He's just around the corner."

She followed him along the path toward the Elephant Forest.

"There he is," Corey said. "That's him, all right."

Corey was right. The African elephant that they had helped bathe was standing at the edge of the Elephant Forest. Hugo was the zoo's oldest elephant: fifty-nine years old, the same age as Ellen's grandma. They had joked about that with Grandma while they washed him.

"Let's see if we can make Hugo purr," Corey said.

The elephants' trainer had told them that elephants sometimes purr, just the way cats do. "They do it when they're content," the trainer had said, "when they're with someone they trust. It's a low, rumbling purr and you might not be able to hear it."

The trainer also said Hugo liked music. He sang a song to Hugo, hoping to make Hugo purr for Ellen and Corey. Hugo seemed to like the song but he hadn't purred.

Together, Corey and Ellen crossed the path and got as close to the elephant area as they could.

"Hey, Hugo," Corey called. "Some of the zebras learned to hula and they're going to Hollywood to star in a movie."

Hugo rubbed his side against the fence.

Ellen blotted out the sound of Corey's voice and focused all her thoughts on the big elephant.

Hello, Hugo, she said in her mind. *I am your friend. I am glad to see you. You are a magnificent elephant.*

Hugo turned his head and looked at Ellen. His trunk reached out toward her, sniffing the air. His wide ears were flat on either side of his head, like giant wings waiting to spread. Ellen suppressed a giggle. Maybe it's the elephants, not the giraffes, that fly around at night, she thought. Like Dumbo.

"Is he doing it?" Corey said. "Can you hear any purring?"

Ellen heard nothing. But the elephant *did* seem to be staring at her. Was he just curious? Could he possibly remember them, from when they gave him a bath nearly two years ago? Or had he somehow received Ellen's mental message?

She beamed it again. *We are glad to see you, elephant friend.*

"I think he remembers us," Corey said. "Wow! Wait until Mom and Dad hear about this."

The mention of their parents reminded Ellen that they were supposed to be watching the gate. "Come on," she said. "We have to stay by the gate. We don't want to miss Mom and Dad."

She checked the entrance area and then returned to the bench, disappointed to see that the giraffe had moved on. Corey kept wandering down the path, trying to see where the dancing zebras were. Finally, to keep him in sight,

Ellen suggested that they take the sleeping bags to the North Meadow and leave them in the tent.

"Maybe Mom and Dad are already there," Corey said. "If they got here just as the zoo was closing, maybe they went in a different gate and they're waiting for us by the tent."

Ellen didn't point out that Mom and Dad had no way to know where the tent was.

They passed the Family Farm area, where children are allowed to pet donkeys, pigs, and sheep. They passed the orangutans and the gorillas. They passed the Nocturnal House, Ellen's favorite zoo exhibit.

It was always dark inside the Nocturnal House, and visitors stood on the walkway surrounded by glass walls. After their eyes adjusted to the darkness, they could look through the glass to the dimly lit treetops on the other side where owls sat, and possums hung by their tails, and giant bats slowly unfolded their wings. When Ellen was in the Nocturnal House, she always felt as if she were hiding in the trees and spying on the nocturnal animals through a secret peephole.

"We'll still stay, won't we?" Corey said. "Even if Mom and Dad don't come?"

"I don't know." Ellen wasn't quite ready to deal with that possibility.

"We have to," Corey said. "I bet a kid in my class that I was going to spend all night at the zoo tonight and if I don't do it, I'll lose ten dollars."

"Ten dollars! Why did you make such a big bet? Why didn't you bet a nickel or a dime?"

"Because I knew I would win." He kicked a pebble and sent it skittering down the path ahead of them. "I don't even have ten dollars," he admitted. "I'll have it on Monday, though, when I win the bet. I should have tried to bet with a whole bunch of kids. If lots of kids had bet that I wasn't sleeping at the zoo tonight, I could collect tons of money on Monday." They caught up with the pebble and he kicked it again. "I should have tried to bet with at least twenty kids. Maybe even thirty."

"I doubt there are twenty kids in your school who would be stupid enough to make a ten-dollar bet," Ellen said, as they approached the North Meadow.

Corey spotted the tent. "There it is," he yelled, as he dropped the two sleeping bags he was carrying and dashed across the meadow. Seconds later, he emerged from the tent, calling, "They aren't in here."

Ellen had known they wouldn't be. When Mom and Dad got to the zoo, they would come to the south gate, as instructed, even if it was late.

She bent to pick up the sleeping bags that Corey had dropped. As she did, she glimpsed a flash of red through the trees. For an instant, she thought it was a person, someone wearing a red coat or a red shirt. But when she turned to get a better look, no one was there.

Probably a red leaf, Ellen thought. A bright autumn leaf, falling from one of the trees.

4

DUSK settled over the meadow. A single star glimmered low in the darkening sky.

Star light, star bright, first star I've seen tonight. The old chant ran through Ellen's mind. *I wish I may, I wish I might, have the wish I wish tonight.*

She closed her eyes briefly. *I wish Mom and Dad would get here.*

She opened the flap of the tent and peeked in. Corey was rummaging in the ice chest.

"Sandwiches," he announced. "And apples and brownies. Let's eat the brownies first."

"We can eat later," she said. "We need to get back to the gate so we don't miss Mom and Dad. They're probably waiting for us."

"What if they aren't there?"

"If they aren't, we'll call Grandpa and Grandma."

"They won't make us come home, will they?"

She knew he was worried about his ten-dollar bet. "I have no idea what they'll say," she said, although she was certain that her grandparents would do exactly that. Most likely, Grandpa and Grandma would come immediately and take them home. Unless Corey could talk Grandpa into staying here overnight and leaving Grandma home by herself. She was sure Corey would try.

"Where are you going to find a telephone?"

"I saw one when we came. It's just on the other side of the ticket booth, near where the taxi stopped."

They started back, past the Nocturnal House. "I want to go in the marsh," Corey said, "and see where the cranes sleep."

Ellen hesitated. The marsh, she knew, was at the corner of the zoo, near the parking lot. She supposed they could go that way and then take the outside path back to the entrance. It wouldn't be much out of the way.

When they reached the Family Farm, they left the main path and went toward the marsh. As they drew near the Animal Health Care building, Ellen thought she heard voices.

She ran to the building and tried the door. It was locked. She knocked loudly. No one came. She stood there for a moment, listening and waiting, but she heard nothing more.

"Hurry up," Corey said. "Maybe the cranes play secret games at night, like duck, duck, gray duck or wingtip tag."

When they reached the first of the wire doors that led into the marsh area, it was locked.

"We can't go in," Corey wailed. "Somebody locked the door."

"Probably the security guard," Ellen said. Somehow she felt better, knowing the guard was at the zoo, taking care of his duties.

Instead of taking the outer path, Ellen retraced her steps and led Corey past the Animal Health Care building again. She could swear she had heard someone talking there. She knocked at the door again. There was no answer.

"The light is out now," Corey said.

"What light?"

"Before when we were here, I could see light under the door. Now I can't."

Then someone *had* been inside. More than one person, if she'd heard voices. Why hadn't they come to the door when she knocked?

"Cross your fingers that Mom and Dad are waiting for us," she said.

As they approached the entrance area, Corey said, "Let's tell Mom and Dad that they missed all the excitement. Let's say a buffalo got loose and it was stampeding down this path, right toward our tent. And you and I waved our arms and got its attention and then we talked to it and got it all calmed down and put it back where it belongs."

Ellen agreed, knowing Corey would do it whether she said yes or not.

Corey didn't get to tell his buffalo story.

As they approached the zoo entrance, Ellen could see that no one was there. She tried not to let Corey see her disappointment. When she made the decision to come to the zoo alone, she had been certain that Mom and Dad would arrive shortly. Now she was no longer sure that she had done the right thing.

"It's lucky for us I always carry money for a phone call," Ellen said. She took off her left shoe and pulled on the piece of tape that kept the quarter from sliding around.

"You said you didn't have any money," Corey complained.

"This is for emergency phone calls only. Mom told me that when she put it in my shoe."

She put her shoe back on, stood up, and followed Corey toward the entrance walkway.

At exactly the same instant, they saw it. Metal fencing completely blocked both the ticket booth walkways where people entered the zoo. The fencing had been lowered from the ceiling. Ellen peered through the fencing at the telephone.

"We could go out the exit turnstile and call," Corey said, "but how would we get back in?"

"We won't. But we have to call and tell Grandma and Grandpa that Mom and Dad haven't come."

"Maybe we can climb backward through the turnstile," Corey said.

They walked to the right, toward the turnstile. When they reached it, Ellen stopped and stared. The turnstile was also blocked by a heavy metal gate.

"It must slide into place after everyone has left for the night," Ellen said.

Corey pushed on the gate but it didn't budge. "It's locked," he said. "Mom and Dad can't get in."

And we can't get out, Ellen thought. Where were her parents? Even with a delayed flight, they should have reached the zoo by now. Had Corey's terrible story been a premonition? Had the plane been hijacked? Had it crashed and burned?

She pushed the negative thoughts out of her mind. Her mother always said there was no point worrying because 99 percent of the things we worry about never happen.

"What if Mom and Dad came and they couldn't get in so they went home?" Corey said.

"If they did, they found our note and know where we are and they'll make arrangements to get in. They're probably calling someone from the zoo right now."

"Mrs. Caruthers isn't home," Corey said. "Too bad."

He didn't sound like he thought it was too bad. He sounded like he was glad his parents might have a hard time getting into the zoo.

Ellen frowned at him. He was probably concocting all sorts of wild stories about what happened during the zoo night camp-out. When his friends found out that his parents weren't here, they would believe anything Corey made up.

As if to confirm Ellen's suspicions, Corey added, "Mom and Dad would make us go to sleep. This way we can stay up all night and have lots of adventures."

"Aren't you even worried about Mom and Dad?" Ellen said crossly.

Corey shrugged. "We can't do anything about it, so why waste time worrying?"

She couldn't argue with his logic.

"The security guard must have a telephone," Ellen said. "I wonder where his office is."

"I don't know. Let's go eat; I'm starving."

Ellen agreed. There must be other telephones; maybe they would find one on their way to the tent. If not, it would be best to stay there and watch for the security guard. They would tell him what had happened. He knew someone was camping in the meadow so he might even come before midnight.

Ellen's stomach growled. Since she and Corey were apparently going to spend at least part of the night alone in the zoo, they might as well go ahead and enjoy the picnic.

It was dark now. Even with her flashlight on, Ellen could see only a few feet ahead of her. The giant trees that were so magnificent in the sunlight, now seemed twisted and sinister.

Ellen shivered. She wished she hadn't left her sweater in the tent. She wished she could find a telephone. Most of all, she wished she had stayed home.

"Let's take the path the other way," Corey said. "We'll still come to the tent and we might see mountain goats tap-dancing. We can stand on the big rocks and the flashlight can be our spotlight, like we're in a theater."

Ellen wondered how Corey could be so unconcerned about their plight. How could he think about dancing goats when they were locked in the zoo all alone?

"It's much longer to walk that way," she said. "We're going straight back to the tent."

"After they tap-dance, they'll do ballet."

"Sure they will. The ducks are probably doing *Swan Lake* right now."

Corey missed her sarcastic tone. "Maybe the mountain goats will fly, too." He grinned at her. "What if ALL the animals sprout wings at night and nobody knows it?" He put his hand in his armpits and, moving his elbows up and down like wings, he galloped down the path.

I might as well talk to the moon, Ellen thought, as she shook her head and started after him. Dancing zebras. Flying goats. What would he think of next?

Moments later, Corey rushed back to her. "Somebody's up there," he whispered, pointing at the path ahead. "And he's trying to break into the little store."

"It's the security person that Mrs. Caruthers told us about. Good. He's probably making sure everything is locked properly." She was glad they had found the security guard. He would take them to a telephone. Maybe he even carried a portable phone with him.

Corey grabbed her arm, forcing her to stop walking. "He isn't checking the locks," he insisted. "He has a tool in his hand and he's trying to pry open a window."

Ellen scowled. "If this is one of your stories and you're trying to scare me, you'd better quit right now," she said.

"No! It's true, I swear it."

Something in Corey's voice made her believe him.

"Where is he?" she whispered. "How far ahead of us?"

"Across from the Elephant Forest. It's the snack shop where we bought popcorn last time we came."

"Did he see you?"

Corey shook his head, no.

"You're sure?"

"Positive. I saw him from behind and I didn't make any noise. I came to tell you right away."

Ellen turned and started in the other direction. "We're going back to our tent," she said.

Corey didn't follow her.

"Come on," she hissed.

"I'm going to spy on the zoo man," he said.

"What? Don't be an idiot."

"Maybe he's a crook. Maybe he steals things from the zoo at night and nobody knows it. If we see him do it, we can tell Mrs. Caruthers." The words came faster. "The police will ask us questions. We'll be detectives. We'll be heroes! We'll get our pictures in the paper."

"If he's a crook, we're going to keep out of his way. Now, come with me."

Corey stayed where he was. "Dad always says when someone is doing something wrong, people should take a stand. He says everyone is scared to get involved."

Ellen hesitated. Corey was right; Dad did say that.

"The zoo man won't see us," Corey said. "We'll stay on the other side of the path. There are trees and bushes to hide in. All we have to do is watch, to see what he does. That's all. And then tomorrow morning we can tell Mrs. Caruthers what we saw."

Ellen switched her flashlight off. Silently, they rounded the curve in the path, staying close to the right-hand edge, near the rhododendrons. As they came to a cleared area that contained a picnic table, Corey stopped and pointed.

Ellen squinted in the dim light. On the other side of the path, about fifty feet ahead, she could make out the dark outline of a building. She knew it was the food building, where her family often bought a treat when they visited the zoo.

She heard a noise like someone hammering lightly on wood. When her eyes focused in the direction of the noise, she saw the outline of a man. He stood at the side of the building, beside the wooden panels which open to make a pass-through counter.

More noise. Corey was right. The man was breaking into the food stand. The panel was probably easier to force open than the door.

Ellen, with Corey beside her, crouched low beside the bushes and watched. She couldn't see exactly what the man was doing but she saw movement and she heard the wooden panel creak.

A light went on inside the food stand. The panel was raised up and hooked to the roof overhang. Through the opening, she could see him clearly now as he pulled out drawers and slammed them shut again. He picked up a bag of potato chips, ripped off one end, and began to eat.

"Details," whispered Corey.

Ellen put her finger to her mouth, warning him to keep quiet. She knew what he meant, though. For awhile, Corey's stories had centered on a make-believe detective who always astounded the police by remembering every detail of the villain's description.

Ellen stared at the man. He looked tall, although it was

hard to be sure when she was crouched so low. Six feet probably. Maybe even taller. Dark hair. A khaki jacket. Jeans.

The man turned, still searching the inside of the food stand. His jacket was open. Ellen saw a red shirt. And it wasn't jeans, it was overalls. Bib overalls. Wouldn't the security guard wear a uniform?

The man stopped moving. He picked up a small box, held it toward the light, and examined it. He laid the box on the counter and bent over it. Something glinted in the light from the bare bulb inside the food stand.

Corey clutched her arm.

The man had a knife. A big knife. He was using it to break open the lock on the box.

That's probably what he used to pry open the panel, too, Ellen thought.

He lifted the lid of the box and reached inside.

Money. He removed a stack of bills and began counting them.

Corey leaned closer and she was afraid he was going to say something. She put her finger to her lips again. The whites of Corey's eyes seemed enormous as he pointed at the man.

Ellen nodded. She watched as the man put the bills in the pocket of his jacket and zipped the pocket shut. Then he calmly sat on the counter of the food stand and continued to eat potato chips.

Ellen dropped to her hands and knees and began to crawl away from the food stand, staying as close as possible to the bushes. She was afraid to stand up, since the man was facing in their direction. Even though they were far beyond the rectangle of light that fell from the open panel to the ground outside, she didn't want to take any chance that he would see movement and come to investigate.

Glancing over her shoulder, she saw that Corey was creeping along too, directly behind her. When they rounded the curve, heading back toward the south gate, Ellen stood up.

Corey stood beside her and slipped his hand in hers. For once, he kept his mouth shut. Ellen took a deep breath and then jogged toward the gorilla house, back to the North Meadow and the safety of their tent.

The moon rose silently, sending a dim light over the zoo. Ellen looked up. The moon was nearly full. A harvest moon, her mother would call it. In her mind, she could hear Mom singing, as she always did when they sat together around a campfire: "Shine on, Shine on, harvest moon, up in the sky."

Mom. Where are you? Why haven't you come?

Ellen wished she had not brought Corey to the zoo. It had seemed right at the time but she had been positive her parents would join them. She hadn't counted on being locked in the zoo alone with Corey all night.

And she certainly hadn't counted on discovering that a thief was prowling around the zoo.

5

"I'M GOING to spy on him some more," Corey said.

"No, you aren't. We're both staying right here in this tent."

They were sitting on their sleeping bags, with the picnic supper between them. There were chicken salad sandwiches, ham and cheese sandwiches, little bags of chips, apples, bananas, and chocolate-frosted brownies. There were cans of apple juice, too, and even a little bag of after-dinner mints.

The basket contained enough for four people, but after nibbling at half a sandwich, Ellen quit. Despite her grumbling stomach and the delicious food, nothing tasted good. She was too nervous to eat.

"We need to gather all the evidence we can," Corey said. "Maybe the security guard does other bad stuff."

"I don't think that man was the guard."

"Then who was it?"

"I don't know. But we'll find out what the guard looks like when he comes past here at midnight. You can spy on him then, from inside the tent. If he isn't the thief, we can tell him what we saw."

"I don't want to tell the guard. I want to be a detective and gather more evidence."

"We don't need more evidence and it would make him angry if he caught us following him."

Corey bit into another brownie. "Well, I'm not staying in this dumb tent all night. I want to walk around the zoo. What good is it to spend the night in the zoo if we don't see anything but the inside of a tent? I want to have an adventure."

"You'll have more of an adventure than you bargain for if that thief catches you spying on him."

"He won't catch me."

"That's right. He won't catch you because you aren't going to do it."

A loud roar from across the meadow made both of them jump.

"A lion," Corey said.

"Be quiet and listen. Maybe we can hear some of the other animals."

They stretched out on top of their sleeping bags and listened.

The lion roared again, a deep throaty noise that ended on a high whine. Ellen closed her eyes and strained her ears to hear more. All was quiet.

It felt cozy in the tent, the way it felt when her family went camping. Outside the tent, there was only silence. Gradually, her tight muscles relaxed.

Ellen took a deep breath and then another.

The silence stretched on.

———

ELLEN and Corey's grandparents squinted at the X ray as the doctor held it in front of the light.

"I'm sorry, Mrs. Howard," the doctor said. "The leg is not healing properly. I'm afraid we'll have to reset it."

"Now? Tonight?"

"The sooner the better. I've already called the hospital and arranged to have you admitted."

"But—"

"You may as well get it over with tonight, Esther," Grandpa said. "You don't want to limp the rest of your life."

"If you like, you can spend the night at the hospital, too, Mr. Howard," the doctor said. "We have several sleeping rooms for relatives to use in cases like this, when we do unplanned surgery at night."

"Yes," Grandpa said. "Yes, I'll do that."

"We'd better call the children," Grandma said, "and make sure Mike and Dorothy got home. We can't leave Corey and Ellen there by themselves."

"Use my phone, if you like," the doctor said.

Grandpa dialed. He waited a moment and then said, "I got the answering machine. That means they've gone on the camp-out."

He waited until the machine made a little *bleep* and then said, "Hello, it's me. Esther and I are on our way to the hospital. She has to have her leg reset and I'm going to stay at the hospital tonight, in case she needs me. I'll call you tomorrow, after you get home from the zoo."

When he hung up, Grandma said, "I'm glad Mike and Dorothy got home in time. I was afraid the plane might be late and Ellen and Corey would have to miss the camp-out."

Grandpa said, "You worry too much."

COREY'S eyes felt heavy. He struggled to keep them open. No matter what Ellen said, he didn't want to waste his night at the zoo by falling asleep. Maybe if he walked around awhile, he wouldn't feel so tired.

"I have to go to the bathroom," he whispered.

There was no response.

"Ellen?"

Ellen was asleep. Quietly, Corey got up from his sleeping bag. He put two apples in his jacket pockets. He found his flashlight, his camera, and the bag of peanuts that he had brought along, in case he got hungry in the night. He slipped through the flap of the tent and started off in the moonlight.

After he went to the bathroom, he would take the long way back to the tent. He would go past the snow leopards and the other big cats. Maybe one of them would roar at him.

Yes. That's what he would do. Heck, if he was going to be at the zoo all night, he had to have some fun. Let

Ellen sleep in the tent if she wanted to. Corey would have his adventure by himself.

ACROSS the zoo, on the other side of the lion area, Tony Haymes walked quietly down the path. He felt good now that he had eaten and even though there had been only fifty dollars in the cashbox, it was better than having no money at all. He also had two bananas and a sandwich in his jacket pocket, along with the cash. It was always nice to know where his next meal was coming from.

He had pulled the panel securely shut and left the snack shop through the door. No one would be able to tell he had been inside the building until they opened the cashbox and found it empty.

Tony smiled. I haven't lost my touch, he thought. Eight months in prison couldn't take away talent like his. Of course, fifty bucks was peanuts compared to Tony's usual haul.

That's what I need, he decided. A big job. Fast. Make enough in a hurry to get me out of the country, let me lie low for awhile. Then I'll start over somewhere else. Mexico, maybe. He'd heard there were ways to make big bucks in Mexico. But in order to get to Mexico he had to do more than pilfer petty cash from a hot dog stand.

Think big, he told himself. Think big. Bank robbery? No. Too risky. All the banks have surveillance cameras these days and he would be recognized. Jewelry store? No. He would need a fence to get rid of the stolen goods and he was out of touch.

He left the African area behind and meandered past the orangutans and great apes. There was a special display outside the monkey house and, curious, Tony squinted in the moonlight to see what it said.

COME MEET THE NEW BABY! We are pleased to announce that a golden lion tamarin monkey was born here on August 2nd. This species seldom reproduces in captivity. The baby is healthy and enjoys having visitors.

Next to the announcement were several snapshots of a baby monkey. Tony stared at the pictures for a long time. The monkey was tiny, no bigger than a doll. In one of the pictures, a person was holding it and the little monkey had its arms wrapped around the person's neck and its head snuggled against the person's chest just the way a little child might.

There was also a newspaper article about the birth of the baby monkey. The headline said: RARE BABY MONKEY ATTRACTS ZOO VISITORS. The story began by saying zoo attendance was up 35 percent since the birth of the baby monkey.

Tony tugged on the glass doors that led inside the monkey house. They were locked. He cupped his hands on the sides of his face and peered inside.

The interior of the building was dimly lit, as if the zoo were trying to match the moonlight of the outdoors. Tony could see glass partitions which separated zoo visitors from the floor-to-ceiling chain link enclosures where the monkeys lived.

Inside the enclosures, he saw trees, fallen logs, and platforms at various heights. In one cage, high up by the ceiling, there was a swing.

Something moved in the cage closest to where he stood. Tony saw a small shape. For a moment he thought it was a squirrel. When it moved again, another, smaller, shape followed and he realized that it was the golden tamarin monkey and her famous baby.

And that's when he knew how he would get enough money to go to Mexico. He would kidnap the baby monkey and hold it for ransom.

It should be a snap. All he had to do was get into the cage and coax the little monkey to come to him. That would be simple enough.

Tony's heart began to pound as he thought of what he would do after he had the monkey. He'd get a room somewhere, hide out, and demand a ransom. The zoo must have plenty of money and if they didn't, they would get it from the public. People who love animals are suckers for animal sob stories. The public would contribute. All the people who had come to the zoo to see the baby monkey would want to help get it back. They'd give money; he was sure of it.

Twenty thousand dollars. Tony leaned his head against the cool glass door and closed his eyes. He would demand a $20,000 ransom for the return of the baby monkey. And he would get it.

But first he had to have the monkey. He squinted through the door again. Even if he broke in, the glass partitions inside looked solid and so did the chain fencing. Even his knife couldn't cut through chain like that; it would take a hacksaw.

Take your time, he told himself. Calm down and think it through before you act.

There had to be some other way to get inside. How do the keepers put food in? How are the cages cleaned? There must be some kind of entrance at the back side of each cage.

His hands dropped to his sides and he started around the outside of the monkey building. He soon came to a wooden door marked "Employees Only."

My lucky day, he told himself, as he used the knife to pick the lock on the door. As he worked, he planned his strategy. He would go through whatever opening was at the back of the rare monkey's cage. He would use the bananas in his pocket to make friends with the mother monkey. While she ate the bananas, he would pick up the baby, step back through the door or hole or whatever it was, and leave.

He would have to move quickly. Even though the monkeys were tiny, they were still wild animals and he wasn't sure what the mother would do if she saw him take her baby. The last thing he needed was to get bit.

If he had to, he would give her his sandwich, to distract her. That should keep her occupied until he and the baby were safely outside the cage.

And once he had the baby monkey? Then what? He would put the monkey inside his overalls and zip his jacket. He would take a cab—tell the driver his infant son was asleep. That would explain the lump in his coat. He would rent a motel room, one of those places where they don't ask for license numbers, just cash on the line. He had the cash, from the snack-shop box.

Tomorrow he would call the director of the zoo and tell him where and when to bring the $20,000. He would leave the monkey in the motel room, go get the money, and be on his way to Mexico.

Yes! Tony thought. It would work! Later, he could figure out exactly how to word the ransom call and arrange the pickup. Right now he needed to get the baby monkey in his jacket and get away from the zoo.

His heart thumped rapidly in his chest and little beads of moisture stood on his upper lip as he opened the "Employees Only" door and slipped silently into the area behind the monkey cages.

———

COREY paused outside the rest rooms, debating which way to go. He was tempted to head north, past the bison and wolves. He bet those wolves would be howling tonight, with the moon almost full. The thought made him shiver with excitement.

He wasn't scared. After all, what could happen to him? Still, it was odd to be here like this, in the middle of the night, with only the zoo animals.

He turned toward the lion area. The lion had roared earlier; maybe it would do so again. If not, he would keep walking, down past the orangutans and gorillas, all the way to the monkey house.

The monkey exhibits were Corey's favorite part of the zoo. Ellen liked the Nocturnal House but all those bats gave him the creeps. He'd take the monkeys any day. Monkeys were silly; they made him laugh. And it was easy to make up stories about what they did because they always did something unexpected.

He wondered if monkeys lie down to sleep at night or if they sit in the trees. Maybe they make little beds in the leaves and lie down and use each other's tails for pillows. Do monkeys dream? Do they sing monkey lullabies to their young?

Corey didn't know anything about how monkeys act at night. Well, he thought happily, this is my chance to find out.

He paused for only a moment near the lion area. When none of them roared, he decided to go on. Even with the flashlight, it wasn't as easy to find his way in the dark as he had thought it would be. He started walking toward where he thought the monkey house was.

Here I come, monkeys, he thought. You're going to have midnight company.

6

THE LION roared again.

Ellen's eyes flew open. For a moment she didn't know where she was or what she had heard. Then she remembered. She sat up, pulled the flap of the tent open, and looked out.

She wondered where her parents were. Something must have gone terribly wrong or they would be here. They would never let her and Corey spend the night here alone. Heck, she and Corey weren't even allowed to spend the night alone at home, in their own house with Prince to protect them. Grandma and Grandpa always came and stayed with them if Mom and Dad had to be gone.

"Corey?" she whispered. "Are you awake?"

There was no answer. He must be asleep. She kept still, listening for animal noises again. She heard nothing. Not even the rhythmic breathing of someone who's asleep.

She reached over toward Corey's sleeping bag. It was empty.

"Corey?"

She groped for her flashlight and shined it frantically around the tent. She was alone.

Stay calm, she told herself. Maybe he went to the bathroom. That's where he must be. She probably heard him leave without knowing it and that's why she woke up.

Ellen stretched and moved her head from side to side, working the kinks out of her neck. She wasn't used to sleeping on the ground.

She wondered if the zoo security man had gone past yet. She had meant to stay awake and watch for him.

She felt thirsty now so she opened the ice chest and removed a can of juice. After a few sips, she looked outside again.

Corey should be back by now. It didn't take this long to walk to the rest rooms and back.

Ellen put the can of juice down. It would be just like him to decide to go off by himself in search of some excitement. Like it or not, she supposed she had better go look for him.

She walked across the meadow to the rest rooms and cracked open the door to the men's side. "Corey? Are you in there?"

There was no reply. If Corey had been to the bathroom, he was gone now.

She wondered which way he would go and decided it was useless to guess. With her brother, anything was possible. He was probably looking for his dancing zebras and flying giraffes.

At least she didn't have to worry that Corey would get lost. He knew his way around the zoo and no matter which way he went, sooner or later he would come back to the North Meadow. She just hoped he wouldn't try to find the thief and spy on him.

The thief must be a zoo employee—a keeper, perhaps, or a maintenance man. She found it hard to believe that anyone who worked at the zoo would also steal from it but the fence went completely around the outside; no one else could possibly get in.

Or out, she thought glumly.

She decided to take the path to her left first, because she thought that path dead-ended at the north end of the zoo. If Corey had gone that way, she would find him for sure.

She had not gone far when a rustling sound came from the right side of the path. She stopped walking and pointed the light in that direction. Then she smiled. On the other side of the fence sat a whole row of wallaroos, a small kind of kangaroo. They were all up on their hind legs and supported by their tails. They sat still, watching her. Their eyes glowed red as her flashlight reflected off them. Apparently, they were curious about her flashlight and had come to see what it was.

Ellen swung her hands back and forth like the conductor of a symphony orchestra, waving the flashlight in loops and circles. Her parents had taken her and Corey to see a laser light show at the Pacific Science Center once; she wondered if the wallaroos thought this was some kind of laser show.

She continued down the path, pausing now and then to shine her light on each side of the path. When she reached the end, she saw that there was a metal gate blocking this entrance, too. She turned and started back.

The only other animal she saw was a snow leopard, which seemed just as fascinated by her light as the wallaroos had been. After watching Ellen for a moment, the leopard went into its den and then, just as Ellen was going to move on, it came back with a baby leopard.

Clearly, the mother leopard wanted to show her baby the amazing light. Maybe the leopards thought a flying saucer had landed in the zoo and she was an alien being. She realized that was exactly the sort of thing Corey would say, so she beamed the light back at the path and continued on.

Even with the almost-full moon, it was difficult to see where she was. The tall trees with their thick dark branches loomed over her. The flashlight made a small circle of light on the path immediately ahead of her but on both sides and behind her the darkness hung close and heavy. The air seemed thick.

Where was Corey? Where were her parents? She felt isolated from the rest of the world, as alone as if she were walking through the jungles of Africa, where the wild beasts roamed free, instead of here in the zoo where they were contained behind fences.

Although the light helped her see where she was walking, it also made her feel more vulnerable. Anyone or anything in the shadows could see her quickly because of her flashlight, while she could see only what she pointed the flashlight directly at.

She switched off the flashlight and went on without it.

She walked more slowly, putting her feet down carefully, feeling with her toes to be certain she was still on the path.

She heard something move behind her. Holding her breath, she stopped and listened. When she didn't hear it again, she turned on her light and aimed it behind her. She saw only a clump of bushes.

Her mouth felt dry. All around her, the leaves whispered secrets and in the distance, a lone wolf howled at the moon. The mournful sound sent a prickle of fear up the back of Ellen's neck.

She took a deep breath and told herself to relax, but she still had an uneasy feeling, as if some unknown danger lurked just around the corner.

EEIIIYYAHHHH!!!

The scream came with no warning, from the area behind her where she had heard rustling, the place where she had just beamed her light.

Ellen jumped, drawing her breath in sharply. She swung around, instinctively putting one hand across her face for protection. With the other hand she waved the flashlight back and forth, shining it from side to side.

"Who's there?" she croaked. It was a wonder she could speak at all; her throat felt like sandpaper.

There was no answer but she heard that same rustling sound again. It was closer this time. She didn't know whether to turn off the light and run, or try to see who (or what) had screamed.

In the split second that she tried to make up her mind, a peacock stepped into the circle of light. His blue and green feathers fanned high above his tail as he strutted. *"Eeiiiaayahh!"* he screamed again.

Ellen stared, her heart thudding in her chest. She had always thought that peacocks—or peafowls as she knew they were properly called—were the most beautiful of birds but she had never heard one cry before. It was harsh and shrill, like a cat in pain. How could such a lovely bird make such an ugly sound?

She took a deep breath, turned, and continued down the path away from the peacock. The light jiggled because her hand was shaking. Anyone's hand would shake after that experience, she thought. Any sensible person would fear for her life if a peacock screamed at her in the dark.

She wondered if Corey had heard the peacock's cry. If so, he was probably running for the tent as fast as he could go right now, convinced that some terrible demon was loose in the zoo.

Well, it would serve him right. He knew better than to go off alone this way. When Mom and Dad heard about it, he would catch heck for sure. If Mom and Dad ever heard about it. *Where were they?*

She came to a fork in the path. She stopped, unsure which way to go. Even though she was familiar with the zoo from previous visits, everything seemed different in the dark. She couldn't look off in the distance for landmarks and she was afraid she might have missed some of the signs along the sides of the path.

I should have stayed in the tent, she thought. Eventually, Corey would return. Maybe he already had and, when he found she wasn't there, had gone out looking for her. It could go on that way all night—missing each other, searching in the dark—unless one of them stayed at the camp.

She took the path to her right. If she was guessing correctly, it would wind past the Nocturnal House and back to the North Meadow. She wondered what the Nocturnal House looked like at night. Was it lighted, so the animals would think it was daytime? After she found Corey, maybe she would go to the Nocturnal House and find out. It was close to the North Meadow; she wouldn't get lost. And it would be fun to see her favorite exhibit under different conditions.

The minute she thought of it as her favorite exhibit, she knew where she would find Corey. The monkey house. Of course. It was always his favorite part of the zoo. He had even told Grandma and Grandpa that he wanted to sleep in the monkey house tonight. Why hadn't she thought of that right away?

She walked faster, shining the light back and forth across the path as she went. She hoped she was on the short cut across the middle of the zoo but even if she was on the outside path, she would end up near the monkeys.

And once I find Monkey Corey, she thought, I won't let him out of my sight again.

7

IN HIS MIND, Corey was already telling his pals about his zoo night adventure. I went exploring on my own, he would say. I tried to find the thief and spy on him some more. It was pitch black out but I turned off my flashlight and sneaked along, hiding behind bushes, to be sure he didn't see me first.

This time, Corey had his camera. If the man stole something else, Corey planned to shoot a picture and catch him in the act. The police would have proof of a crime.

Corey imagined himself showing the picture to the police and being interviewed by TV and newspaper reporters. He saw himself getting a medal for bravery. Most of all, he thought how exciting it would be to open the newspaper and see his own picture.

The images of glory faded when Corey realized he had been walking a long time and not paying attention to where he was. He should have come to the monkey house by now.

He turned on his light and saw water. A huge hippopotamus lifted his head and opened his mouth. His white teeth shone in the beam of light like a toothpaste ad.

Corey promptly forgot he was The Great Detective. He wondered if the hippo was hungry. Last fall, on the TV news, he had seen the hippos eating whole pumpkins left over from Halloween.

He took an apple out of his pocket. It would be like shooting baskets, only easier, to feed the hippo an apple. Of course, an apple wouldn't seem like much to the hippo. It would be like a person eating one sunflower seed.

Then he remembered that Grandpa had said he shouldn't feed any of the animals because they are on special diets, so he ate the apple himself and walked on. Although he listened carefully and looked in all directions, there was no sign of the thief.

He's probably breaking into the other food stands, Corey thought. Maybe he steals money from them every night. The police and the zoo authorities were certainly going to be glad to learn about this. He and Ellen would be heroes. Maybe they really would get their pictures in the paper. Or maybe just *he* would get his picture in the paper, since he was the one who was going to spy on the man some more and collect additional evidence.

Maybe he should forget about visiting the monkey house. Maybe he should keep hunting for the thief.

No. The zoo covered many acres and the man could be anywhere. He'd look for him again after he found out what monkeys do at night.

It took him longer than he thought it would to find the monkey house. After he left the hippos, he didn't see anything else he recognized. He hadn't thought it was possible for him to get lost in the zoo but he was. He kept on until his flashlight caught a sign with animal pictures on it. One picture was a monkey; an arrow pointed which way to go.

The sign said "Primates." Corey had noticed that the zoo signs and maps always said primates and he didn't understand why. Everyone he knew, even Grandpa and Grandma, called it the monkey house.

He pushed eagerly on the monkey house doors and then sagged against them in disappointment. The doors were locked.

Pressing his face against the glass, he looked inside. Dimly, he saw the benches in the center of the house and the trees in the enclosures nearest the door. He squinted his eyes into narrow slits, trying to spot one of the monkeys.

Something moved in the cage nearest the door. Corey looked that way. It was, he knew, the cage where the tamarin monkeys lived. Grandma and Grandpa had brought him to see the baby monkey after it was born and Corey had entered the zoo's contest to choose a name for the baby. He had suggested Poppy but the zoo committee chose Shadow.

Shadow's mother, Sunshine, was leaping back and forth, running wildly from one side of the cage to the other. Corey stared. He had assumed the monkeys slept at night, but apparently this was their exercise time.

The lights came on inside the monkey house. Corey tried to see who had turned them on but he saw no one. The lights must be on an automatic timer. In the other cages, the monkeys seemed startled by the sudden light. They stretched and looked around.

Sunshine continued her frenzied activity. Several times, she ran to her baby, who was perched partway up one of the trees, and then ran off again.

A banana flew through the air and landed near Sunshine; she did not pick it up.

Was it feeding time now? In the middle of the night? If so, it meant that one of the monkeys' keepers was on duty. That's who turned on the lights. Corey craned his neck, trying to see who had thrown the banana. From his place outside the front doors, he could not see the far corner of the golden tamarins' cage; he could not see who had thrown the banana.

Corey knew Ellen would want him to speak to the keeper. He should explain that he and Ellen were here alone and ask to use a telephone. But if he did, the keeper might make Corey and Ellen go home.

Another banana sailed toward Sunshine. She ignored this one, too. Corey had never seen a monkey act so agitated. Did they always get this excited about being fed?

And then he saw the reason for the mother monkey's distress. Someone had entered the cage from the back side, and was moving slowly, with one hand upraised, toward the tree where the baby monkey sat. The entrance was partway up the back of the cage and the man was on a narrow platform in the tree branches. Corey instantly recognized the tall man in the overalls.

Corey swallowed. It was the same man who broke into

the food stand and took the money. What was he doing now? There wouldn't be any money to steal in a monkey cage.

Corey put his hands on the sides of his face, trying to see the man better. He had wanted to spy on the thief. Well, here was his chance. He would hide here and when the man left the monkey house, Corey would follow him. He would watch to see if the man broke into any other food stands and stole any more money.

Was the man one of the keepers? Was it his job to check on the monkeys at night, to be sure they were OK?

The man crouched and sat motionless on the platform for several seconds. The mother monkey continued to race back and forth. Because of the thick glass partitions, Corey could not hear anything but he was quite sure Sunshine was chattering.

The man reached in his pocket, removed a square package, and tossed it to the ground. A sandwich? Is that what the monkeys eat at night? Corey wondered. Shouldn't the man have unwrapped it? The package had barely hit the ground when the man lunged, reached one arm down into the tree, and plucked the baby monkey from the branch.

The man tried to stuff the baby monkey inside his jacket while the monkey struggled to get away. The mother monkey leaped toward the man; he kicked at her and she retreated.

Holding the little monkey firmly with both hands, the man turned quickly and disappeared through the opening at the back of the cage, closing the door behind him.

The mother monkey went wild. She careened up and down, back and forth, so fast that it looked like she was doing trampoline tricks.

Corey's scalp tingled as he realized what he had witnessed. He felt like a bolt of lightning had just zigzagged from his ears to his toes, leaving all of his nerves crackling with electricity.

He was sure that the tall man was not supposed to take Shadow out of the cage. He was not supposed to feed the monkeys, either. He was not, Corey realized, a zoo employee at all. No zoo employee would act the way this man was acting.

If he doesn't work at the zoo, how did he get in? Who was he? Why would he want to take a monkey? To set it free? Corey had seen a TV special once, about animal rights activists who had freed some caged animals from a traveling circus in order to call attention to their improper care.

But the Woodland Park Zoo was known all over the world for the good way they treated the animals. That's why Grandpa and Grandma always went to the charity auction. They said the zoo had even trained some of the rare tamarin monkeys to survive in the wild and had then set them free in the rain forests in Brazil.

It wouldn't do any good to turn a monkey loose in the city of Seattle. It would never survive.

Maybe he planned to sell it. Some people want exotic pets. Was there a black market for stolen monkeys? Had the man taken animals before? Corey didn't remember hearing about any stolen animals but he wasn't very faithful about keeping up with the news, except for the Seahawks and the Mariners.

Corey wished he could get to a telephone, to call 911. That was the emergency number and Corey was sure this would be considered an emergency. He couldn't call 911 when the telephone was on the other side of the fence.

He needed help but try as he might he could not think of how to get it. Even if he ran to the gate and yelled, no one would hear him. The only thing on the other side of the gate was the zoo parking lot and there wouldn't be anyone there at night.

He decided the best thing to do was his original plan: follow the man and watch him closely. He would see exactly what the man did with the monkey; he could report everything to the police tomorrow morning.

Specific, he told himself. Get the specific details.

Corey turned away from the glass doors. He wondered how the man had gotten inside the monkey house. There must be a back door of some sort. Corey had to find it fast and get evidence of what he had just seen. He would take a picture of the man with the baby monkey.

He hurried around the side of the building, toward the back of Shadow's cage. He found the door easily; it was standing wide open and the lights inside were on.

Corey squatted down a few feet to one side of the door. He put down his flashlight and looked through the viewfinder of his camera. If the man left the lights on, Corey might be able to get a picture without using the flash.

"*Chit-chit-chitchitchit.*" The frantic cries of the little

monkey came from inside the door. Corey could hear the mother monkey's screams now, too.

Just as Corey peered through his camera, the lights went off. He lowered the camera. He couldn't use the flash; the man would see it for sure and know that Corey was watching him.

"Damn it!" the man muttered. "Hold still. Stay in there."

The man's back was to him. Corey stayed low. As long as he didn't move, he was sure the man wouldn't see him. There were scuffling noises and the man cursed again.

The man kicked the door, to close it, and started toward Corey. The man's hands were clutched across his chest. Corey couldn't see any monkey but he knew the man was holding one.

The man's arms kept moving, as if he were having trouble holding the monkey. Twice he stopped and struggled with the bulge in his jacket.

A few more feet, Corey thought, and he'll be past me. Then I'll follow him. I'll find out where he takes the monkey. I'll stay behind him and spy on him all night long.

The dark shape of the man loomed over him. Corey held his breath.

And then the man yelped in pain.

Thunk! Fur brushed past Corey's face. Instinctively, he reached out and tried to grab the monkey. The tail slipped through his fingers just as the man dove downward.

The man's hands closed around Corey's arm. He gasped in surprise. Then he grabbed Corey's shoulders and hoisted him to his feet. He muttered something that would get Corey grounded for a month if he ever said it.

Chattering wildly, the baby monkey ran past them and disappeared into the night.

"Who the hell are you?" the man hissed. Before Corey could reply, he added, "You just made me lose $20,000."

Corey had never heard anyone sound so angry. So full of hate.

"I didn't do anything," Corey protested. "The monkey got away all by itself. We have to find it! What if it climbs over the fence?" Corey thought of the heavy traffic on Aurora Avenue or North 50th Street. He shuddered.

"Damn thing bit me." The man shook one hand several times and then put his mouth briefly on his wrist. He spat.

Corey stepped backward but the man quickly gripped him again. His fingers dug into Corey's arms as he leaned closer, staring at Corey. "Maybe," he said slowly, "there's more than one way to collect a ransom."

Corey twisted, trying to wriggle loose. The strap on his camera broke and the camera fell to the ground. "You're hurting me," he said.

"You think that hurts? You don't know what it is to get hurt."

Corey remembered the knife.

He didn't say anything else.

8

ELLEN was lost. She didn't understand how it could have happened, but she didn't know where she was or which way to go to find the monkey house. How could she be so turned around in a place she had visited so many times?

She should have taken a map. Maybe the maps show where telephones are located. But she hadn't known she'd be alone, searching for Corey. And she hadn't known how scarey the zoo would seem at night.

The moon disappeared behind some clouds; it was even darker now than it had been earlier. The path seemed endless and she had no idea whether she was still on the shortcut or whether she had somehow followed another path by mistake. When she waved her light around, nothing looked familiar.

She saw another food stand and moved cautiously toward it. When she was next to it, she stopped and listened in case the thief was inside. She heard nothing.

This, she decided, was the most horrible night of her life. She had looked forward to it so much and now everything had gone wrong. If only she had waited at home until Mom and Dad got there, instead of rushing away in a cab.

"You can't solve a problem by saying, *if only*." That's what Mom always said. Ellen trudged onward.

The beam from her flashlight hit fencing. Ellen stopped and raised the light higher; the fencing continued. She recognized the Aviary. That isn't where she had thought she was, but at least she had her bearings now. The Aviary was close to the monkey house. She had just taken the long way to get there.

Relieved, she walked faster. With any luck, Corey would be in the monkey house. He was probably jumping on one of the benches, scratching his armpits, or hanging by his knees from a railing, pretending to be a monkey in a tree. She would insist that he return to the tent with her and stay there until morning. No more wandering around the zoo in the dark.

Just ahead, she heard a shrill chattering. A monkey?

Yes. There it was again, even louder this time, and she was sure it was a monkey. The monkey didn't sound very happy. It sounded upset, as if someone were teasing it.

The closer she got to the monkey house, the more distressed the monkey sounded. It seemed to be only one monkey and it sounded like it was in pain. Was it hurt? If so, she knew Corey wasn't responsible. Her brother was silly and made up wild stories but he was basically a good kid and he loved the monkeys. He would never hurt one of them.

Light from the monkey house shone out through the glass doors. Ellen saw it and began to run. By the time she got to the monkey house, the chattering had stopped.

The monkey house was locked. Ellen looked through the glass doors. In the first cage, she recognized one of the rare golden lion tamarins that Grandma and Grandpa had brought her to see, when a baby monkey was born. The monkey was clearly upset, rushing frantically back and forth in its cage.

When she looked closer, she could tell it was the mother monkey, Sunshine, the one Ellen had watched as it nursed her baby. What could have happened to distress her so? Was her baby sick? Ellen could not see the baby monkey. It must be in the far corner, she thought, where she couldn't see.

Although she was certain the monkey was making noise, the soundproof glass of the cages and the thick doors of the building prevented her from hearing it. Ellen wondered how she heard the chattering earlier when she couldn't hear it now. Were there monkeys elsewhere in the zoo?

The monkeys in the other cages moved about restlessly while Sunshine leaped hysterically from the tree to the ground and back again.

Ellen heard the chattering again, fainter now. It came from behind the building. From outside. Maybe it was Corey, pretending to be a monkey. She hurried in that direction, flashing her light around. "Corey?" she called. "Are you here?"

"*Chit-chit-chit-chit.*" The excited chattering retreated.

Ellen waved her light back and forth across the back of the building. A door marked "Employees Only" stood slightly ajar. The wood around the lock was splintered; someone had broken in.

Oh, Corey, she thought. Surely you wouldn't have done this. You said you wanted to sleep with the monkeys but you wouldn't do a stupid thing like this. Would you?

Of course not. She answered her own question. Corey was no hoodlum. He didn't go around vandalizing public property and he definitely would not do anything to scare the monkeys. Grandma and Grandpa had taught them that animals have feelings, much like people have. Grandma even carried a list in her purse, of companies that don't test their products on animals. She wouldn't buy soap or shampoo or perfume unless the manufacturer was on her list. Grandma said she didn't want some poor rabbit blinded just so she could smell good.

Ellen continued around the outside of the building, aiming the light toward the ground. Something crunched under her shoe. Looking down, she saw peanuts spilled on the path. Then she noticed red drops on the path near the peanuts. She leaned down to look more closely.

Blood. There were drops of blood on the path behind the monkey house.

Ellen's breath came faster. Had someone hurt the baby monkey? Is that why the mother was so upset?

The man she had seen carried a knife. After he broke into the food stand, he must have broken into the monkey house, too. But why? Who was he? Not an employee of the zoo. She was convinced of that.

But if the man they had seen did not work at the zoo, how did he get in? Where was the security guard? Had they just missed him, or had something happened to him? The questions bounced in her brain like the bumper cars at the county fair.

She stared down at the path. Corey had brought peanuts with him. Were these some of his? How did they get spilled?

Don't jump to conclusions, she told herself. Anyone could have spilled peanuts on the ground. She swung the flashlight in a wider circle, and froze. There, lying on the path a few feet in front of her, was a camera. She picked it up and turned it over. Her hand began to shake.

Mom had taped the small identification tag on the camera before Corey went to camp last July. Corey Streater, it said, and gave the telephone number. Corey treasured his camera. He would never be careless with it.

Ellen aimed the light at the path again and found Corey's flashlight.

Something terrible had happened to her brother. She knew it. He would never leave his flashlight and his camera like this.

Why was blood on the ground? Was it monkey blood—or human?

Where was Corey?

I have to find him, Ellen thought. First, I'll go back to the tent. He's had plenty of time to explore the zoo and if nothing has happened to him he might be back at the tent by now. If he's there, we'll stay inside the tent until morning if I have to sit on him the rest of the night.

If he isn't there . . .

She didn't want to think about what she would do if he wasn't there.

She headed back toward the tent. Please be there, Corey, she thought. Please, please be there.

She never made it back to the tent.

9

As ELLEN passed the Nocturnal House, she heard voices inside.

Her first instinct was to rush in, to see who it was, but she forced herself not to. Instead, she eased cautiously toward the door that leads to the viewing walkway. She pushed it only until she could hear clearly through the crack. It was light inside, to make it seem like daytime for those animals.

"What's a kid like you doing here alone in the middle of the night?" The man's voice was angry. "What'd you do, run away from home?"

"I'm on a camp-out," Corey said.

"Sure, you are. And I'm the Boy Scout leader."

"My grandparents bought the camp-out at a charity auction."

"Your grandparents are here, too?" The man sounded alarmed.

"Yes," Corey said, without hesitation. He was so convincing that for a moment Ellen wondered if Grandpa and Grandma had come to the zoo while she was off looking for Corey. "My sister's here, too," Corey continued, "and both my brothers and my mother and father, and all of my aunts and uncles and cousins. Even some of our neighbors."

"You're lying," the man said. "If all those people were camping out at the zoo, I would have heard them."

"You'll hear them soon," Corey said, "because they'll be looking for me."

There was a brief silence. Then the man muttered, "Well, they won't find you. You and I are going on a little camp-out of our own and we're going to stay there until all those relatives of yours cough up twenty grand."

"You mean you're going to hold me for ransom?" Corey's voice was higher than usual and the question ended with a little squeak.

"Smart kid. Now shut up and let me think."

"But my parents don't have any money," Corey said. "My father is crippled and blind and my mother has AIDS from a blood transfusion that she got. Neither of them can work. There's no way they can pay you a ransom."

Ellen's jaw dropped. She had heard Corey tell some crazy stories before but this one topped them all.

"People who go to charity auctions have money. Now shut up!"

Silence.

Ellen eased the door closed and stood outside in the darkness. Her throat felt tight. She wanted to burst into tears and run back to the tent and hide, but she knew she couldn't do that. Somehow, she had to help Corey. She had to get him away from the man.

I'll climb the fence, she decided. I take gymnastics lessons; I'm strong. I'll go back to the south gate, climb the fence, and call the police.

She hurried along the path, walking as quickly as she could in the dark. When she was past the house where the great apes live, she turned on her flashlight again and began to run. Past the Family Farm, past the open-air theater, past the food stand. By the time she reached the south gate, she was out of breath. She stood for a moment, panting, and looking up. There were brick walls on both sides of the entrance. Wooden lattice, covered with vines, made a canopy overhead for several feet in front of the walls. There was no way she could get through that.

She went toward the exit turnstile until the brick wall ended and a chain link fence began. She would have to climb the chain link fence.

You can do it, she told herself. You MUST do it. It's the only way to save Corey.

She stretched up and grasped the fence above her head. Wedging the toe of her right shoe into the fence, she pulled herself up. She tried to get her left foot positioned, too, but when she put her weight on her right foot, it slipped out of the wire fencing. The holes in the fence were not big enough to allow her to get a solid foothold.

She dropped back to the ground. Quickly, she tried again. This time, she managed to lift herself onto her right foot but was unable to put her left foot in the fence. She clung to the fence, leaning into it, unwilling to jump down and start over but unable to continue. She held on tightly with her right hand, leaned over, and untied her left shoe. She kicked her heel against the fence until the shoe came off and fell to the ground. Now she could curl her toes around the fencing. Through her sock, she could feel the wire and grip it.

She removed her other shoe the same way and then, feeling like one of the monkeys, she began to climb. One hand up, one foot up. Next hand. Next foot. Although she knew she must hurry, she climbed cautiously. Even without her shoes, it was difficult to get a solid grip. Twice, one foot slipped out of the wire but she was able to hold on with the other until she could regain her balance.

Reaching above her head, she felt the top of the fence. She was almost there. Going down wouldn't be so hard. She could let her feet slide down the other side of the fence and just hang on with her hands. All she had to do was make it over the top.

She grasped the top tightly with both hands and pulled herself up. She swung her left leg up and crooked her knee over the top. Her leg hit barbed wire.

She reached out, feeling gingerly with her hand. From the top of the fence, three strands of barbed wire angled out toward the parking lot. The cuff of her jeans was caught on the first strand. She tugged. It held fast.

There was no way she would be able to climb over barbed wire. She tried to kick her left leg free. Her fingers ached, from hanging on to the fence. She kicked again. And again. A piece of barbed wire pierced her sock and cut her ankle.

She gave another furious kick. She heard the sound of her jeans tearing and tried to stop in midkick but it was too late. As the material gave way, she lost her balance and fell.

She clutched frantically at the wire as she fell, trying to grab on and stop herself. Her fingers slid too fast; her hands bumped helplessly down the fence and she thudded to the ground.

As she started to sit up, a sharp pain shot through her left shoulder. She lay back down and waited for the pain to subside.

Tears stung her eyes as she lay huddled at the bottom of the fence. She wasn't going to make it over the top.

Gently, she poked her shoulder and winced at the touch of her fingers. A broken collarbone? Bad bruise? She wasn't sure what was wrong but she knew it hurt. Her scratched ankle hurt, too. She would probably have to get a tetanus shot tomorrow, on top of everything else. Then she felt guilty for feeling sorry for herself when Corey was being held hostage.

She did not try to scale the fence again. It wouldn't do Corey any good if she fell off the fence and killed herself. She would have to get help some other way.

She found her shoes and put them back on. Then, holding her left arm close to her side and trying not to move it, she started back along the path toward the Nocturnal House.

How long had she been gone? Ten minutes? Fifteen? Were the man and Corey still in the Nocturnal House? She didn't turn on her flashlight, for fear the man was nearby and would see her.

As she walked, she tried to think. Where was the security guard? Had something happened to him? Or was he somewhere on the zoo grounds, able to help her and Corey if he knew they needed it? How could she reach him?

There had to be other telephones somewhere. Where? She couldn't stumble around the zoo in the dark all night, hunting for a telephone. Corey needed help fast.

When she got back to the Nocturnal House, she eased open the door again and listened. Silence. Ellen's throat felt tight. They had left. The man had taken Corey somewhere and now she would never find him again.

Just as she let go of the door, she heard a slight sniffling noise. She recognized it immediately as the sound Corey always made when his allergies acted up or when he had been crying. She could almost hear her mother saying, "Corey, stop that sniffling. If your nose is running, get a tissue."

They were still inside. Maybe the man was hiding, unsure how many people were looking for Corey.

She tiptoed a few feet away from the Nocturnal House, where she wouldn't be seen if the man decided to leave. Quickly, she figured out a plan.

She would yell out, as if she were calling to other people, that she had found Corey. She would make it sound like a whole group was on their way to the Nocturnal House.

Had the man believed Corey when he said there were other people on the camp-out? Probably. After all, it was unlikely that Corey would be here alone.

The man probably thought there were others here. If

he did, her plan might work. The man might run away rather than taking a chance that he would be surrounded by a mob of angry relatives. And then she and Corey would run, too, and hide somewhere until morning, or until help arrived.

Even if the man didn't run, the security guard might hear her yell and come. He was probably looking for them anyway. It must be after midnight. If the guard checked the tent and found it empty, he would be alarmed. He would try to find them.

By now, maybe Mom and Dad were home and had called the police or the president of the zoo or someone. Even if Mom and Dad weren't home yet, Grandpa and Grandma would be back by now and would find the note. Help might be on the way already.

Maybe I shouldn't yell quite yet, Ellen thought. Maybe I should wait awhile. Stay right where I am and wait for someone to come. Except the security guard might NOT be looking for them. Mom and Dad might NOT be home. Help might NOT be on the way.

She took a deep breath, planted her feet firmly on the path outside the Nocturnal House and yelled as loudly as she could, "This way, everybody. I think I've found him." She waited a few seconds and when nothing happened, she yelled again. "He's over here. In the Nocturnal House. Come on, everyone! This way!"

The door of the Nocturnal House burst open. With the light behind them, the silhouettes of the tall man and the small boy were plainly visible.

Ellen gasped. The man had one arm firmly around Corey's neck. In his other hand, he held the long sharp knife. "If anybody takes one more step," the man said, "this kid won't live."

What have I done? Ellen thought. She stood still, staring in horror at her brother and the man with the knife.

The man looked around. His eyes stopped briefly on Ellen and then, after waiting for a few more seconds, he looked at her again and said, "Come here."

He knows I was bluffing, Ellen thought. He knows I'm the only one out here. She whirled and started to run.

Behind her, Corey cried out.

Ellen stopped and looked back. The man held the knife in the air now, pointed toward Corey's chest.

She couldn't run away. Slowly, she turned and walked toward the man. "Who are you?" she whispered. "What do you want with us?"

10

Inside the Nocturnal House, the man kicked at the wall. "Of all the rotten luck. Just when everything was rolling my way, I get saddled with a couple of brats."

"You don't have to be saddled with us," Corey said. "You could let us go."

"Sure. And have you go screaming to Mama and Papa."

"They aren't . . ." Corey stopped.

The man's eyes narrowed. "They aren't what? They aren't here? That's what you were going to say, isn't it?"

Corey didn't answer.

The man nodded his head slowly, as if the pieces of a puzzle had fallen into place. "You kids are here alone. That's why nobody came when you yelled. And that's why you're going to do exactly as I say. Because there's no one to rescue you."

"There's a security guard," Ellen said. "He's on his way here right now."

"No, he isn't."

"Why are you being so mean?" Corey said. "We didn't do anything bad to you."

"No? Well, the rest of the world did. But not anymore. Old Tony's in charge now and you kids are going to make me a bundle of cash. Twenty grand, to be exact."

"Why do you need money so badly?" Ellen asked. "Don't you have a job?"

"Job?" The man started to laugh. "Don't you have a job?" he repeated, as if it were the funniest joke he'd ever heard.

Ellen and Corey looked at each other. Corey shrugged his shoulders.

"What's so funny about having a job?" Ellen said. "Most people have one."

The man quit laughing. "I'm not most people. I'm Tony Haymes. You won't find me grubbing around for eight hours every day, breaking my back so the boss can get rich. No way. Old Tony's too smart for that.

"If you don't have a job," Corey said, "how do you pay your bills?"

"I've been living rent-free." The man started laughing again. Ellen looked at Corey and rolled her eyes. This guy was some kind of a wacko.

"When you're smart enough," the man said, suddenly serious again, "you don't need a job. You can get plenty of bucks without working."

"You steal money, don't you?" Corey said.

"I take what I deserve."

"It's wrong to steal."

"What are you, my conscience?" The man looked at

them with such loathing that both Corey and Ellen took a step backward.

"If you get caught," Corey pointed out, "you'll go to jail."

"Tell me about it."

The way he said, "Tell me about it," made it clear that he already knew firsthand about going to jail. Ellen shuddered. Who was this Tony? And how were she and Corey going to get away from him?

"Listen hard," Tony said. "This is what we're going to do and I don't want any screwups."

Ellen looked at him. She needn't have worried about remembering specific details, when they watched him rob the snack store. The details of this man's face were etched in her brain. She would never forget this face, this voice. Never.

"We're going to spend the rest of the night in the ticket booth, right next to the gate. No matter what we hear or who we see, we're going to be quiet. You got that?"

Ellen nodded. Beside her, Corey nodded, too.

"Good. Because one peep out of either one of you and the other one will never talk again."

Ellen swallowed. Corey slid his hand into hers and held tight. In his other hand, he still clutched the remains of his bag of peanuts.

"As soon as the zoo opens in the morning," Tony said, "we'll be out of here." He jerked his head toward the door. "Let's go."

He made them walk in front of him. Slowly, they went past the flamingos, and down the path past the great apes.

Ellen knew there was one big flaw in the man's plan.

They couldn't spend the night in a ticket booth because the ticket booths were on the other side of the barrier.

She didn't tell the man that, though. Let him think what he wanted. The longer he kept her and Corey on the zoo grounds, the greater the chance that they would be rescued. This is where Mom and Dad would look for them.

Ellen had put the flashlight in her pocket before the man opened the door. She left it there. The slower they walked, the better the chances that help would come.

Corey tugged on her sleeve. She leaned down but kept walking.

"I'm going to escape," Corey whispered.

"No!" Ellen said. "Don't do something stupid."

"What are you kids whispering about?" Tony demanded. "I told you to be quiet and I meant it."

Just then, Ellen stumbled on an uneven part of the path. If Corey hadn't caught her sleeve, she would have fallen. Instantly, Tony was there, too. He grabbed her arm but Ellen knew he was not trying to help her; he only wanted to make sure she didn't run away.

"No tricks," he hissed.

They kept walking. Ellen was unsure where they were. Gradually, she became aware that Corey was dropping the peanuts out of his bag. One by one, every few feet, he took a peanut and let it slide from his fingers to the ground.

He's leaving a trail, she realized, like Hansel and Gretel. He's making a trail so that if anyone is looking for us, they'll know we came this way. Maybe her brother was smarter than she thought.

She reached up and unclasped one of the barrettes from

her hair. Then she lowered her hand and dropped the barrette, flinging it slightly to the side so that it would land on the grass and not make any noise. A few minutes later she did the same with her other barrette.

Without the barrettes, her hair hung in her eyes but she didn't care. It was more important to leave clues than to be beautiful and the barrettes were better clues than the peanuts because they could be identified as Ellen's.

Of course, clues were only helpful if someone was looking for them. As far as she knew, nobody was. Grandma and Grandpa might not have found the note; they might have decided to sleep at their own house since they thought Mom and Dad were here at the zoo. And Mom and Dad—well, who knows what they thought or where they were.

"*Chit-chit-chit.*" The soft sound was behind them. Ellen and Corey stopped. So did the man.

"Who's there?" Tony said.

There was no reply.

Corey nudged Ellen and when she leaned toward him he said, "That's the baby monkey."

"Let's go," the man said.

They walked on. Ellen felt as if all of her senses were working on overload. Her eyes struggled to see in the dark; her ears strained to hear any sound; her taut nerves were poised to react, if necessary.

Ahead in the dark, the lion roared.

Behind them, the man cursed.

He's nervous, too, Ellen thought. He didn't plan on having us show up and he isn't really prepared to take us with him.

Maybe Corey was right. Maybe they should try to escape. If they both ran at the same time, disappeared into the darkness in different directions, he couldn't catch both of them. Maybe he wouldn't even try. Maybe he would let them go.

A small voice in her mind answered, but what if he does catch one of you? What then?

There are two of us, she reasoned, and only one of him. Maybe we could jump on him and overpower him.

He's bigger, the small voice replied. And he has a knife.

Before she could continue the debate with herself, Corey took the decision out of her hands. When the lion roared again a few seconds later, Corey whispered, "The moat." And then, before Ellen had time to react, he raced toward the sound of the lion.

"Hey!" Tony yelled.

Immediately, Ellen took off in the opposite direction. She turned on the flashlight and waved it back and forth, acting as a decoy so Corey could get away. She knew exactly where he planned to go. Because she had come to watch Grandma and Grandpa fish from the lion's moat, she knew precisely how the lion's enclosure was laid out. Corey knew, too. There was a metal fence, to keep the people out, and inside the fence there was tall grass that led to a cliff which dropped downward to the moat. It was a long way down and the water in the moat was deep.

As long as Corey stayed on this side of the moat, he would be safe from the lions but he was counting on the fact that the man wouldn't know that. Only someone who had observed the lion area carefully would realize that a person could go under the fence and still be perfectly safe. Corey was betting that Tony wouldn't look for him on the other side of the lion's fence.

Ellen heard footsteps behind her. The man was after her, not Corey. She would have to turn off her light. If she didn't, he would catch her for sure. She switched off the flashlight and turned to her right. She put her right arm out in front of her as she ran, so she wouldn't bump into anything. Her left shoulder didn't throb anymore but she kept that arm close to her chest anyway.

It was impossible not to make noise as she stumbled through the tall ferns and scrub alder. She pushed on and found herself on one of the paths again.

Her outstretched hand hit something. Quickly, she felt a metal railing with more than one rung. But what was on the other side? She ducked down and crawled between the rungs. She was in tall grass now and she stayed on her hands and knees. After only a few feet, as she put one hand out to move forward, she felt nothing. Air. Empty space. She was at the edge of a drop-off.

She heard a splashing sound from below and realized she must be above the hippo pool. She couldn't think of any other water at this end of the zoo.

She tried to remember how far it was from the top of the overhang, where she apparently was, to the water. About four feet, she thought. Close enough that she could probably slide down without hurting herself.

She wondered how dangerous hippos are. What would they do if a person dropped down into their pool, swam across, and escaped out the other side? Do hippos ever attack humans?

As Ellen crouched on the edge of the overhang, she heard movement behind her. Another peacock? An animal? Or the knife-wielding thief?

The man did not have a flashlight. Thank goodness for that. At least he would have to come within a few feet of her in order to find her.

If it was the man, and he saw her, she decided to take a chance on the hippos.

And then she saw him. He stopped about eight feet to her left, on the other side of the railing. He didn't look toward the pool. He turned his back to the water, leaned his elbows on the guard rail, and stood still. She was certain his eyes were scanning the path and the bushes; he was looking and listening, trying to find her.

Ellen hardly dared to breathe. Light clouds drifted across the moon again. The man was a black silhouette, looming beside her.

COREY ran. He didn't hear anyone coming after him; the man must be chasing Ellen. He hoped the man didn't catch her. Maybe it had been wrong to bolt like that. He had been thinking only about how to escape. He didn't think that he might put Ellen in jeopardy.

The lion's area should be just ahead. He knew all about where the lions can and can't go, from when he had come to watch Grandma and Grandpa fish in the moat. His plan was to squeeze under the fence and go to the edge of the cliff, behind the trees. It would be hard for anyone to see him there, even in the daylight. In the dark, it would be impossible.

The man would be afraid to go into a place where wild lions live. He wouldn't know about the steep cliff that went to the edge of the moat or about the hidden fence at the bottom. He wouldn't know that the lions couldn't get to the cliff, even if they swam across the moat.

"*Chit-chit-chit.*" The sound came out of the dark. It was the same sound he had heard a few minutes ago. It still sounded to him like the baby monkey. Maybe Shadow was following him.

Corey stopped running and looked around but it was too dark to see what had made the noise. He wished he hadn't left his flashlight by the monkey house.

He should have reached the lions by now. Had he been mistaken about where he was when he broke away from the man? What if he had run the wrong way? Had he gone in circles, the way people do when they're lost in the woods?

Corey waited, listening.

"*Chit-chit-chit.*" There it was again, just to his right. He thought it was Shadow, but what if he was wrong? Maybe it was Tony, pretending to be a monkey so Corey would come closer.

Where was he? Which way were the lions?

There was a rustling in the bushes. Corey saw only the outlines of trees and shrubbery. He squinted, trying to see if there was a small animal shape, too.

"*Chit-chit-chit.*" The sound came from behind him

now. Corey turned and saw movement at the base of a tree. It was the baby monkey.

Corey dropped to his knees. "Hello," he whispered. "Don't be scared." He held out one hand, in case the monkey wanted to sniff his fingers the way dogs do when they first meet a person.

The monkey didn't move. Corey inched closer. If he could catch the baby monkey, he would do it. The little monkey would be safe with him and Corey could keep it until they were rescued. Ordinarily, he would never try to catch a wild animal but this was an emergency. He could make sure that Shadow didn't escape from the zoo and get hit by a car or some other terrible fate.

"Good little monkey," Corey whispered. "Good Shadow." He moved closer.

"*Chit-chit-chit.*"

Slowly, Corey crept closer to the baby monkey. He wished he could tell the monkey not to be afraid.

He should have paid more attention to Ellen's science fair project. Ellen told him how to talk to Prince, and Corey tried a few times, but he never could concentrate the way he was supposed to. Instead of focusing on Prince, he always made up stories in his mind, imagining what Prince might say to him. Ellen sent the same thought, over and over, but Corey got bored with the same thought and soon gave up trying.

If Ellen were here, she might be able to talk to the monkey, tell it that they were his friends and he would be safe with them. Ellen might be able to coax the monkey to come to him.

But Ellen wasn't here. She was somewhere in the dark

zoo, fleeing from the evil man. What if the man had caught her? He would be angry because they had tried to escape; what would he do to Ellen?

It's my fault, Corey thought miserably. If I hadn't pretended to see Mom and Dad, we would not be alone in the zoo with a madman. What if he caught Ellen and took her out of the zoo and hid her somewhere and tried to collect a ransom and Corey never saw Ellen again? What if . . .

Corey felt something brush his sleeve. Startled out of his horrible fantasy, he looked down and saw the baby monkey standing beside him.

Slowly, Corey put his hand forward and stroked the monkey's head. The monkey didn't move. Corey petted it again. Gently, he put his other hand on the monkey's stomach and picked the monkey up.

He held it against his chest and the monkey snuggled against him.

"It's OK," Corey whispered. "You're safe with me."

As he stood up, the monkey put its arms around Corey's neck. I'll go back to the monkey house, Corey thought. That's probably the last place in the zoo that the man would go now. I'll be safe there and I can put Shadow back in the monkey cage, where he belongs.

I'll find the main path again, and stay on it until I come to the monkey house.

"Don't be scared," he told the monkey. "I'll take you back to your mother."

He was not at all sure of his directions but he started out, carrying the baby monkey. Sooner or later, he would come to something he recognized and then he would know which way to go.

He walked slowly, cuddling the little monkey against him. He wished someone could take a picture of him. He wanted to remember always how it felt to hold the baby monkey. Maybe, when he grew up, he would work in a zoo. He would protect animals like the golden lion tamarin and keep them safe.

There were bushes with thorny spikes around him now; the sharp spines snagged his shirt as he pushed his way through. He tried to think where in the zoo he had seen bushes like these. Was it over by the llamas or in front of the hippo pool? He couldn't be clear over by the llamas; he had not run that far.

He must be near the hippos. Yes, he was near the hippo pool which meant he was close to the main path. Soon he would find it. Soon he could start back to the monkey house.

11

ELLEN's legs ached. She had crouched there, beside the hippo pool, for several minutes. Why didn't the man leave? He must be waiting for her to move, to make a noise, so that he would know where she was.

Well, Ellen wasn't going to move. Her legs felt like they were rusted shut at the knees and might never straighten out again but she stayed still.

The man cursed. He turned around, hit the railing with his fist, and cursed again. Then, muttering to himself, he walked away from the pool.

Relief flooded through Ellen. He was leaving. She was safe. She could stay right here at the edge of the hippo pool until morning, and he wouldn't find her. He wouldn't find Corey by the lion's moat, either, she was sure of that, and by morning someone would come looking for them.

Her taut muscles relaxed slightly.

She heard the sound of the man moving away from her.

"HA!" he shouted. "I got you, you little bugger!"

Ellen gasped. She scrambled to her feet and whirled in the direction of the man's voice. Her legs, numb from her cramped position, threatened to buckle. She reached for a tree trunk to steady herself.

She heard Corey's scared voice. "Let go of me."

Tears of frustration stung Ellen's eyes. Corey wasn't safe by the lion's moat. He was back in the clutches of the man with the knife. What had gone wrong? Did Corey get mixed up in the dark and run the wrong way?

"*Chit-chit-chit-chit-chit.*"

There it was again. The same sound she had heard earlier.

"Stop it!" Corey cried. "You're scaring him."

Him? Who was with Corey?

"Be quiet and do what I say."

"*Chit-chit-chit-chit.*"

"You made him run away!" Corey said.

"Call your sister," the man commanded.

Ellen didn't move. She held her breath.

"Ellen?" Corey sounded panicky now.

"Call her again. Louder."

"Ellen!" He was crying now; she could tell by the way his voice quavered.

Ellen was quiet. If she let the man know where she was, she and Corey would both be hostages again. That wouldn't help Corey. If the man didn't find her, maybe she could still sneak away and get help.

"She can't hear me," Corey sobbed.

"How do you know? Do you know where she went?"

Ellen heard Corey gulp, the way he always did when he was trying not to cry. "She was going to hide by the lions."

What's he doing? Ellen wondered. Why does he want the man to go back to the lions? Corey must think he can still get away and hide by the moat. Why else would he say that?

Silently, she pleaded with her brother. Don't do anything foolish, Corey. Don't try to escape again. It isn't worth the risk. Just do what the man tells you to do and I'll get help.

Somehow.

Ellen's head throbbed. She wished she could take a couple of aspirin. She knew there were probably some aspirin in the first-aid kit that Mrs. Caruthers had left in the tent but the tent was on the other side of the zoo. It might as well be on Mars, for all the good it did her.

She heard movement. Neither the man nor Corey said anything more but Ellen could hear the sounds as they moved farther away from the hippo pool. If she followed, would the man hear her? She couldn't go the other direction; the hippo pool was there.

She waited until she couldn't hear them anymore. Then, moving as cautiously and quietly as she could, she made her way toward the railing and returned to the path.

She tried to think if there were any parts of the zoo she had not been that night, places where there might be a telephone. Did the security guard have an office somewhere or did he just walk around all night? Where WAS he? If she couldn't get out of the zoo, she had to do something to bring help here. But what?

There were plenty of dry leaves on the ground; she could rub sticks together to get a spark. A fire would bring help.

The animals were fenced in. What if the fire blazed out of control? She couldn't start a fire at the zoo, not even to help Corey.

An airplane buzzed high overhead. Ellen pointed her light straight up in the air and turned it on. Then she put her hand over the end and blocked out the light for a second. She rapidly put her hand on and off the light so that if anyone was looking down from the sky, they would see the light flashing on and off.

Dot, dot, dot; dash, dash, dash; dot, dot, dot. She tried to flash an SOS signal, using the Morse code. She hoped she was remembering the code correctly. She had learned a few signals as a science project last year but she hadn't used the code since she finished the project. Still, the three dots, three dashes, three dots, stuck in her mind and she flashed it several times, until she could no longer hear the airplane.

She knew the chances were slim that anyone in an airplane would see her small light. She had flown once, when her family went to Disney World. She remembered sitting next to Dad, looking out the window of the plane at the tiny houses down below. They had seemed like toys rather than real buildings.

Before they landed in Florida, Dad had pointed out small patches of blue, no bigger than postage stamps, and told her that those were swimming pools. They had laughed together when Dad said he hoped the pool at their motel was bigger than that.

Dad, she thought, *why haven't you come? What happened to you?* She knew something was terribly wrong, or her parents would be here by now. And Grandma and Grandpa, too. If they had got home, they would have checked the telephone machine; they would have seen her note. And they would immediately have arranged to get in the zoo. But none of it had happened. *Why not?*

She tried to think what to do.

I'll have to scream, she decided. I'll go to the gate and I'll scream for help as loudly as I can.

Probably the man with the knife would hear her but maybe someone else would hear her, too. Someone who could help. She knew it was a risk but she decided it was a chance she had to take. She had to do something and, since she couldn't get out of the zoo, yelling seemed to be the best way to bring help in.

With the decision made, she felt better. She paused a moment, trying to think where her chances of being heard would be the greatest. It would have to be where there wasn't a parking lot between the fence and street. Otherwise, no one would hear her, no matter how loudly she yelled.

Maybe, she thought, I should go through the Elephant Forest. She was close to that and she knew the back side of the Elephant Forest adjoined Aurora Avenue North, which was one of the main streets in Seattle. She didn't know exactly how close the street was to the back of the zoo, but she had heard cars going past when they were bathing Hugo.

She wasn't afraid to go into the Elephant Forest. She was fond of the giant beasts.

She moved cautiously, trying not to make any noise.

Although her shoulder didn't hurt much anymore, she was glad there was a way into the Elephant Forest that did not require climbing.

She slid down the gully into the clearing at the edge of the Elephant Forest. Except for getting the seat of her jeans dirty, it was an easy slide. At the bottom, she found wooden poles with cables between them—impossible for an elephant to get past, but no problem for a girl. She slipped between two cables. She didn't see or hear any elephants. She hoped it wouldn't frighten them for her to yell for help from their territory. She hurried across the clearing and entered the brush and trees of the Elephant Forest. Ahead, on the far side, she heard an occasional car.

Yes, this was the right place to call for help. It was as close to people as she could get.

It seemed to take forever to make her way through the undergrowth and, as she made her way around shrubs and trees, she knew it would be easy to go the wrong way. She kept listening for the sound of traffic ahead, and went toward it.

Ellen reached the back fence, and gripped it with both hands. She glanced once behind her, listening carefully, but heard nothing. She had no idea where the man and Corey were now.

"HELP!" Ellen yelled. "I'm trapped in the zoo. Someone help me. Please! HELP!!"

Through the trees, she saw the headlights of a car. She

pointed her flashlight toward the car, and waved it back and forth. "HELP!" she shouted, so loudly that it made her throat hurt. She kept calling, over and over, for what seemed like five or ten minutes. "Help. Help!"

And then she heard something, or someone, moving toward her from behind. Had she frightened an elephant? Was one of the beasts stomping toward the sound of her voice?

"HELP," she yelled again.

"HELP," echoed another voice, directly behind her.

Corey.

"Shut up!" commanded the man.

Before Ellen could run away from the voices, the man's hand grabbed her arm.

He had heard her cries.

He had found her.

12

THE AIRPORT shuttle bus stopped at the Streaters' house. Mr. Streater paid the driver.

"Home never looked better," Mrs. Streater said, as she unlocked the front door. "Hello, Prince. Did you miss us?"

"I am exhausted," Mr. Streater said.

They carried their luggage to their bedroom.

Mrs. Streater peered into Ellen's bedroom and then into Corey's. "All the sleeping bags are gone," she said. She turned on the lights in the room she used as an office. It contained a hide-a-bed, and when they had company it doubled as a guest bedroom. It was where Ellen and Corey's grandparents slept when they stayed overnight.

"Nobody's home," Mrs. Streater said.

"Did you think they would be? I knew your folks would take the kids to the zoo, when we didn't get here on time."

"I knew Father would go on the camp-out but I didn't

think Mother would actually sleep in a tent with a cast on her leg."

"Your mother has always been a good sport. And she does love the zoo."

"She probably couldn't stand to stay behind and miss out on the fun," Mrs. Streater said.

"Maybe it's just as well our plane had engine trouble and we had to land in Portland. This way your parents went on the camp-out, after all."

"They'll have tales to tell in the morning," Mrs. Streater said. "Especially Corey."

"It *is* morning. It's after midnight and I am going straight to bed."

"Don't you want to see if there are any messages?"

Mr. Streater shook his head. "We can't return any calls at this time of night anyway. I'll listen to the messages tomorrow."

Mr. and Mrs. Streater got ready for bed. "I wonder if Ellen and Corey are asleep," Mrs. Streater said.

"I doubt if Corey will close his eyes—or his mouth— all night."

Mrs. Streater turned out the light.

Prince whined and pawed at the side of the bed.

"Go lie down, Prince," Mr. Streater said.

Prince whined and pawed again.

"Do you suppose they were so excited about the camp-out that they forgot to feed Prince and let him out?" Mrs. Streater said.

"Anything is possible."

Mrs. Streater sighed, turned on the light, and got up. "Come on, Prince," she said.

"He probably just wants two dinners," Mr. Streater grumbled.

Mrs. Streater went to the kitchen and turned on the light. She put Prince out the back door. While she waited for him to come back, she noticed the piece of paper on the telephone machine.

"Dear Mom and Dad:

We are waiting for you at the zoo."

Quickly she read the rest of Ellen's note. "Mike!" she called. "Mother and Father didn't take the kids to the zoo. Ellen and Corey went by themselves. They took a cab."

Mr. Streater came to the kitchen and looked at the note. "Your folks must have met them there after they went to the doctor. They would never allow the kids to stay there overnight alone. Neither would the zoological society."

Mrs. Streater dialed her parents' home. "There's no answer," she said.

"Of course not. Your folks are at the zoo, having the time of their lives."

Mrs. Streater let Prince in and fed him.

"Are you coming to bed or not?" Mr. Streater rubbed one bare foot on top of the other.

"I'm going to listen to the messages. Just in case there's something from the kids that we need to know."

Mr. Streater leaned against the refrigerator and yawned.

She pushed the button to play back messages and began to jot down names and telephone numbers. One message was Mrs. Streater herself, saying that she and Mr. Streater were in the Portland airport and didn't know when they would get home. There were several "bleeps" on the machine after that, indicating that someone had called but left no message.

"All those calls were probably us, too," Mr. Streater said.

The next message on the machine was from Mrs. Streater's father. He said, "Hello, it's me. Esther and I are on our way to the hospital."

Mr. Streater snapped to attention. Mrs. Streater reached for him and clutched his pajama sleeve while they listened to the rest of the message.

When they heard, "I'll call you tomorrow, after you get home from the zoo," Mr. Streater said, "I don't like this. I don't like this one bit."

Mrs. Streater turned off the answering machine without listening to the rest of the messages. "Where are the kids?" she said. "Even Corey would know better than to stay at the zoo alone."

"Let's not panic. Maybe someone from the zoological society stayed with them."

"But wouldn't they call and tell us that?"

"Maybe they did. Let's listen to the rest of the messages."

They turned the machine back on and played the rest of the messages. There was nothing from Ellen, Corey, or anyone from the zoological society.

Mr. Streater said, "Let's call Mrs. Caruthers."

Mrs. Streater looked up her number and dialed it. After six rings, a sleepy male voice said, "Hello?"

"I'm sorry to disturb you so late at night," Mrs. Streater

said, "but I need to speak with Mrs. Caruthers. It's urgent."

"She isn't here. This is her son."

"Do you know anything about the children who were going to camp overnight at the zoo? This is their mother and we had plane trouble and didn't get home on time. We have a note saying that the children went to the zoo."

"That's right; the kids are at the zoo."

"Do you know where? If we go there now, do you know where we can find them?"

"You can't get in now. All the gates are locked at night."

"Are you certain that's where the children are?"

"Positive. Ma called a little while ago and she said the kids got there a half an hour late. She was glad she didn't have to wait any longer than that because . . ."

"Do you expect her home soon?" Mrs. Streater didn't mean to be rude and interrupt, but she was anxious about Ellen and Corey.

"She won't be home until morning."

"Oh," Mrs. Streater said. "She stayed, then?"

"She said she couldn't leave, not when . . ."

"How kind of her!"

The voice at the other end stifled a yawn.

"Thank you so much," Mrs. Streater said. "I'm sorry I woke you up. We'll go to the zoo first thing in the morning to bring the kids home."

She hung up, turned to Mr. Streater, and said, "Mrs. Caruthers stayed at the zoo. Wasn't that nice of her?"

"She probably didn't have any choice. Corey probably refused to leave."

"We must do something special, to thank her. Maybe we could send flowers."

"Well, let's wait until daylight to order them," Mr. Streater said, as he returned to the bedroom.

"As long as I'm up, I'm going to call the hospital," Mrs. Streater said. "Maybe someone can tell us how Mother is." Just as she reached for the telephone, it rang.

"This is Jeff Caruthers. You called for my mother a few minutes ago. I was kind of fuzzy minded on the phone but after you hung up, I realized exactly what you had said. Aren't you at the zoo now?"

"No. That's why I called you. Our plane was late and we just got home."

"Ma said the kids came to the zoo alone and met you there a few minutes later. She said she left as soon as you arrived."

"She isn't with them? She didn't stay at the zoo?"

"Ma's at the hospital. My sister's having a baby."

"Then who's with Ellen and Corey?"

"I don't know. Ma thought you were."

Mrs. Streater's hand shook as she hung up the phone and called the police.

"I need help," she said. "I think my children are alone at the Woodland Park Zoo."

13

"Stop yelling," the man said, as his arm tightened on Ellen's shoulder.

She tried not to cry but the pain from his hand on her shoulder was excruciating. Blinking back tears, she glared up into his angry eyes.

"Some people heard me," she lied. "Their car slowed down and I saw them point at me. They've gone for help."

"You're bluffing." The man's other hand gripped the back of Corey's shirt. "Even if you aren't, no one can get in here. I should have got rid of you kids as soon as I found you," he growled. "I should have tied you up, too. Or locked you in the snake house."

Too? thought Ellen. Who else is tied up?

"I had the baby monkey," Corey whimpered. "I was taking it back to its mother but he grabbed me and made me lose it." The man yanked Corey's shirt and Corey gulped, to keep from crying.

"Stand still and be quiet," the man said. "I need to think."

A twig snapped. Ellen jumped. Beside her, she felt the man stiffen. Was the baby monkey following them? She peered into the darkness and she knew the man and Corey were doing the same. A large shape moved toward them from Ellen's right and Ellen realized it was an elephant.

They are such big, strong animals, she thought. If only I had their strength. If only they could help us.

And then she thought, maybe they can. The trainer had told her that elephants have the reasoning ability of a third grader. He said some elephants understood thirty different commands. If the elephants were that smart, maybe she should try to talk to them. Maybe they would get her message.

She tried to block everything else out of her mind, the way she did when she sent her thoughts to Prince. It wasn't easy to do when she was so frightened but her weeks of practice helped.

She concentrated only on the large, dark shape that ambled toward her through the trees. *Friend elephant. Help us. We are your friends and we're in danger. Please help us.*

The elephant stopped. It stood quietly for a moment while Ellen silently repeated her urgent plea. *Friend elephant: help us.* The elephant moved its trunk back and forth, sniffing.

Ellen heard movement from her left now. Another elephant?

The first elephant lifted its trunk and trumpeted. The

loud, sudden noise sent chills down Ellen's arms. Was it answering her? Or did it trumpet because it somehow sensed her fear and Corey's? Maybe it just wanted to warn the other elephants that there were strangers in the Elephant Forest.

Farther back in the forest, a second elephant answered.

"We're going to have an earthquake!" Corey cried. "A BIG earthquake."

"What are you talking about?" the man said.

Ellen wondered the same thing.

"Listen to them," Corey said. "The elephants do that when they're scared. They can sense earthquakes before people can. Before the last big earthquake in San Francisco, all the elephants in the San Francisco Zoo trumpeted, just that way, to warn the other elephants that they were in danger. The keeper at the San Francisco Zoo said they wished they had listened to the elephants and left town before the earthquake hit."

For a moment, Ellen believed him and wondered how he knew what had happened in San Francisco. Then she realized it was another of Corey's tall tales. He was trying to frighten the man. Perhaps if the man got scared enough, he would run away, to try to save himself from disaster.

"Corey's right," Ellen said. "We read about it in *Junior Geographic* magazine. The elephants started trumpeting about ten minutes before the earthquake began."

"One man who was visiting the zoo that day got a broken leg during the earthquake when a tree fell on him," Corey said. His words spilled out like water from a pitcher, flowing faster and faster, the way he always talked when he got into one of his stories. "Afterward, he said if he had known that the elephants were trying to warn him, he would have run far away from the zoo and gone somewhere safe to hide, like a basement. Instead, his leg was crushed under the tree and he was almost trampled when the elephants stampeded."

The first elephant stepped closer. Its trunk reached toward them, as if wanting to touch or smell them. The man leaned backward.

Ellen tuned out Corey's voice. She focused all of her energy on sending her thoughts to the elephant. *Good elephant, help us! We need you. The man is evil. Please help us escape.*

The elephant trumpeted again; other elephants replied. There were more of them now and they all seemed close.

Behind her, on the other side of the fence, Ellen heard another car go past. In front of her, and from both sides, she heard movement. Although Ellen could make out only three distinct shapes, she knew that there were several more elephants nearby.

They trumpeted again. And again. The sound filled the night. It bounced back from the paths, from the trees, from the stars.

If the security guard was anywhere on the zoo grounds, Ellen thought, surely he would come to investigate. He would hear the elephants and come to see what was wrong. Even the cars whizzing past on Aurora Avenue would hear this much noise. Maybe someone would wonder what was wrong and call the police.

Keep calling, good elephants. Bring help.

There was another loud eruption from the elephant

chorus. A tingle of excitement prickled Ellen's skin. She was sure the elephants recognized that she and Corey were in danger and they were responding in the only way they could. Would their cries for help work? Would someone hear them and come?

"An earthquake's coming," Corey repeated. "The elephants know that an earthquake's coming."

"Let's get out of here," the man said.

"You'll get away faster if you go alone," Ellen said.

The man grabbed Corey's arm in one hand and Ellen's arm in the other. He started away from the fence, pulling them with him. "We're staying together," he said, "until I collect my ransom. Now, move it."

The elephants kept calling. It was a steady clamor with first one and then another sounding the alarm.

The man moved around the first elephant, keeping lots of space between it and them. Even in the dim light, Ellen could see that it was watching them. Its huge ears were spread wide and its trunk was raised in the air. Just as they passed it, the elephant let out a mighty blast.

The man began to run. Ellen and Corey stumbled along beside him.

The clouds lifted and the full moon once again shed its eerie light. The second elephant approached from their left and the man swerved away from it. Propelled by the man's hands on their arms, Corey and Ellen crashed through the woods while the elephants continued their uproar.

They zigzagged through the elephant obstacle course, making wide swings around each elephant that they saw. Once, the man didn't see an elephant approaching from the side and it reached out its trunk and touched the back of his neck.

The man cried out and then ran even faster. Ellen held her right arm in front of her face, trying to shield herself from scratchy branches that they passed.

They came to the edge of the forest and started across the clearing toward the gully.

The man stopped. Just ahead, Ellen saw a huge elephant blocking their way. It was Hugo, the enormous elephant that they had helped wash. The trainer had said Hugo was ten feet tall and weighed more than six tons. Looming before them in the dim light, he looked even bigger than that.

Behind Hugo, Ellen saw the gully that led out of the Elephant Forest. They could not get out unless Hugo moved.

The man walked to his right, shoving Ellen and Corey in that direction. Hugo turned that way, too. The man moved the other way. Hugo did the same. His ears fanned out to full size.

"Damn elephant," muttered the man.

Ellen looked up, directly toward the small eyes of the enormous old elephant. *Help us, Hugo*, she pleaded silently. *We're your friends and we need help.*

The elephant swayed slightly from side to side as his upraised trunk fanned the air. His big ears framed his face like giant bookends; his long ivory tusks gleamed in the moonlight.

The man let go of Corey and Ellen. He withdrew the knife from his jacket pocket.

"No," Ellen said. "You can't."

Hugo lifted his trunk higher and gave a tremendous bellow.

"The earthquake is starting!" Corey yelled.

"Oh," the man said. He sounded breathless now, and not as menacing as before. In the pale moonlight, the whites of his eyes were wide with horror. "Oh," he repeated.

"Earthquake! Earthquake!" shouted Corey.

"RUN!" Ellen screamed as she bolted away from the man. "Corey! This way!"

The elephants responded raucously.

There was no way to get around Hugo and up the gully, so Ellen dashed back across the clearing and into the forest, toward the other elephants. Despite the size and the frenzied trumpeting, she did not fear the animals as much as she feared the man. The elephants, she felt sure, were trying to help her.

Ellen knew the man was terrified of the elephants. And he was afraid of an earthquake, too. Ellen didn't think he would chase her now, not back into the Elephant Forest. Instead, he would try to save himself. He would try to get around Hugo, leave the Elephant Forest, and try to find a place where he might be safe in an earthquake.

She hoped Corey was right behind her. The elephants were making so much noise that she couldn't tell if he was running with her or had gone in a different direction. Either way, they would meet at the back of the Elephant Forest. She and Corey could go back to the fence and shine her flashlight at the cars going past until someone noticed and came to their aid.

Corey screamed. The high-pitched shriek pierced the air in a brief interlude between trumpetings.

Ellen looked back over her shoulder.

Corey had not been fast enough.

The man had caught him.

14

Tony had his hand on Corey's arm.

Ellen got a sick feeling in her stomach.

"No!" she cried, as she ran back toward Corey and the man. "Don't hurt him. I'm coming back. We'll go with you. We'll be quiet and do whatever you say." Her cries were smothered by the trumpeting of the elephants; she realized the man could not hear her.

The ground shook. Instantly, the thought flashed through her mind: it really is an earthquake. Corey wasn't making it up, after all.

But then she realized that the earth was shaking because all the elephants were hurrying forward, approaching the clearing. The whole herd was stomping its way toward her. She had always been surprised at how little noise an elephant makes when it moves but now, in their excitement, they crunched shrubbery underfoot and the forest trembled.

Corey screamed again. The man yanked on Corey's arm. Corey wriggled free, stumbled, and fell to the ground.

Ellen rushed toward him. In a brief lull between trumpetings, she called, "I'm coming. We won't try to run again. I promise."

"You kids can't be trusted," the man growled. "If I don't get rid of you now, I'll never make it out of here."

Ellen ran toward the man, wondering frantically if she was strong enough to tackle him. Maybe if she came in low, from behind, the blow would make him fall down. She had to try; she couldn't let him hurt Corey.

Corey kicked at the man, trying to knock the knife out of his hand. The man cursed and lunged at Corey.

I can't get there in time, Ellen thought. Tears rolled down her cheeks and made salty puddles in the corners of her mouth.

Corey kicked again.

The man held the knife high. It stopped above his head for a fraction of a second and then plunged downward.

Ellen screamed.

Just before the blade reached Corey, Hugo turned his head, stretched out his trunk, and pushed the man's arm. The knife whizzed past Corey's ear and clinked against the cable.

"What the . . . ?" Tony jumped and looked over his shoulder. Hugo loomed over him. Hugo's trunk reached out toward Tony again, whipping back and forth like a huge gray snake, barely missing Tony's face. At the edge of the clearing, the other elephants trumpeted.

The knife dropped to the ground.

Tony backed away from Corey, keeping his eyes on Hugo. Hugo stared back, his ears still straight out sideways and his trunk writhing.

Corey crawled through the dirt and grabbed the knife. He jumped again, reaching for Ellen's hand. Together, they stepped away from Hugo and the man.

Tony spun around and dashed across the meadow.

Hugo lunged after him.

Instead of running into the forest, Tony ran to his right. Almost immediately, he knew he had made a mistake.

There was a fence. A high fence. Unable to climb over it, Tony turned to run the other way but it was too late. Hugo stood directly in front of him now. Tony pressed his back into the fence. Hugo lowered his head, to butt Tony.

The other elephants stamped out of the forest. They moved across the clearing to get closer to Hugo, their trunks thrashing about wildly.

One elephant smashed a small tree flat to the ground with one foot as it crashed forward. When it got to Hugo, it stopped and watched, its trunk uplifted, its huge ears spread wide. A half moon of elephants stood around Hugo, like army tanks ready for battle. One after another, they trumpeted.

"Help!" shouted Tony. "Help! HELP!!"

As soon as Hugo stepped toward the man, Ellen and Corey scrambled and clawed their way up the gully, sending dirt and rocks showering down behind them. When they reached the top, they ran down the path.

"Get rid of the knife," Ellen gasped. "If he gets away from Hugo and catches us, we don't want him to be able to get it again."

They passed the high shed where the giraffes stay at night. The fence in front of it was low and Corey flung the knife over the fence into the tall grass and shrubs that grew in front of the shed.

They pounded down the path. Ellen had a stitch in her side from running but she knew they couldn't stop. As they rounded the curve where the zebras had been earlier, they saw a light.

"Zoo security," called a man's voice. "Who's there?"

They stopped running. At long last, they had found the security guard.

Ellen and Corey both talked at once, trying to explain who they were and what had happened.

"I just came on duty," the man said. "Where is the other guard? Have you seen him?"

"No."

"What about the night veterinarian or the keeper?"

"We haven't seen anybody except the man with the knife," Ellen said, "and Hugo has him."

"Hugo who?"

"Hugo the elephant."

"What do you mean, Hugo has him?"

"He has the man trapped against the fence," Corey said, "and he's going to butt him with his head."

"Oh, no!" the guard said. "He'll crush him!"

"He's doing it to help us," Ellen said. "He saved our lives."

The security guard wasn't listening. "You kids stay

here," he commanded. "I called the elephants' trainer when I heard the elephants making such a ruckus. He's on his way. Stay right where you are and I'll try to calm Hugo until the trainer gets here. I don't know where everybody else is but if anyone comes by, send them to the Elephant Forest."

Ellen was only too glad to quit running. She sank down on the path and Corey sat beside her.

"If Hugo kills the man," Corey said, "will they punish him? Will they think he went crazy and that now he's too dangerous to live in the zoo anymore?"

"Oh, I hope not," Ellen replied. Had it been a horrible mistake to ask the elephants for help? If Hugo hurt the man, it was her fault. If they lock Hugo up, Ellen thought, I'll never forgive myself.

"Look!" Corey said.

Ellen looked where Corey pointed. Through the trees, she saw blue lights flashing around and around.

"Police!" Corey cried.

They scrambled to their feet and dashed toward the lights. "Help!" Ellen shouted. "We're in here. Help!"

She saw more lights now and heard voices. "We're here," she cried again. Searchlights suddenly flooded the whole area with brightness. Ellen and Corey stopped running and blinked their eyes, trying to adjust to the harsh, unexpected light.

"There they are," someone yelled.

Moments later, Ellen saw her parents. Her parents and what looked like an entire squad of police officers. Her mother was crying. Her father kept saying, "Oh, thank goodness," over and over.

Mr. and Mrs. Streater ran forward. Mrs. Streater hugged Corey while Mr. Streater hugged Ellen and then all four of them hugged each other at the same time.

A red minivan screeched to a halt just outside the gate and a man jumped out. "I'm the elephant trainer," he said to the police. "I had a call from zoo security that the elephants were restless. What's going on?"

"There's a man in the Elephant Forest," Ellen said. "He had a knife and he tried to kidnap us but all the elephants trumpeted and then Hugo went after him."

"Hugo is going to kill the man," Corey said.

The trainer sprinted down the path toward the elephants. All but one of the police officers raced away, too.

"Who is the man?" the police officer asked Ellen and Corey. "Did he tell you his name? Do you know why he was here?"

"His name is Tony something," Ellen said.

"He stole money from the zoo and he was going to hold us for ransom," Corey said. "He was going to lock us in a room and not feed us and then make you pay billions and billions of dollars to get us back."

"It would have been worth it," Mr. Streater said, as he hugged Corey one more time.

The director of the zoo arrived, and wanted to know what was happening. He said Jeff Caruthers had called him. After the police officer explained, the director said, "It couldn't be Hugo. He's our most gentle, well-trained elephant. He would never be aggressive toward a human."

"It was Hugo," Ellen insisted. "But he didn't attack

the man. He only defended us. He saved Corey's life. And probably mine, too."

The director headed for the Elephant Forest.

"They may need my help," the officer who had stayed with the Streaters said. "I'll be back as soon as I can." He rushed away.

Corey said, "I want to go, too."

"We're staying as far away from that horrible man as we can," Mrs. Streater said.

"The police have guns," Corey said. "What if they shoot Hugo?"

Mr. Streater frowned. "I don't think they would destroy an animal whose home has been invaded. The trainer would use a tranquilizer gun, to make Hugo fall asleep."

"He didn't have time to get a tranquilizer gun," Ellen said, choking on a sob as she spoke. She knew she sounded hysterical but she was unable to control her voice. "Hugo attacked the man in order to save us. If Hugo sees us now and knows that we're safe, maybe he would leave the man alone."

Mr. and Mrs. Streater looked at each other.

"Please?" Ellen said. "He saved our lives. If there's any chance that we can help him, we should do it."

"Let's go," said Mr. Streater.

"Hurry!" said Mrs. Streater.

They rushed down the path toward the Elephant Forest. Thanks to the floodlights that the police had brought, they could see where they were going. Ahead, the elephants trumpeted again.

When they reached the gully, they stopped and looked down. A semicircle of police officers surrounded Hugo. The other elephants had retreated to the edge of the clearing and stood watching.

Hugo still had the man pinned against the fence. Hugo wasn't actually touching him but he kept flicking his trunk from one side of the man to the other. Whenever Tony tried to move, Hugo put his head down, as if he were going to butt Tony with it.

The zoo director stood beside Hugo. The trainer stood against the fence, to Tony's left, where Hugo could see him. The trainer was talking to Hugo, giving him gentle commands.

A crackling sound came from a walkie-talkie that was attached to the belt of one of the officers. The trainer put his finger to his mouth, signaling to be quiet. Ellen saw the officer push a button, to turn the walkie-talkie off.

"Back, Hugo," the trainer said. He held his hand up, with the palm toward Hugo, and pushed it slowly through the air. "Back," he said again.

Hugo lifted one front leg.

"Back, Hugo." The trainer repeated the gesture.

Corey nudged Ellen in the ribs and pointed. She looked where he was pointing and saw two police officers with their guns drawn. She bit her lip to keep from crying out to them not to shoot Hugo.

15

THE TRAINER continued to give clear, short commands. Hugo folded his ears back against the sides of his head, instead of sticking them out sideways. Ellen thought that was a good sign.

The other elephants lowered their trunks. None of them moved or trumpeted.

No one spoke. All Ellen could hear was the faint, low voice of the trainer.

"Back, Hugo." Each time he gave the command, the trainer gestured again.

The big elephant turned his head slowly from side to side. His trunk sniffed the air.

When he looked in her direction, Ellen waved at him. Maybe he would recognize her and know she was safe.

Corey waved, too.

"Back, Hugo. Back."

Hugo stepped backward, away from the fence.

"Good boy;" said the trainer. "Back. Back."

Hugo moved backward again.

The trainer stepped away from the fence, toward Hugo. He motioned to Tony to go behind him.

Tony staggered away from the fence, into the waiting arms of a police officer.

Ellen began to tremble. It was as if all of the fear that had consumed her for the past two hours needed to shake itself out of her body. Her legs quivered so badly that she wasn't sure she could stand up. She felt her mother's arms go around her and guide her to a bench. Gratefully, Ellen sat down.

"It's Tony Haymes," said one of the officers whose gun had been ready. "The con who escaped from the state penitentiary yesterday."

Mrs. Streater plopped down on the bench beside Ellen. "Oh, my," she whispered.

"We thought you were going to shoot Hugo," Corey said.

"I'm glad we didn't have to," said the officer.

"So am I," said Ellen. "I think the man was more dangerous than the elephant."

The police officer who had originally stayed with them came over to the bench.

"I'd like to ask you some questions now," he said.

"Corey," Mr. Streater warned, "you must tell the exact truth and nothing more."

Corey got a hurt look on his face. "I wouldn't lie," he said indignantly.

While they were explaining everything that had happened, the other police officers walked out of the elephant area and started down the path. Tony Haymes, with his hands behind him in handcuffs, walked with them.

Ellen watched him go.

The police officer said, "He was in for armed robbery before. When another sentence is added to the first one, he'll probably be locked up for the rest of his life."

What a waste, Ellen thought. The man didn't look more than twenty-two or twenty-three years old. If he had worn clothes that fit properly, he might even have been good looking. Now he would spend his entire adult life in prison.

He thought he was so smart, not getting a job like other people. Well, he didn't look smart now. He looked scared.

He glanced once at Ellen. The anger and hatred that had flashed from his eyes earlier were intensified now, as if he thought it was her fault that he was going back to prison.

Ellen knew better. No matter how much Tony blamed the rest of the world for his problems, he was responsible for what he did. No one else was.

As Ellen watched him pass, the edges of her fear melted a little, replaced by pity. Tony Haymes would not marry or have children. He would never go to a football game or walk on a beach or go fishing. He would never take a vacation and he would never again visit a zoo. She wondered how the chance for some fast money could possibly be worth all those years behind bars.

Corey watched the man walk past, too. "He tried to steal the baby monkey," Corey said.

"The golden lion tamarin?" asked the zoo director.

"Is that a rare one?" asked the police officer.

"Yes," said the director.

"But it got away," Corey said. "Shadow is loose somewhere in the zoo."

"Unless he climbed over the fence," said Ellen.

The director asked them exactly what had happened with the monkey and where it was last seen. Then he hurried off, giving orders to the security guard.

The police officer talked to them for a long time. Finally he said, "We may want to question you again later, but for now you can go home."

"We aren't going home," Corey said. "We're camping overnight at the zoo."

"You can't be serious!" Mrs. Streater said. "Do you really want to stay here after all that's happened?"

"Under the circumstances," said Mr. Streater, "I think we'll cut the camp-out short and go home now."

"But we can't!" Corey cried.

Ellen knew he was worried about his ten-dollar bet but she didn't say anything.

"There isn't any danger now that the police have caught the bad man," Corey said. "And you're here, to stay with us."

Mr. and Mrs. Streater looked at each other. "It's three o'clock in the morning," Mrs. Streater said.

"So the night is shot anyway," Corey said. "We might just as well stay."

Mr. Streater laughed.

The zoo director returned. "We found the guard who was on duty until one A.M.," he said. "He was in the

Animal Health Care office, tied up and gagged. He tangled with Tony Haymes early in the evening."

"Is he all right?" asked Mrs. Streater.

"Only his pride is injured. He said that one of the llamas got kicked by another llama and had a badly shattered leg. The night keeper and the vet took her to Pullman, to the Washington State University veterinary hospital. The guard was placing a call for replacement help for tonight when Tony Haymes jumped him."

"Even after all that has happened," Mr. Streater told the director, "my son wants to spend the rest of the night here at the zoo."

"It's all right with me, providing you stay in the North Meadow," the director said. "All the animals are restless because they heard the elephants trumpeting. And we'll be searching this area for the baby tamarin. I don't want the animals made even more nervous over unnecessary flashlights or noise."

"I'm too tired to do anything but sleep," Ellen said.

"Please, Dad?" Corey said. "It means a lot to me."

Yes, thought Ellen. Ten dollars.

"Ellen?" Mrs. Streater said. "What about your sore shoulder? Do you want to go home?"

Ellen looked at Corey's anxious face. "Oh, my shoulder's OK," she said.

"If we don't sleep here tonight," Corey said, "we'll never get to do it."

"I suppose since we're here, we might as well stay," Mr. Streater said.

"This family," said Mrs. Streater, "will be the death of me."

Corey smiled. Whenever his mother said that her family would be the death of her, he knew it meant she was going to go along with whatever it was that the rest of them wanted to do.

"I do want to call the hospital, though," Mrs. Streater added, "and find out exactly what's happened about Mother's leg."

"There's a telephone just ahead," said the director. "It's outside the rest rooms, near the great apes and the Family Farm."

Ellen groaned. How had she missed it? She must have passed within a few yards of the telephone, but in the dark she had not seen it.

Mrs. Streater was on the phone for several minutes. When she hung up, she said, "Grandma's leg was reset and she's sleeping now. She'll be home in a few days."

They started toward the North Meadow. Even though the searchlights had been turned off, the zoo didn't seem as dark as before. The trees were less menacing and the night sounds were friendly. Ellen's head even stopped aching.

Several times, Corey scampered ahead and returned, like a puppy whose owner doesn't go fast enough on a walk. Once he said, "Be quiet when you go around the curve. This is where the zebras do the hula."

"What next?" said Mr. Streater, but Corey had already left again.

"We'll have to sleep in our clothes," Mrs. Streater said, when they reached the tent. "We didn't bring pajamas."

"Have a sandwich," said Corey.

Ellen thought that was the best suggestion Corey had made all night.

While they ate the rest of the picnic food, each one told in detail exactly what had happened that night—all except the fact that Corey had deliberately misled Mrs. Caruthers. When Mr. and Mrs. Streater assumed that Corey thought he saw them, Ellen didn't tattle on him. She had a feeling Corey already regretted what he had done.

Mr. and Mrs. Streater explained how they waited five hours in Portland. "We called several times and always got the machine. We thought Grandpa and Grandma had come to the zoo with you."

When she heard how her parents had gone to bed but Prince whined until they got up again, Ellen said, "Prince is a hero. If he hadn't scratched and whined, you wouldn't have found our note until morning." Secretly, she wondered if Prince might have received her thoughts long distance, when she asked the elephants to help. Had he known she and Corey were in danger? Was he trying to help them, too?

Ellen put disinfectant on the scratch on her ankle and then, at last, everyone settled into their sleeping bags.

Ellen lay for a long while, unable to fall asleep despite her weariness. She was finally drifting off when she heard, "*Chit-chit-chit.*"

Ellen's eyelids sprang open. Had she dreamed it or had she heard a soft animal sound just outside the tent?

She listened. She heard her mother's even breathing; her dad gave a soft snore. Then it came again. "*Chit-chit-chit.*"

"Ellen? Mom? Dad?" Corey's whisper came from the darkness.

"Mom and Dad are asleep," Ellen said. "Did you hear that noise?"

"It's Shadow," Corey said. "I'm going to catch him."

Ellen unzipped her sleeping bag and sat up. She saw Corey lift the flap of the tent and step out. Quickly, she followed him.

"*Chit-chit-chit.*" The sound was louder now. It came from a small clump of bushes directly behind the tent.

Corey sat on the ground near the bushes. Ellen sat behind him. Neither of them spoke. A tiny face peeked out from behind the bushes. Then the little monkey ran to Corey and, without hesitating, climbed into Corey's lap.

Corey put his arms around the baby monkey. "This time," he said, "I really *will* take you back to your mother."

"This time," said Ellen, "you are not wandering about the zoo alone. I'm waking up Mom and Dad."

Mr. Streater found the zoo security man. He said the director and some other zoo employees were still searching the area near the hippo pool, where the baby monkey had escaped from Corey. Soon the baby was reunited with its mother.

By the time Ellen crawled back into her sleeping bag, she could see the first faint tinge of pink light in the morning sky. She fell asleep instantly and slept soundly until voices outside the tent woke her. She saw that her parents were already up.

Mr. Streater poked his head in the tent and said, "Wake up, kids."

Corey moaned and rubbed his eyes. "I want to sleep some more," he mumbled.

"There's someone here from the newspaper," Mr. Streater said. "He wants to take your picture with Hugo and with the baby monkey."

Corey bounded up, all trace of sleepiness gone.

Ellen followed him out of the tent.

A man with a camera bag stood with Mr. and Mrs. Streater. He held a notebook and pencil. The zoo director was there, too, and the reporter was writing down what the director said.

"Hugo is normally a gentle animal," the director said, "but when he sensed danger, he responded. He could easily have crushed Tony Haymes against the fence. He didn't do it, even though the other elephants were trumpeting and running."

"What made them start?"

"They trumpeted," the zoo director said, "because they heard the children call for help. Then, when three people ran through the Elephant Forest, the elephants got more excited and followed them."

Ellen wondered why the reporter didn't ask her and Corey the questions. After all, they were the ones who were there when everything happened.

"I asked the elephants to help us," Ellen said. "Hugo held Tony against the fence because I told Hugo we were in danger."

The reporter looked startled.

"Ellen," said Mrs. Streater, "I don't think . . ."

"She learned how to talk to animals, for a science project," Corey explained.

The reporter smiled at Ellen and Corey but didn't write anything in his notebook.

The zoo director said, "There were strangers in the elephant enclosure, yelling and disturbing them. Naturally, the elephants reacted by trumpeting and attempting to defend themselves."

Ellen could tell that, except for Corey, no one believed that Hugo and the other elephants had received and understood her messages.

Had the elephants heard her silent cries for help? Did Hugo know what she said?

The zoo director's explanation was logical, she had to admit that. Still, she couldn't help feeling that, last night, the elephants had known what she was trying to tell them.

There was no way to prove it, of course. She wouldn't even include Hugo in her science fair project, since there was no way to document more experiments. But she believed, and would always believe, that he had understood.

"Are we going to have our picture in the paper?" Corey asked.

"Indeed, you are," said the reporter. "First, I want to shoot one of you in front of the tamarin monkey cage and then we'll take one with Hugo."

"Maybe we could be IN the monkey cage," Corey suggested, "looking out through the wire. And what if we sat on Hugo's back?"

"Corey . . ." Mr. Streater said.

Ellen combed her hair with her fingers and tried to

make it stay back out of her eyes. She wished she hadn't thrown away her barrettes last night. Nobody had followed her trail anyway and now she looked like a kitchen mop, just when she was getting her picture taken for the newspaper.

The trainer was at the Elephant Forest, to help Hugo pose.

Ellen's heart filled with love and gratitude when she saw the great gray beast. As she entered the elephant area, she looked up at Hugo and saw that he was gazing down at her.

She stared into his eyes. *Thank you, Hugo,* she thought. *Thank you, dear elephant friend, for helping us.*

Corey nudged Ellen with his elbow. "Listen," he whispered. "Do you hear that?"

Ellen nodded. She smiled up at Hugo. *Thank you,* she repeated. *You saved our lives. We love you.*

"He's purring!" Corey said breathlessly. "I can hear him."

That night, the picture was on the front page. It showed Ellen and Corey standing in front of Hugo. Hugo's trunk rested lightly on Ellen's shoulder.

The headline said, TERROR AT THE ZOO.

Ellen read the article and started to laugh. "Listen to this," she told Corey, and then read one paragraph out loud: "The representative of the Woodland Park Zoological Society who arranged the camp-out was not present. She was at Swedish Hospital, where, at four A.M., her daughter gave birth to twins."

"See?" Corey said. "Nobody ever believes me."

HORROR
AT THE
HAUNTED
HOUSE

Special thanks to
Myra Karp of Wedgwood World, Seattle,
and to Daisy Makeig-Jones

Omnibus Edition ISBN 978-0-545-78469-6

12 11 10 9 8 7 6 5 4 3 2 1   14 15 16 17 18 19/0

Printed in the U.S.A.   40

First Scholastic printing, September 2014

FOR BRETT MICHELLE
October 31, 1989

Chapter 1

H ey, Ellen! I'm going to have my head chopped off!"

Over the din on the school bus, Ellen Streater recognized her younger brother's voice. She peered through the window. Corey waved and ran along the sidewalk.

Ellen's best friend, Caitlin, nudged Ellen with her elbow and muttered, "I'm glad he's your brother, not mine."

As the yellow bus wheezed to a stop, Corey yelled again. "I'm going to have my head chopped off!"

Ellen was used to her brother's fanciful stories but she wished he would wait until she got home. As she stepped off the bus, she heard her classmates snickering.

Corey danced with excitement. "It's going to happen in a haunted house," he said. "Mr. Teen is going to chop my head off with a big knife."

The bus rumbled away. Ellen started down the sidewalk toward home with Corey bouncing beside her. "You sound awfully happy for someone who's about to be murdered," she said.

Corey giggled. "I won't *really* get my head chopped off," he said, "but it will look like I do. There's a big wooden contraption with a rope and a fat sharp knife and Mr. Teen wears a black hood with only his eyes showing. I get to put my head on a wooden block and then Mr. Teen lets go of the rope and all the people watching will think the knife cut off my head. There's even going to be fake blood."

"Exactly who is this Mr. Teen?" Ellen said.

"He's Grandma's friend. She told me all about it."

Ellen raised her eyebrows. Grandma's friend? Corey's stories ordinarily did not include real people. Was he telling the truth, for a change? Or at least his garbled version of the truth?

"Are you making up a story?" she said.

"No! Grandma fixed it so we could get killed in the haunted house."

Ellen stopped walking. "WE?" she said. "Am I supposed to get my head chopped off, too?"

"Oh, no," Corey said. "You get tied up and burned at the stake."

"I can hardly wait."

Ellen saw her grandmother's car parked in the Streaters' driveway. She hurried inside, gave Grandma a quick hug, and said, "Would you please tell me what's going on?"

"How would you like to participate in a Halloween haunted house?" Grandma said.

"That depends on whether I come out of it dead or alive."

Grandma laughed. "I don't think Mrs. Whittacker would ask you to do anything dangerous."

Mrs. Whittacker was Grandma's best friend. She had no grandchildren of her own so she frequently baked cookies for

Ellen and Corey and always gave them a small gift on their birthdays.

"Mrs. Whittacker is President of the Historical Society and her group is renovating Clayton House, the mansion that was donated to the city. It's a gorgeous old house and Mr. Clayton also donated the furnishings. There are antique music boxes, hand-carved tables and chairs, an extensive collection of Wedgwood, stained-glass lampshades—I could go on and on. The Historical Society plans to turn the mansion into a museum, with the Clayton treasures on display, but they need funds in order to get the house ready for public viewing."

"So they're making it into a haunted house," said Corey. "And we get to be in it. We'll be famous! Maybe we'll get our picture in the paper."

"It's being called the Historical Haunted House," Grandma said. "Each room will be a horrible scene from history, and people will pay to take the tour. Many local celebrities are donating their time to act as characters in the scenes. They'll reenact the duel between Alexander Hamilton and Aaron Burr in 1804 and the stabbing of Julius Caesar and . . ."

"Who were they?" said Corey.

"You'll need to find that out," said Grandma, "if you want to enter the prize drawing. All of the scenes except one will be historically accurate. When people finish viewing the haunted house, they can write down which scene is not based on fact and all the correct answers will be entered in a drawing. The prize is one hundred dollars. There will be twenty scenes in all—even a medieval torture chamber."

"Are you sure Mom and Dad will let us do this?" asked Ellen. A stabbing and a torture chamber did not sound like the sort of event her parents would normally approve of.

"I called your mother," Grandma replied, "and she said it is OK with her if you want to help, since the scenes *are* authentic. You'll get a history lesson and the money is for a good cause."

"Tell her about my part," Corey said. "Tell her about me getting my head chopped off."

"Corey will be Prince Rufus, who was beheaded at the age of ten," Grandma said.

"I get to scream," Corey said. "Loud." His eyes sparkled. "Tell her about Mr. Teen," he said.

"Who?" said Grandma.

"Mr. Teen. The one who's going to wear a black hood and chop off my head."

Grandma looked confused for a moment and then started to laugh. "Not Mr. Teen," she said. "Guillotine. That's the name of the instrument with the knife. The man in the black hood will be Mike McGarven."

"Mighty Mike?" said Corey. "The D.J.?"

Grandma nodded.

"Wow," said Corey. "I'm going to meet Mighty Mike. Wait till Nicholas hears this." He picked up the telephone and began punching his friend's number.

Ellen didn't blame Corey for being excited. Mighty Mike was a popular disc jockey, known for his wicked sense of humor. Lots of kids listened to his program every Saturday, when he played the Top Ten songs and made jokes about them. Corey should have a wonderful time acting in the haunted house with Mighty Mike, and Corey's buddy, Nicholas, would surely be impressed.

"Corey says I'm going to get burned at the stake," she said.

"That's right," said Grandma. "You'll be Joan of Arc, Maid of Orleans."

"I've heard of her," Ellen said, "but I don't remember exactly what she did. Was she the one who heard voices and led the army into battle?"

Grandma nodded. "It should be one of our best scenes. You'll wear a long gown and be tied to the stake and the flames will leap around your bare feet."

"Oh, goodie," said Ellen.

"You won't really get burned, of course. They do everything with mirrors and tricks and optical illusions."

Corey hung up the phone. "The line's busy," he said.

"Who else is in my scene?" Ellen asked.

"I don't know. Mrs. Whittacker didn't say."

"That's all I do? Just stand there?"

"And scream," said Corey.

"There's a meeting of all the volunteers," Grandma said. "You'll be told then exactly what you're supposed to do."

"Maybe a movie producer will come," Corey said, "and he'll see me get my head chopped off and he'll hire me to scream in a horror movie." He raised his arms, with his hands like claws, made a horrible face, and lurched around the room.

"Mom and Dad won't let us go to horror movies," Ellen said, "so I doubt if they'd let you be *in* one."

Corey quit lurching. "They might, if I got paid thousands of dollars."

"The Historical Haunted House will be open from seven to ten for five days before Halloween," Grandma said, "so it will take quite a lot of your time. On Halloween night, it will be from six to midnight."

"I have to miss trick or treat," Corey said. "But it will be worth it."

Ellen agreed to help at the haunted house. It would be fun,

especially if she got to work with a celebrity like Mike McGarven. She could hardly wait to tell Caitlin. Ellen had never met anyone famous and she was quite sure none of her friends had, either.

Mrs. Streater came home then and heard all the details. While Grandma (and Corey) talked, Ellen wondered which celebrity would be in her scene.

"We get to scream," Corey said again. "Ellen screams while she burns and . . ."

"I don't think Joan of Arc screamed," Mrs. Streater said. "She prayed."

"Well, *I* get to scream while they chop off my head. The louder, the better."

"Just don't scream *after* you're supposedly beheaded," Grandma said. "Once the blade drops, you must lie completely still and be quiet."

"That'll be a first," said Ellen.

"It should be quite an event," Mrs. Streater said. "With so many radio and television personalities participating, the haunted house is certain to get lots of publicity."

"Mrs. Whittacker thinks the Historical Society will raise all the money they need to rewire the mansion," Grandma said. "We also hope that when people realize how many unusual items are in Clayton House—the furniture and the Wedgwood collection and all the rest—they will want to come back when the museum opens to see everything when it's properly lighted and displayed."

"What if the magic trick doesn't work right," Corey said, "and Ellen really catches on fire? The people watching would think Ellen's screams were part of the act. What if nobody untied her and . . ."

"Stop it," Ellen said, "or you'll *really* get your head chopped off."

"Nothing will go wrong with the magic tricks," Mrs. Streater said. "A real fire would be too dangerous; it will be a fake fire."

Ellen went to the kitchen to get a snack. As she took the first bite, Corey screamed—a shrill, bloodcurdling shriek that lasted several seconds.

Ellen jumped and dropped her banana. Prince, the Streaters' dog, whined and ran into the living room, sniffing the floor.

Ellen heard Grandma say, "Land's sakes, Corey! You scared me half out of my skin."

"Just practicing," Corey said.

"This family," said Mrs. Streater, "will be the death of me."

"Next time," said Grandma, "warn me before you practice."

Better yet, thought Ellen, don't practice at all.

"The orientation meeting is next Saturday morning," Grandma said, as Ellen returned. "I'll pick you up at nine o'clock. Mrs. Whittacker said if I bring you to the meeting, we can come early and she'll give us a personal tour of the mansion before the others arrive."

Ellen was glad to hear that Grandma would be there, too. Corey didn't mean to act up in public but he was so unpredictable. She never knew what he would say or to whom. If Ellen was going to be introduced to a lot of TV stars, she didn't want her little brother embarrassing her by making up one of his stories —or by deciding to practice his screaming in the middle of the meeting.

Chapter
2

Ellen peered through the windshield, eager for her first glimpse of Clayton House.

"I've driven past the Clayton property dozens of times," Grandma said. "I never thought I'd be on this side of the iron gates."

The long, curving driveway wound past a fountain. Water sprayed ten feet into the air while a sculpted cherub danced in the mist. Flower beds overflowed with gold and rust chrysanthemums; ducks and geese swam lazily on a pond.

"It's like a park," said Ellen.

"Forty acres," said Grandma.

"There's the house!" yelled Corey.

Grandma parked the car and they all gazed at the mansion.

As Ellen looked at turrets, gables, and several different kinds of chimneys, she felt a quick pang of apprehension. Clayton House seemed grim and unapproachable.

"It will be a perfect haunted house," said Grandma.

A porch with fancy pillars wrapped itself around the front of the house and a matching porch hugged the left side of the second story. A small balcony with an ornate wrought-iron railing extended from an upper room on the right side.

Grandma said, "Either the architect had a restless imagination, or else the house was designed by committee. The back doesn't seem to match the front and the sides are completely different from each other."

"I wish we lived here," said Corey. He pointed to the room with the balcony. "I'd take that room so I could sleep outside all summer."

Despite the parklike grounds, Ellen was glad she didn't live in Clayton House. But Grandma was right—it would be a great haunted house.

Mrs. Whittacker met them at the door. She led them into the great entry hall, where a huge staircase curved upward, its banisters intricately carved to resemble swans and cherubs. Sunlight streamed through a large stained-glass window, painting colored designs on the polished wooden floor. The walls were of wood, too, and all were carved in various designs.

"Samuel Clayton made his fortune in lumber," Mrs. Whittacker said. "When the mansion was built, his lumberyards were right next door." She waved her hand at the decorative woodwork. "He was one of the first to use steam-powered woodworking machinery. Previously, this sort of thing had to be done by hand. The machines made it so easy that Mr. Clayton got a bit carried away. He used fine wood throughout the house. Rosewood. Mahogany. Even satinwood."

"I never heard of satinwood," Ellen said.

"It's an East Indian tree." Mrs. Whittacker pointed to a yellowish-brown panel. "This is made of satinwood. Feel it."

Ellen touched it. The wood felt smooth and rich.

"Where do the wedge trees grow?" asked Corey.

"I beg your pardon?"

"The wedge trees. That the Wedgwood comes from."

Mrs. Whittacker managed not to laugh as she explained that Wedgwood is a fine earthenware, made by the Wedgwood Company in England.

"You mean *dishes*?" Corey said.

"That's right. You'll see the Wedgwood when we go upstairs, including some pieces which were made in the eighteenth century."

"Some are two hundred years old," said Grandma.

"Even older than you," said Corey.

"The Wedgwood collection is worth more than $200,000," said Mrs. Whittacker.

Ellen imagined living in such a building. The entryway alone was larger than the Streaters' entire house. It may be elegant, she thought, but it certainly isn't very homey.

All her life, Ellen had experienced strong feelings for places. When she went into a house, she knew if the people who lived there loved each other or if they were angry or afraid or sick. It wasn't something she could explain—in fact, she had never tried—but her feelings were invariably correct.

She had always disliked visiting a particular aunt and uncle because whenever she was in their home, it seemed filled with anger and the feeling made her uncomfortable. When the aunt and uncle divorced last year, her parents and grandparents were shocked. Ellen wasn't surprised; she sensed years ago that Uncle Ted and Aunt Cheryl did not like each other.

When she was only six, Ellen told her mother that a neighbor, Mrs. Lantow, was sick. When Mrs. Streater inquired, Mrs.

Lantow cheerfully said her health was fine. Months later, the Streaters learned that Mrs. Lantow had undergone chemotherapy treatments for cancer but had told no one.

Clayton House didn't contain feelings of anger or illness but Ellen sensed no love or joy, either. Despite the comfortable temperature, the house felt cold; with all the elegant furnishings, the mansion seemed empty. Something sinister hung in the air, as if the walls knew a secret evil that was not apparent to visitors.

Corey and Grandma were awed by the splendor; Ellen felt vaguely uneasy. She pushed the feeling aside and concentrated on Mrs. Whittacker's voice.

"The house was built in 1864," Mrs. Whittacker said. "At that time, Mr. Clayton used the lower level for his business. He had an office, meeting rooms, and a display room. The servants' quarters were also on this floor, along with a small kitchen and dining room. The main kitchen and dining room are upstairs, where the Clayton family lived."

Ellen had never heard of a house with more than one kitchen.

"There are four fireplaces on the lower floor," Mrs. Whittacker continued, "each one different." She guided them from room to room.

One fireplace was made of black and gray marble, imported from Italy. Another was a pale blue onyx, so translucent it seemed to be formed of wax. A third was surrounded by satinwood, heavily carved. Ellen's favorite was the one made from Mexican silver, with a hearth of white mahogany.

When Mrs. Whittacker led the way to the next room, Ellen lingered behind, admiring the silver fireplace. She wondered if the Claytons ever actually lit fires in their exquisite fireplaces. Flames would look lovely, reflected in the gleaming silver.

Lightly, she ran her fingers over the shiny metal, marveling at its beauty.

"Don't touch that!"

Ellen jerked her hand away and turned toward the harsh voice.

A middle-aged woman stood behind her.

"Silver tarnishes," the woman said.

"I'm sorry. I didn't mean to tarnish the silver. It's just so beautiful and I . . ."

"Well, keep your hands to yourself from now on," the woman snapped.

Ellen swallowed and twisted her fingers together, not sure if she should answer or not. She stared at the woman's excessive green eye shadow.

Grandma, Mrs. Whittacker, and Corey returned. "Oh, it's you, Agnes," Mrs. Whittacker said. "We heard voices; I thought perhaps Ellen had bumped into Lydia." She laughed, as if she had just told a joke.

The woman smiled graciously. "Your friend and I were having a cozy little chat."

Ellen quickly crossed the room and stood beside her grandmother. If that was a cozy little chat, she thought, I'd hate to have an argument with this woman.

Mrs. Whittacker said, "This is Agnes Munset, a talented artist who specializes in ceramics. She's agreed to be curator of the museum's Wedgwood collection."

"Don't you own the Potlatch Gallery?" Grandma asked, after the introductions were finished.

"Yes."

"I've been there many times," Grandma said. "I especially like your pansy vases. I've given several as wedding gifts."

The woman who had scolded Ellen was all sweetness and charm as she discussed her gallery and her art work. Ellen couldn't believe the transformation. Agnes even asked Corey how old he was and then told him he looked much older.

Corey beamed.

When Mrs. Whittacker led them upstairs, Ellen was glad Agnes Munset didn't follow.

As they neared the top of the stairs, Corey said, "Who's Lydia? You said you thought maybe Ellen had bumped into Lydia."

"I was just teasing Agnes," Mrs. Whittacker said. "Lydia is our ghost."

"Your *what?*" said Grandma.

"Oh, didn't I tell you? The mansion really *is* haunted."

"Now, Marie," said Grandma, "be serious."

Mrs. Whittacker winked at Ellen and Corey. "There *are* stories," she said, "that the ghost of Lydia Clayton, Samuel's first wife, was often seen around Clayton House in the years after her death."

"I hope I see her," Corey said.

"You might," Mrs. Whittacker said. "Lydia's ghost was here just last month."

"Have you seen her?" asked Grandma.

"No," Mrs. Whittacker admitted.

"I didn't think so. Has Agnes?"

"Agnes refuses to discuss the ghost. She says such supernatural prattling is beneath a woman of her talent and education. But the electrician who came to measure the dining room and give us an estimate for upgrading the wiring and installing spotlights swears he felt her presence." She paused and then added, "Of course, the electrician is also a member of our Historical

Society and he just happens to be in charge of publicity for the Historical Haunted House."

"And it would certainly be good publicity," Grandma said, "if rumors of a real ghost should start to circulate."

"Wouldn't it, though?" said Mrs. Whittacker.

"I hope I see Lydia," said Corey. "If I do, I'll ask her how it feels to be a ghost. Does it hurt when she goes through walls? Do ghosts ever eat? Are there animal ghosts, or only people? If I see her, I'm going to ask her if I can dress up like a ghost, in a sheet or something, and go with her to see where all the ghosts live. I bet she'd let me, if I promised to be really quiet for the whole day, so nobody noticed me."

There is no way, thought Ellen, that her brother could ever be really quiet for a whole day.

What did Mrs. Whittacker mean when she said the ghost was felt? Exactly how does one *feel* a ghost? Ellen frowned. She already sensed something menacing about the mansion. Her encounter with the museum's curator was upsetting, too, and now there was talk of a ghost. The huge old house, beautiful as it was, gave her the creeps.

"If you see the ghost," Corey said to Ellen, "send her to me. I'll ask her to visit my class at school."

"You are not going to see any ghost," Grandma said.

Ellen hoped she was right.

Chapter
3

Fairylustre. A perfect name, Ellen thought, as she gazed at the exquisite octagon-shaped bowl. The outside of the bowl showed a castle, with a bridge and archways in black, purple, green, and gold. The inside depicted winged fairies, outlined in gold. The fairies flew through the air, perched on toadstools, and hid from imps and other tiny people.

Ellen loved fairies. When she was little, her two favorite books had illustrations of fairies. She had asked to hear those stories so often that eventually she memorized them and "read" them to herself, long before she really knew how to read. She used to tape cloth wings to her dolls and pretend that they were the fairies in the stories, flying through the air. And three years in a row, she insisted on having a fairy costume for Halloween.

Ellen no longer played with dolls, but she kept a small glass fairy on her dresser, for good luck. She still had her fairy books, too. The octagonal bowl was even more beautiful than the illustrations in Ellen's books.

"You may hold it, if you like," Mrs. Whittacker said. "Until we have enough money to install spotlights, it's difficult to fully appreciate these pieces unless you pick them up."

Ellen hesitated. Mrs. Whittacker had said that even the small pieces of Fairylustre were appraised at more than two thousand dollars. What if she accidentally dropped it? Still, there was something compelling about the shimmering colors that made her want to touch them, and she longed to see the fairies up close. She picked up the bowl and turned it slowly around, examining each fairy. "It's beautiful," she whispered.

"The full name is Wedgwood Fairyland Lustre," Mrs. Whittacker said, "but it's usually shortened to Fairylustre. It was made between 1915 and 1931."

No wonder Mrs. Whittacker was excited about turning Clayton House into a museum. Treasures such as the silver fireplace, the carved banisters, and the Fairylustre should be displayed where people could enjoy looking at them.

Ellen laughed. "Look, Grandma," she said and she pointed to the shoes on a flying fairy.

Grandma looked and laughed, too. She told Mrs. Whittacker, "I've always said Ellen needs fairy shoes."

"I always wear out my tennis shoes on *top*," Ellen explained. "I get holes in them, right over my big toes. Mom accuses me of walking with my toes pointed straight up."

"Let me see the fairy shoes," Corey said.

"They point upward," Ellen said, as Corey bent over the bowl.

"Do you want to hold the bowl too, Corey?" Mrs. Whittacker asked.

Corey nodded. Ellen started to hand the bowl to him and

then stopped. The bowl was suddenly cold and a damp chill spread up her wrists.

Ellen stared at the bowl. It felt like a bowl sculpted of ice, with a fan behind it blowing the cold air toward Ellen.

"It's my turn," Corey said, reaching for the bowl.

Ellen handed it to him but the feeling of cold stayed on her arms. She watched her brother carefully. He didn't seem to notice anything unusual about the bowl. If he felt the cold, she was sure he would say something about it. Corey was not known for keeping still when anything unusual happened.

Corey held the bowl for only a moment. "You'd better take it back," he told Mrs. Whittacker. "Sometimes I get the dropsies."

As soon as the bowl was safely back on the shelf, the cold disappeared from Ellen's hands. She waited a moment and then touched the Fairylustre bowl. There was no cold air, no icy feeling. Ellen jammed her hands in her pockets and stepped away from the shelves of Wedgwood.

"Let's go see the pig," Corey said.

"What pig?" Ellen said.

"Some king of Norway was murdered in a pigpen," Corey said, "and that scene is going to have a real pig in it. Mom told me."

"I think Corey's more interested in the horror scenes than he is in fine old ceramics," Grandma said.

"The pig won't be here until the haunted house opens," Mrs. Whittacker said.

Ellen wondered if the pigpen murder was the scene that wasn't based on truth.

"The dining room is the only room of the mansion that won't be made into a scene from history," Mrs. Whittacker said.

"Instead, we'll display the Wedgwood collection and some of the finer pieces of furniture in here."

The rest of the volunteers began arriving then and everyone assembled in what Mrs. Whittacker called "the second drawing room" to get their instructions.

As soon as they were seated, Ellen nudged Corey with her elbow and whispered, "Did you feel anything odd when you held that bowl?"

"Like what?"

"It seemed cold to me. And while we were holding it, I felt a cold wind blowing on my arms."

"I didn't feel anything."

"Why did you give the bowl back so quickly?"

Corey shrugged. "I was afraid I'd drop it. And I wanted to see the pig."

Ellen didn't say anything else. She kept thinking of what Mrs. Whittacker had said about someone feeling the ghost's presence.

Corey apparently had the same thought because he suddenly shouted, "Maybe it was Lydia!" Everyone turned to look at him.

"Shhh!!" Ellen said.

"What?" said Grandma. "What was Lydia?"

"Oh, nothing," Ellen said. "Corey's just telling me one of his stories."

Grandma chuckled and the other people quit staring.

Corey whispered to Ellen, "Maybe the cold air you felt was really a ghost." Corey's eyes were wide and serious.

It made her nervous to have him say what she had been thinking. "It was probably just my imagination," she said. "Old houses like this give me the heebie-jeebies."

"Well, if you feel it again," Corey said, "tell me so I can feel it, too." He was thoughtful for a moment. "Don't tell Grandma," he said. "If Mom and Dad find out there's a real ghost here, they might not let us do the haunted house. Maybe we should keep the ghost a secret."

"We don't know that there is a real ghost," Ellen said. She did not point out that she wasn't the one who shouted Lydia's name to a roomful of people the second the idea popped into her mind.

"What are you two whispering about?" Grandma asked.

Corey and Ellen answered exactly together: "Nothing."

Ellen wished she hadn't told Corey about the cold feeling. He said he wanted to keep it a secret, but he always blurted out whatever came into his head. She wondered why she had felt the cold air and he didn't. Did she only imagine it? She would have to be careful or her parents would think she was making things up, the way Corey does.

While Mr. and Mrs. Streater encouraged Corey's imagination, they also worried that he would forget to distinguish between what was true and what wasn't. Mr. Streater often said he thought Corey had the potential to be a first-rate writer—and also the potential to be a first-rate liar.

Perhaps, Ellen decided, a door had opened, causing cold air to blow across her hands just when she held the Fairylustre bowl. Yes, that must be what had happened.

The meeting began. Mrs. Whittacker explained to the group of volunteers exactly how the Historical Haunted House would work. Ellen tried to listen carefully but it was hard to concentrate when there were so many well-known people in the room. She recognized two sportscasters, several TV news people, the weatherman from Channel Five, and a woman who did a cooking show that Ellen's mother sometimes watched.

A part of her mind kept thinking about the Fairylustre bowl and the cold wind.

Partway through the meeting, Ellen sensed that someone was watching her. When she glanced around, everyone in the room appeared to be looking straight at Mrs. Whittacker. Still, Ellen couldn't shake the feeling that someone was staring at her.

You're getting jumpy, she told herself, and the haunted house hasn't even started yet.

When the general instructions were finished, each person was told which room his or her scene would be in. Corey's scene was in the conservatory and Ellen's was in the parlor. Maps of the mansion were distributed. Ellen couldn't imagine living in a house so big that people needed maps to find their way around.

"Someone from the Historical Society will be in each room, to assist you," Mrs. Whittacker said. "Please find your assigned room and go there now."

"If you can find your own way," Grandma told Ellen, "I'll go with Corey to the conservatory."

Ellen studied the map. The parlor and the conservatory were both upstairs, across the hall from the main dining room where all the Wedgwood was displayed.

"We'll be in adjoining rooms," she told Corey.

"Good," he said. "You can meet Mighty Mike, too. I wonder what he looks like." Corey seemed to have forgotten all about the ghost of Lydia Clayton.

As Ellen walked toward the parlor, she wondered who else would be in her scene. One of the newscasters? The weatherman? The cooking school woman? Ellen entered the parlor and stopped in dismay as she saw which Historical Society member had been assigned to the Joan of Arc scene. Agnes Munset.

"Yours is the only scene with just one person," said Agnes.

"We all felt that extra actors would dilute the impact of watching young Joan burn at the stake."

Ellen tried to hide her disappointment. She wasn't going to work with a celebrity, after all.

"I'll tie you to the stake each night," said Agnes, "and I'll start the machine that makes the fake fire. Then I'll need to take care of other duties. I assume you know what you're supposed to do."

Ellen said, "I'm supposed to stand still and look saintly."

Agnes nodded. "That's exactly right," she said. "Let's try it once, to be sure everything works properly."

Scenery flats, painted to look like shop fronts and crowds of people, loomed across the back and both sides of the room, making it look like the village square of Rouen, France, in the year 1430. In the center of the scene, a pile of sticks and branches waited. If it had not been for the small platform in the middle of the pile—and the rough hewn 2 × 4 going straight up from the middle of the platform—the scene would have seemed like preparations for a homecoming bonfire or some other town celebration.

On the back of the platform, not seen from the public viewing area, three steps led upward. Ellen climbed them and stood on the platform with her back to the stake. It rose several feet above her head.

"Cross your arms and put your hands on your shoulders," Agnes said.

Ellen did.

Agnes tied Ellen to the 2 × 4 with rope. She wound the rope around Ellen, just below her shoulders, and again at the waist. Using another length of rope, she bound Ellen's ankles to the stake.

"It should be loose enough that you can wiggle out if you need to," Agnes said. "Of course, you shouldn't do that when there's an audience."

Even with the rope fairly loose, it made her feel helpless to be lashed to the stake.

Agnes flipped a switch and Ellen heard a crowd shouting. The angry voices filled the room.

"Witch!"

"Heretic!"

"Death to the traitor!"

Ellen's skin prickled.

When Mr. Streater had learned that Ellen and Corey were to be in the haunted house, he urged them to study the characters they played. Corey had not yet bothered to learn about Prince Rufus but Ellen had read everything she could find about Joan of Arc.

She learned that Joan was a French patriot and mystic who lived more than five hundred years ago. When Joan was in her teens, she believed she heard the voices of saints directing her to lead the French army against their English invaders. Obeying the voices, she inspired the soldiers and led the French to victory.

Then, during an attempt to liberate Paris, Joan was taken prisoner and accused of witchcraft. A church court condemned her. Before her death, she publicly declared the justice of France's cause and the authenticity of the voices she heard. Twenty-five years later, legal proceedings cleared her name and her condemnation was annulled. And in 1920, the Roman Catholic Church declared her a saint.

Ellen felt sorry for Joan of Arc. A lot of good it did to clear her name after they had already killed her.

Her only "crimes" were patriotism and a belief that she heard the voices of saints. Why were her accusers so angry?

When Ellen had asked her father about it, he said people can always find good reasons to do terrible deeds and that the real lesson of history is to stay calm and not be too quick to judge other people.

As she listened to the angry voices, Ellen wished the people who condemned Joan of Arc had not been so quick to judge.

Agnes hit another switch. As the lights dimmed, Ellen felt as if she stood in the middle of a fire. Red and yellow lights whirled at her feet in a way that made the pile of sticks appear to be burning. She heard the crackling of the flames, with the shouting crowd still in the background. To her amazement, she also smelled smoke.

"I can smell it!" she said.

"Several of the exhibits have smells as well as sight and sound," Agnes said. "Technicians from the Provincial Museum in Vancouver, British Columbia, helped us prepare them."

Ellen leaned her head against the stake and looked upward. Joan of Arc must have been terrified, with the flames leaping around her ankles and the wild crowd cheering as her clothing caught fire. How did she keep from struggling and screaming? How did she manage to stand there calmly and pray?

"It's perfect," Agnes said. She stood now in the viewing area, behind the ropes that would keep the public at the far end of the parlor. "You look exactly like Joan should look."

"Thanks." Perhaps, Ellen decided, she had judged Agnes too hastily. Maybe she wasn't mean, after all.

Agnes turned off all the special effects and untied the ropes. Since Ellen didn't have to practice with anyone else or rehearse any lines, she finished before Corey did.

While she waited for Grandma and Corey, Ellen went back into the dining room to look at the Fairylustre again. Each piece was different; each had exquisite colors. Not all of the Fairylustre pieces had fairy scenes, however. One had tiny drops of gold forming a spider web pattern. Another, a large vase, pictured a twisted, dry tree with demon's heads instead of leaves, and bats hanging on the branches. At the foot of the tree, a white rabbit with pink eyes, wearing a pink jacket, seemed to be running for his life. Ellen wondered if there were stories depicted on the Fairylustre or just random scenes.

Behind her, Ellen heard Corey's excited voice. "Wait till you hear me scream, Mighty Mike. I'm going to practice until I'm the best screamer in the world."

I hope he practices when I'm not around, Ellen thought.

She leaned close to the vase, noticing new details. As she did, she had the same sensation she'd had earlier, that someone was watching her. As she looked around at the empty room, she felt a sudden chilling breeze, as if someone had just opened a door or window directly beside her. A prickle of fear ran across her scalp.

Ellen straightened and backed away from the Wedgwood. There were no windows in this room and the only door was the one to the hallway. The cold air continued to brush against her. She shivered and turned to leave. The cold air swirled around her, surrounding her. Ellen stopped.

Was it a magic trick, something rigged up especially for the haunted house?

She took a deep breath, trying to control her pounding heart. Be logical, she told herself. She looked carefully around the dining room for any wires which might lead to concealed fans or air-conditioning vents. Maybe the electrician had fixed it so the air-conditioning system would produce sporadic blasts of frigid air. Maybe it was a publicity stunt. Mrs. Whittacker said the electrician was in charge of publicity.

But this room wasn't going to have a haunted house scene; this room was only a display of furniture and the Clayton family's Wedgwood collection. There would be no reason to scare people who came to admire the museum pieces.

The walls in the dining room were plainer than the rest of the mansion so that full attention could be focused on the rows of recessed china cupboards which held the Wedgwood collection. She saw no wires. No vents. No way to make a blast of cold air turn on and off.

It's the ghost, Ellen thought. It's the ghost of Lydia Clayton. The cold wind seemed to blow from all directions at once. Ellen wanted to run away from it but she felt as if roots had grown down through the bottoms of her feet and anchored her to the floor.

Maybe the electrician had not tried to start a rumor. Maybe when the electrician got close to the Wedgwood he was warned away by Lydia's ghost. Afterward, he was probably embarrassed when other members of the society laughed at his report of a ghost and so he pretended that he had made it all up as a way to get publicity.

"There you are!" Corey's voice at the dining-room door jarred Ellen into motion. The cold wind vanished. "Come and meet Mighty Mike," Corey called.

Ellen ran out of the dining room. Although the cold air did not follow her, she felt chillled to the bone, anyway.

"That's what I like," Mighty Mike said, as Ellen dashed toward him, "a fan who's eager to shake my hand."

When Ellen and Corey got home, they sat around the table

with their parents, eating tuna sandwiches, while Corey told all about the mansion and the pig and Mighty Mike. All, that is, except the part about a ghost. To Ellen's relief, Corey was too excited about Mighty Mike and about pretending to get his head chopped off to talk of anything else.

"You're awfully quiet," Mrs. Streater said to Ellen.

"She hasn't had a chance," Mr. Streater said, looking at Corey.

"Ellen felt the ghost!" Corey said.

Ellen kicked him under the table. She might have known he couldn't keep anything secret.

"I mean, there was a statue there and we pretended it was a ghost and Ellen . . ."

"Let Ellen tell her part herself," Mrs. Streater suggested.

"I'm alone in my scene," Ellen said, "but there are lots of special effects. You can even smell the fire."

"And there's weird music," said Corey. "It gets loud right when the big knife comes toward my head."

Ellen didn't mind letting Corey do the talking. She was anxious to be alone, to ponder what had happened. She needed to think about the cold wind that she thought was the ghost of Lydia Clayton.

After lunch, Ellen took a hot shower. The water poured over her, warming her at last.

The ghost was watching me, Ellen decided. I sensed it during the meeting and again in the dining room. She watched me and then she tried to—to what? To scare me away?

Why me? Ellen wondered. Out of all the dozens of celebrities and volunteers and Historical Society members who were at Clayton House today, why was I the only one who felt the ghost?

Chapter
4

As Mrs. Streater had predicted, the Historical Haunted House got plenty of publicity. Hundreds of tickets were presold. Many of Ellen's friends planned to attend and they all promised to come to the Joan of Arc scene. Caitlin said she would try to come more than once.

On opening night, the volunteers arrived two hours early, to allow time for a final dress rehearsal. The Historical Society had clearly been busy since the orientation meeting. The outside of the mansion was now shrouded in huge spider webs, making the building look as if the doors had been shut for a hundred years. Eerie music drifted across the grounds. The water in the courtyard fountain was green and slimy and the cherub in the center of the fountain was gone, replaced by an evil-looking sea serpent.

"I may not have to pretend I'm scared," Corey said, as they climbed the steps and entered the mansion. The entry hall was transformed. The carved woodwork and somber furniture which had seemed so impressive in the sunlight looked melancholy in the gloomy semidarkness. Strange sounds came from every direction: creaking doors, a muffled scream, the whoosh of unseen wings. Small eyes—rats? snakes?—glowed from corners and discordant music drifted down the great carved staircase.

Corey slipped his hand into Ellen's. She squeezed it, to reassure him, but she wished she could turn around and leave. Let somebody else stand in this creepy place every night for a week, tied to a stake.

Just then, the lights went on and Mrs. Whittacker's voice came over the loudspeaker. "By now, I'm sure you all can see how effective the Historical Haunted House is going to be. The lights will remain on for thirty minutes. All volunteers please take your places."

Ellen hurried to the parlor, put on her costume, and climbed to the platform where Joan of Arc would burn at the stake.

Her rehearsal went smoothly. First a woman from the Historical Society gave her some stage makeup and showed her how to apply it. There was foundation, eye shadow, blush, and lipstick.

"Without makeup," the woman explained, "you would look far too pale under the special lights. You're supposed to be Joan of Arc, not her ghost."

The casual remark annoyed Ellen. She did not want to think about ghosts.

"You may keep the makeup," the woman went on. "It will be more convenient for you to put it on at home each day before you come."

When the makeup woman left, Agnes tied the ropes around Ellen's ankles, waist and shoulders, turned on the various switches, and watched for a few minutes from the viewing area. Then she turned everything off, untied Ellen, and told her she was free to do whatever she wanted until she heard the announcement that it was time for all actors to take their places.

Ellen peeked into Corey's room. Mighty Mike, wearing a long black robe and a black hood, stood beside the guillotine. Corey lay with his head on a wooden block, grinning gleefully.

"Should I scream now?" Corey asked.

"Let's save the screaming for when we have an audience," Mighty Mike replied. "We wouldn't want you to overdo it and lose your voice."

Maybe *you* wouldn't, Ellen thought, but it would be a whole lot more peaceful at home.

While she waited, Ellen decided to see how she looked with the makeup on. She remembered seeing an ornately framed mirror in the room where the Wedgwood was. She entered the dining room and looked in the large oval mirror which hung just inside the door. She had never worn makeup before and she thought the eye shadow made her eyes seem enormous. She wondered how Corey felt about wearing makeup.

She left the mirror and wandered over to the Wedgwood display. Some of the older pieces, such as the black basalt, got only quick glances. Mrs. Whittacker said it was old, expensive and highly collectible, but Ellen didn't think it was particularly pretty. Other pieces, like the creamware, were much more attractive but she didn't look at them long, either. She focused her attention on the Fairylustre. She was drawn to it, feeling connected on a deep level, as if she herself had painted the small green fairies and embellished their long, sweeping wings with gold.

She stood warily for a moment, wondering if the chill breeze would appear. It did not. Ellen relaxed and began to admire the fairies.

The Wedgwood was carefully arranged by date, with a small brass plaque identifying each piece. The earliest was a large black urn. The plaque said it was made in 1768. Next was a set of cream-colored dishes with a rose and green design on the border. The Fairylustre was much newer. Ellen wasn't interested in any of the other patterns or types of Wedgwood, only the Fairylustre. Of course, the dim lighting, which had been designed for formal candlelight dinners in the old dining room, did not show the pieces to the best advantage. It was easy to see why Mrs. Whittacker planned to use some of the haunted house profits to install spotlights.

Ellen's favorite piece, the small octagonal bowl, was tipped slightly, so that viewers could see the inside as well as the outside. Ellen longed to hold it again but she didn't dare pick it up without permission.

For the first time, she realized why people have collections. She began to understand why someone would care so much about an old bowl that they would pay thousands of dollars for it. If I were rich, she thought, I would buy a piece of Fairylustre with fairies on it. She liked the vase where a spider web was made entirely of tiny gold dots, too, but the pieces that showed the fairies were the ones she liked most.

The purple, green, and gold colors of the fairyland scene on the octagonal bowl were truly lustrous. Even in the dim light, they shimmered and Ellen thought she had never seen anything so beautiful. She wished she could meet the artist; clearly it was someone who loved fairies as much as Ellen did.

The voice of Agnes Munset came over the loudspeaker. "Ten minutes until we open. All actors please take your places. Ten minutes until we open."

Ellen took one last look at the octagonal Fairylustre bowl, trying to imprint every detail on her memory so that she could think about it later.

Then she turned and hurried toward the door. As she did, she caught a glimpse of movement in the mirror. When she looked, two faces gazed back at her from the mirror, her own and another.

Ellen glanced back over her shoulder, wondering who was behind her. The room was empty.

With her heart racing, she looked at the mirror again. The other face was still there. It was a young woman with light brown curls, wearing a long-sleeved, white nightgown with lace at the throat. She might have been pretty except for the expression on her face. Ellen had never seen anyone look so sad.

Her unhappy eyes stared straight at Ellen and her mouth slowly opened, as if she wanted to cry out for help but could not speak. Her arms lifted and her hands stretched toward Ellen, beseeching her to—to what? To help her? How?

Ellen stood still, unable to move or speak. The back of her neck prickled as she stared at the face in the mirror.

Agnes's voice came again. "All actors should now be in their places."

Ellen glanced quickly around the room again. She was still alone. When she looked back at the mirror, she saw only her own reflection. The sad woman had disappeared.

Ellen hurried across the hall. As she took her place on the platform in the Joan of Arc scene, her breath came fast, as if she'd been riding her bike uphill. The face in the mirror had to be one of the special effect tricks that had been set up throughout the haunted house. Still, it had startled her so much that her heart was still pounding. She wondered how they could make the face so realistic. For a moment, Ellen had been convinced that the woman was standing directly behind her.

Before they left for home that night, Ellen took Corey into the dining room to show him the face in the mirror. She didn't tell him about it; she wanted it to surprise him, the way it had surprised her.

She led him in, pretending she wanted to show him a fairy scene on one of the dishes. "See the mushrooms?" she said. "And the toadstools? I think the fairies use them for chairs."

Corey glanced at the Fairylustre without really looking. "Mighty Mike is going to the Rose Bowl game this year," he said, "and he's going to ride a horse in the parade. He gets to go the week before and see how they make the floats for the parade. He says they make whole scenes out of flowers. I have to watch the Rose Bowl parade on television because I might see him and if the camera is pointed at him, he'll wave to me."

Ellen turned away from the Fairylustre and started toward the door. There she was again. The sad woman in the mirror was behind her, arms outstretched, beseeching. Ellen waited for Corey to notice but he just kept chattering about Mighty Mike's visit to the Rose Bowl parade.

Ellen stopped walking and pointed at the mirror. "Look," she said.

Corey looked up. "What?" he said.

"See the woman? I wonder how they do that."

"What woman?"

"The woman in the mirror."

"I don't see any woman in the mirror."

Ellen looked at Corey to see if he might be teasing her. Then she looked at the mirror again. She saw her own face. To the left, and not quite as tall, was Corey's face. And in between them, taller than both, was the woman in the nightgown.

"You don't see her, standing between us?" Ellen said.

Corey shook his head. "All I see is you and me. Is it supposed to be a trick mirror?"

"Change places with me," Ellen said. "Stand where I'm standing and then look."

They traded places. Ellen could still see three faces in the mirror. "Do you see her now?" she asked.

"Nope. They've probably turned it off for tonight."

Ellen stared at her brother. Why couldn't Corey see the face? Ellen saw the curls and the nightgown and the sad eyes just as clearly as if the woman had been standing directly beside her. She saw the hands, stretching toward Ellen, as if begging her to grab hold.

"Let's go," Corey said. "Mom will be waiting for us and I'm hungry and I want to tell her about the Rose Bowl parade."

Silently, Ellen followed her brother out of the room. It was not, she knew, a trick mirror. A trick mirror would work for everyone, not just for one person.

Mrs. Whittacker stood by the front door when Ellen and Corey went down the stairs. "You're the last to leave tonight," she told them.

"We were in the dining room," Corey said. "Ellen wanted to show me the trick mirror but it was already shut off."

"What trick mirror?" said Mrs. Whittacker. "There isn't any trick mirror in the dining room. We didn't put any haunted house scenes in the dining room because we don't want to distract attention away from the displays."

"I was only kidding," Ellen said.

Mrs. Whittacker went out with them and, using a key,

locked the door. "We had a special deadbolt installed," she said, "so it takes a key to unlock the door, even from the inside. With so many people coming through the mansion, we thought it best to take some security precautions."

"Aren't you going to turn off the lights?" asked Corey. "It would waste energy to leave them on all night."

"They're on a timer. They all go out automatically in half an hour."

"There's Mom," Ellen said.

Corey dashed to the car and began telling his mother about Mighty Mike's trip to the Rose Bowl.

Ellen rode home in silence. Twice, she had seen a woman in the mirror. Who? Lydia Clayton? That was the most sensible explanation, if you could call it sensible to see a ghost. Was it possible for a ghost's image to show up in a mirror even when the ghost itself was invisible? Why couldn't Corey see it? Why didn't the bowl feel cold to him when he touched it?

Until she got involved in the haunted house, Ellen had never thought much about ghosts. She wasn't sure if she believed in them or not. She didn't know anything about them, really.

But she knew one thing: the face she saw in the mirror was not her imagination. It was real.

Chapter
5

Ellen had a plan.

The second night of the haunted house, she headed straight for the dining room. If she saw the woman in the mirror again, she would ask Mrs. Whittacker to look at the mirror. Surely Mrs. Whittacker would see the woman's reflection, too.

If Mrs. Whittacker didn't see it, Ellen wasn't sure what she would do. She didn't have to decide, because when she looked in the mirror, she saw only herself. She waited a moment but nothing happened. She walked away and came back to the mirror. She still saw only her own reflection. She didn't have to show Mrs. Whittacker, after all. With relief, she turned her attention to the Fairylustre.

Again, she was drawn to the octagonal bowl with the paintings of the fairies. She remembered how, as a little girl, she had read her fairy books over and over, unable to get enough of them. She felt the same way now; she wanted to hold the bowl and to examine the fairies up close.

As she looked at the bowl, the room seemed suddenly cold and damp. Ellen shivered and hugged herself for warmth. The cold air intensified but it was all on her face, not her back, and she realized it came from the shelves of Wedgwood.

She squinted at the shelves, trying to figure out exactly where the icy blast originated.

Then she gasped. Her hands flew to her mouth and she stepped backward.

Two transparent hands floated up from inside the large black urn that was the oldest piece of Wedgwood in the Clayton collection. They were a woman's hands with tapered fingernails and they looked absolutely real, except that Ellen could see right through them.

Slowly the hands drifted toward Ellen. The fingers were outstretched, the way the hands of the woman in the mirror had been, as if the owner of the hands was begging.

Ellen took another step backward. The hands followed. They floated toward Ellen, the fingers rippling slowly, as if they were somehow pulling themselves through the air.

With a shock, Ellen realized that the hands were the source of the icy air. The chill wind blew out of them, straight toward her. Instead of blowing past her, as an ordinary breeze would, it doubled back, swirling around her face and shoulders, lifting her hair and then letting it fall again.

Ellen tried to speak, to tell the hands to go away, but her mouth felt glued shut. She wanted to scream for help but she couldn't. She was unable to utter a sound. She felt like a statue, fastened in concrete to that spot in the floor, unable to move or speak.

The hands came closer. The air grew colder.

One of the hands reached toward Ellen's face, as if to touch her. When the fingers were almost to her cheek, Mrs. Whittacker's voice announced, "Ten minutes until we open. All actors in place, please."

The sound jarred Ellen free from her fear. With a great burst of energy, she turned and ran out of the room. As she passed the mirror, she saw a reflection of the hands. They were floating back toward the shelves. Ellen looked behind her. The hands disappeared inside the black urn.

It was the ghost. Ellen had no doubt about that. Even the clever people who had designed the haunted house could not invent floating hands with cold air blowing out of them.

Agnes was waiting to start the Joan of Arc sound effects when Ellen rushed into the room.

Ellen stopped, her heart beating a rapid rhythm as she caught her breath.

"What's wrong?" Agnes asked. "You're white as a ghost."

"The ghost isn't white; she's transparent," Ellen said. "I saw her—the real ghost—over there, in the dining room. I was looking at the Fairylustre and two hands came floating up out of a big urn. I felt cold air and I could see right through the hands. She tried to touch me. The hands reached for my face." The memory of it made Ellen shudder.

Agnes stared at Ellen for a long moment. "Let me be sure I understand," she said. "You believe you saw a pair of hands come out of the Wedgwood?"

"Yes! I swear it really happened."

"Where are the hands now?"

"When I ran away, the hands went back inside the urn."

"I see."

Ellen could tell that Agnes was skeptical. "I saw the ghost last night, too," Ellen said. "Only last night it was a whole person, not just hands, and I saw her in the mirror by the dining-room door."

"You saw a woman's reflection?"

"Yes, but when I turned around, no one was there."

Agnes was silent for a moment, as if trying to decide what she should say. Finally she said, "Why do you keep going back to the dining room, if it scares you?"

"I like to look at the fairy scenes. The dining room doesn't scare me; it's the ghost that scared me. Why don't you believe me?"

"I just spent five minutes listening to your brother insist that purple people from Jupiter will land on the balcony outside the parlor tonight. Now you tell tales of ghost hands in the Wedgwood."

"Corey's always making up stories. This really happened."

"I told Mrs. Whittacker it was a mistake to have children in the haunted house, but she was determined to use the two of you. I can still find someone else to be Joan of Arc, if you're upset. Should I?"

Ellen hesitated. She knew Agnes hoped she would say yes, and she was tempted. It would be comforting to go home tonight and not come back—but she had told all of her friends to come and see her be Joan of Arc. She couldn't tell Caitlin that she was dropping out and she couldn't let Mrs. Whittacker down; Mrs. Whittacker was counting on her. Besides, she could just hear Corey if she quit doing the Historical Haunted House because she was afraid of a ghost. Everyone in three counties would hear all about it and, since nobody else had seen the ghost, they would think Ellen was just jittery.

"No," she said slowly. "I don't want to quit; I want to be Joan."

"Well, stay away from the dining room, since you don't seem to have a problem anywhere else. Now let's get your hands tied so I can turn things on in here. It's almost seven o'clock and people are lined up waiting to get in."

Ellen stood with her back against the stake and crossed her arms against her chest. She felt the rope as Agnes loosely tied it around her shoulders.

"Staying out of the dining room won't make the ghost go away," Ellen said.

"Nearly three hundred people went through the haunted house last night," Agnes said. "Most of them stopped in the dining room and not a single person said anything about any ghost."

"Then why have I seen it twice?"

"*If* you've seen it twice, both times in the dining room, I should think you would stay out of there. You know what the Wedgwood collection looks like; don't look at it anymore."

It seemed an odd remark from the woman who was curator of the new museum. Shouldn't she encourage people to look at the Wedgwood—to study it and appreciate it?

"If you have any more problems," Agnes continued, "I'll speak to your parents about finding a replacement."

Agnes flipped the switches which started the Joan of Arc scene. The flames seemed to leap and dance around Ellen's feet. The noise of fire crackling and voices shouting filled the room. Usually, the realistic sound track for the Joan of Arc scene transported Ellen backward in time. This time, she hardly heard it.

When the first group of haunted house patrons entered, Ellen closed her eyes and tilted her head back, the way she always did, as if she were beseeching God to save her. But she wasn't thinking about Joan or about burning at the stake.

Behind her closed eyelids, she saw a pair of ghostly hands, moving slowly toward her face, trying to touch her.

Ellen pondered what to do. If she told her parents, she knew they would insist that both she and Corey drop out of the haunted house. If they believed she had seen the ghost, they would want to protect her from any further encounters. If they didn't believe her, they would want to protect her from her own imagination. Either way, Ellen would feel like a baby. And Corey would be outraged if he had to give up his chance to scream with Mighty Mike.

She knew her parents loved her and they always tried to do what was best for her. She also knew that sometimes she had to solve her own problems. She had been terrified when she saw the hands. If she ran away now, she would feel cowardly and defeated. She would always wonder if she gave in too easily.

But how does one stand up to a ghost? How could she conquer her fear?

Knowledge.

The word popped into her mind as if it had been caught behind a trapdoor and had just sprung loose. Knowledge. Grandma always said that people fear the unknown. They are afraid of different cultures, of new ideas, of religions that depart from the safety of what they have been taught.

I will learn about ghosts, Ellen decided. I will learn about Lydia Clayton. If I see those hands again, I'll be prepared. I'll pay close attention to exactly how they look and what they do. Maybe I should start a journal, the way I kept track of my experiments in animal communication. She could imagine what the Science Fair judges would think of an experiment in human/ghost communication.

At closing time, Ellen asked Mrs. Whittacker how she could learn more about the Clayton family.

"There are some old diaries," Mrs. Whittacker said.

"Could I read them?"

"Of course. But you'll have to do it at the Historical Society's library. We don't allow any one-of-a-kind volume to leave."

She gave Ellen the address and told her the library was open on Saturdays from noon until four.

Ellen looked to see if Corey was ready to leave. He was still helping Mighty Mike clean up their scene and prepare the fake blood for the next day.

She glanced across the hall toward the dining room. What would happen if she waited for Corey in there? Would the ghost appear? She inched toward the door. The dining room was empty.

Actors from other scenes chatted as they left for the night. Ellen heard Mighty Mike's booming laugh. There are people nearby, she thought. They would hear me if I had to yell for help.

She threw back her shoulders and walked toward the shelves of Wedgwood. She stopped in front of the Fairylustre display.

Almost immediately, she felt the icy air. It swirled toward her, surrounded her, and then seemed to condense, to draw into itself. Ellen felt as if she were being sucked into the center of a small hurricane.

The wind stopped as quickly as it had begun. At the same moment, Ellen felt an icy hand on her shoulder. The individual fingers gripped her through her blouse but when she looked, she saw nothing.

"What do you want?" Ellen whispered.

A second hand touched her other shoulder. Together they pushed Ellen forward until she stopped at the rope which kept the public away from the Wedgwood.

Ellen knew that the ghost of Lydia Clayton wanted her to look at the Wedgwood.

The cold pressure increased, pushing on Ellen's shoulders until she ducked under the rope and stood directly in front of one of the Fairylustre vases. She leaned down until her face was only a few inches from the shelf.

Despite her closeness to the beautiful vase, Ellen hardly saw the lustrous colors or the golden spider webs. She could think only of the cold fingers on her back.

"Get away from there!"

At the sound of Agnes's voice, the cold hands evaporated, leaving a tingly feeling on Ellen's shoulders.

Ellen clutched the rope, feeling unsteady, as she turned to face Agnes.

"You have no business being inside that rope," Agnes said. "That's how things get broken."

Ellen nodded and ducked under the rope, away from the Wedgwood.

"What are you doing in here?"

"Waiting for my brother."

"You can wait for him in the conservatory. I thought we agreed that you wouldn't come in the dining room anymore."

"I wasn't scared this time."

"Well, it's after ten; this room is closed. And even if it weren't, I don't ever want you to go behind the rope again. Is that clear?"

"Yes."

"I mean it, Ellen. If I find you in here again, you'll be

replaced as Joan of Arc. I will tell Mrs. Whittacker that you can't be trusted to stay away from the Wedgwood."

Ellen didn't know what to say so she was silent. She let go of the rope and walked toward the door. As she passed Agnes, the woman put out a hand to detain her. "Why were you leaning so close just now? Why were you examining that vase?"

Ellen was not about to tell her the real reason—that she was leaning toward the vase because she felt two icy invisible hands on her shoulders, pushing her that way. If she did, she knew there would be someone else playing Joan of Arc tomorrow.

Instead, she said, "No particular reason. That's just where I happened to be standing."

Agnes's frown softened slightly. A flicker of emotion flashed across her face. Relief? But why did she care which piece of Fairylustre Ellen admired? There was something odd about this conversation, something that didn't quite make sense. Maybe Agnes had seen the ghost, too, but didn't want to admit it. Maybe she was afraid that Ellen would tell and that it would somehow have a bad effect on the museum.

Ellen tried to think it through on the way home but it was hard to concentrate with Corey chattering from the back seat.

"Mighty Mike says he'll take me to the radio station someday when he isn't working and take me in the studio and show me where he plays the Top Ten songs every Saturday. And he says he'll show me where they broadcast the news. And he's even going to buy me lunch at the cafeteria, where all the radio and TV guys eat."

"He must have taken quite a shine to you," said Mrs. Streater.

"He says I scream better than anyone and that if they ever

do a mystery on the radio and they need someone to scream, he's going to call me."

Lulled by the rhythm of the windshield wipers, Ellen began to relax. She tuned out Corey's voice—something she had learned, from necessity, to do with ease—and replayed in her mind the scenes in the Clayton mansion.

Lydia Clayton's icy hands had pushed Ellen toward the Wedgwood collection because she wanted Ellen to look closely at it. Why?

There's something she wants me to see, Ellen decided. Some piece in particular? Maybe there is one piece that was her favorite and she wants to make sure I notice it.

Tomorrow, Ellen decided, I'll go to the Historical Society and ask to read those old diaries.

If she knew more about Lydia Clayton, she might be able to figure out what the ghost was trying to tell her.

Chapter
6

What secrets would the diaries divulge? What would she learn about Lydia Clayton? Ellen arrived at the Historical Society's office promptly at noon the next day, filled with anticipation. She asked to see the Clayton family diaries, hoping she might soon understand the strange events at Clayton House.

The woman in charge hesitated, as if debating whether to trust Ellen with the diaries.

"Mrs. Whittacker suggested that I read them," Ellen said, "and I'll be careful."

The woman nodded and brought the diaries to Ellen.

There were three slim volumes, each with a soft leather cover embossed in gold. The pages inside were a thin parchment, yellowed with age. The writing had been done with brown ink, in a flowery script. The first letter of each paragraph was double size and full of curlicues.

Ellen carried the diaries to a table and began to read. Some of the writing was difficult to read and the language was hard to understand. Ellen hadn't known the English language had changed so much. After an hour of straining her eyes and her brain, Ellen closed the first volume and paged through the others, feeling discouraged.

She had hoped that the diaries would be personal accounts of life at Clayton House, perhaps written by Lydia herself. Instead, most of the diary entries were about the interior of the house and the furniture. All were signed by someone named Franklin Haller. Since Mr. Haller included details of cost and shipping arrangements for the furniture, the diaries read more like a designer's ledger than a personal history. Ellen wished she had gone for a bike ride with Caitlin instead of coming here.

"Did you find what you were looking for?" asked the woman who worked in the library.

Ellen shook her head. "I wanted to read about Lydia Clayton," she said.

The woman's eyes twinkled. "Do you like ghost stories?" she said, and then laughed at Ellen's surprised look. "You aren't the first to be fascinated by the reports of Lydia's antics," she said. She walked to a shelf of books, reached up, and removed one. Handing it to Ellen, she said, "Try this. It's a short biography of Lydia Clayton and includes the stories about her ghost."

"Thank you."

As she read, Ellen was fascinated by the woman who had lived so long ago. Lydia was only sixteen in 1866 when she married Samuel Clayton and went to live in his grand mansion. A spoiled girl who was used to having her own way, she threw a fierce temper tantrum the first time her husband went to England on a business trip. To placate her, he brought her a gift —a set of creamy white dishes with a hand-painted green and rose border design. The dishes were creamware, made by Wedgwood, and Lydia fell completely in love with them.

After that, the only gift she ever wanted was more Wedgwood and she devoted much of her time to her collection. She studied the old pieces and cataloged her new ones. "Her Wedgwood," according to the biographer, "was her passion and her delight."

Lydia and Samuel Clayton had a son they named Josiah, after Josiah Wedgwood. Lydia adored her baby and spent every waking moment with him. When little Josiah died of whooping cough at the age of four months, Lydia was inconsolable and never fully recovered from her grief. She became a recluse, spending all of her time with her beloved Wedgwood.

A year after Josiah's death, another son, Paul, was born. It was a difficult birth which left Lydia weak and ill. When Paul was only six weeks old, Lydia got pneumonia and died. On her death bed, she made her husband promise that he would always keep her Wedgwood.

Ellen pitied Lydia Clayton. She lost her first baby and didn't live to raise her second one. The unfortunate girl lived in the mansion only five years, and died when she was just twenty-one.

Ellen continued to read. Two years after Lydia's death, Samuel Clayton remarried. The union turned out to be an unhappy one. His new wife, Caroline, desiring to decorate the mansion to her own tastes, sold the Wedgwood collection, without her husband's knowledge, to a wealthy land baron who intended to give it to his daughter as a dowry.

When the land baron's workman arrived to pack the Wedgwood, he was forced out of the room by what he described as "a cold hurricane of such force that I thought the roof would fly off the house."

Once outside, the weather was calm and sunny but the worker refused to go back inside and try again. Insisting that supernatural forces were at work in the Clayton mansion, he believed he had been given a clear mandate not to pack the Wedgwood.

The land baron cancelled the deal, and Samuel Clayton found out what had happened. He forbade Caroline to sell the Wedgwood and he continued to add to the collection until his own death.

The incident with the land baron's workman was the first of what would be many reports of cold winds, moans in the night, and fleeting apparitions in the Clayton mansion. Local people, many of them jealous of the Clayton family's wealth, gossiped that Lydia Clayton's ghost was still guarding her worldly treasures, even after death.

The reports of hauntings continued for several years, with Caroline the main victim. Caroline, already jealous of her pretty predecessor, complained bitterly to Samuel that Lydia's spirit refused to leave Clayton House. More than once, Caroline tried to pack the Wedgwood away in storage, hoping that Samuel wouldn't miss it. He always noticed and insisted it be returned to its original shelves.

Caroline never had children and when she suffered a miscarriage, she told Samuel that it was caused by a fall she took as she fled from Lydia's ghost. Since no one witnessed the fall, there was no proof of her story, but Samuel, who longed for another child, decided to have Lydia's coffin dug up and burned. He intended to put Lydia's cremated remains in the Wedgwood and told Caroline, "She loved those dishes more than she loved me. She wants them in death, just as she always wanted them in life."

Caroline, however, refused to have Lydia's remains in the house and so Samuel gave up the plan.

Reports of ghost sightings continued to plague Samuel until his death from smallpox in 1895. He often blamed Caroline for the hauntings, saying that if she had allowed Lydia to be cremated and her remains placed in the Wedgwood, the ghost would quit haunting Clayton House. Caroline also died of smallpox, just a week after Samuel.

Years later, Samuel's great-grandson developed a passion for Wedgwood. "In particular," the book said, "Edward Clayton was fond of a new Wedgwood line called Fairyland Lustre. More than once, he declared that his great-grandmother, Lydia, would have liked the brilliant colors and the imaginative scenes."

Ellen reread that paragraph three times. Even though the pieces in the collection were dated, it had not occurred to her until now that Lydia Clayton lived long before the Fairylustre was made. If Lydia had never owned any of it, why would her ghost care about it now? Why did the hands push Ellen toward it, as if she wanted to be sure Ellen noticed it?

Whatever his feelings about Lydia's ghost, Samuel Clayton kept his promise about the Wedgwood. In his Last Will and Testament, he made sure his heirs would honor Lydia's request, as well. He left the mansion to his son, Paul, on condition that the entire Wedgwood collection must stay right where it was.

Paul not only followed his father's command, he perpetuated it in *his* will, and his heirs did the same. Samuel's great-grandson, Edward, was the last of the Clayton line. The book didn't say so, but Ellen knew he was the one who left the mansion to the city, to be managed by the Historical Society. Ellen wondered if the gift had specified that the famous collection of Wedgwood be kept or whether the Historical Society had made that choice.

After Samuel and Caroline died, there were no further reports of a ghost. The gossips of the time decided that it wasn't the Wedgwood Lydia wanted, it was her husband. The writer of the book agreed, claiming that, with the death of her husband, Lydia's restless spirit was finally at peace and her ghost was gone forever.

Ellen turned to the copyright page of the book. It was published in 1945. What had happened in the decades since then?

Were there other, unreported ghost sightings? Too bad no members of the Clayton family were still alive. The people who had lived in Clayton House would be the logical ones to see a ghost, if she appeared. But if Lydia's ghost had been seen, surely there would be some mention of it in newspapers.

Fleeting apparitions, the book said. It was a perfect description of the reflection of the woman in the mirror.

Ellen asked the Historical Society woman if this book was the most recent publication there was about Lydia Clayton.

The woman nodded. "From time to time, rumors of a ghost circulated, but none were ever documented. Eventually, they always faded away."

What did the ghost want, Ellen wondered, more than a century after her death? Why, after so many years without any proof of a ghost, would Ellen feel the icy wind which had chilled the land baron's workman so long ago?

The Wedgwood, of course. The reason was somehow connected to Lydia's treasured collection. But surely she would not object to showing the Wedgwood in a museum setting. The pieces were in no danger; they were beautifully displayed. As soon as the Historical Society spent the haunted house money, the Wedgwood would have special lights, to show it off even more. If the ghost truly loved these dishes, she should be happy to see people admiring them.

Ellen thanked the woman for letting her read the books. As she rode the bus home, she decided to go to the mansion early that night, to give herself time to examine the Wedgwood exhibit before she dressed in her Joan of Arc costume. Corey wouldn't mind going early. If he could, he would take his sleeping bag and stay at the haunted house all night.

Until now, Ellen had been interested only in the Fairylustre. She was attracted to the fairies, not the dishes themselves. Now, after reading about Samuel and Caroline and the ghost, Ellen was interested in all the Wedgwood and eager to study the older pieces. She would have to be careful, though. She couldn't let Agnes catch her in the dining room again.

Chapter 7

Everything went wrong.

Corey agreed to go an hour early that night but when Ellen told her mother, Mrs. Streater said, "You'll have to check with Grandma and Grandpa. We have tickets for the Seattle Repertory Theatre tonight so Grandma and Grandpa will drive you to the haunted house and pick you up afterward. What time do you want to leave?"

"Five o'clock. That would get us there at five-thirty instead of six-thirty."

"All right," Mrs. Streater said. "Be sure Grandpa and Grandma don't have to wait around with you. They're planning to go out to dinner after they drop you off."

When Ellen tried to reach her grandparents, she got their telephone answering machine. She left a message but they didn't call back. She tried two more times, just in case they were home but had forgotten to check the machine; each time she got the recording.

At five-thirty, she gave up. Grandpa and Grandma were scheduled to pick them up at six and obviously they had gone somewhere else first. She would just have to find a different time to study the Wedgwood.

When they arrived at the haunted house, they were astonished to see a long line of people waiting to get in.

"Looks like you're going to be busy tonight," Grandpa said.

"Mighty Mike's been talking about it on the radio," Corey said.

"This is wonderful," Grandma said. "They'll easily raise enough money to finish renovating the mansion. And I'm so proud of you two for all the time you're putting in. Grandpa and I brag to all our friends about it."

Ellen raced to the parlor and hurried into her costume. She had already applied her makeup at home and had helped Corey with his, too. She was all ready fifteen minutes before the doors opened. Just time to sneak across to the dining room and take a good close look at the big urn that the hands came out of.

But when she stepped out the parlor door, she nearly bumped into Agnes.

"Where are you going?" Agnes asked.

"To check on Corey," Ellen said. "Mighty Mike wasn't here yet when we arrived so I thought I'd better make sure their scene is ready."

"Mike's here," Agnes replied. "It's a good thing, too. You should see the crowd outside. If we can get everyone in place, we're going to open the doors early. Come on, I'll get your scene started."

Reluctantly, Ellen climbed up the steps to the platform and waited for Agnes to tie her to the stake. Agnes worked quickly, pulling the rope tighter than usual. She flipped the switches, said, "See you later," and left.

So much for coming early to look at the Wedgwood, Ellen thought. Maybe she would be able to sneak over to the dining room for a few minutes afterward.

The haunted house ran overtime. It seemed like half of King County decided to come that Saturday night. Instead of closing the doors at ten, it was 10:20 when the last visitors finally shuffled out. The time passed quickly for Ellen as she listened to what people viewing the scene said about it. Parents sometimes explained to children who Joan of Arc was and many people shrieked in horror at the idea of someone being burned alive.

That night was especially fun because Caitlin and some of Ellen's other school friends came. Although Ellen could not distinguish faces in the dim light, she recognized their voices. It took willpower not to smile when she heard Caitlin squeal, "Look! Ellen's on fire! Oh, I can't watch!"

Usually, Ellen could slip out of the rope at closing time, whether it was tied or not. That night, the rope was too tight. She had to wait for Agnes to come and untie her. She tapped her foot impatiently. Why had Agnes been so careless when she tied the rope?

An uncomfortable thought struck Ellen. Had Agnes tied her this tight on purpose, so she couldn't leave the room without Agnes knowing it? Was this Agnes's way of guaranteeing that Ellen didn't go back in the dining room? Why would she care whether Ellen got scared or not? Certainly not because she was fond of Ellen.

Mrs. Whittacker made an announcement on the loud-speaker: "Everyone please leave as quickly as possible tonight."

I'd love to, Ellen thought. She heard other actors talking and hurrying past the door to the parlor. She didn't call to them to untie her because she expected Agnes to arrive any second. When Agnes didn't appear, Ellen wished she had asked someone else to help her but by then the hall outside the parlor was empty. Where was Corey? He could untie her. You would think her brother would come to look for her.

When Agnes finally came, she looked surprised to see Ellen.

"I thought you'd be on your way home by now," she said.

"I can't get loose. The rope is too tight."

"Oh, my," Agnes said. "I'm so sorry. I certainly did not intend to tie the rope that tight." She quickly untied Ellen and apologized again. Ellen felt guilty for suspecting that Agnes had done it on purpose.

Agnes walked out of the room with Ellen and accompanied her down the stairs to the great hall. Corey was waiting for her there.

"I wondered where you were," he said.

"I couldn't get untied."

"Oh. I thought you were probably looking in the mirror again."

Don't say it, Ellen thought. Don't mention the ghost in front of Agnes.

"There's Grandpa and Grandma," Ellen said. "Good-night, Agnes."

On the way home, Grandpa and Grandma told them about the new restaurant they'd been to and Corey told more Mighty Mike stories. When Grandma asked Ellen how her scene had gone, she said merely, "OK."

"Ellen's mad," Corey said. "She wanted to go early to look at the fairy dishes some more."

"After the haunted house ends and the museum officially opens," Grandma said, "we'll go some Saturday and spend as much time as you like."

"Thanks," Ellen said. Usually, Grandma knew just how to make her feel better. This time, she had mixed feelings. She did want to study the Wedgwood but she wanted to do it now, not some vague time in the future. Once the haunted house was over, she would not want to come back to Clayton House, even to see the Fairylustre.

Corey was more excited than usual on the way home because his teacher and some of his third grade classmates had come that night. Nicholas and his parents were there, too.

"I waved at Miss Thorson," Corey said, "just before I got my head chopped off."

ELLEN went right to bed. Most nights, she read for half an hour but that night she quit after only two pages, even though she was in a good part of her book. She didn't know why it was such hard work just to stand and pretend she was being burned alive, but she felt totally worn out.

The dream partially awakened her. As Ellen struggled to open her eyes, she was aware that she had dreamed of the ghost. Usually, Ellen had a hard time remembering her dreams. It always irritated her when Corey sat at the breakfast table and related a long and involved story that he said he had dreamed. She often wondered if his dreams were really so vivid that he could remember all the details, or whether he merely invented stories as he lay in bed at night and then, the next morning, he thought he had dreamed them.

This time, she knew she had dreamed and the dream was so realistic that she could not pry herself loose from it. In her sleep, she had grown suddenly cold. Now, in her half-sleep, she shivered and pulled the blankets tight under her chin. The cold continued. An icy fog surrounded her bed, swirling around her face and seeping down under the covers.

Ellen turned on her stomach and burrowed her face in her pillow but the bone-chilling air swept across the back of her neck. As she moved her head, trying to get away from it, she felt a hand on the back of her neck. The fingers lay like five slender icicles across her skin.

Ellen tried to open her eyes, wanting the dream to end, but her eyelids felt glued together. She was sinking, swirling, drowning in a sea of ice water. Her teeth chattered and she began to shake uncontrollably.

Someone moaned, a low, groaning whisper in her ear. "Ohhhh." The moan slowly formed a single word: "Ohh . . . end." The word was spoken laboriously, as if it were a great effort for the person to speak at all. When she heard the voice, Ellen was finally able to snap out of the sleep state.

She raised her head and blinked into the darkness, still shivering.

"Ooohhh . . . end," the voice said again, and Ellen realized that it hadn't been a dream at all. She rolled over, fully awake now, her eyes staring wide into the black bedroom. When she sat up, the cold hand slid from her neck to her shoulder. The icy air still surrounded her; the ghostly voice echoed loudly in her ears.

"Are you Lydia?" Ellen whispered.

Silence.

"What do you want?"

Silence.

"I don't know what you want. Why did you come here? Why are you haunting me?"

The hand left her shoulder. The cold air now seemed concentrated directly in front of her.

"Aaahhh . . . end."

End, what? Ellen wondered. End of me? End of my life? Was the ghost threatening her? Why?

Ellen forced herself to move. She lifted her hand out from under the covers and reached the lamp that sat beside her bed. As soon as she clicked it on, the voice stopped. The cold air vanished.

Ellen looked around her room. She saw nothing unusual. Her jeans and sweatshirt were still draped across the chair, where she had left them. Her poster of the Woodland Park Zoo hung on the wall next to the window. Her radio still sat on her desk; her library book lay on the floor beside the bed, where she had sleepily put it last night, just before she fell asleep.

And her bedroom door was still shut. Tight. The ghost had materialized in Ellen's bedroom without opening or closing the door.

End. End. What could "end" mean?

Even though she no longer felt the icy hand on her neck or the cold air around her, Ellen continued to shiver. It was partly from cold, partly from fear, and partly from relief that the ghost had left.

It was bad enough to see ghostly hands or an image in a mirror when she was at the Clayton mansion. It was far worse to have the ghost materialize in Ellen's bedroom, while she was sound asleep. For the first time in her life, Ellen felt unsafe in her own home.

The mansion was a spooky old house and even without all the sinister scenes being acted out, stories of Lydia's ghost had been reported there for years. But Ellen knew of no record of the ghost ever straying beyond the Clayton property.

As she lay there, trembling and wondering what to do about this strange midnight visitor, there was a soft knock on her door. Ellen tensed and clutched the blanket even tighter under her chin.

"Ellen? Are you awake?"

"Yes, Mom. Come in."

Her mother opened the door. "Is anything wrong? I got up to go to the bathroom and saw light under your door."

Ellen hesitated. Should she tell her mother about Lydia? She was tempted to pour out the whole story but she stopped herself. Not yet, she thought. Mom can't do anything to keep the ghost from coming, so why worry her?

"Nothing's wrong. I just couldn't sleep."

"Do you feel all right? You look pale." Mrs. Streater walked to the bed and put her hand on Ellen's forehead. "No fever," she said. "Your face is cool."

"I had a bad dream," Ellen said.

"Want to tell me about it?"

"I—I dreamed there was a ghost in my room. She touched my neck and she tried to tell me something but all I could make out was the word, 'end'."

It didn't seem quite so scary, now that she was telling Mom about it. Especially when she pretended that it had only been a dream.

"What did the ghost look like?"

"I couldn't see her. I just felt her hand and heard her voice. And I could feel cold air all around me."

"That's the funny thing about dreams," Mom said. "Even though you didn't *see* the ghost, you knew it was a woman. If it had really happened, you wouldn't know if it was a man or woman unless you saw the person."

Ellen didn't say she knew it was a woman because it was not her first encounter with the ghost. She didn't want to mention the ghost's reflection in a mirror.

"I've worried that this haunted house would give Corey nightmares," Mrs. Streater said. "Usually he's the one who has such realistic dreams. Maybe I should have worried about you instead. Not that my worrying ever makes any difference, anyway."

She patted Ellen's shoulder. "You don't have to finish at the haunted house, you know," she said. "If all those horrible scenes start to bother your sleep, I'll just tell Mrs. Whittacker that you can't do it any longer."

"Don't do that," Ellen said. "I want to finish." If she didn't, Grandma and Grandpa would be disappointed, to say nothing of Mrs. Whittacker. And Corey would be furious.

No, she would finish out the week. With the light on and Mom beside her, her courage returned. So did her curiosity. In spite of her fear, she was fascinated by the ghost, and puzzled. Why could she see Lydia and feel the ghost's presence when no one else could? Why did the ghost follow her home? What was Lydia trying to say, with her strange-sounding *ooohheenndd*?

Ellen was determined to find some answers and the place to do it was at the haunted house. She would manage to elude

Agnes and study the Wedgwood. One way or another, she would figure out what Lydia wanted her to see.

After Mrs. Streater left, Ellen turned off the light and lay still for a long time, unable to go back to sleep. She kept expecting the ghost to appear again.

When she finally fell asleep, she slept uneasily, waking often. The ghost did not return.

Chapter
8

*T*rue *Ghost Stories.*

The Streaters were browsing in a book store when Ellen saw the title in a special display of Halloween books. She opened it at random and began to read.

"Sometimes," she read, "a haunting is determined by what happened on the site years before." Like Lydia, she thought, who first appeared because Samuel's second wife tried to sell all the Wedgwood.

She continued to read, flipping from one chapter to the next and reading a sentence here, a paragraph there. When her parents were ready to pay for their purchase, Ellen asked if they would also buy the ghost book.

"Haven't you had enough of ghosts?" Mrs. Streater said. "I should think that is the last thing you would want to read right now."

Ellen was glad Mom didn't say anything about a bad dream.

"The book looks really good," Ellen said, "and I don't have anything to do when we get home." She had learned long ago that, while her parents usually said *no* to requests for new games or faddish clothes, they often said *yes* if she or Corey wanted to buy a book. It annoyed Corey, who could never sit still long enough to read more than a few pages, but even when Ellen was small, she had preferred book stores to toy stores. She had memorized the fairy books when she was three and then, with Grandma's help, she had learned to read before she started school. She still loved to read and often read her favorite books more than once.

When her parents looked uncertain about *True Ghost Stories*, Ellen added, "I suppose I can always watch television." Mrs. Streater agreed to buy the ghost book.

As soon as they got home, Ellen settled into a comfortable chair and, with great anticipation, began to read. She was glad the haunted house wasn't open on Sunday. The afternoon and evening stretched lazily before her like the first day of summer vacation.

Knowledge. The best way to fight fear is with knowledge. She had learned about Lydia Clayton's life from the biography. Now she would learn about ghosts. If she collected enough separate bits of knowledge maybe they would somehow fit together, like pieces of a puzzle.

She read straight through until dinner. The book was fascinating. Still, Ellen did not feel that she understood Lydia yet. Every ghost, it seems, is different and has its own reasons for doing what it does. She wished she knew what Lydia's reasons were.

After dinner, she stretched out on the sofa and kept reading.

"I'll say one thing for you," Mr. Streater remarked, "when we buy you a book, our money isn't wasted."

Ellen didn't hear him. She was reading a theory that some ghosts only appear at specific times of the year. One ghost always haunted a certain house at Christmastime. Another came only on the anniversary of a violent thunderstorm during which a favorite cocker spaniel was struck by lightning.

This wasn't true of Lydia, Ellen knew. According to the biography at the Historical Society library, Lydia had been seen in different seasons of the year.

The book said ghosts materialize most often in the dark but this didn't seem always true of Lydia, either. True, Lydia had disappeared from Ellen's room as soon as the light was turned on. But the dining room of the haunted house was lit when Ellen saw the hands and it wasn't dark when she saw Lydia's reflection in the mirror.

Ellen had nearly concluded that, while the book was interesting, it didn't pertain to her situation when she read about a man who sold his house and moved because he believed the house was haunted. He frequently heard footsteps in the night and claimed he could *smell* a ghost. He became so nervous he could not sleep and after months of restless nights, he moved.

On the first night in his new house, he heard the same rushing of footsteps which had become so familiar in the old house. He also smelled the distinctive odor of the ghost he thought he had left behind. After three months, he moved again and the story repeated itself. It became clear that it wasn't the houses that were haunted—it was the man himself. A ghost had attached itself to him and followed him wherever he went. Even moving to a different country failed to help.

Ellen quit reading and thought about that. What if the ghost of Lydia Clayton had decided to follow Ellen? Lydia had never left Clayton House before, or at least had never been seen away from it, until she appeared in Ellen's bedroom. What if Lydia kept haunting her? What if she continued to appear, night after night? Ellen shuddered, remembering how she felt as she was roused from a sound sleep by the cold fingers on her neck and the strangled sound of "Oohh . . . end."

She put the book aside and went to get a glass of milk and a cookie. Mr. Streater was in the kitchen making his lunch for work the next day. When he saw Ellen he said, "If you're interested in ghosts, why don't you look them up in our encyclopedia?"

"Good idea," Ellen said. She couldn't very well say that she had come to the kitchen to get away from ghost stories—not after begging her parents to buy her the book. Besides, her dad loved it when she and Corey used the encyclopedia. Whenever they asked him a question that he couldn't answer, he suggested that they look it up in the encyclopedia. Sometimes Ellen suspected he said that even when he knew the answer.

"Ghosts" were in Volume 13, which seemed appropriate. After a lengthy section on primitive religions, she read, "It is believed that certain people have psychic abilities which allow them to perceive that which other people do not sense, both in sight and hearing, just as some animals can see, hear or even smell that which humans cannot."

Ellen read that part again. Maybe this explained why she could see, feel, and hear the ghost even though no one else was able to. She thought back to the time when she knew, without being told, that Mrs. Lantow was sick. She had known about Uncle Ted and Aunt Cheryl's unhappiness.

Do I have special psychic ability? she wondered. The mention of animals who see and hear what humans can't made her remember how she had tried, last summer, to communicate with Prince as a Science Fair experiment. She had been successful in getting Prince to obey her unspoken commands. She had also communicated with an elephant at the zoo, although she couldn't prove that. Maybe she had unusual psychic powers. Maybe that's why Lydia had chosen her. Or maybe Lydia had no choice in the matter. Maybe Lydia was always there but Ellen was one of the rare people who could see her.

Knowledge. Ellen kept coming back to the idea that if she learned enough about ghosts, she would somehow be able to deal with Lydia. She finished her snack, put on her pajamas, and finished reading *True Ghost Stories* in bed.

It ended by saying that a person would learn far more about ghosts from just one personal encounter with one than by reading a hundred books on the subject. If that's true, Ellen thought, I'm already something of an expert.

That night, Lydia came again. Ellen woke shivering and knew, even before she heard the moan, that the ghost was back. She pulled the covers up over her face and squeezed her eyes shut tight. It didn't help. The icy air penetrated her blanket.

Ellen pretended not to notice. She lay still, hardly breathing. She heard a muffled, "Ooohhh . . . end," and did not respond.

Maybe if I ignore her, Ellen thought, she'll grow tired of bothering me and leave.

The mattress began to shake. It wasn't a gentle rocking movement, like the vibrating bed she and Corey had seen demonstrated at the county fair. It was instead a violent motion, as if a person stood at each corner of her bed and raised and lowered the mattress. At the same time, it tilted from side to side, until Ellen was afraid she would be flipped into the air like a pancake.

She clenched her teeth and clung to the bedding. The shaking grew more frenzied.

Ellen flung the blankets back, uncovering her face. "Stop it!" she said, trying to keep her voice low.

Immediately, the bed quit shaking.

"What do you want?" Ellen whispered.

The cold air that had pressed against her moved away. She felt it swirling a few feet in front of her, like a miniature tornado. Seconds later, the swirling stopped. The ghost appeared.

Ellen saw all of her. It was the same woman whose reflection Ellen had seen in the mirror. She wore the same long white gown, with lace at the wrists and throat.

"Lydia," Ellen said. It was a statement, not a question.

"Ooohhh . . . end." The ghost had a greenish glow to her, especially her huge eyes.

Frantically, Ellen tried to remember everything she had read about ghosts, wondering what she should say or do.

"Why have you come here?" Ellen said. She thought of turning on the light but her mother might notice and Ellen wanted answers, not more questions.

The ghost held up her hands and beckoned to Ellen.

"You want me to follow you?" Ellen said.

The ghost beckoned again.

Ellen shook her head, no. She felt safe in her bed, though she wasn't sure why, the way the bed had been lurching just then.

The ghost held out one hand to Ellen, as if urging her to take it and follow.

"No," Ellen said, but even as she spoke, she swung her legs over the side of the bed and sat up. Her feet found her slippers and slid into them.

Moving as if she were in a trance, Ellen took her bathrobe from the blanket chest at the foot of her bed and slipped her arms into it. She turned and faced the ghost.

She had to look up because the ghost was taller than Ellen. She saw the back of the ghost's head as it moved toward Ellen's bedroom door. When it reached the door, it disappeared.

I should get back in bed, Ellen thought. I should turn on the light. If Mom comes, I can say I wanted a drink of water. But her mind seemed to belong to one person and her body to another. Even as she told herself what to do, she did exactly the opposite.

Feeling as if she had been hypnotized, Ellen quietly turned the knob and eased the door open. She peered out. The ghost stood in the hallway, waiting for her.

It floated down the stairs. Ellen followed.

It flowed through the living room. Ellen followed, though she went around the furniture instead of moving through it as the ghost did.

The ghost went to the front door and disappeared. As Ellen approached the door, she heard the click-click of Prince's toenails coming toward her across the floor. She stopped.

Prince nudged Ellen with his muzzle, wanting to be scratched. The feel of his fur, the everyday gesture of rubbing his head, brought Ellen out of the dreamlike state she had been in. She stood there, quietly stroking Prince's fur.

Prince growled. The ghost reappeared on the inside of the door.

"Shush, Prince," Ellen whispered. "No bark."

Prince growled again.

The ghost did not appear to notice. She lifted her arms again and beckoned for Ellen to follow her.

Ellen shook her head. "I can't," she said. "I'm not allowed to leave the house at night, without telling my parents." It was true and, for once, Ellen was glad to abide by her parents' strict rules.

The ghost came closer. Prince bared his teeth and moved between Ellen and the door.

"What do you want?" Ellen whispered. "You can't expect me to follow you around in the middle of the night when I don't know what you want or where you're going."

The ghost's mouth opened and a low, strangled sound came out. Ellen sensed it was a supreme effort to speak, but the effort failed. The luminous green eyes looked so sad that Ellen expected to see tears flowing down the ghost's cheeks.

The whole room was filled with frigid air. The ghost lifted her arms and beckoned again, imploring Ellen to follow.

Prince growled.

Ellen's fingers closed around Prince's collar.

"Come, Prince," she said. She turned and fled across the living room, up the stairs, and back to her own room, with Prince beside her. She closed her bedroom door. "You can sleep in here tonight," she told Prince. She wondered if Prince had actually seen the ghost or if he had only sensed something was there.

She got back in bed and sat propped against two pillows, staring at the closed door.

I will probably never sleep again, she thought. I'll be too nervous about being awakened by a ghost. I'll die of lack of sleep, if I don't die of fright first. Or else I'll tell someone what's going on and get committed to a mental institution.

Why did I follow her downstairs? Ellen wondered. I should have stayed in bed. Does she have some power over me, to make me do what she wants me to do? Or was I still half-asleep until

Prince came along and brought me to my senses? What if Prince had not been there? Would I have followed Lydia? Followed her where?

Where had Lydia planned to go? To Clayton House? That was much too far for Ellen to walk, although perhaps a ghost had no sense of distance. Lydia just materialized wherever she wanted to be. Maybe she thought Ellen could do the same.

Too bad I can't, Ellen thought. If I could, I would materialize in the dining room of the mansion when Agnes isn't there and try to figure out if there's something about the Wedgwood collection that Lydia is trying to show me.

Eventually, Ellen dozed, awoke, dozed again, and finally fell asleep.

Lydia did not return.

Chapter 9

Are ghosts logical? Ellen wondered. If they aren't, Lydia's strange behavior will never make sense, no matter how hard I try to explain it. If they are, then I must discover what Lydia is trying to tell me.

Ellen's head told her to stay out of the dining room. Her curiosity told her to examine the Wedgwood again.

The next night, Ellen and Corey got to the haunted house later than usual, arriving just in time to get to their places before the doors opened. As Ellen hurried through the great hall and up the stairs, she hoped Agnes wouldn't be annoyed with her for being so late. There had been an accident on the freeway and traffic was a mess.

When Ellen entered the parlor, Agnes wasn't waiting. Moments later, Mrs. Whittacker announced on the loudspeaker, "All actors in place, please. The doors will open in five minutes."

Since Agnes wasn't there, Ellen turned on the switches herself to start all of the special effects for the Joan of Arc scene.

Then she got on the platform and held her hands behind her, as if they were tied.

Mrs. Whittacker rushed into the room. "I nearly forgot!" she cried. "I'm supposed to get your scene ready tonight."

"Where's Agnes?"

"She's sick. She called this afternoon and I couldn't find anyone to replace her. We expect a small crowd tonight, since it's Monday, so I thought we could manage but someone from Sheltering Arms showed up to make a video and I had to show her around."

As she spoke she wound the rope around Ellen's knees and shoulders and tied her to the stake. "I see I didn't need to panic. I might have known you would start all your special effects without any help. You and Corey are wonderful."

Mrs. Whittacker hurried away just in time. The first visitors of the night entered the viewing space as Ellen closed her eyes and tried to look saintly.

As the fake crowd shouted, "Witch! Heretic!" and the real audience murmured their sympathy and fright, Ellen's excitement grew. She could inspect the Wedgwood tonight, to see if it held some clue to what Lydia wanted Ellen to know. She could go behind the rope and examine each piece as much as she wanted, without worrying that Agnes would find her and order her out of the dining room.

Mrs. Whittacker came promptly at ten to untie Ellen. As soon as she put her shoes on, Ellen hurried across the hall to the dining room. It was empty. She glanced in the mirror as she passed it and saw only her own reflection. Good. Maybe Agnes *and* Lydia would leave her alone long enough for her to get a good, close look at the Wedgwood collection.

Quickly, she crossed the room to the Wedgwood display and ducked underneath the rope. She had already decided that she would begin with the earliest pieces and examine each one in order. It had occurred to her that maybe Lydia was trying to get her to admire the older Wedgwood, the pieces Lydia herself had collected. Until now, Ellen had focused all her attention on the Fairylustre and perhaps Lydia didn't like that.

As she leaned toward a tea server from Lydia's original creamware set, she heard footsteps behind her. When she looked around, no one was there. Probably one of the actors rushing down the hall, she thought, eager to get home.

She turned back to the Wedgwood and heard the footsteps again. She remembered the man in the book, the one who had moved so many times but no matter where he went, he heard the same footsteps of a ghost. She realized that she, too, was hearing phantom footsteps, not real ones. Instead of looking behind her, she kept her eyes straight ahead, trying to concentrate on the dishes.

Seconds later, Lydia materialized. She looked exactly the way she had looked the night before, in the same long gown. She stood at the far end of the display, with her arms outstretched.

Instead of being scared this time, Ellen was annoyed. This was her only chance to look at the Wedgwood without having Agnes interrupt her. "What do you want?" she said.

"Oooohhh . . . end."

"I'm trying to figure out what you want," Ellen said crossly. "It would be easier if you quit popping up all the time and scaring me."

The ghost signaled for Ellen to come closer.

Ellen ignored her. She continued to look at the older dishes, one piece at a time. She didn't touch them because she was afraid she might accidentally drop one but she put her face only a foot or so away from each one and examined it carefully.

"Aaaahhend." The ghost motioned again, urging Ellen to the Fairylustre part of the display.

"Hey, Ellen. Are you ready to leave?"

She jumped at the sound of Corey's voice and then looked quickly toward the ghost. Lydia had vanished.

"I'll be there in a minute," Ellen said.

"Are you looking at those dumb old dishes again? I don't see what's so great about them. If you want to look at dishes, all you have to do is open the kitchen cupboards at home."

"The kitchen cupboards at home do not contain anything like this," Ellen said.

"I've figured out a way to earn some money so I can have a bike," Corey said.

"Oh?"

"I'm going to give screaming lessons."

Ellen rolled her eyes and did not answer.

"I'll bet there are lots of kids who would like to be able to scream as good as I do. Mighty Mike says I'm the best screamer he's ever heard, even counting people on TV. So I decided I could charge fifty cents apiece and teach all the other kids how to scream. Nicholas is my first student."

"Well, don't do it at our house," Ellen said. It was bad enough to hear Corey practice his screaming without listening to his friends, as well.

Ellen stood now in front of the Fairylustre. She had already studied it so many other times, she didn't think it was what Lydia wanted to show her, but she looked again anyway, just because she liked it.

"I can't decide if it should be private lessons or a whole bunch of kids at once," Corey said. "What do you think?"

"I think . . ." Ellen stopped. "Corey," she said. "Go get Mrs. Whittacker."

"You think Mrs. Whittacker would want to take screaming lessons?"

"Just do what I say. And tell her to hurry."

"I wasn't going to start the lessons tonight."

"Run!"

As Corey trotted out of the dining room, Ellen kept her eyes fixed on the bottom shelf of the Fairylustre display. Her heart quickened with excitement. This must be what Lydia had been trying to tell her. This was what the ghost wanted her to see.

In a few minutes, she heard Corey and Mrs. Whittacker returning. Corey was explaining how the screaming lessons would work.

As soon as Mrs. Whittacker was in the dining room, Ellen dared to take her eyes off the shelf and turn around.

"What is it?" Mrs. Whittacker said.

"A bowl is missing."

"What? Are you sure?"

"We've been robbed!" Corey yelled.

Ellen pointed to the bottom shelf. "One of the Fairylustre bowls is gone," she said. "It's always been there, on the bottom shelf. It's octagonal shaped and it has fairies and a bridge."

Mrs. Whittacker looked where Ellen was pointing. Her hands flew to her face and she drew in her breath sharply. "You're right," she said. "I know which bowl you mean."

"The purple people from Jupiter must have come," said Corey.

"It's the bowl I held that first night," Ellen said. "That's why I remembered it."

"Wow," said Corey. "How could they steal a bowl when there were so many people in here?"

"Not everybody who goes through the haunted house bothers to look at the museum displays in here," Ellen said. "Maybe one person was in here all alone and just went under the rope and helped themselves."

"Or maybe," said Corey, "it wasn't the purple people. Maybe it was a gang of thieves and they've had it planned for a long time. One of them pretended to be with the Historical Society and he told all the people that this room was closed tonight and then he stood guard while the other thieves went in and . . ."

"We mustn't jump to conclusions," Mrs. Whittacker said. "We don't know for sure that the bowl was stolen."

"It's gone, isn't it?" Corey said.

"I must call Agnes," Mrs. Whittacker said. She hurried through the upper kitchen to her office, with Ellen and Corey following her. Ellen knew her parents were probably waiting outside by now to take her and Corey home, but she didn't want to leave in the middle of a mystery.

As they entered Mrs. Whittacker's office, Ellen said, "Please don't tell Agnes that I'm the one who discovered that the bowl was stolen."

"Why not?" Corey said. "You're practically a detective. The police will interview you. You'll probably get your picture in the paper."

"I don't want my picture in the paper," Ellen said. "Not for this."

Mrs. Whittacker dialed the phone and waited. "Agnes? One

of the bowls is gone. The small octagonal Fairylustre; the one with the castle and bridge." She was quiet for a few moments, listening. Then she sighed, clearly relieved. "Oh, thank goodness," she said. "I was afraid someone had stolen it. I guess I forgot to tell you that we aren't supposed to remove it from the mansion. Yes. Yes, I can understand that. Well, I hope I didn't wake you; I realize it's late to call, especially when you aren't feeling well."

As Mrs. Whittacker continued to talk, Ellen quit listening, since the bowl was obviously safe. Instead, she thought about the ghost. Lydia must have wanted her to notice that the bowl was gone. That's why she motioned for Ellen to go to that end of the display. Maybe that's what she wanted last night, too, when she tried to get Ellen to follow her out the front door.

If that's so, Ellen thought, this might be the end of the haunting. I discovered the missing bowl, it's been accounted for, and all is well. Maybe I won't see Lydia anymore.

Relief flooded her. Even though she had stood up to Lydia earlier that night, she had secretly dreaded going to sleep again, for fear she would awaken to a cold wind on her face.

"What did she say?" Corey asked, as soon as Mrs. Whittacker hung up.

"She has it. She took it to her studio to repair a tiny chip on the inside of the rim. She took it home on Saturday, repaired it on Sunday, and planned to bring it back today. She hadn't thought to tell me, since she expected the piece to be back in place before I arrived tonight. When she got sick, of course, the bowl did not get returned."

"I didn't see a chip," Ellen said.

"Neither did I. That's why we're so fortunate to have Agnes. She notices everything, including the smallest flaws. And with her special training, she's able to do repairs even on old pieces. She restored a china bowl for me, one that belonged to my mother, and it's impossible to tell where she did it. The collection is in good hands."

"Rats," said Corey. "I was hoping it was stolen." Then, seeing the look on Mrs. Whittacker's face, he added, "I would want you to get it back and not have it be broken. But I thought the police might come and investigate. Maybe Ellen would have been a witness. Maybe she would have to go to court and tell how she knew that the bowl was gone and I would have to go, too, to tell how I ran and got you. Maybe . . ."

"Maybe you had better see if your parents are waiting for you," Mrs. Whittacker said.

They were. As usual, Corey ran ahead and began talking the minute he opened the car door. By the time Ellen reached the car, Mr. and Mrs. Streater had heard all about how Ellen and Corey had thought a bowl was stolen but it turned out that Agnes had taken it home to fix it.

Mrs. Whittacker walked out with Ellen and talked to Mr. and Mrs. Streater for a few moments. "I don't know how we would manage without these kids of yours," she said.

As the Streaters' car passed the gates at the end of the Clayton driveway, Ellen tuned out Corey's voice and thought about Lydia.

The first time Ellen felt the cold wind, she had been looking at the octagonal bowl. Agnes didn't take the bowl home until Saturday night. By then, Lydia had appeared to Ellen, one way or another, several times. If the fact that a bowl was missing wasn't what Lydia wanted her to notice, what was it? What did she want?

Ellen's anxiety quickly returned.

That night, Ellen awoke, feeling cold. The clock beside her bed said 2:30 A.M. For a moment, she feared Lydia was in her room again.

She lay quietly alert but did not see the ghost, nor did she feel a wind or the pressure of icicle fingers. Maybe I just got uncovered, Ellen thought. Maybe that's why I woke up.

She snuggled under her blankets and closed her eyes. Then she heard something. She raised her head, listening. The sound came again.

Prince was whining. He wasn't outside the door, trying to get in, as he sometimes did at night but she was sure she had heard him whine. He must have whined earlier, too; that must be what awoke her.

Prince never needed to go out during the night. Was he sick? Worried, Ellen swung her legs over the side of the bed. She put on her robe and opened her bedroom door. The whining came again.

She followed the sound into the living room and stopped. Lydia glided toward the front door. Although she was clearly visible, she was also transparent. Ellen saw Lydia and, at the same time, she saw her father's favorite reclining chair, which was directly behind the ghost.

Prince whined again and Ellen realized the ghost was not alone. As Lydia moved, Corey followed, a few steps behind her. Prince was next to Corey, pawing at the floor and whining, obviously trying to get Corey's attention.

"I'm not supposed to go anywhere without telling Mom or Dad first," Corey whispered.

Lydia moved ahead of him and beckoned for him to follow.

As Ellen watched them, she felt as if she were viewing a home video. She heard their voices and saw their actions but she did not feel like she was actually there in the living room with them. The scene had an other-worldly quality, a feeling of unreality, and she felt oddly detached from it. It was the same trancelike sensation she had experienced the night she almost followed Lydia out the door.

Corey stepped closer to Lydia. "If I go with you to Clayton House, will you come and visit my class at school?"

The ghost beckoned again.

"That would be so cool," Corey said. "If I tell Nicholas and the other kids I saw a ghost, they'll think I'm just making up a story. But if I bring you with me, they'll know it's all true."

Lydia floated through the front door.

Corey hesitated for only a moment. Then he said, "Wait for me," opened the door and went out. Prince tried to go with him, but Corey pushed the dog back, slipped through the opening, and shut the door.

As the door closed, Prince barked. Ellen's feeling of unreality vanished and she snapped into action. She dashed across the room, flung open the door, and rushed out. Prince ran ahead of her, barking frantically.

"Corey!" Ellen yelled. "Get back here!"

At the sound of Ellen's voice, Lydia looked back and raised her arms. Her entire body glowed with an eerie green light.

"Aahheenndd," she called.

Corey stopped walking. As Ellen approached him, she saw that her brother's eyes were closed. Was he walking in his sleep? He had talked to Lydia, as if he were fully alert. Yet, now he seemed like a zombie, the way Ellen had felt the first time, when she followed Lydia from her bedroom to the front door. She had felt that way again just now, watching Corey with Lydia. If the ghost had some power over Ellen, the power clearly worked on Corey, too.

Prince stood protectively between Lydia and the children. A low growl rumbled deep in his throat and the fur along the ridge of his back stood straight up.

Ellen gave Corey a gentle shove. "Get back in the house," she said.

"Aaa . . . end," Lydia implored. She motioned for Ellen to go with her. The glowing green eyes were enormous. They pleaded silently for Ellen to obey.

"No," Ellen said. "We cannot go with you. Corey is too young to follow you around the streets in the middle of the night. And so am I."

Ellen grabbed Corey's hand and pulled him toward the house. The porch light went on and Mr. Streater stepped out the door.

"What's going on?" he demanded.

Ellen blinked in the sudden light. Prince trotted toward Mr. Streater and Ellen knew without looking that Lydia was gone. "Corey was walking in his sleep," she said. "Prince woke me."

"We must have forgotten to put the chain lock on when we went to bed last night. Thank heaven you heard Prince."

Corey opened his eyes and looked around, as if wondering where he was.

"It's all right, son," Mr. Streater said. "You were walking in your sleep."

"No, I wasn't. I was following a ghost. She wanted me to go with her and then she was going to come to visit my school."

"You were dreaming," Mr. Streater said. "Prince heard you moving around and woke Ellen up."

"It was only a dream?" Corey sounded disappointed. "I thought the ghost was here."

Ellen knew it was better for Corey to think he had dreamed the whole episode. Otherwise, there was no telling what he would do in an effort to take Lydia to school with him. He'd probably sit up tomorrow night, waiting for Lydia to appear so he could leave with her.

When she was back in bed, Ellen lay awake for a long time. Why had Lydia chosen Corey this time? Had she given up haunting Ellen? Or had she hoped that if Corey followed her Ellen would, too?

Was Ellen wrong to let her father believe that Corey had dreamed about the ghost? If she told her parents what was really happening, what would they do? What could they do?

Ellen wished she had never agreed to help with the haunted house.

Chapter
10

Hey, Ellen!" Corey waved from the sidewalk. "We got a video of you on fire."

"Is it X-rated?" asked a voice from the back of the school bus.

Caitlin giggled but Ellen glared out the window. Moments earlier, she had been the center of attention as a group of boys who had gone through the haunted house asked her opinion about which scene was the fake one. Now Corey was spoiling it. She would have to ask her parents to keep Corey away from the bus stop until she was off the bus and it had left. The other kids must think she came from a family of circus freaks.

She stepped off the bus but before she could speak Corey said, "The video shows all the scenes from the haunted house. It has me screaming and you getting burned at the stake."

"Whose video is it?"

"Grandma brought it."

That surprised Ellen. Her grandparents had refused to come

to the haunted house because Grandma said she couldn't bear to watch Ellen and Corey in such dangerous situations, even when she knew they weren't real.

"Did Grandma and Grandpa look at the video?"

"Not yet. They're going to watch it with us. Grandma says she thinks she can stand to watch me get my head chopped off on screen if I'm sitting beside her, perfectly safe."

Ellen laughed.

"Maybe a Hollywood producer will see it and offer us movie contracts."

"I doubt that."

"Grandma said they might use part of it on TV on Halloween night, to advertise the haunted house. If they choose our scenes, a producer might see us. Mighty Mike's going to advertise us on the radio, too."

Despite her annoyance at her brother, Ellen walked faster. It would be fun to see a video of the haunted house, especially the Joan of Arc scene.

"Here are the stars of the show," Grandpa said, as Ellen and Corey got home.

"Where did you get the video?" Ellen asked.

"Mrs. Whittacker had a copy made for us. Someone from the staff of Sheltering Arms took it last night, so they can show it to Mr. Clayton, and Mrs. Whittacker thought we would enjoy having a copy to keep."

"Mr. Clayton?" Ellen said. "What Mr. Clayton?"

"Edward Clayton. The man who gave the mansion to the city."

"He's *alive?*" Ellen had assumed the mansion was willed to the city when the last of the Claytons died.

"He's in a nursing home, Sheltering Arms. He's quite old and unable to care for himself. He had private care at home for some years but he said he missed talking to people his own age so now he's at Sheltering Arms. The Director of the nursing home had the haunted house filmed for him."

"Let's look at the video," Corey said.

As scenes from the haunted house appeared on the television screen, Ellen's mind was in a whirl. It had not occurred to her that one of the Clayton family was still alive. She wondered if Lydia had ever appeared to him. Perhaps he knew things about the long ago hauntings—family stories that would not be in a published biography of Lydia.

Corey's bloodcurdling scream on the video brought Ellen's attention back to the screen.

"Good heavens," said Grandma.

"Rewind it," said Corey. "Let's play that part again."

Grandpa reversed the video and played Corey's part again. This time, everyone except Corey covered their ears.

Corey said, "Do it again."

"Later," Grandma said. "We want to see Ellen's part."

When the video showed King Haakon the Great of Norway being murdered by his soldiers in a pigsty, Corey declared, "That's the fake scene. What would a King be doing in a pigpen? Maybe I'll win the money."

"Mrs. Whittacker said the actors are not allowed to enter the drawing," Ellen said.

"I know," said Corey. "I tried. So I told Nicholas about the pigpen and he entered the drawing and if he wins, I get half."

"Shh," said Ellen. "Here's my part."

The screen now showed the village square and the distant

crowds. The shouting was clearly heard as the camera moved closer to Joan of Arc: "Witch! Heretic!" The flames leaped and hissed.

Grandma reached for Ellen's hand. "I'm not sure I can watch this," she said.

"Too bad they couldn't get the smoke smell on video," Ellen said. She felt like she was watching someone else, not herself. Joan had her eyes closed and her head back so her face tilted toward heaven. Her lips moved slightly, as if in silent prayer. People standing near the video camera could be heard saying things like, "Oh, that poor girl. Imagine what it would feel like."

Ellen blinked and leaned closer. A chill ran down the back of her neck. "Stop it for a minute," she said. "Please."

Grandpa hit the *pause* button.

Ellen stared at the screen. She saw herself, lashed to the stake, with the fake fire at her feet. And beside her on the platform, she saw Lydia.

"What are you looking at?" said Corey.

Ellen glanced at her grandparents and Corey. They were watching the same television screen she was. Didn't they see the ghost?

"Do you want to look at this part again?" Grandpa asked.

"No," said Ellen. "For a moment, I thought I saw someone else on the platform with me."

She held her breath while the others looked at the screen.

"Nobody there but Joan," said Corey.

"You probably got a glimpse of one of the painted figures in the backdrop," said Grandpa. "Do you want to see the rest now?"

Ellen nodded but she barely watched the rest of the video.

She had never sensed Lydia's presence during the Joan of Arc scene yet the ghost evidently had been there with her while the video was taken. How many other times was Lydia with her and she didn't know it? It was creepy enough to have a ghost appear out of nowhere; it was even creepier to think that the ghost was following her around when she wasn't aware of it.

Why couldn't anyone else see her? If the ghost got captured on film, then everyone who looked at the film should be able to see her. Yet, Ellen was the only one who did.

When the video ended, Grandpa and Grandma applauded.

Corey said, "Let's look at it again."

"We'll leave it here," Grandpa said. "Your parents will want to see it when they get home and you can look at it as much as you want."

"I'll fast-forward it to the part with me and Mighty Mike," Corey said. "Maybe I can use it to demonstrate when I give my screaming lessons."

Ellen saw Grandma and Grandpa exchange an amused glance but neither of them asked Corey what lessons he meant.

"Do you know if Mr. Clayton can have visitors?" Ellen asked.

"I could find out," Grandma said. "I have a friend at Sheltering Arms, recovering from a broken hip. I've been meaning to go and visit her."

"Maybe I could go with you," Ellen said, "and if Mr. Clayton can have visitors, I'll talk to him."

"That's a lovely idea," Grandma said. "So many patients in nursing homes never get visitors."

"Why don't you go now," Grandpa suggested. "I'll stay here with Corey."

Ellen and Grandma looked at each other and nodded agreement. Ellen was afraid Corey would want to go along, but he preferred to stay home and watch himself and Mighty Mike on video.

Ellen had never visited a nursing home so she wasn't sure what to expect. Sheltering Arms was spacious and bright, with bouquets of flowers in the lobby. Several elderly people in wheelchairs sat just outside the front door, enjoying the sunshine.

Grandma inquired at the desk and learned which room her friend was in. The nurse said that Mr. Clayton could have company. He was in Room 4, just down the hall.

Ellen hesitated in the doorway of Room 4. The door was open but the old man in the bed had his eyes closed. She didn't want to awaken him. As she wondered what to do, a nurse's aide bustled past. "Mr. Clayton," she called cheerfully, "you have a visitor."

The eyes opened at once and Mr. Clayton looked at Ellen. "Do I know you?" he asked.

"No," Ellen said.

"Good. I was afraid I was supposed to recognize you."

Ellen introduced herself and said she had a part in the haunted house.

He chuckled. "They showed me the movie," he said. "I hardly recognized the place. Looked like I hadn't hired a housekeeper in years." He squinted at Ellen. "Which part did you play?"

"I was Joan of Arc."

"Ah, yes. And a fine job you did of it." He motioned to the single straight chair in the room. "Have a seat. I'd offer you something to drink but this is the butler's day off." He laughed at his own joke and Ellen relaxed.

She looked around the small room. Mr. Clayton had a bed, a nightstand, and a small dresser with a television set on it. There were no rugs, no pictures on the walls. The spare furnishings were a sharp contrast to the elegant mansion.

"Do you miss your house?" she asked.

"No. It was too much for me. I loved it all my life but it is time to let someone else maintain it. Too bad I never married. Never had any children to pass it all on to."

"It was nice of you to give it to the city," Ellen said. "This way, lots of people will enjoy it."

"I hope so."

Ellen wondered how to approach the subject of Lydia.

"I can still go back, you know," Mr. Clayton said. "In my mind. I'm lucky that way. Some people my age have memory trouble but I can still go back and visit Clayton House, anytime I want. In my mind, I can wander from room to room and see all the furniture and remember the good times, when I was young."

"I like the Mexican silver fireplace," Ellen said.

Mr. Clayton smiled. "So many treasures," he said.

"I like the Fairylustre, too."

"Oh, the Fairylustre. That was always my favorite. In fact, I acquired most of the Fairylustre pieces."

"Tell me more about it," Ellen said.

"It's odd," Mr. Clayton said. "The appreciation of the Wedgwood seems to be something you are born with, like an ear for music. Certain people love it immediately; others are unimpressed with even the most beautiful pieces." Ellen thought of Corey.

"Neither of my parents particularly cared for it," Mr. Clayton went on. "As far as they were concerned, the Wedgwood was just some dusty old dishes that Great-grandmother Clayton had been fond of. But even as a small lad, I loved it. Too much, it seems, for I have the distinction of being the only person to break one of the original pieces. I was only three or four at the time but I can still remember the horrified reaction of my nanny when she discovered that, while she was chatting with one of the maids, I had removed a creamware plate and dropped it, smashing it into a dozen pieces. When I was older and my business was prospering, I sought out several fine old pieces. That's when I bought the Fairylustre."

"My favorite is an octagonal bowl," Ellen said. "It has a castle on it."

"I know which one you mean. I bought that for myself for my fortieth birthday present. More than forty years ago."

He laughed at Ellen's surprised expression. "When you don't have any family, sometimes you have to buy your own birthday present," he said.

"You picked a good one."

"Why did you come here? A pretty young girl must have plenty to do besides visit an old codger like me."

"I wanted to know more about your house and the Wedgwood. And . . ." She blurted it out before she lost her nerve: "I wondered if you know anything about the ghost."

"Ah. So that's it. The ghost stories are circulating again. I suppose that's to be expected when the whole building's been turned into a haunted house."

"I wondered if—if you ever saw her."

Mr. Clayton looked at Ellen so intently that Ellen dropped her eyes. When he spoke, his voice was barely a whisper. "You've seen her?"

Ellen nodded. "At least, I've seen some ghost and I think it's Lydia."

"When? What happened?"

It was a relief to talk about it. Once she began, the words came quickly, and the whole story poured out: the mirror, the floating hands, the night visits, and Ellen's belief that Lydia was trying to tell her something or show her something.

"I have the feeling she wants me to help her," Ellen said, "but I don't know what she needs or how I can help."

When she finished, Mr. Clayton said, "She isn't a bad ghost, you know. She's never hurt anyone. She only appears when something is wrong or when she's worried."

"Do you think she doesn't like the haunted house?"

"More likely, someone is disturbing the Wedgwood. My instructions to the city made it quite clear that the Wedgwood collection is to be displayed on the same dining-room shelves where it was when I moved out. The pieces are not to be moved."

"That's where it is," Ellen said, "in the dining room. They're going to install some brighter lights but the shelves aren't being changed."

"And no one is rearranging the Wedgwood or handling it?"

"Only Agnes."

"Who?"

"The curator of the museum. She's a potter, with her own gallery, and she's been doing some repair work on the Wedgwood."

Mr. Clayton frowned. "What kind of repair work?"

"She took home the little octagonal bowl that I like so much. It had a small chip and she fixed it."

Mr. Clayton's voice rose. "Someone chipped the Fairylustre? How? They aren't allowing the public to handle it, are they?"

"No. The area is roped off, to keep people back. I don't know how it got chipped. I only know that Agnes took it home to repair it."

Mr. Clayton thumped his fist on the bed. "When I turned that collection over to the Historical Society," he said, "it was in mint condition. If they're being careless with it, I may have to enforce my right to rescind the agreement."

Ellen licked her lips. She hadn't meant to stir up trouble or upset Mr. Clayton. She only wanted to learn about Lydia. "Did you ever see the ghost?" she asked.

"Twice. Both times when I was just a lad." He smiled, remembering. "The first time, I had picked some flowers in the garden and needed a vase to put them in. I went to the dining room and reached for the first piece of Wedgwood on the shelf. Instantly, I felt a chill and had the sensation of cold hands on my arm, restraining me. It frightened me so much, I ran out of the room and put my flowers in a glass jar from the kitchen."

"What happened the second time?"

"The second time, I was about ten years old. It had rained for a week and I was bored and irritable because I wanted to play outside. Having a somewhat active imagination, I decided to stir up some excitement by staging a robbery."

Ellen smiled. It sounded like the sort of scheme Corey would dream up.

"My plan was to hide some of the Wedgwood in my bedroom and then wait for someone, probably the downstairs maid, to notice that it was gone. Remembering how my nanny reacted to the broken plate, I thought the maid would scream and carry on hysterically and the whole household would come running. I put four or five pieces under my bed, after carefully wrapping them in bath towels. Nothing happened. The maid didn't notice they were missing. My parents didn't mention it." He shook his head. "Later, I wondered if they knew all along what I had done and had decided not to give me the satisfaction of reacting. At any rate, I slept that night with the Wedgwood under my bed and in the night, Lydia woke me. She grabbed me by the shoulders and shook me awake. I was so terrified, I couldn't scream. When she stood beside my bed and pointed to the floor, I knew what she wanted."

"What did you do?"

"I got up and returned all the Wedgwood to the proper place, right then, in the middle of the night, and I never touched it again. I never told my parents that I'd seen the ghost. They had always ridiculed the old ghost stories and I didn't want to confess what I'd done. That was the last time I ever saw the ghost. When I was older and found out how valuable the Wedgwood is, I decided the ghost was worried that I would be careless and break another piece. Later yet, when my father died and I learned about the baby's remains, I wondered if she was nervous that I would find them and dispose of them inappropriately."

"Remains?"

"Josiah's remains. Lydia could not bear to part with her baby, so she had the infant's body cremated and then put the cremated remains in a piece of her Wedgwood. Cremation was rare back then and Samuel told no one about this, fearing that Lydia would be considered insane. The secret was kept until his death; his Will divulged that Josiah's remains were in the oldest piece of Wedgwood, a black urn. He also stated that the Wedgwood collection must not be moved or sold. Those instructions have been honored by all of my family. When I wrote up my agreement with the city, I was quite specific about that."

"Maybe that's what Lydia is trying to tell me—that she doesn't want Josiah's remains disturbed."

"They won't be, as long as the Wedgwood is left where it belongs. I must say, I'm distressed to learn that this Agnes person took some of the Fairylustre home with her. Even though Josiah's remains are in a basalt urn, not the Fairylustre, my directions were for the entire collection."

He picked up a small tablet and pencil from the nightstand and wrote something down. "I have an appointment with my attorney tomorrow," he said. "I'll ask him to remind the City and the Historical Society of our agreement regarding the Wedgwood. They really must be more careful. Perhaps they'll need to post a guard, to be sure nothing else gets chipped."

When he finished writing, he winked at Ellen. "Should I tell my attorney that the ghost of Lydia is unhappy and causing trouble with Joan of Arc? Or do you think he'd assume I'm losing my mind?"

"It might be best not to mention Lydia." She felt more relaxed, hearing Mr. Clayton joke about the ghost. "I wonder, though, why me? Why can I see her and nobody else can? I haven't moved any of the Wedgwood. If she was trying to protect the urn, I should think she would appear to Agnes."

"Maybe she's tried."

Puzzled, Ellen waited for him to explain.

"There's an old saying from Confucius that goes, 'Everything has its beauty but not everyone sees it.' I think that's true of more than just beauty. The ghost might be there but only a person who is highly aware of feelings and vibrations will be able to see her. Some people are more psychically tuned in to the whole universe than ordinary people are."

Ellen thought of the other times when she had sensed, as Mr. Clayton put it, feelings and vibrations—situations that other people had not perceived. She could think of dozens of examples of times when she intuitively knew something that the people with her did not sense.

"Corey saw her, or seemed to," Ellen said, "when he was asleep."

"Perhaps in the sleep state, he was more receptive."

"Do you think she wanted to show Corey whatever it is she's been trying to show me?"

"Probably. Or perhaps she used your brother as a way to get you to go with her, hoping you would follow him."

"I almost did."

"I have a picture of her," Mr. Clayton said. "It was in a packet of old photographs that I found after my parents died. She's identified on the back as Lydia and I recognized her as the ghost who appeared the night I hid the Wedgwood under my bed."

"Is the picture here?" Ellen asked. "Could I see it?"

Mr. Clayton directed her to open the bottom drawer of his dresser and take out a small metal box. When she gave it to him, he opened it and looked through the contents for a minute. He selected a yellowed photograph and handed it to Ellen.

The smiling young woman in the picture held an infant. She looked so happy that for a moment it did not seem possible that she was the sad-eyed ghost. But the hair was the same and the face and—Ellen realized with a start—even the white night-gown with lace at the throat. Ellen turned the picture over. On the back it said, "Lydia and Josiah."

Ellen had felt all along that the apparition she saw was the ghost of Lydia Clayton. The picture proved she was right.

Grandma came to the door then and told Ellen it was time to leave. Ellen introduced her to Mr. Clayton.

"Thank you for coming," he told Ellen, as she put the metal box back in the drawer. "Except for my attorney, you're the first visitor I've had."

"Don't your friends ever come?"

He shook his head sadly. "That's the bad part about living to be eighty-one," he said. "Most of my friends have already died."

"I'll come again," Ellen promised. She liked hearing Mr. Clayton's stories of when he was young and it had felt good to talk about Lydia with someone who understood. Most of all it was a relief to know that he, too, had seen the ghost. Impulsively, she asked, "Do you want me to bring you anything next time?"

"Blueberry muffins." He answered so quickly that Ellen giggled. "The food here isn't bad," he explained, "but they never serve blueberry muffins. They were always my favorite."

"I'll make some myself," Ellen told him. "I can't come tomorrow, because tomorrow is Halloween and the haunted house opens early, but I'll try to come on Saturday."

"Next time, Ellen Streater," he said, "I'll know your name."

As Grandma drove Ellen home, she said, "All the money in the world and the only thing he wants is a blueberry muffin. How nice that you thought to ask him."

Ellen did not answer. She was planning what she would do at the haunted house that night. She would look inside the oldest piece of Wedgwood, the big black urn. She would see if the remains of Josiah Clayton had been disturbed.

Chapter
11

She wasn't afraid anymore. Mr. Clayton said Lydia had never hurt anyone and she believed him. Besides, the photograph of the happy young mother with her baby had made Ellen want to help the ghost if she could. *She's a troubled spirit,* Ellen decided, *and for some reason she thinks I'm the one who can help her. Well, perhaps she's right; maybe I can help. I'm going to try.*

Once, on a vacation, the Streaters had wandered through an old graveyard in a small town, reading the headstones. Ellen remembered asking her parents why so many of them said, *Rest in Peace.* Mom explained that many people believe unhappy souls become ghosts and wander the earth. Those who are happy have a peaceful eternal sleep.

Lydia was clearly an unhappy soul and Ellen wanted to help her. She felt sorry for anyone, even a ghost, who was in such anguish.

Besides, if she could solve Lydia's problem, whatever it was,

Lydia would quit haunting her. Even though she was no longer afraid of the ghost, she did not relish the idea of being awakened again in the middle of the night by an ice-cold hand on her neck. Or of always wondering if Lydia, unseen and unnoticed, was standing beside her.

All she had to do was figure out what Lydia wanted her to know. If the ghost was only worried about the remains in the urn, why did she urge Ellen toward the Fairylustre?

Lydia always repeated the same word, a moaning sound with "end" as the last syllable. Ellen started going through the alphabet, thinking of words that ended with end. Amend, attend, bend, blend, commend, defend, dividend, fend, friend.

She stopped. Could it be "friend?" Was Lydia trying to tell her that she meant no harm, that she was Ellen's friend?

She continued through the alphabet—intend, lend, mend, offend, pretend, recommend, send, spend, tend, trend, upend. None of the others made any sense in connection with the ghost. Friend did.

That night, Ellen walked through the great hall with a sense of anticipation. If Lydia appeared, she planned to ask her if that's what she meant. Surely the ghost would be able to give some sign if Ellen was right.

After she slipped into her Joan of Arc robe and removed her shoes and socks, she still had a few minutes to spare before it was time for Agnes to tie her, so she hurried into the dining room. The octagonal Fairylustre bowl was back in its usual place. Ellen ducked under the rope to get a closer look. She wondered if she might be able to see where Agnes had repaired the chip.

The bowl looked the same as it always had. Carefully, she picked it up, turning it around and around in her hands. She saw no hairline cracks nor any evidence of glue. She ran one finger around the rim of the bowl, feeling to see if it was smooth or uneven. She could detect no place that felt like a repair.

She turned the bowl again, to admire her favorite scene, and then stopped. The shoes of the fairy flying over the bridge were slightly different than they had been. Before, the toes of the shoes pointed up, with tiny gold balls on the tips. Now, one of the fairy's shoes went straight ahead, instead of up. Ellen examined the shoes carefully. The balls on the tips of the toes seemed slightly bigger, too.

How odd that Agnes would make such a change. Ellen wondered if she should say something about it. Probably Agnes would want to correct the mistake, if she knew. The whole point of restoration was to put a piece back exactly like it was originally.

She also wondered how the bowl got damaged. There wasn't any chip that first day, when Mrs. Whittacker showed her the Fairylustre. If there had been, surely one of them would have noticed it.

Ellen put the octagonal bowl back on the shelf. She would be glad when the new lights were installed. Even the shimmery Fairylustre seemed dull tonight, as if it needed to be dusted.

She went to the other end of the display, wondering if she dared peek inside the black urn to see if it contained fragments of human bones. As she approached the urn, Lydia appeared.

There were no preliminaries this time. No cold wind or running footsteps. No icy hands. She was just there, suddenly and completely. As usual, she motioned for Ellen to come closer.

"Ooohhh . . . end."

Behind her, through her, Ellen could see the shelves of Wedgwood.

Ellen spoke softly. "Lydia, are you trying to tell me that you want to be my friend?"

Lydia moved closer.

Ellen stayed where she was, hoping that she had guessed correctly about the word, *friend*.

"Ooohhend."

"Friend?" Ellen asked again, enunciating carefully: "You are my friend?"

The ghost stopped moving. The terrified expression in her eyes disappeared. "Foohhend," she whispered.

"Yes, I understand. You want to be my friend."

The ghost nodded her head.

"Friend," Ellen repeated.

The ghost quickly reached out and Ellen felt the cold hand on her arm.

Ellen gulped but did not flinch. "I want to be your friend," she said. "I'll help you, if I can."

Lydia spun Ellen around, pushing her back toward the Fairylustre.

"I saw the bowl," Ellen said. "I found the mistake Agnes made, when she repaired the chip. Is that what you're trying to show me?"

Lydia did not answer. She moved in front of Ellen, pulling her closer to the Fairylustre.

"I'll tell Agnes about the mistake," Ellen said. "I'm sure she'll be able to correct it."

Lydia tugged harder. Ellen sensed an urgency, as if the ghost feared that Ellen would not act quickly enough. Maybe, she thought, it isn't the repair job that's bothering Lydia. Maybe it's something more personal.

"I know about the black urn," Ellen said. "Mr. Clayton told me. Is that what's troubling you? Are you afraid someone will disturb what's in it? Are you worried about your—about the remains of your baby's body?"

As soon as Ellen said *the remains of your baby's body*, Lydia screamed. It was not a low moan, like before, but a horrible, wrenching shriek, a blending of a woman's voice with some unearthly cry. It was a sound unlike anything Ellen had ever heard.

She jumped and felt gooseflesh rising all over her body. As the sound died away, Lydia disappeared. Realizing such a scream was sure to attract attention, Ellen quickly moved away from the shelves and back to the public viewing area. She couldn't let Agnes catch her examining the Wedgwood.

To Ellen's surprise, no one came into the dining room. She thought surely Corey would want to know who had uttered such a scream but neither her brother nor anyone else approached. Was Ellen the only person who had heard that awful cry?

It wasn't going to be easy to help Lydia. Ellen wasn't at all sure what to do next.

It was almost seven o'clock, so Ellen returned to the parlor to wait for Agnes. She wondered how to tell Agnes about her mistake on the Fairylustre bowl without making her angry. She supposed she could tell Mrs. Whittacker instead but that seemed like a mean trick on Agnes, since Mrs. Whittacker was Agnes's boss.

As it turned out, she didn't have a chance to tell Agnes anything before the haunted house opened. Agnes dashed in at one minute to seven, quickly tied Ellen to the stake, started the special effects and left again.

While she pretended to be Saint Joan, Ellen thought back over everything that had happened so far. Lydia seemed to want to show her something about the Fairylustre bowl but for the life of her, Ellen couldn't figure out what. It had not been the fact that the bowl was missing. Apparently, it was not the poor repair job, either. What, then? What did Lydia see that Ellen did not?

At ten, when the haunted house closed, Agnes failed to come and untie Ellen. She tried to wriggle loose but the rope was too tight. Fortunately, she spied Corey and Mighty Mike as they passed the doorway on their way out.

"Corey!" she called. "Agnes forgot to untie me."

Mighty Mike quickly loosened the knots and the rope fell to the ground. "Thanks," Ellen said. She bent down to put on her shoes and socks.

"I'll meet you downstairs," Corey said. "I want to walk with Mighty Mike."

"I'll be a couple of minutes," Ellen said. "I have to talk to Agnes." She had decided the best approach would be to tell Agnes privately about the mistake. That way, Agnes could correct it without embarrassment.

Ellen went through the doorway at the far end of the dining room and crossed the kitchen to the pantry which had been converted to an office for Mrs. Whittacker and Agnes. As she approached, she heard Agnes's voice. Ellen realized she was talking to someone.

The office door was partway open. Ellen peered in. Agnes sat behind the desk, smoking a cigarette, with her back to the door. "This is my last night," Agnes said. "No more Clayton House."

Ellen stopped. What did she mean? Was Agnes quitting?

"I had a bit of a scare last night," Agnes said. "Mrs. Whittacker noticed that one of the bowls was missing. I had taken it home with me on Saturday, after everyone left, because I couldn't tell from my photograph if I had done one of the fairies exactly right. Then I got sick and couldn't work on the bowl and couldn't return the original, either. Just my luck, she noticed it was missing and called me. I made up a story about repairing a chip and she bought it with no question. I never did get to compare the original bowl to mine."

Ellen's heart began to thud against her ribs. She couldn't see who Agnes was talking to.

"I've switched all but two pieces," Agnes continued, "and I'll do those two tonight, as soon as everyone's cleared out of here."

Agnes started to swivel around on the chair. Ellen flattened herself against the wall, behind the door, where Agnes couldn't see her.

Agnes kept talking. "Some of mine have been on the shelves for two weeks now and nobody can tell the difference. I told you I was good, Harry, and this proves it."

Ellen sidled away from the office door. She tiptoed back through the kitchen and into the dining room. She ducked under the rope and went straight toward the octagonal bowl. She picked it up and rubbed it carefully across her sleeve, to remove any dust. Then she looked at it closely.

It wasn't the lighting that made it seem duller tonight. It *was* duller. It was duller and the fairy's shoes were wrong and Ellen knew it was neither old nor valuable. She was not holding a piece of Wedgwood Fairylustre.

She was holding a fake.

Chapter
12

At last, Ellen knew what Lydia wanted her to see.

Why didn't I notice sooner? she wondered. How could I have been so dense?

She put the bowl back on the shelf and walked slowly past the other pieces. One of the Fairylustre vases didn't seem quite right to her, but she wasn't sure exactly why. She could not tell if the blue and white pieces were authentic or not. She couldn't tell the creamware, either, or any of the other pieces.

She stared for a long moment at the big black urn. Was it the same urn she had looked at that first day? Or was it a reproduction?

Even though she had studied the Wedgwood frequently in the last week, she could not tell which pieces were original and which were copies. Except for the Fairylustre bowl. That was a reproduction, for sure.

Agnes said she switched all but two pieces. If all of these

are imitations, Ellen thought, where are the originals? What has happened to the Wedgwood collection? Where are Josiah Clayton's remains?

Probably Lydia kept urging Ellen to look at the Fairylustre because that's what Ellen most admired. If she was going to realize a copy had been substituted for the real piece, it would most likely happen when she was looking at the Fairylustre.

Ellen felt stunned, short of breath, the way she had once when she was playing basketball and got the wind knocked out of her. She also felt angry. What right did Agnes have to steal these treasures? Ellen supposed Agnes planned to sell the real pieces. Maybe she already had. They might be gone, welcomed into private collections, anywhere in the world. They might never be recovered, might never again stand on the shelves of Clayton House.

Ellen thought of Mr. Clayton, lying in his bed at Sheltering Arms, giving his home and his treasured works of art to the city so that people like Ellen could enjoy them. How was he going to feel when he learned that the curator of the museum had stolen his beloved Wedgwood?

Well, she isn't going to get away with it, Ellen thought. Maybe the real pieces haven't been sold yet. Maybe there's still time to get them back.

She turned and ran across the dining room and down the stairs. She would tell her parents everything and they would call Mrs. Whittacker. Better yet, they could call the police. Maybe the police would come to Clayton House and catch Agnes yet tonight. She said she still had two pieces to switch.

Ellen rushed across the great hall. Corey was not standing by the door, where they usually met. No doubt he got tired of waiting for her and was already out in the car with whichever of their parents had come to pick them up, babbling about how good he had screamed tonight or telling yet another Mighty Mike tale.

She grabbed the door handle and pulled. Nothing happened. She pulled again. With a sinking feeling, Ellen realized the door was already locked. Mrs. Whittacker must have thought all the volunteers had left; she had gone out and locked the door behind her.

Ellen knew it took a key to unlock it, even from the inside. She did not like the idea of going back to the office and admitting to Agnes that she was locked in. She didn't particularly want to talk to Agnes at all—not until she'd been to the police with her discovery.

Before long, her parents would try to get in and would realize what had happened. But it might take a long time before they could reach Mrs. Whittacker or someone else who had a key.

Ellen would have to go and find Agnes, in order to get out. She went back upstairs and down the hall toward the dining room. Agnes was probably still in her office, talking to her friend.

As she walked, Ellen made up a story to explain why she had stayed in the mansion. She would tell Agnes that she thought Corey was still inside and she had gone to look for him. By the time she realized he had left without her, the door was locked. Unlike her brother, she was not used to making up stories but she certainly could not tell Agnes the real reason why she lingered so long after closing.

Her mind was on what she would say to Agnes as she entered the dining room and headed for the door to the kitchen.

She didn't see Agnes crouched beside the bottom shelf of Wedgwood.

Ellen was nearly to the kitchen door when she was hit by an icy blast of air so strong that she was forced to stop walking.

"Not now, Lydia," she said.

The moment she spoke, she heard a gasp behind her. Whirling around, she saw Agnes, still crouched beside the collection. On the floor beside her was a cardboard box. A piece of Fairylustre was in her hand. She stood up, quickly putting the Fairylustre on a shelf.

"Why are you still here?" Agnes said.

"I got locked in."

"What were you doing for so long?"

Ellen opened her mouth to give the story she had made up but before she could begin, Agnes said, "You were in here again, weren't you? You're the one who rearranged all the Wedgwood."

"No."

"I suppose you thought it was funny to put the newer pieces down at that end, where the dates are in the eighteen hundreds and put the old creamware up here."

"I didn't do that," Ellen said.

"I was in here personally while the public was here, to be sure that nobody got too close. The collection was in the proper sequence then. Someone rearranged it after the haunted house closed."

"It wasn't me."

"None of the other volunteers has shown any interest in the Wedgwood. Only you."

"I didn't move them around." She had to clamp her teeth tight together to keep from saying that Agnes was the one who had been messing with the Wedgwood, so why was she accusing Ellen?

"It won't do you any good to deny it," Agnes said. "I've already talked to Mrs. Whittacker about you. I caught her before she left and warned her that you can't be trusted to leave the collection alone and that she should watch you carefully until the haunted house closes, to be sure you stay away from it."

Ellen's mouth dropped open in astonishment. Then her eyes narrowed as she realized what Agnes had done. She wanted to be sure that nobody discovered that the real Wedgwood was missing. She wanted as much time as possible to get away, and she knew Ellen had examined the pieces thoroughly and might just notice that something wasn't right, so she made up a story about Ellen rearranging the Wedgwood, to be sure Mrs. Whittacker didn't allow Ellen to get too close to it.

Fury crackled through Ellen's veins. She was so angry, she wished she could point at Agnes and have bolts of lightning come out the ends of her fingers. She didn't even want Agnes to unlock the door for her. She just wanted to get away from that horrible woman.

"I'm going to call Mrs. Whittacker," she said, "and ask her to come and let me out." She turned and strode toward the kitchen door.

"Stay away from my office!" There was an undercurrent of panic in Agnes's voice.

Ellen kept walking.

Agnes started after her, tripped on the cardboard box, and fell against the shelves. Two vases toppled at the impact and smashed to the floor.

"Oh!" Ellen cried, as she looked at the shattered fragments. "Were they the real ones?" As soon as the words were out of her mouth, she realized what she had said. Her voice seemed to echo in the huge dining room. The real ones, the real ones.

"The real ones?" Agnes repeated. There was such animosity in her eyes that Ellen recoiled. They stared at each other for a moment.

"Harry!" Agnes shouted.

The kitchen door opened and a man wearing a blue ski parka ran into the dining room. He stopped when he saw Ellen. "Who's she?" he asked.

"She knows," Agnes said.

"What? You told this kid?"

"Of course not, you idiot. I don't know how she found out."

Ellen stepped backward, toward the dining-room entry.

"Now what do we do?" the man said.

"We'll have to take her with us."

"Oh, no. I'm not taking some kid across the state line."

Ellen tried to swallow but her throat was so tight, nothing moved.

"Do you have a better suggestion?" Agnes asked.

"We'll lock her in your office."

"With the telephone." Agnes looked disgusted.

"We can tie her up. Nobody will be back here until tomorrow afternoon. That's enough time for us."

"They'll come looking for her long before tomorrow afternoon," Agnes said. "They're probably trying to locate a key right now. We have to get moving, Harry. We're out of time. I'll get the last box; you get her in the car."

Ellen whirled and ran toward the door. The man's footsteps thumped on the floor behind her.

She ran into the hallway. He drew closer.

"There's no place to run," he called. "You're locked in here with us."

Straight ahead was the Joan of Arc room. Ellen knew there was no exit from that. To her right, the stairway led to the great hall and the front door; since it was locked, there was no point going that way. She ran to her left, toward the bedrooms. Bedroom doors sometimes lock from the inside.

She ran past the conservatory, where Corey and Mighty Mike did their scene every night, and past the library where the Julius Caesar scene took place. She saw a door ahead, a door that Mrs. Whittacker had not opened that first night, when she took them on a tour of the mansion.

She reached the door, turned the knob, and flung it open. It was not a bedroom. It was a linen closet. She whirled around and saw the man approaching, just a few yards away.

Ellen's mind raced, trying to decide what to do. She could try to run past him; maybe if she ducked, just as she got to him, she could elude his grasp. Or she could kick him. She could kick him in the groin and then run.

Ellen was not a fighter. She avoided conflict if she could and the thought of purposely kicking another person, with the intent of hurting him, was abhorrent to her. But it would be even worse to be forced into the car and be taken hostage by this man and Agnes.

There was no time to debate her options. The man lunged toward her. Ellen swung her foot toward him as hard as she could but he was too quick. It was as if he had anticipated what she would do and was ready for it.

As her foot lifted toward his groin, he clasped his hands together into a single fist and brought it down, hard, on Ellen's shin. The blow forced her foot away from him and, instead of kicking the man, she kicked the wall. Ellen yelped as streamers of pain flew up her leg. She dropped to her knees.

The man unclasped his hands and reached for Ellen's shoulders.

Before he could grab her, the lights went out. The entire mansion was plunged into darkness. In front of her, Ellen heard the man curse.

Quickly, she rolled to her left and then crept away, moving forward, groping along the wall with her hand. She remembered that all the lights were on a timer. No doubt Agnes would have to go to some central control in order to turn them on again. That would take at least a couple of minutes—long enough for Ellen to hide, if she could just get away from the man now.

Behind her, she heard the man thumping the wall with his hands, as he tried to find her.

She crawled past the door to the library and the door to the conservatory. Hardly daring to breathe, she felt for the entry to the parlor. If she could get in there, she could hide under Joan of Arc's platform. She thought she could find her way to the platform, even in the dark. The man would not know where to look. If he found the door to the library, he would probably go in there, thinking she would enter the first room she came to. Even if he went in the parlor, he wouldn't be familiar with the Joan of Arc setup. He wouldn't know where to search.

If Agnes knew how to turn the lights back on, or got a flashlight, they still might not find her under Joan of Arc's platform.

Time, she knew, was on her side. By now, she was sure her parents were trying to get in. Maybe Mrs. Whittacker was already on her way back, with the key.

She crawled on. She must be near the entrance to the parlor.

A shuffling sound approached from her right. The man was moving down the center of the hallway, sliding his feet as if he were on skis. He was apparently trying to cover as much of the floor as possible without raising his feet.

Ellen scrunched tight against the wall, disappointed that the man had not gone into the library or the conservatory. The shuffling feet came closer. She held her breath.

The slight sliding sound of his shoes on the floor drew even and she was aware of his presence beside her. He passed her, moving slowly, as if he had his hands outstretched, trying to find her. Ellen remained on her hands and knees. After awhile, the man shouted for Agnes and Agnes yelled something in return.

Maybe they will decide to run for it, Ellen thought, and leave me here.

She found the parlor door and turned in, seeing the room in her mind and remembering how it was arranged. The public viewing area was first, then the thick velvet rope that kept viewers from going too close. She found one of the brass poles that held the rope and crawled past it.

There was a long expanse of floor next, made to look like a cobblestone street. Then would be the pile of sticks and branches, with the platform concealed on the backside.

She crawled faster now, eager to get under the platform. Her outstretched hand came to the brush pile. She crept around to the back. She felt the platform steps.

As she tried to move the sticks far enough away from the platform to allow herself to get underneath, the lights came on. Blinking in the sudden brightness, she yanked quickly at the platform, moving it just enough so she could squeeze through.

When she ducked down, her sweater snagged on one of the sticks. Tugging furiously, Ellen tried to disentangle herself. She heard footsteps running down the hallway toward her. This time, she knew it wasn't Lydia. These footsteps were real and they were far more dangerous than those of the ghost.

She jerked her arm, tearing the sweater.

"There she is!" cried Agnes.

Chapter
13

Ellen kicked and screamed. She clung to the wooden platform, getting splinters in the palms of her hands, but Harry and Agnes were too strong.

They dragged her away from the platform. Harry held her arms behind her back. "There's no way we can take her along," he said. "She'll slow us down too much."

"We'll tie her here," said Agnes, "to the stake." She grabbed the rope as Harry pushed Ellen up the platform steps and against the stake. He held her arms to her sides while Agnes wrapped the rope around and around, pulling it as tight as she could.

They wound more rope around Ellen's ankles and then around Ellen's waist. As Agnes reached around Ellen's face from behind to pull on the rope, Ellen bent her head and bit Agnes's hand as hard as she could. Agnes yelled and jerked her hand away.

The ropes cut into Ellen's skin. She knew there was no point trying to wiggle loose; she would only get rope burns.

"The last of the Wedgwood's in my car," Agnes said. "Bring the car around to the front and I'll meet you there."

Harry bolted out of the room. To Ellen's surprise, Agnes did not follow him. Instead, she waited until she was sure Harry was gone. Then Agnes turned back.

"Sorry, kid," she said. "But you should have minded your own business." She took a cigarette lighter out of her pocket. "I've worked for months on this job and I'm not letting you spoil it now."

She flicked the lighter twice. When a tiny flame appeared, she bent down, holding the lighter against the pile of sticks and brush at Ellen's feet.

Stunned by the realization of what Agnes was doing, Ellen stared silently.

"You've been practicing for this scene all week," Agnes said. "Now you can see what it's really like to burn at the stake."

Ellen screamed.

"There is no one to hear you." Agnes held the lighter steady against a twig. A tiny wisp of smoke curled upward toward the ceiling of the great mansion. In her mind, Ellen heard the sound effects from the Joan of Arc scene: the fire crackling, the shouts of the crowd. "Heretic!" "Witch!"

The twig caught. The bright yellow and blue flame stretched toward the other sticks. Ellen screamed again.

"A fire is a clever twist," Agnes said. "I wish I had thought of it sooner."

"You'll get caught," Ellen said.

"They won't be able to tell from the ruins that the charred vases and bowls weren't the real Wedgwood."

"My brother knows," Ellen said. "That's why I stayed here,

so I could detain you until he gets back with the police." In her panic, the lie rolled easily off her tongue.

"Corey doesn't know," Agnes said. "If you had both discovered that the Wedgwood was missing, you would both have run to tell someone."

More twigs caught fire. The smoke grew darker.

"They'll think we forgot to untie you," Agnes said, as she held her lighter to the other side of the brush pile. "They'll think something went wrong with this old, faulty wiring, and that you were not able to free yourself to escape the fire. It will be called a tragic accident."

A larger stick began burning. The flames spread outward.

Ellen closed her eyes. She couldn't bear to watch as the twigs and branches, one at a time, caught fire. Was it possible that her life would end like this? That she would never see her parents and Corey and Grandpa and Grandma again?

She shivered.

Her eyes flew open as she realized she had shivered because a strong icy wind was blowing at her back.

The wind surged past Ellen with such force that the heavy stake pushed against Ellen's back and she had to struggle to stay upright.

It blew across the platform, surrounding the pile of brush.

Agnes's head jerked up. "What the . . ?" she said.

The flames sputtered. The wind swooped back and forth, howling in its severity. The fire flickered, smoldered briefly, and then went out.

Quickly, Agnes tried to relight it.

The cold wind went mad. It swirled around Agnes, blowing her hair into her eyes. It lifted the smaller branches into the air so that they flew around Agnes, scratching her arms and face.

Desperately, she flicked the lighter again, but each time, as soon as the flame flared up, the wind blew it out.

"What's going on?" Agnes cried.

"It's the ghost," Ellen said. "I told you there was a ghost in here."

"That's nonsense. There are no ghosts." Agnes's hand shook as she frantically worked the lighter.

The wind centered itself beside her and blew with such force that the cigarette lighter fell from her fingers. It dropped into the pile of sticks.

"You've angered the ghost," Ellen said, "and now she's going to get you."

Agnes reached into the pile of brush, trying to retrieve the lighter. The wind became an indoor tornado, enclosing her. She abandoned the lighter and hunched over, shielding her face with her hands.

More of the smaller twigs and sticks were caught in the whirlwind and began blowing around and around Agnes.

"Harry!" she yelled. "Help!"

"He can't hear you," Ellen said. "He went for the car. No one can hear you except me and the ghost. And she is my friend."

"Make her stop!" Agnes cried.

Ellen said nothing.

Agnes twisted suddenly away from the pile of brush. She turned and ran toward the door but before she got there, the cold wind stopped, the swirling branches dropped to the floor, and Lydia materialized in the doorway.

The ghost looked much worse than the other times Ellen had seen her. For an instant, Ellen thought it was a different ghost altogether. The face was haggard, with sunken cheeks, and there were no eyeballs —just deep hollow, empty sockets. She gave off a strong, putrid odor —like rotting meat that's been left in a warm garbage can.

But she wore the same lace-trimmed white gown, and the curly, shoulder-length hair was exactly like Lydia's. And then she made the same unearthly cry that she had made earlier, when Ellen asked her about the remains in the Wedgwood.

The ghastly cry was even louder than before and the high ceiling in the parlor made the horrible sound echo on and on. Ellen's pulse throbbed in her throat, in rhythm with the repulsive reverberation.

Ellen could not take her eyes from the apparition. Never had she seen anything so obnoxious. And yet, she felt no fear. She knew that Lydia was trying to help her. If the ghost had not intervened, the entire pile of brush would be burning by now, and Ellen with it.

"Aaaeeeiiigghhh!" As she cried this time, Lydia lifted her arms, as if to enfold Agnes and draw her close.

Agnes grabbed a large branch from the pile of sticks and lunged at the ghost. Gripping the limb with both hands, Agnes held it shoulder high and aimed it directly at Lydia's head.

The branch passed easily through Lydia's body. As it did, she made a low, guttural sound, like a wild animal growling.

Agnes opened her mouth but no sound came out. She dropped the branch. She backed away from Lydia.

Lydia raised her hands and reached for Agnes's throat.

As the ice-cold hands touched Agnes's skin, she fainted, falling in a heap just inside the doorway.

The ugly, foul-smelling apparition instantly vanished. In its place, stood the same sad young woman that Ellen had always seen before.

Downstairs, voices called, "Ellen? Are you in here?"

"Up here!" she shouted. "In the parlor!"

Lydia disappeared.

Footsteps thundered up the stairs.

"In here," Ellen cried again.

She expected to see Mrs. Whittacker. Instead it was a police officer, followed closely by Corey.

"I told you she was in trouble," Corey said. "A flying saucer could land on that little balcony and purple people from Jupiter might try to kidnap Ellen." Seeing the inert Agnes on the floor, he knelt beside her. "The purple people from Jupiter have killed Agnes!" he yelled.

Even with his mouth going as usual, Ellen was glad to see her brother. Her parents were right behind Corey.

"She isn't dead," Ellen said. "But she tried to kill me. She stole all the Wedgwood and put fake pieces on the shelves and when I found out, she tried to set fire to Clayton House."

"We realized you were locked in," Mrs. Streater said, "and we couldn't reach Mrs. Whittacker, so we called the police."

The officer began to untie Ellen. "When we arrived," he said, "we found a man sitting out in front in a car, with the engine running."

"That's Harry," Ellen said. "He and Agnes tied me up."

Agnes groaned and sat up. She looked at the police officer and groaned again.

"How did you knock Agnes out, when she had you tied up?" Corey asked.

"I didn't. She fainted." Ellen looked at Agnes, wondering if Agnes would say anything about the ghost.

"I didn't faint," Agnes said. "I slipped and hit my head on the floor."

"No," said Ellen. "She saw the ghost of Lydia Clayton, and

she fainted." She rubbed her arms, where the rope had cut into them.

The police officer raised his eyebrows and looked at her.

"Somehow, everyone forgot to untie Ellen tonight," Agnes said. "I was just leaving, when I heard her call. I came up to untie her but I tripped on one of these branches. I must have knocked myself out when I fell."

"Agnes tried to start a fire," Ellen said. "She and Harry tied me here and then she was going to burn Clayton House and me with it. The twigs were already starting to burn when Lydia's ghost blew out the flame."

"That's ridiculous," Agnes said. "Why would I burn down my place of employment? *I* wouldn't collect any insurance. And there certainly was no ghost involved."

"Are you sure it wasn't purple people from Jupiter?" Corey said.

"Just like my kids," said the police officer to Mr. and Mrs. Streater. "Terrific imaginations."

Mr. and Mrs. Streater looked at each other, as if wondering what to believe.

"It wasn't my imagination," Ellen said. "I've seen the ghost before. The other times, I was the only one who could see her but this time, Agnes saw her, too."

"Ellen doesn't normally make up stories," Mr. Streater said.

"I do seem to smell smoke," Mrs. Streater said.

"Mighty Mike and I untied Ellen," Corey said. "Before we left, we came in here and Mighty Mike untied the rope."

"Mighty Mike McGarven?" said the officer. "The D.J.?"

"You can call him and ask him," Corey said. "He'll remember."

"There's where the fire was," Ellen said. She pointed to the charred black places where the twigs had started to burn.

The officer bent to look more closely. "There's the cigarette lighter," he said, reaching into the pile of wood and picking Agnes's lighter off the floor.

"Did you scream?" asked Corey.

"Yes."

"Good." Corey smiled in satisfaction. "She learned how from me," he said, but the police officer was no longer listening to Ellen and Corey. He was busy telling Agnes her rights.

"You could have been killed," Mrs. Streater said, as she hugged Ellen.

"And this beautiful mansion might have burned to the ground," said Mr. Streater.

"Did you really see the ghost?" asked Corey.

"Yes."

"Did you ask her about visiting my class at school?"

Ellen gave him a disgusted look. "I had a few other things on my mind," she said.

"Well, if you see her again, be sure to ask."

A second officer arrived. "I didn't find any drugs or weapons on the guy," he reported, "but another squad car took him for questioning. There are several boxes of old dishes in the car that look like they might be valuable."

"The Wedgwood!" all the Streaters said, together.

"And he had two plane tickets for London in his pocket, leaving at midnight tonight."

"Looks like you'll miss your flight," the first officer said to Agnes, as he snapped handcuffs on her and led her away.

The other officer questioned Ellen awhile longer and then thanked her and told the Streaters they could go.

"But you didn't call the newspaper," Corey said. "Aren't you going to call the newspaper and have someone come and take our picture?"

"Not this time," said Mr. Streater.

"We could wait awhile," Corey said, "until they get here."

"This family," said Mrs. Streater, "will be the death of me."

Chapter
14

"Those were the best blueberry muffins I ever ate," Mr. Clayton said. "How you had time to make them with all the goings on last night, I'll never know."

"I stayed home from school today," Ellen admitted. "I was worn out."

"Small wonder. I heard the news story about you this morning. How you caught that Agnes person and her partner."

"Not the whole story."

"Oh?"

"Lydia saved my life—and she saved Clayton House from burning. But Agnes denied seeing the ghost and the police officer thought I was making that part of the story up."

"Why would you do that? You told the truth about everything else, didn't you?"

"Of course. I wouldn't lie to the police. But apparently Corey had been bombarding them with his outlandish theory that I was kidnapped by purple people from Jupiter, so when I started talking about a ghost, the officer ignored me, too. It was the best part of the whole episode and he didn't believe me."

"So tell me. I'll believe you."

Ellen smiled at him and told him everything, exactly as it had happened. "She looked horrible, much worse than the other times."

"Maybe a ghost appears one way to her friends and another way to her enemies."

"I'll never be afraid of her again," Ellen said, "no matter how she looks. If she hadn't blown out the fire, I would not be here today, talking to you."

Mr. Clayton shook his head. "It's hard to believe that anyone would set fire to Clayton House, let alone try to murder you."

"Agnes was in big financial trouble. Mrs. Whittacker found out this morning that Agnes owed a huge amount in back rent for her gallery and had other debts, as well. She and Harry had already shipped all of Agnes's gallery pieces to London and had rented shop space there."

"No doubt they planned to sell the stolen Wedgwood."

"Mrs. Whittacker says they'd have no trouble finding buyers."

"So Lydia saved your life." Mr. Clayton nodded his head, looking satisfied. "I always did think she was a kindly ghost, not at all like the stereotype that everyone fears."

"The police called my house this morning. They had a list of the Wedgwood from the Historical Society and they found all the missing pieces in Agnes's car."

"What about the pieces that broke, when Agnes fell?"

"They were fakes that Agnes had made."

"Thank heaven."

"As we were leaving Clayton House last night," Ellen said, "I pretended I'd forgotten my jacket and ran back upstairs alone. I was hoping I could see Lydia and thank her, but she wasn't there."

"You may never see her again. She doesn't need you anymore, now that they've recovered all the Wedgwood, unharmed."

"It would be a relief not to be haunted anymore but I would like a chance to tell Lydia how grateful I am."

"I imagine she knows that, without being told."

"When Mrs. Whittacker came over this morning, she said that Josiah's remains were still in the urn. She knew about them and had been worried, too. She said to tell you, all of the Wedgwood is back on the shelves in their original places and they won't be moved again."

"One piece will be," Mr. Clayton said.

"I don't think so," Ellen replied. "Mrs. Whittacker seemed determined to make sure that nothing like this happens again."

"*I'm* removing one piece," Mr. Clayton said. "The octagonal Fairylustre bowl. I told my lawyer this morning to withdraw it from the list of pieces that I'm giving to the city."

"I don't understand." Ellen looked at the small dresser top, already crowded with Mr. Clayton's television, a box of tissues, and some shaving equipment. "Aren't you afraid it will get broken, if you keep it here?"

"I don't plan to keep it here. It's yours."

Ellen stared at him.

"If it hadn't been for you, the entire collection would have been lost. The little bowl seems like a fitting reward."

"I don't need a reward," Ellen said. "Besides, Lydia is the one who should be thanked."

Mr. Clayton chuckled. "Lydia got what she wanted," he said. "It pleases me to give the little bowl to someone who appreciates it and will love it as much as I always have."

"Thank you," Ellen said. "I'll treasure it always." Her smile faded. "But Lydia might not like it if I take the Fairylustre bowl. What if she keeps haunting me?" Even though Ellen was no longer afraid of Lydia, she did not relish the idea of being awakened in the night by cold hands on her face.

"Lydia has appeared only when the Wedgwood was in danger. She first came back, years ago, when Caroline Clayton kept trying to get rid of the Wedgwood. As a small boy, I was clearly a threat."

"The first time I felt the ghost was when Mrs. Whittacker handed the Fairylustre bowl to Corey."

"Exactly. Another small, and probably careless, boy. I believe Lydia was determined that the Wedgwood not be harmed and her baby's remains not be disturbed. Since you are the one who prevented that from happening, she should be happy to see you rewarded. And I know you would be careful with the bowl."

"If Lydia appears tonight at the haunted house, I'll tell her about your gift and ask her if she'd object."

"I don't think you'll see Lydia again. I think the ghost appeared only because the Wedgwood was being stolen and the black urn removed from Clayton House. Now that the whole collection is safe, there's no reason for her to be restless."

To her own surprise, the idea of never seeing Lydia again disappointed Ellen. When she thought about that, she realized she had been hoping she would see the ghost once more, but this time looking happy, the way the smiling Lydia looked in Mr. Clayton's old picture as she cuddled her precious baby.

As she thought of the picture, a new idea hit Ellen. "I wonder," she said.

"Yes?"

"I wonder if what she really wants is to be near her baby."

Mr. Clayton looked startled. "What do you mean?"

"The biography of Lydia said she became a recluse after Josiah died, spending all of her time with her Wedgwood, but the biographer didn't know about the baby's remains. Maybe Lydia was really only trying to stay close to all she had left of Josiah. Maybe she *still* wants that. I saw her hands come out of the black urn."

Mr. Clayton looked thoughtful. "Perhaps Samuel had the same idea. Maybe that's why he suggested digging up Lydia's coffin, cremating her body, and putting her remains in the Wedgwood. He might have guessed how Lydia felt."

"But Caroline wouldn't let him do it," Ellen said.

"And he couldn't tell Caroline his real reason because she didn't know about Josiah's remains."

"Maybe it isn't the Wedgwood Lydia cares about; it's Josiah."

Mr. Clayton nodded. "I think you're right. All these years, she's been trying to tell someone to bury her baby's remains where she is buried, so they can be together. How did you think of this?"

"Lydia looked so happy in your picture and she looks so sad now. I just tried to figure out what would make her happy again."

"I'll have it done immediately. Lydia's buried in the Clayton family plot so it will be no problem and this will insure that Josiah's remains are never disturbed in the future. I should have thought of this long ago."

"Perhaps it's just as well you didn't have Josiah's remains buried sooner. Lydia may not care about the Wedgwood, once her baby's remains are no longer in the urn, and if Lydia had not appeared, Agnes would have succeeded in stealing the Wedgwood."

Grandma entered Mr. Clayton's room. "Are you ready to leave?" she asked Ellen. "It's Halloween, you know. I have to buy goodies in case anyone comes for trick or treat. I don't dare buy candy bars ahead of time, or Grandpa eats them."

Ellen took Mr. Clayton's hand. "Thank you again. It's the best present I ever got."

Looking serious, he shook a finger at Ellen. "There's one string attached," he warned. "You must bring blueberry muffins again."

"I'll come every Saturday."

HALLOWEEN. The final night of the haunted house. Ellen wondered if she would see the ghost one last time.

At home, Mrs. Streater said, "Corey went to a Halloween party at Nicholas's house and he isn't back yet. You won't need to leave for another hour."

"In that case," Ellen said, "I'm going to take a nap."

Ellen rarely slept in the daytime but the stress and excitement of the last few days had worn her out and with Corey gone, the house was quiet, for a change.

She turned on her radio, stretched out on her bed, and closed her eyes. The music soothed her and she felt her muscles relax. For the first time in several days, she fell asleep without worrying that she would be awakened by a ghost.

When the song ended, a shrill, fearsome scream jolted Ellen's nerves. She gasped and raised her head from the pillow, scanning the room. For an instant, she thought Lydia was back and that something else was wrong. Then she heard Mighty Mike say, "The scream you just heard was Prince Rufus; he will get beheaded tonight, beginning at . . ." Realizing it was a promotional spot for the haunted house, Ellen reached for the radio knob and switched it off.

There is no escaping my brother's voice, she thought. Even when he isn't here, I have to listen to him scream.

AS ELLEN stood tied to the stake that night, the sound effects of the crackling fire seemed more frightening than ever. The bright, artificial flames looked real as they flickered upward and the smoke smell stung her nostrils. When she looked down at the pile of brush and twigs, she saw blackened ones and knew they had been charred the night before.

I came so close, Ellen thought, and she was flooded with gratitude. Without Lydia, the experience of being burned alive would have been a horrible reality.

There was a huge crowd that night and many more people than usual took time to admire the Wedgwood collection. A beaming Mrs. Whittacker declared that Ellen's brush with danger and Agnes's arrest had certainly resulted in some fine publicity. People who ordinarily would have ignored the Wedgwood collection now stood in line to see the dishes that were so old and valuable a respected artist had ruined her career by replacing the real pieces with replicas.

"Ticket sales surpassed our goal by 20 percent," Mrs. Whittacker said. "We have enough money to replace the wiring, renovate the kitchen, and have some left over for future improvements."

Ellen decided it was just as well the newspapers and television stations did not know about Lydia. If they had broadcast news of a brave ghost who put out a fire, stopped a fleeing thief, and prevented a murder, Clayton House would be so jammed with gawkers that the haunted house would never be able to function.

Shortly after midnight, Ellen removed the Joan of Arc gown for the last time and joined the crowd who had gathered in the great hall to watch Mrs. Whittacker draw the winning name from those who correctly guessed which scene was not factual. Corey and Mighty Mike were already there and Ellen saw Corey wriggling with impatience as he waited to see if Nicholas's name was selected.

Mrs. Whittacker quieted the group by holding up a large glass bowl filled with slips of paper. "As you can see," she said "many people correctly guessed that the fictional scene was the one in the conservatory. No Prince Rufus was beheaded at the age of ten."

"*I* was the fake?" Corey's horrified voice rang out. "*I* was the fake and the pigs were real?"

As Mighty Mike consoled Corey and Mrs. Whittacker reached into the bowl for the winning name, Ellen slipped away. She went back upstairs and into the dining room.

She looked at the beautiful little Fairylustre bowl, its shimmery colors gleaming. As she thought of all the people who must have admired it that night, she decided to leave it where it was. It belonged to her and she would treasure that knowledge, but she wanted to have it displayed with the rest of the Wedgwood, where other people could enjoy it, too.

She held the bowl for a moment, turning it slowly. It was still hard to believe that anything so beautiful was hers. The thought made her glow with pleasure.

I'll have a little plaque made, she decided, a small brass plaque that says: *This piece is on loan from Ellen Streater*. I'll leave my Fairylustre bowl here in Clayton House, with the rest of the Wedgwood. She felt Lydia would approve of her decision.

Ellen walked to the other end of the display and stood in front of the oldest piece of Wedgwood, the black urn which contained the cremated remains of Josiah Clayton.

Did Lydia already know of Mr. Clayton's plan to bury Josiah's remains for all eternity beside his loving mother? Had she been present, unseen, at Sheltering Arms when Ellen wondered if the hauntings were motivated not by greed over her Wedgwood collection but by Lydia's love for her child?

"Lydia?" she whispered. "Are you here?"

Silence.

"Can you hear me, Lydia? If you can, please give me a sign."

Nothing. There was no cold air, no breeze, no hint that anyone other than Ellen was in the dining room. Ellen looked over her shoulder, toward the mirror. She saw only her own reflection.

"Lydia?" She said it louder this time, even though she knew that if the ghost were present, she would hear Ellen's voice at any sound level.

Silence.

Ellen waited a moment before she spoke again. "I want to

thank you, Lydia. You saved my life and I will always remember you."

Nothing. No hands, no face in the mirror, no chill.

Ellen stood quietly for a few more minutes. As she gazed at the shelves of Wedgwood, she realized that all the feelings of apprehension that she'd had about the house initially were gone. There was no more tension in the air, no coldness. The sinister vibrations which had disturbed her on her first visit were no longer here. Clayton House felt serene.

Ellen laid her fingers on the old black urn. Lightly, she caressed the piece which contained the last remains of Lydia Clayton's baby. As her hands moved slowly across the surface, she knew Mr. Clayton was right. She would not see Lydia's ghost again. She could only hope that her words of thanks, or her thoughts, were somehow perceived by the ghost.

Ellen smiled at the old Wedgwood urn.

"Rest in peace," she said softly. "Rest in peace, my friend."

DANGER
AT THE
FAIR

FOR MARK EDWARD KEHRET
September 21, 1992

Omnibus Edition ISBN 978-0-545-78469-6

12 11 10 9 8 7 6 5 4 3 2 1   14 15 16 17 18 19/0

Printed in the U.S.A.   40

First Scholastic printing, September 2014

PROLOGUE

ELLEN STREATER stared into the darkness as the hall clock struck twelve.

Midnight. The perfect time for ghosts and spirits, she thought. If he's ever going to hear me, it will be now.

She sat up and swung her legs over the side of the bed, searching with her toes for her slippers. Silently, she moved to her dresser, feeling along the top until her hand closed over the small silver elephant.

It was the first time she had intentionally touched the elephant since the night of the accident. Then, overcome with rage and grief, she had unfastened the chain and flung the elephant into the wastebasket. "You didn't bring good luck," she had said. "You brought terrible, horrible luck."

The next day, someone—Ellen assumed it had been her mother—retrieved the elephant and put it on Ellen's dresser. It had lain there all these months, growing dusty, a reminder of the worst day of her life.

1

It was not what Grandpa had intended, when he gave it to her.

"I know how much you like the elephants," he had told her, "and an elephant with its trunk curled up is a symbol of good luck. When you wear this, you'll remember our fun trips to the zoo."

It had been a special gift, chosen especially for her. Now, as she stood in the midnight blackness, Ellen hoped the silver elephant might somehow help her make the connection she longed for. More than anything, she wanted her words to be heard and understood.

Cupping the elephant and its slender silver chain in her left hand, she held it close to her heart and whispered, "Grandpa? Wherever your spirit is, I hope you can hear me. I want to tell you what happened today. Maybe you already know. Maybe you were part of it."

She paused briefly, wondering where to begin. With the strange message? With the Tunnel of Terror? With the realization that someone wanted to kill her?

Ellen took a deep breath, squeezed the silver elephant, and began with breakfast that morning.

CHAPTER

◈ 1 ◈

"HERE COMES The Gruesome Green Ghoul!" Corey Streater, with his arms above his head and his fingers spread like claws, lurched into the kitchen.

His sister, Ellen, took another bite of toast and ignored him.

"Eat your breakfast, Corey," Mrs. Streater said, "or you won't be ready to go to the fair when Nicholas and Mrs. Warren get here."

"I'm ready now," Corey declared. "I'll eat breakfast at the fair, as soon as I ride the Tilt-a-Whirl and The River of Fear."

"You'll eat breakfast right here," Mrs. Streater said. "It's probably the only decent food you'll get all day."

"The Gruesome Green Ghoul eats people," Corey said. He grabbed Ellen's arm and pretended to take bites from her wrist to her elbow, as if her arm was corn on the cob.

Ellen jerked her arm away, glad that she was going to the fair with Caitlin and would not have to put up with her little brother's nonsense. "I wouldn't go on that River of Fear ride if you paid me," Ellen said.

"Is that the big enclosed ride that stays on the fairgrounds year-round?" Mrs. Streater asked.

"That's the one," Ellen said. "Some kids that rode it last year told me it's the scariest ride they were ever on."

"Good," Corey said, as he spread peanut butter on a slice of toast. "When I grow up," he continued, "I'm going to invent The Gruesome Green Ghoul ride and I'll go to all the fairs and run it and pretend to eat people."

"*If* you ever grow up," Ellen said.

"My ride will fly upside down and rotate in circles and whip back and forth, all at the same time, and you'll have to ride it standing on your head with bare feet. You'll get strapped down so you don't fall off and there'll be this huge green blob, like a giant amoeba, that bites at your toes and then . . ."

"Don't expect me to ride on it," Ellen said.

"The Gruesome Green Ghoul ride will be the scariest ride ever invented," Corey said. "Even scarier than The River of Fear. I'll make a trillion zillion dollars, and spend it all on corn dogs."

"You forgot to take the bandage off your face," Mrs. Streater said.

"I didn't forget," Corey said. "I like it. It's the best Batman bandage I ever saw. I'm going to wear it for a whole year." He took a drink of orange juice and then screamed as loudly as he could.

Ellen dropped her toast.

"What's wrong?" cried Mrs. Streater.

"Just practicing," Corey said. "I plan to go on every ride and I'm going to scream and scream and scream."

"Don't overdo it," Mrs. Streater said. "You're still hoarse from that throat infection. If you scream all day, you'll lose your voice altogether."

"Hallelujah!" said Ellen.

A horn beeped in front of the Streaters' house.

"It's Nicholas!" Corey yelled. "I'm leaving!"

"Good," said Ellen.

"Be careful," Mrs. Streater said. "Stay with Mrs. Warren and do exactly what she tells you."

Corey dashed out the door.

His mother called after him, "Don't eat too much junk!" but Corey did not hear her. He was lurching toward the Warrens' car, shouting, "Here comes The Gruesome Green Ghoul."

Mrs. Streater poured herself a cup of coffee and sank into a chair opposite Ellen. "Did you ever notice," she said, "how quiet it seems right after Corey leaves?"

Ellen laughed.

"I hope he behaves himself," Mrs. Streater said. "Fairs and carnivals can attract some rather seedy characters and you know how Corey is, always imagining that he's a spy and other people are dangerous criminals."

"Mrs. Warren will watch him."

Mrs. Streater nodded. "Yes. Your father says I worry too much. But trouble always comes in threes, you know, and I can't help wondering what the third will be."

A terrible windstorm in January had uprooted a fir tree and sent it crashing across the Streaters' garage, causing extensive damage. Then, in March, they lost Grandpa. Ellen thought no trouble could be as bad as that and she knew from the sad look on her mother's face that Mrs. Streater was thinking the same thing.

A dark sense of foreboding swept through the sunny kitchen, pushing aside the warmth of the August morning. Quickly, Ellen finished her toast and carried her dishes to the sink. Trouble coming in threes is nothing more than an old superstition, she told herself. What could be more safe than the county fair?

◇　◇　◇

"DON'T VOLUNTEER any information," Mitch Lagrange told his wife, as they waited to cross the border from Canada to the United States. "Answer questions pleasantly but don't say anything more."

"I'm not stupid," Joan Lagrange replied.

Mitch looked in the rearview mirror at his nine-year-old stepson, Alan. "You pretend to be asleep," he said.

Mitch pulled the car up to the enclosure where the border guard sat.

"Where do you live?" the guard asked.

"Seattle."

"How long were you in Canada?"

"Overnight."

The guard looked around Mitch and addressed the next question to Joan. "What did you do there?"

"We took my son to the Vancouver Aquarium." She pointed to the back seat, where Alan lay with his eyes closed.

The border guard nodded and waved them on their way.

"I knew they wouldn't have a stolen vehicle report yet," Mitch said. "I doubt the owner has even realized the car is missing. Still, it's a relief to get across the border without any problem."

"Portland, here we come," Joan said, "to collect our ten thousand smackeroos."

Mitch stayed just under the speed limit as he drove south on Interstate 5. "I wish I could open it up," he said, "and see how fast this beauty will go."

"When you're driving a stolen Mercedes with counterfeit license plates," Joan replied, "you don't take chances."

"This handles like a dream," Mitch said. "It's a shame to strip it and sell the parts."

"We'll get twice as much for the parts as we would for the car," Joan said, "so don't get any funny ideas." She consulted the map of Washington State. "The turnoff for the fair in Monroe is Highway 2," she said. "But do we *have* to waste a day visiting your brother? If we keep going, we'll be in Portland in time for lunch. The fair is fifteen miles out of our way." She looked at the map again. "Monroe doesn't even rate a red circle on the map. It's only a tiny black dot, like a period."

"I owe it to Tucker, to see how he's doing."

"You don't owe him anything."

"We should have posted bail when he asked us," Mitch said.

"We didn't have an extra three thousand dollars sitting around."

"We could have come up with it, if we had tried." Mitch exited the freeway and headed east on Highway 2. "It's been hard on Tucker the last six months, working for a carnival in order to stay on the move after he jumped bail."

"It wasn't our fault he got caught faking car accidents so people could turn in false claims to their insurance companies. Why should we have to bail him out?"

Half an hour later, Mitch handed two dollars to the parking lot attendant and pulled the Mercedes into the line of parked cars at the fair.

"There's a Ferris wheel," Alan said, "and a big roller coaster. This is going to be fun."

"Let's work the fair, Mitch," Joan said.

"Are you crazy?"

"It would be like old times, picking pockets for a living."

"No, thanks," Mitch said. "What if we got caught?"

"We won't get caught. And even if we did, we'd be let off with a warning or a small fine. A little country fair, way out in the boonies like this, won't have a decent police department. They probably can't even check fingerprints or get computer data."

At the mention of fingerprints, Mitch stiffened. His greatest fear was to have his fingerprints checked, although Joan didn't know that. He had never told his wife about his past; she thought he had always been Mitch Lagrange and Mitch saw no reason to enlighten her. Joan could never tell someone else what she didn't know herself.

"I used to outsmart them in Los Angeles and San Diego," Joan continued. "We won't get caught here."

"Maybe not, but why stick our necks out when we don't need the money? We'll make ten grand on this car deal and it's a sure thing, with no risk now that we've made it across the border."

"We need a little excitement," Joan said. "The car business is boring."

"Bor-ring," echoed Alan.

"Good," Mitch said. "Boring means no trouble."

"We could cut Tucker in on the day's take. We'll find a way for him to help and give him fifteen or twenty percent."

"I'll help," Alan offered, "if you give me twenty percent, too."

Joan laughed.

"Please, Mitch?" Alan said. *"Please?"*

"People bring money to a fair," Joan said. "We could help them get rid of it."

Mitch shook his head.

She gave him that odd narrow-eyed look, the one that always made him wonder if she suspected he had concealed his past when they married last year. As if to confirm what he was thinking, Joan said, "Don't be so paranoid. Sometimes you act as if you're wanted by the feds. All we want to do is pick a few pockets."

"I'll bet my *real* dad would do it," Alan said.

Mitch sighed. He hated it when Alan said things like that when Mitch tried so hard to be a good father.

"My *real* dad isn't chicken," Alan said.

Mitch wanted to say, "Your real dad is a fool who spends more time behind bars than free." Instead he said, "Oh, all right. We'll try it for awhile."

CHAPTER

◈ 2 ◈

THE DARK gold lettering gleamed in the afternoon sun:

FORTUNES TOLD.   PALMS READ!
SEE INTO YOUR FUTURE
What Message Will the Spirits Have for You?

Ellen and her friend Caitlin stood beside the Ferris wheel at the fair and read the writing on the side of the large trailer. Painted ferns, flowers, and rainbows surrounded the words and a trio of angels, painted in pink, gold and white, hovered above the message. Across the bottom, in smaller letters, it said:

The Great Sybil Sees All, Knows All
Two dollars admission.

"Let's do it," Ellen said. "Let's have our fortunes told."

"No way. I'm not wasting two dollars on some fake in a turban who pretends to see things in a crystal ball."

"It would be fun," Ellen said. "She might tell you there's a handsome stranger in your future."

Caitlin ate a handful of popcorn. "The only thing I want to know about my future is whether or not I'll make Drill Team and I doubt if any carnival gypsy knows that."

"I'm going to do it," Ellen said. "I've always wanted to have my fortune told." She took two dollars out of her wallet.

Caitlin frowned. "What if she sees something bad in your future? Would you want to know?"

Ellen hesitated.

"Oh, forget I said that," Caitlin said. "The Great what's-her-name won't pretend to see anything bad. It wouldn't be good for business."

"What do you mean, *pretend*?" Ellen said, acting shocked. "The Great Sybil sees all and knows all; it says so right here." She grinned at Caitlin.

"If I want to listen to someone who sees all and knows all," Caitlin said, "I can hear my mom, for free."

Ellen gave her money to the bored-looking man who sat in a small ticket booth at the entrance to the fortune-teller's trailer.

"Go right in," he said. "The Great Sybil waits to enlighten you."

Caitlin, rolling her eyes, whispered, "The Great Fake waits to bamboozle you."

Despite Caitlin's cynicism, Ellen eagerly opened the door and stepped inside. She expected a dark, gloomy room, with heavy draperies, glowing candles, and possibly incense burning. Instead, the trailer was filled with greenery. Plants of all kinds grew in large redwood tubs and brass pots. Tendrils of ivy climbed the walls, crossed the ceiling, and descended the other side, intertwined like braids. Bright red blossoms covered a large cactuslike plant and a hint of rose petals filled the air. Ellen felt as if she stood in a jungle or an exotic greenhouse.

"Welcome." A tall woman, her black hair tied back with a green ribbon, stepped from behind a huge philodendron. Despite the warm day, she wore a fringed shawl over her blouse, and a long green skirt. She carried a large tin watering can. "I am The Great Sybil. And you are?"

"Ellen. Ellen Streater."

"Ellen. Wise and understanding, like a light in the dark."

"Excuse me?"

"Your name. Ellen. It comes from the Greek, Helene, meaning, 'A woman whose wisdom and understanding are like a light in the dark.' "

"I didn't know that." Ellen wanted to write that down, so she could tell Caitlin the exact words, but it seemed awkward to take out a notebook and start writing in the middle of a conversation, as if she were a newspaper reporter.

Ellen looked around. A small couch, covered in dark brown velvet, snuggled under a gigantic fern. Two straight wooden chairs, with a small bare table between them, stood in the center of the room. She wondered if she should sit down.

"Names are important," the woman said. "When a person is given the right name, it helps to shape that person's destiny."

"What does your name mean?" Ellen asked.

The woman looked surprised, as if no one had ever asked that before. "Sybil is Greek, also. It means 'prophetess.' "

"That fits. Did your parents name you that or did you choose the name when you started your fortune-telling business?"

"My name has always been Sybil," the woman said sternly, as if Ellen had insulted her.

"Oh. I thought it might be a business name, the way authors sometimes use a pen name."

"No. Sit, please." The Great Sybil gestured in the direction of the table and chairs. She put the watering can on the floor.

Ellen sat on one of the chairs, keeping her hands in her lap where they were hidden by the table. Trying not to be too obvious, she opened her shoulder bag, took out a small notebook and pencil, and wrote, "Helene: wise and understanding. Light in the dark."

After dimming the lights, The Great Sybil sat across the table from Ellen. "Do you have any special concerns?" she asked. "Is there something in your future that worries you?"

"No. I just thought it would be fun to have my fortune told."

"There is a blue aura about you," The Great Sybil said, "which indicates you are good at communication. Perhaps we will be able to get a message for you from the spirits."

"Spirits?" Ellen said. "What spirits?"

"The beings who live among us, unseen."

Ellen said nothing.

"You look doubtful," The Great Sybil said. "Most people willingly accept that other beings may live in outer space. So why not here? If spirits can exist on Mars or Jupiter or in between and beyond, why can't they exist here on Earth, as well? Just because we can't see them doesn't mean they aren't here. We don't see television transmissions, either, but we turn on our sets, confident that there will be a picture."

Maybe Caitlin was right, Ellen thought. Maybe I shouldn't be doing this.

The Great Sybil smiled at her. "Do not be nervous," she said. "The spirits are kind and loving. There is nothing to fear. Close your eyes, please."

Ellen did.

"Breathe deeply. Relax."

Ellen took a deep breath and then another, feeling the tension ease out of her shoulders.

"That's right. Clear your mind. Think only of the sky and the clouds and the sunshine. Open your heart to whatever message the spirits might have for you today."

The woman's voice was low and soothing. Ellen tilted her head back slightly as she imagined blue sky and clouds like fat cauliflowers overhead.

"Loving spirits," said The Great Sybil, "come to us today. Look down on your friend, Ellen, who seeks wisdom and understanding."

Behind her closed eyes, Ellen imagined a gathering of angels, like the three painted on The Great Sybil's trailer, floating over the fairgrounds toward them.

"Oh, spirits," droned The Great Sybil. "We give you our love and friendship. What message do you have for Ellen today?"

The trailer was still. None of the sounds of the midway seeped through. Ellen, feeling half-asleep, waited.

"Ellen is ready, spirits," whispered The Great Sybil. "Ellen is open to receive her message."

Whack!!

Ellen's hands jerked upward and slammed the notebook onto the tabletop. Her right hand stiffened on the pencil and the pencil raced across the paper. Startled, Ellen opened her eyes and stared at her hands. The pencil moved rapidly across the notebook page but Ellen had no idea what she was writing. She tried to stop writing but the pencil continued its hectic scribbling. It was as if her hand belonged to someone else.

When the notebook slammed onto the table, The Great Sybil opened her eyes, too. Ellen heard her draw in her breath, as if in astonishment.

It lasted only a few moments. Then, as suddenly as it had begun, the pencil stopped writing and Ellen's hand relaxed.

"What happened?" Ellen said.

"What did you write?" The Great Sybil asked.

"I didn't write anything. I mean, I don't know what I wrote." She squinted at the paper but in the dim light she could not make out the words. "The pencil just started moving and I couldn't do anything about it. It was as if my hand belonged to someone from outer space and wasn't connected to my brain at all."

She stopped. Maybe this was a prearranged trick, something that happened to everyone who paid to have their fortunes told. Yet, the woman looked genuinely surprised.

The Great Sybil put her hands on the table and, leaning toward Ellen, whispered, "So. You are one of the gifted ones."

Ellen said nothing. If this was all a show, the fortune-teller was a terrific actress.

The Great Sybil flung her arms wide, as if to embrace the entire room. "Thank you, spirits," she said. Her vibrant voice sounded tinged with awe. Clearly, she had not expected this to happen. "Ellen and I thank you for your kindness."

Ellen's pulse pounded in her throat.

The Great Sybil said, "You have received a wonderful gift,

Ellen. In all my years of fortune-telling, this has never happened before. You are able to open the channels of communication between this plane of existence and the next. The spirits can speak through you."

Ellen felt goose bumps rise on her arms.

The Great Sybil's eyes glowed; her excitement filled the room. "Let us read the message the spirits sent you." She rose and turned the lights brighter.

Ellen looked at the piece of paper. "It isn't my handwriting," she said. "The words lean backwards, the way a left-handed person's writing sometimes does."

"Of course, it wouldn't be your handwriting," The Great Sybil said. "*You* wrote nothing. One of the spirits wrote the message, using your hand—your body—as a tool. It's called automatic writing; psychics can sometimes do it."

"I'm not a psychic," Ellen said.

"Many people have talents of which they are not aware. What does your message say?"

Ellen looked at the paper again. At the top of the page in her own, round script, it said, "Helene: wise and understanding. Light in the dark." Below those words, in the odd slanted script, was the message.

Ellen read aloud: *It is for you to know that the smaller one faces great danger. He will pay for his mistake. It is for you to know that the paths of destiny can be changed and the smaller one will need your help to change his. You will know when it is time. Do not ignore this warning.*

She finished reading aloud and then quickly read the message again, to herself.

"May I see it?" The Great Sybil asked.

Ellen's hand shook slightly as she tore the slip of paper from the notebook and handed it to The Great Sybil. "What does it mean?" she asked.

"Is there a young child in your care?"

"No."

"Do you do baby-sitting, perhaps?"

"I baby-sit for my neighbors sometimes but they have two little girls. The message is about a boy."

"Who are you with today?"

"My friend Caitlin. We're looking at the exhibits and going on the rides and . . ." Ellen stopped. "My brother came, too," she said. "Corey."

"Your younger brother? A small boy?"

"He's nine. He came with his friend Nicholas, and his friend's mom."

"Perhaps there is danger ahead for Corey."

Despite the warm room, Ellen shivered slightly. She remembered her mother saying, "Trouble always comes in threes."

"I advise you to keep a close watch on Corey for a few days."

Ellen thought, that'll be a switch; usually he spies on me. Aloud she said, "I'll try."

"Good. The spirits occasionally use automatic writing when they have an urgent message to communicate," The Great Sybil said. "It is not wise to ignore the spirits."

"What spirits?" Ellen asked. "Who sent this message?"

"I don't know that. Your guardian angel, perhaps, or a spirit who loves you, or one who loves the small person who will be in danger. The important thing is not who sent the message; it is what you do about it. You have been offered a chance to change the small one's destiny. Perhaps, even, to save his life."

"But the message is so indefinite. I don't know for sure who the small one is or what the danger is or when it's going to happen. How can I help someone when I'm not even sure who I'm supposed to help?"

The Great Sybil gave the paper back to Ellen, pointing at the line that said, *You will know when it is time.* "You will know when it is time," she said. "Trust the spirits."

"I would be more trusting if I knew who the message was from."

The Great Sybil said, "Have you lost a loved one recently? Someone who would feel close to you, even though they are no longer with you?"

Grandpa.

The word exploded in Ellen's brain, sending fragments of fresh grief through her entire body. Her eyes swam with tears.

"You have," The Great Sybil said.

Ellen nodded. "Grandpa," she whispered.

"Perhaps your message is from him."

Ellen stared at the woman. Was it possible? Could the odd warning somehow be a message from Grandpa?

"Sometimes a loved one who has recently gone on tries to contact those who are left behind, to let them know that he or she still exists. In your case, perhaps your grandfather sees a danger that could be avoided and he wants to help."

Images flashed through Ellen's mind: the look on Dad's face when he told her and Corey that a drunk driver had hit Grandpa's car; Grandma crying at the memorial service; the hollow feeling Ellen got when she saw Grandpa's favorite chair, forever empty. She was not yet used to having him gone; the idea that his spirit might have written her a note was more than she could face.

Snatching the piece of paper from the table, Ellen sprang to her feet. Caitlin was right; she should not have come here.

"Wait!" said The Great Sybil, as Ellen rushed out the door. "We must talk further."

Brushing tears from her cheeks, Ellen stumbled down the trailer's steps.

The Great Sybil called after her, "Please come back! I can help you. We'll do another reading, for no charge."

Ignoring the woman's words and the startled man in the ticket booth, Ellen ran away from the trailer.

CHAPTER

◈ **3** ◈

THE FERRIS WHEEL stopped with Corey and Nicholas in the top bucket. "Hi, clouds!" yelled Corey. "Hi, sun! Look at us: we're on top of the world!"

He leaned forward to look down on the fairgrounds, causing the bucket to sway. Nicholas gripped the bar and pressed his back stiffly against the seat.

Below the Ferris wheel, crowds of people moved in all directions, eating, talking, enjoying the fair. "Maybe I'll see Ellen down there," Corey said. He turned sideways and looked over, causing the bucket to sway even more.

"Sit still," said Nicholas.

Corey craned his neck, searching in all directions for a glimpse of his sister. She was always too wimpy to go on the Ferris wheel and he wanted her to see him way up here in the sky, like a bird. He tucked his hands in his armpits and flapped his elbows up and down, like wings. "I'm a woodpecker," he said. "No, I'm an eagle, flying to my nest."

"Hold still," said Nicholas.

"Nicholas, look!" Corey stopped flapping and started to stand up as he pointed over the edge of the bucket. Nicholas grabbed Corey's shirt and yanked him back down.

"That man stole a purse!" Corey cried. "He took it out of a baby stroller." Corey's voice rose and he talked faster in his excitement. "I saw him! Look! There he goes! The woman must have left her purse in the stroller basket and that man with the shopping bag helped himself and he put her purse in his bag and now he's going to get away. She doesn't even know he did it."

Details, Corey reminded himself. Good witnesses have specific details. He tried to see what it said on the man's shopping bag but the man was too far away.

Corey waved both hands over his head and yelled at the man who ran the Ferris wheel. "Bring us down! Hurry!!"

Nicholas had heard Corey tell wild stories too many times to believe him without questioning what Corey said. "The man was probably the woman's husband," Nicholas said. "Maybe he's going to buy their lunch."

"He isn't. He's a thief. I'll bet there are police and F.B.I. agents all over the fair, looking for him."

The Ferris wheel began to turn but it stopped again with Corey and Nicholas in the nine o'clock position. Corey still hung over the edge of the basket. "He's getting away," he said. "He's clear over there now, by the stand that sells pineapple on a stick. He went in that big building." He waved at the Ferris wheel operator again. "Hurry!" he shouted. "We have to get off! We have to catch a criminal."

The basket finally stopped at the bottom and the attendant pulled back the bar so Corey and Nicholas could get off.

21

"Why didn't you bring us down sooner?" Corey demanded. "Couldn't you hear me yelling?"

"You and thirty others." The operator turned to an older couple who stood in line to get on the Ferris wheel. "Kids," he mumbled. "They can't wait to get on a ride and then they can't wait to get off."

"Maybe that woman is a wealthy princess and there were millions and millions of dollars in her purse," said Corey, as he and Nicholas went through the exit gate for the Ferris wheel ride. "Maybe she's a rich movie star or a famous singer. When we identify the thief, she'll probably give us a big reward and we'll go on every ride six times and have money left over."

The boys went toward where Corey had seen the man take the purse. A group of people crowded around a woman who held a toddler. She was talking to a uniformed fair security guard.

"I left it in the stroller while I put Jennie on the little car ride," the woman said, "and when I came back, it was gone. All my money! All my credit cards!" She started to cry. "Even my driver's license!" Seeing her mother in tears, the toddler began to cry, too.

"Are you a princess or a movie star?" Corey asked. "Did you have millions of dollars in your purse?"

"Are you kidding?" sniffed the woman.

"Run along, son," said the guard.

"I saw the man who took the purse," Corey said. "I was on top of the Ferris wheel and I saw him do it." Corey talked faster and faster, his eyes round with excitement. "He was carrying a big shopping bag and he put the purse in the bag and then he left. Maybe he is a dangerous criminal. Maybe he's wanted by the F.B.I. and we'll be famous for catching him and we'll get our picture in the paper."

"Can you describe the man?" the guard asked.

Corey tried to remember. He was sure he would recognize the man if he saw him again but it was hard to describe him. "He was kind of average looking," Corey said.

"What was he wearing?"

"Pants. And a shirt. They were both dark colored." He knew his description was too vague but no matter how hard he tried, he couldn't recall anything unusual about the man, except the shopping bag. "He carried a big white bag," Corey said, "with red and blue lettering." He beamed at the guard, certain that the shopping bag was the perfect clue.

"Like that one?" The security guard pointed.

Corey looked. A man walking past carried a white paper shopping bag that said MADE IN THE U.S.A. in red and blue letters.

"Yes!" Corey said. "Exactly like that." He looked closely at the man. "That isn't him, though," he said, "but maybe it's his partner. Sometimes criminals work in pairs. You had better talk to that man quick, before he gets away. Look in his bag and see if the purse . . ."

The guard interrupted. "One of the commercial exhibitors gives those bags away," he said. "There are probably two hundred people walking around today carrying bags exactly like that."

"There's another one," Nicholas said, pointing at a woman.

"Oh," said Corey.

The guard took a small notebook from his shirt pocket, wrote down a phone number, and handed the paper to Corey.

"If you think of anything that would help identify the thief," he said, "please call this number."

Corey nodded and put the paper in his pocket. Phooey. For a moment, he had thought he would be a hero. He could almost see the newspaper headline: LOCAL BOY FOILS THIEF!! And, under the headline, a picture of Corey, accepting a reward from the grateful woman after she got her purse back.

"Be alert," Corey said, as he and Nicholas walked away. "We might see him again."

"I didn't see him the first time," Nicholas said.

◇ ◇ ◇

CAITLIN waved from a shady bench near the Tilt-a-Whirl ride. Ellen sank down on the bench beside her.

"So, how was it?" Caitlin said. "Did you find out if I made Drill Team? Do you know who you're going to marry? Did you learn if you'll be rich or . . ." she stopped talking and put her hand on Ellen's arm. "Ellen?" she said. "Are you OK? You're white as a snowman." She looked closer. "You've been crying."

"I got a warning," Ellen said.

"She gave you bad news?"

"The Great Sybil didn't. I got a message from the spirits."

"What kind of a message?"

"It's a warning that something bad is going to happen, probably to Corey. I think the message is from—from Grandpa."

"But your Grandpa . . ." Caitlin clamped her lips together. "We ought to complain to the Fair Board," she said. "That fortune-teller has no right to upset you this way, pretending she can talk to the dead."

"She wasn't pretending. Oh, Caitlin, it was so strange."

"I'm sure it was. Strange and well-rehearsed. Those people are all phonies; you know that, as well as I do."

Ellen shook her head. "It wasn't fake," she said. "The Great Sybil was just as shocked as I was."

"Oh, sure." Caitlin patted Ellen's arm. "I know you miss your grandpa," she said. "It's been real hard for you since his accident, but you have to be realistic, Ellen. If that woman really could communicate with people who have died, she wouldn't be traveling around in a tacky painted trailer, charging two bucks to read fortunes. You notice there's no long line of people waiting for her to enlighten them."

Ellen looked down at her hands. She knew Caitlin made sense, yet she couldn't shake a sense of misgiving.

"If your grandpa's spirit could send a message," Caitlin said gently, "why wouldn't he have sent it to your grandma, or to your mom?"

"Maybe I'm the only one who can communicate. Remember when I worked in the Historical Society's haunted house and the ghost of Lydia Clayton spoke to me and nobody else could hear or see her?"

"That was different. You were in Lydia's former home and she had a problem that she needed your help with."

"This time, Corey has the problem and Grandpa—or some other spirit—is trying to help."

"If it's true that you are the one who can communicate, you would not need The Great Sybil as an intermediary. The spirits could talk directly to you." Caitlin lowered her voice. "If your grandpa's spirit wanted to tell you something, I don't think he would whisper in your ear when you're at the fair. He would do it when you were home alone and could pay close attention."

Caitlin stood up. "Forget about The Great Sybil. She's nothing but a phony and your so-called message is only a trick. Let's go pig out on cotton candy."

Ellen stood, too. How could she explain what had happened in that plant-filled room? Caitlin had not been there. She didn't witness Ellen's pencil darting across the paper as if it were alive. She didn't see the look of excitement on The Great Sybil's face or hear the awe in her voice.

As Ellen followed Caitlin toward the cotton-candy stand, she put her hand in the pocket of her jeans and touched the piece of paper. She wished she could believe that Caitlin was right and the warning was merely a trick. It would be much easier to laugh it off, as if it were a silly message in a fortune cookie.

But what if it was real?

What if Corey was destined for some terrible danger?

And what if Grandpa was trying to warn her?

CHAPTER
◆ 4 ◆

"WHAT HAPPENED? That girl was crying." The bored man came out of the ticket booth and approached The Great Sybil, who stood in the trailer's open doorway.

"She had a message from the spirits."

"Oh, sure. What did you tell her, Sybil? You have to be careful with kids that age. Get them all upset and they run to their parents and you'll end up with the State Attorney General's office closing us down."

"I didn't tell her anything. It was a real message."

"Are you serious?" The man stepped inside the trailer and closed the door behind him. "What happened?"

"She was holding a pencil and a notebook and the spirits did automatic writing."

"Holey-moley." The man slumped into one of the chairs. "How long has it been, thirteen years? Fourteen?"

"Fifteen. When I started charging for my services, the spirits quit coming. Fifteen long years ago."

"Fifteen years since you actually had any communication, and then it happens with some hysterical kid who can't handle it."

"She wasn't hysterical. She got a warning and then, when I asked if she had recently lost a loved one, it hit a nerve. Apparently, her grandfather died not long ago."

"Oh, great. She's going to run home crying and tell Mama that she talked to Grandpa, who died last week. The cops should be here any minute. Geez, Sybil, you need to be more careful."

"Careful! How was I to know this would happen? I was just as surprised as the girl was when that pencil started to move." The Great Sybil sat opposite the man, put her elbows on the table, and leaned her chin on her hands. "It was glorious, Willie," she said. "It was just the way it used to be, when I still had my talent."

"Why?" he said. "Why now, after all these years, are you suddenly able to do it again?"

"I can't. The girl can."

"You led her into it, didn't you? You got her relaxed and called the spirits to come?"

"Yes. But they didn't come to me, they came to her. I was merely a spectator."

"She paid her two dollars, just like everyone else. She bought a ticket before she went in." Willie frowned. "You've always said you lost the talent after you started charging money to do readings. You said the spirits quit coming because it was a business for profit, not a true spiritual search."

"The girl, Ellen, made no profit. Her search was genuine."

"What do you plan to do if the girl's parents show up, angry because you misled their daughter and upset her?"

"I didn't mislead her! If anyone asks, I'll tell them the truth. She got a message."

Willie shook his head. "The truth is, you've hoaxed people out of their money for fifteen years. Now, I'm the first to admit I encouraged you. When you first lost your talent, I told you to fake it and who would know the difference? The way I see it, if people want to spend their money, we'd be foolish not to take it. Still, it's hard to believe that after fifteen years of hoaxes, you are suddenly the witness to a real message from the spirits."

"It's been more than a hoax, all these years," The Great Sybil said. "I've made a lot of people happy because of the 'messages' they got. They've come in here anxious and upset and I've sent them away calm and optimistic. Is that so terrible?"

"You tell them what they want to hear," Willie said, "whether it's true or not."

"This time, I didn't. I swear it, Willie. This time, the spirits spoke. If anyone asks, that's what I plan to tell them."

"Well, it makes me nervous," Willie said. "If any more kids want to buy tickets, I'm going to say they have to be eighteen or older in order to get in."

◈ ◈ ◈

"THE MESSAGE wasn't whispered in my ear," Ellen told Caitlin. "It was written on my notebook paper, by my pencil, held in my hand."

The two girls sat in the top row of the arena where Caitlin's cousin was scheduled to show his sheep. They were early, so it was a quiet place to talk.

Ellen handed Caitlin the message and watched Caitlin's expression change from scorn to concern as she read it.

"That is scary," Caitlin said, as she handed the paper back to Ellen. "It is definitely not your handwriting and I don't see how it could be a trick, either. Not when it was your own pencil and you were holding it."

"It doesn't look like Grandpa's handwriting, either," Ellen said. "But who else would the message be from?"

"Maybe it's from your guardian angel."

"That's what The Great Sybil said. I didn't know you believed in angels."

"My aunt says everyone has a guardian angel," Caitlin said. "She prays to hers every day, asking the angel to keep her safe."

"Sort of like a fairy godmother?"

"Not exactly. Aunt Catherine says we each have an angel who is always with us, to guide us and help us. Sometimes, when we think we have a good idea, it's really our angel who puts the idea into our head. Aunt Catherine even asks *her* angel to talk to other people's angels. When we went on our vacation last year, she had her angel ask my angel to be especially watchful over me while I was away from home."

"Does she ever get written messages from her angel?"

"No," Caitlin admitted, "but I suppose all angels are different. When I was little, I used to imagine that my guardian angel sat on top of my bookshelf at night, watching me sleep, and shooing away any goblins. It was comforting."

"You never told me this before."

"It isn't the sort of thing that comes up in ordinary conversation. I always wanted to think Aunt Catherine was right, but it's been a long time since I believed there was an angel on my bookshelf."

"Whoever it is from," Ellen said, "the message makes me nervous."

"What are you going to do about it?" Caitlin asked.

Ellen shrugged. "What *can* I do?"

"Are you going to tell your parents?"

"No. Mom would get upset and Dad would say The Great Sybil is a fake and tell me never to go back."

"What about Corey? Will you tell him?"

"I don't know. I don't want to worry him and I'm afraid if I tell him, he'll blab to my folks. You know what a motormouth he is."

Caitlin nodded. "Still, if he's going to be in danger, maybe you should try to warn him. He might be more cautious."

Ellen looked again at the slip of paper in her hand. "The danger is some time in the future," she said. "I don't think I'll say anything to Corey just yet."

"Maybe you'll get another message," Caitlin said.

"What do you mean?"

"Well, *you* did the automatic writing, not The Great Sybil. Maybe you can get messages from the spirits any time you want."

Ellen did not answer. What if Caitlin was right? What if she could contact—contact who? She was not at all sure she wanted to receive more messages from the dead. Not even Grandpa.

◈   ◈   ◈

COREY raised his arms high above his head, aimed at the red spot in the middle of the stack of wooden milk bottles, and threw the ball as hard as he could. Thunk! It hit almost in the center of the spot, toppling six of the bottles. The remaining four bottles wavered for an instant but remained upright.

"Phooey!" said Corey.

"Sorry, son," said the man who ran the bottle-throw booth. "Care to try again?" As he spoke, he picked up the fallen bottles and restacked them.

Corey dug into his pocket for three more quarters. Even though he thought seventy-five cents was way too much money just for a chance to throw a ball at a stack of wooden milk bottles, Corey was determined to win one of the stuffed dinosaurs that hung from the ceiling of the booth.

"You aren't doing it again, are you?" asked Nicholas. "You've already lost four times." He finished his corn dog and wiped the mustard from his mouth with his sleeve.

"I want that Tyrannosaurus."

"It would be cheaper to go to the toy store and buy one."

Corey wished Nicholas wouldn't be so practical. It spoiled Corey's grand dream of telling everyone how he won the giant stuffed dinosaur at the fair. Won it! For free! Just by throwing a ball and knocking over some wooden milk bottles.

"Win a dinosaur!" yelled the man, as a group of boys approached the booth. "Only seventy-five cents to win one of these giant, authentic, stuffed dinosaurs."

"Let's go ride the roller coaster," Nicholas said.

"I'm going to try one more time," Corey said. He plunked his money on the counter. The man quickly swept it into his apron pocket and handed Corey another ball.

Corey licked his lips and rubbed the ball between his hands. Using his best Little League pitching form, he flung the ball toward the stack of bottles. This time, the ball hit exactly where he aimed, square in the middle of the red spot. The top three bottles flew off and all of the bottom bottles except one toppled immediately. That one rocked back and forth so violently that the top of the bottle hit the floor before it straightened again. Then it rocked slower and slower until it finally stopped in an upright position.

"Sorry, son," said the man. "Care to try again?"

"I hit the spot!" Corey said. "I hit right in the middle."

"Must have been a shade to one side," said the man.

"It wasn't! I hit dead center!"

"Win a dinosaur!!" yelled the man, covering up Corey's voice. "Step right up and try your luck. Only seventy-five cents for a genuine, authentic stuffed dinosaur."

"I should have won, shouldn't I, Nicholas? That ball hit right smack where it was supposed to."

"I wasn't watching," Nicholas admitted. "Just as you threw it, that kid tripped and dropped his ice-cream cone and I got distracted." Nicholas pointed to where a woman comforted a crying boy. A chocolate ice-cream cone lay in the sawdust at the boy's feet.

A man standing near the boy said, "Don't cry, little boy. I'll give you some money to buy another ice-cream cone." He reached toward his back pants pocket and then began frantically searching all of his pockets. "It's gone," he said. "My wallet is gone."

Corey and Nicholas looked at each other in surprise. "Another robbery?" Corey said.

CHAPTER

◆ **5** ◆

COREY LOOKED around for the man with the shopping bag but did not see him. A group of curious people now surrounded the crying child, his mother, and the frantic man.

"I had my wallet when I bought my ticket to get in," the man said to no one in particular, "and I got it out to use my telephone credit card awhile ago."

"You probably left your wallet in the phone booth," suggested the woman with the little boy. "I did that once."

"Maybe it's still there," the man said. He hurried away.

"Let's go ride the roller coaster," Nicholas said.

"That bottle guy is cheating," Corey said. "One of those bottles is rigged so it won't fall over no matter where the ball hits. We ought to spy on that man and see how he does it and report him to the Fair Board. I bet nobody ever wins a dinosaur. Those same dinosaurs have probably been hanging there for a million years."

"That's why he calls them authentic," said Nicholas. "If we're going to ride the roller coaster before my mom comes back, we'd better get going."

Corey shoved his hands in his pockets and stomped away from the bottle-throw booth. He *did* want to ride the roller coaster and he knew that if he and Nicholas waited until Nicholas's mother was with them, she might say no. Mrs. Warren had allowed the boys to go off on their own while she went to the flower exhibit only after they promised to stay together and to meet her in exactly one hour. She did not make them promise not to go on any scary rides but they both knew it was only because she hadn't thought of it.

In addition to the Ferris wheel, they had already ridden The Giant Lobster Claw and the Tilt-a-Whirl. Corey screamed so much on The Giant Lobster Claw that his throat hurt but he didn't mind. Half the fun of going on a scary ride was being able to scream as loudly as possible. If there was a prize for Best Screamer at the Fair, Corey was certain he would win it.

While they waited in line for the roller coaster, they ate strawberry ice-cream cones and looked across the midway toward The River of Fear. A wooden stairway led to a platform that was as high as the top of the Ferris wheel. People climbed the stairs and waited on the platform to begin the ride.

"The River of Fear ride is working again," Corey said. Earlier, there had been a rope at the bottom of the stairs, with a CLOSED sign hanging from it.

A recorded spiel boomed from speakers at the top of the platform: "Experience a death-defying descent down Whiplash Waterfall! Travel through the Tunnel of Terror! Meet the monsters of Mutilation Mountain! Are you brave enough to ride

The River of Fear? YES!! Astonish your friends! Climb the platform now and begin the journey of a lifetime. RIDE THE RIVER OF FEAR!!"

"After we do the roller coaster," Corey said, "let's ride The River of Fear."

"My mom will have a heart attack if she sees us up there."

"She'll have a heart attack if she sees us on the roller coaster, too."

"True. She still wants me to ride the little fire trucks in kiddieland."

Corey laughed. He knew Nicholas was exaggerating but he also knew Mrs. Warren would never allow the boys to go on anything as exciting and dangerous-sounding as The River of Fear ride. Since The River of Fear was enclosed, it was impossible to tell, without going on it, exactly how scary it was. For Corey, that was part of the appeal.

The boys got in the roller coaster car, buckled the safety strap, and pulled the metal bar forward. As the car climbed, swooped, climbed again, turned, and plunged toward the ground, Corey closed his eyes and screamed and screamed and screamed. This was great! Ellen could probably hear him screaming clear across the fairgrounds.

When the ride ended, he turned to Nicholas and tried to say, "Let's do it again," but he was so hoarse the words didn't come out. Maybe his mother was right; he should not have screamed quite so much.

One look at Nicholas told him that Nicholas wouldn't want to ride again, anyway. All the color had drained out of Nicholas's face and he had one hand clamped over his mouth.

Corey climbed out of the car. When Nicholas started to stand, he swayed and sat down again, resting his head on the metal bar. Corey helped Nicholas out of the ride. Nicholas walked bent over, holding his stomach. There was a small picnic area nearby and Nicholas staggered to one of the picnic tables, sat on a bench, and leaned his head on his arms.

A stand selling curly fries stood next to the picnic area. Corey sniffed the air and decided to buy some. He loved to dip the spirals of deep-fat-fried potatoes into catsup and eat them.

He carried the heaping container of curly fries to the picnic table, along with a paper cup filled with catsup.

Nicholas still had his head down. Corey nudged him. When Nicholas looked up, Corey held out the curly fries and croaked, "Want some?"

Nicholas looked as if Corey had offered him poison. He shook his head violently and turned the other way, so he couldn't see Corey eat.

Corey munched the curly fries, hoping Nicholas would feel better soon. He also hoped his voice would come back before they rode The River of Fear. It wouldn't be as much fun to be scared if he couldn't scream.

"There you are." Nicholas's mother approached the picnic table. When she reached the boys, she put her hand on Nicholas's forehead. "You're sick, aren't you!" It was a statement, not a question. "You probably ate too many of those fatty French fries."

"No, he didn't," whispered Corey. "All he ate was a corn dog, a bag of taffy, two scones, some onion rings, a Polish sausage, and an ice-cream cone."

"Ohhh," said Nicholas, as if it made him sicker to hear the words.

"Your voice!" cried Mrs. Warren. "Corey, what happened to your voice?"

Corey tried to say, "I think I screamed too much," but even the whisper was gone now. His words were much too faint for anyone to hear. He pointed at the roller coaster.

"You went on the *roller coaster*?"

Nicholas groaned again and Corey realized he should not have pointed.

"Well, it's small wonder you're sick, Nicholas," his mother said. "I thought you had more sense than to ride on a roller coaster. It's a miracle you're alive to tell about it. We're going straight home and put you in bed."

To Corey's surprise, Nicholas did not argue. He nodded meekly, as if bed sounded good to him.

Corey poked Nicholas's arm and then pointed at The River of Fear. Nicholas shook his head and put his hand over his mouth again.

Phooey. What rotten luck for Nicholas to get sick before they could go on the best ride of all.

"Come along, Corey," said Mrs. Warren.

"I'll ride home with Ellen," Corey wheezed.

"What's that? I can't hear a word," said Mrs. Warren.

Corey pointed to himself and mouthed the words, "My sister."

"I think he wants to stay here and go home with Ellen and Caitlin," Nicholas said.

Corey nodded vigorously.

"I can't leave you here by yourself," Mrs. Warren said. "Where is your sister?"

Corey dropped to his hands and knees at Mrs. Warren's feet.

"Good heavens," said Mrs. Warren.

Corey mouthed the words, "Baa, baa."

Mrs. Warren looked at him, blinking nervously.

"Caitlin's cousin shows sheep for 4-H," Nicholas said. "Maybe Ellen is in the sheep barn or the show arena."

Corey nodded again.

"We go past the 4-H buildings on our way out of the fair," Mrs. Warren said. "If your sister is there, we'll ask if you can stay with her."

She took Nicholas by the arm and led him away from the midway. Corey trailed behind, eating his curly fries. As they passed the bottle-throw booth, he saw a group of girls, each buying a turn to throw. He wanted to shout, "Save your money! That guy cheats!" but without a voice, all he could do was feel sorry for the girls.

When they reached the 4-H complex, Mrs. Warren said, "We'll look in the show arena but if your sister isn't there, we can't traipse all around hunting for her."

Corey was relieved to see Ellen and Caitlin sitting in the top row of the show arena. Corey nudged Mrs. Warren and pointed at the girls. Mrs. Warren waved at Ellen.

Ellen waved back.

"What happened to your brother's face?" Caitlin asked.

"He got cut when he fell off the monkey bars at the park," Ellen said. "It's healed now except for a scab across his cheek but he insists on wearing that stupid Batman bandage."

"Nicholas and I will wait here," Mrs. Warren said, "while you go up and ask Ellen if it's all right for you to stay and go home with her."

Before Corey could do so, Nicholas bolted toward one of the trash cans that stood just inside the door. He leaned into the trash can and threw up. Mrs. Warren handed him a tissue to wipe his mouth, then turned to Corey. "Stay with your sister," she said.

"I will."

Mrs. Warren put her arm around Nicholas and pushed open the door.

Corey wished Nicholas wasn't sick. It wouldn't be half as much fun to scream on the scary rides alone. Ellen never wanted to ride anything except the merry-go-round. He sighed and turned toward the steps to join Ellen and Caitlin.

"Sorry," said a voice at his elbow. "No food is allowed in the stands."

Corey went outside to finish his curly fries. As he emerged, he heard someone crying loudly. Looking toward the noise, he saw the same boy who had been near the bottle-throw booth. Once again, the boy was crying and pointing at an ice-cream cone on the ground while his mother tried to calm him. That kid, thought Corey, should buy ice cream in a cup and eat it with a spoon.

"Hey!!"

Corey looked at the gray-haired man who had shouted.

"Someone took my wallet!" the man yelled. "Everyone stay where you are! Call the police!"

Corey could hardly believe his ears. *Another* pickpocket? He quickly scanned the crowd of people, most of whom reacted to the man's shouts by clutching their own wallets and purses.

There he was!

The man in the dark shirt with the MADE IN THE U.S.A. shopping bag was easing past the people who had stopped to stare at the shouter.

Corey tried to yell, "That's him! He's the thief!" but he

could not make a sound. Corey watched as the man moved quickly through the crowd, shaking his head at the other people as if to say, *How terrible.*

Corey couldn't let the man get away. Forgetting his promise to stay with Ellen, he took off across the fairgrounds after the thief.

CHAPTER

◦ 6 ◦

"I'M GOING to go talk to The Great Sybil again," Ellen said.

"Now?" said Caitlin. "The 4-H kids are bringing their sheep in. We'll miss Ben."

"You can stay and watch the sheep show. I'll come back here when I'm finished."

"Are you sure you want to go back there?" Caitlin said. "All this talk about danger and spirits and messages from dead people makes me nervous."

"I want to ask The Great Sybil some questions," Ellen said, "and I won't get to the fair again without my parents."

Caitlin nodded sympathetically. "Say no more," she said. "My mom would never let me visit The Great Sybil, either. Do you want me to tell Corey anything if he shows up? Should I ask him to stay here until you come back?"

"I doubt he'll be back. He and Nicholas planned to ride on every ride and eat something from every food booth. Corey's been saving his allowance for weeks so he could blow it all at the fair."

"Maybe the great danger is that he'll get sick from eating too much junk food at the fair," Caitlin said.

"Not when he's with Mrs. Warren. She's really careful about good nutrition. Whenever Nicholas comes to our house, he always wants candy because he never gets it at home; Nicholas says his mother would rather eat broccoli than fudge."

Spectators poured into the arena as the exhibitors led their sheep into position. Bleats and baas filled the air, along with broadcast directions from the judges, telling the exhibitors how to line up.

Ellen started down the steps, eager to see The Great Sybil again. Now that she was over the first shock and had thought about it awhile, the idea of being able to communicate with Grandpa excited her. If she really could get a message and prove that it was from him, maybe Grandma would stop crying so much. And maybe her own heart would heal. It wouldn't seem as bad to have Grandpa gone if she knew his spirit still existed.

Behind her, Caitlin said, "Wait. I'll go with you. I've seen Ben show his sheep before but I've never seen someone get a message from a spirit."

Ellen shook her head. "It's nice of you to offer," she said, "but I know you want to watch the sheep competition and it's almost ready to start."

"I don't want you going back there alone," Caitlin said firmly, as she followed Ellen to the exit. "This whole thing is too weird."

Ellen smiled gratefully at her friend. "I could wait and go after Ben shows his sheep," she said.

"No," Caitlin said. "This is more important than sheep."

They left the show arena and headed toward The Great Sybil's trailer.

◇ ◇ ◇

COREY DASHED after the man. When he caught him, he planned to grab the shopping bag and summon help. As soon as the police found the victim's wallet in the man's shopping bag, they would arrest the man. Probably the woman's purse was still in the shopping bag, too. Corey might get his picture in the paper yet.

The fairgrounds were crowded, making it difficult for the man to move fast without attracting attention. Since he didn't know anyone was chasing him, Corey gained on him quickly.

Just outside one of the exhibit halls, Corey caught up. He approached the man from behind and grabbed the shopping bag, pulling it out of the startled man's grasp. He tried to yell, "Help!" at the same time but he only managed a faint wheeze.

"Give me that!" the man said, as he tried to take back the bag.

Corey crossed his arms and held the bag handles tightly against his chest. He looked around him for one of the uniformed security guards who had responded when the woman's purse was stolen, but none was in sight.

"Why, you sneaky little thief!" the man said. He grabbed Corey's shoulder and turned to two teenaged boys who stood nearby. "This kid is trying to steal my bag," he said.

The boys instantly grabbed Corey's arm and pried his hands loose from the shopping bag. "That was a stupid move, kid," one of them said.

"*He's* the thief," Corey rasped but in addition to having no voice, he was out of breath from running and he could tell the boys did not understand him.

The boys handed the bag back to the man.

"Thank you," he said.

Corey glared at him. This time he paid attention to the man's appearance. Medium height. Brown hair. Dark blue shirt and pants. A gold wristwatch. There was nothing remarkable about the man's appearance and Corey realized that he probably dressed in a nondescript way on purpose. If he wore a wild-colored plaid shirt or a T-shirt with a saying on the front, witnesses would be able to remember him. This way, he blended into the crowd and slipped away unnoticed.

"Are you going to call the cops?" one of the teenagers asked.

"No," the man said. "He has probably learned a lesson."

In frustration, Corey tried to wriggle free. He knew the man didn't want to call the cops because if the police came they would discover who the guilty person really was.

The man turned and walked toward the entrance of the building.

Corey twisted and jerked. He pointed at the man's shopping bag and tried to whisper, "Thief."

"Knock it off, kid," one of the teenagers said. He and his buddy, each firmly holding one of Corey's arms, ushered him away from the building. "You're lucky that guy didn't turn you in," the older boy continued. "If you keep this up, you'll be spending the night in the juvenile detention center."

The two boys kept a tight grip on Corey until they had walked for several minutes. Corey glared at them, studying their faces and memorizing what they wore. When the police finally arrested that pickpocket, Corey intended to give a complete description of these two boys. Maybe they would be arrested, too, for obstructing justice. Maybe *they* would spend the night in the juvenile detention center.

◇ ◇ ◇

AS ELLEN and Caitlin approached The Great Sybil's trailer, a white-haired woman was walking away from it. When she saw the two girls, she smiled and said, "Are you girls going to have your fortunes told?" Without waiting for them to answer, she went on, "It's well worth the price. The Great Sybil gave me the most wonderful news."

"She did?" Caitlin said.

The woman dabbed at her eyes but Ellen could tell her tears were happy ones. "Harold is at peace," the woman said. "I can stop worrying about him."

Wondering who Harold was, Ellen said, "How did The Great Sybil know?"

"Oh, she talks to the spirits," the woman said, "and they answer her. She specifically asked if Harold is all right and she was told, yes, he is. I can't tell you how much better I feel. I've been terribly worried about Harold. He wasn't ready to go, you know. He didn't want to leave me and he wanted to watch the grandchildren grow up. It happened so fast; we didn't have time to adjust to his sickness and, boom, he was gone. Ever since, all these months, I've worried that Harold couldn't rest in peace because . . ."

Ellen broke in to ask, "Did the spirits answer in writing?" She felt rude for interrupting but she had a feeling the woman would talk all day, given half a chance.

"Writing? How could spirits write anything?"

"They talked, then?" Caitlin said. "You heard someone?"

"Oh, no, my dear. I heard nothing. If I could hear such

things myself, I wouldn't need to pay a spiritualist, now would I? The Great Sybil heard the spirits and told me what they said."

"But how do you know she got an answer?" Caitlin said. "What if she made it up?"

The woman frowned. "Why would she do that? She never knew Harold. She can't possibly care if he is happy or not." The woman's smile returned. "I'm going to be able to sleep tonight, without taking a sleeping pill, for the first time since Harold passed on. The Great Sybil said I won't need pills anymore, now that I know Harold is at peace."

"I'm glad for you," Ellen said.

"Me, too," Caitlin said. She nudged Ellen and started to walk on. "It was nice talking to you," she said over her shoulder.

"When you girls get your fortunes told," the woman said, "I hope your news is as good as mine." She walked away, smiling and nodding at everyone she passed.

When the woman was no longer within hearing range, Caitlin said, "Do you think The Great Sybil really got a message about that woman's husband, or do you think she pretended, knowing what the woman wanted to hear?"

Ellen shrugged. "Does it matter? Either way, the woman is happy."

"I guess most people believe what they want to believe," Caitlin said.

"The trouble is," Ellen said, "I don't know what I want to believe. One part of me thinks it would be great if I could communicate with Grandpa. Another part of me says I'm asking for trouble if I try again. Also, there's Corey to consider, assuming he is 'the small one' in the message. If he is going to be in danger, I want to help him and I don't see how I can, without more information."

They had reached the ticket booth. "Hello," Ellen said to the man inside.

He barely glanced up from the newspaper he held before he said, "Sorry. You have to be eighteen or over."

"The Great Sybil told me I could come back without paying."

The man put down his paper and looked directly at her. "Aren't you the kid who was here earlier today?"

"Yes. I need to see her again."

"Sorry. She's out."

Ellen and Caitlin looked at each other. Their eyes agreed: *He's lying.*

Ellen, with Caitlin right behind her, marched to the door of the trailer and knocked.

"Hey!" the man called after them. "I told you Sybil isn't in."

The door opened.

"I am glad you returned," The Great Sybil said.

The man stepped out of the booth and hurried toward them. "Sybil," he said, "I don't think you should do this."

"I have to," The Great Sybil said. "Please come in, Ellen. And?"

"This is my friend Caitlin," Ellen said. "I told her about the automatic writing."

"Welcome, Caitlin. Pure one."

Caitlin looked questioningly at Ellen as they stepped inside.

"Caitlin," explained The Great Sybil, "is from the Greek name Katharos, meaning 'pure one.' It honors St. Catherine of Alexandria who escaped martyrdom on a spiked wheel in the fourth century."

"No kidding," said Caitlin.

"Be seated, please."

Ellen sat on the couch, leaving room for Caitlin to sit beside her. The Great Sybil sat on the same chair as before. "Do you wish to try again to contact the spirits?" The Great Sybil asked.

"Yes. I want to ask who the message is from and when the danger will be."

The Great Sybil nodded.

"You'll need the paper and pencil again," Caitlin reminded her.

Ellen reached in her shoulder bag and removed her notebook and pencil.

"Maybe you will get a spoken message this time," Caitlin said to The Great Sybil. "Maybe the spirits will speak to you."

"No," The Great Sybil said. "It is Ellen who will receive any messages." Ellen wondered why she sounded sad; she had seemed thrilled earlier, when the automatic writing occurred.

Ellen carried the pencil and notebook to the table and sat opposite The Great Sybil. She kept her hands on the table, with the pencil poised, ready to write. "I'm ready," she said.

The Great Sybil dimmed the lights and said the same calming words she had used before, about deep breaths and looking at the sky.

This time, although Ellen kept her eyes closed, she remained tense. Instead of imagining blue skies and fluffy clouds, Ellen's mind focused on the pencil she held. She gripped it tightly, expecting it to jolt into a frenzied scribbling.

"Ellen has a question, loving spirits," The Great Sybil said.

"She needs your help in knowing when the little one will face danger."

Nothing happened.

"We come to you in love," The Great Sybil said. "We ask you to tell us when to expect the danger."

They waited. The pencil remained still.

"Is the one who sent the message here with us? If you are, please let us know your identity."

Nothing. After five minutes of silence that seemed to Ellen more like an hour, they gave up.

"The spirits do not always choose to answer us," The Great Sybil said, after Ellen had opened her eyes and the lights were bright again. "Or perhaps they do not always hear our requests. We will have to try another time."

As Ellen and Caitlin walked away from The Great Sybil's trailer, Caitlin said, "If I were you, I would forget all about that so-called message. Before you went in there the first time, I was positive that she was a fake. Then you convinced me that the automatic writing really happened. Now I think it was all a hoax, after all. The reason it didn't work this time is that I was there, watching."

"When it happened, it seemed so real."

Caitlin unwrapped a stick of gum and offered half to Ellen. "Maybe so, but it is odd that you would get a message when you were there alone but nothing happened when I was looking. If the whole thing was genuine, why didn't it happen the second time? If there is really danger in Corey's future, and the spirits want to help, why did the spirits ignore you?"

"Maybe I was too nervous. I couldn't relax this time; I kept waiting for the pencil to start writing."

Caitlin said, "I think it was all a trick. Maybe she does it with magnets or some kind of ink that's already on the table but it's invisible until it touches paper or—oh, I don't know how but I think it was all faked somehow, just like she pretended the spirits spoke to her and told her what that woman wanted to hear about her husband."

"That was different," Ellen said. "That woman asked a specific question. And her message was not in writing."

"If a person is dishonest in one situation," Caitlin said, "how can you trust them anywhere?"

They entered the sheep arena just as the judges began handing ribbons to the owners of the champion sheep.

"Look!" said Caitlin. "Ben got a red ribbon; that's second place."

Ellen said, "I'm sorry I've ruined your day. You missed seeing Ben show his sheep and we've hardly gone to any of the exhibits yet, all because I wanted to get my fortune told."

"Don't worry about it," Caitlin said. "The Great Sybil was more interesting than any exhibit. Besides, Mom and I are coming tomorrow. I can see the rest of the exhibits then."

"In that case," Ellen said, "would you mind if we go home early? I'm worn out."

As the girls walked to the bus stop, Ellen was glad tomorrow was the last day of the fair. She wanted The Great Sybil and her tricks to leave town as soon as possible. *If* they were tricks.

Everything Caitlin said about the automatic writing being faked made sense but deep inside herself, Ellen still believed she had received a true message. It might be possible to make the writing appear on the paper but how could anyone have caused Ellen's hand to jerk without touching her? How could her inability to control her own body be a trick?

Corey was not home yet when Ellen arrived. She tried to

read but she couldn't concentrate; she flipped the TV from channel to channel and saw nothing interesting. What's the matter with me? she thought. Ever since Grandpa died she had felt edgy, as if she expected another tragedy. Now her uneasiness was multiplied tenfold as she listened for Corey to burst in, chattering about what he and Nicholas did at the fair.

I never thought I'd be eager to hear my brother's voice, she thought, trying to laugh away her tension. Usually when Corey was home, she wanted to plug her ears.

She was sure Corey was perfectly fine. After all, Mrs. Warren was with him and she was one of those fussy mother-hen women who hardly let Nicholas out of her sight. Nothing could happen to Corey when he was with Mrs. Warren. Still, Ellen would be glad when Corey was safely home.

CHAPTER

◦ 7 ◦

"SOME KID knows what we're doing."

Mitch Lagrange opened the trunk of his car and put the MADE IN THE U.S.A. shopping bag inside, next to the five other MADE IN THE U.S.A. bags that were already there.

"How could he?" Joan asked. "We haven't worked the same area twice all day and no one has acted the least bit suspicious. How could some kid catch on?"

"I don't know, but I'm telling you this boy has it figured out. He ran after me, grabbed my bag, and tried to accuse me." Mitch slammed the trunk shut. "Luckily, there's something wrong with his voice and he couldn't make himself heard. I pretended he was trying to take the bag away from me and two teenagers stepped in and acted like big macho heroes. They held the kid while I walked away from him."

Mitch unlocked the car door and slid behind the wheel. Joan got in the passenger's side and Alan sat in back.

"How old was he?" Joan asked.

Mitch shrugged. "About the same age as Alan, I'd guess. Maybe eight or nine."

"What does he look like?"

"Just an average-looking kid, except he had a big Batman bandage on his face. Brown hair. Jeans. A T-shirt with elephants on it—from a zoo, I think."

"Did his parents see you?" she asked.

"He was alone."

"Are you sure? If he was only eight or nine, somebody must have brought him to the fair."

"There wasn't anybody with him when he ran after me," Mitch said, "but by now he's probably blabbed to his parents or whoever brought him. We'll have to quit. We can sit here and wait until Tucker gets his dinner break."

"No!" said Alan. "You promised we could work until Uncle Tucker can meet us."

"I didn't know some junior detective would show up and accuse me of stealing."

"I want some more ice cream."

"You've had enough ice cream," Mitch said. "We've bought a dozen ice-cream cones today."

"I never get to finish them. I always have to pretend I'm falling and spill them on the ground."

Joan chuckled. "You're getting to be a fine little actor," she said. "I almost believed you myself last time, the way you cried and carried on."

Alan smiled. "Let's move to Hollywood," he said. "Maybe I'll get a job in a TV show."

"I don't like it," Mitch said. "Maybe we shouldn't even wait to eat dinner with Tucker. All we need is some little kid going to the cops."

"Today has been the best day of the whole summer," Alan said. "Maybe even the best day of my whole life. We got tons of wallets and purses. We even got that video camera. Let's keep that. Can we, Mitch?"

"Be quiet, Alan. I'm trying to think."

"This is way more fun than delivering a dumb old car," Alan said. "And you said we could do it all afternoon. You promised."

"Alan!"

Alan said, "Mom! You promised, too. You said if I did my part good, I could have some of the money. You said we could do it until Uncle Tucker's dinner break."

"We did say that, Mitch," Joan said. "Now that we know about the boy, we can watch for him. There can't be more than one kid that age running around with a Batman bandage on his face and elephants on his shirt. If we spot him, we'll back off."

"I don't like it," Mitch repeated. "We've done well this year; we've made a lot of money. I don't want to blow it over a two-bit pickpocket incident."

"Just work until dinnertime, when we meet Tucker," Joan said. "We promised Alan and it's been such fun, working a crowd again. It's like when I was first on my own and had to pick pockets in order to eat."

"If we get caught by the cops, your meals will be provided by the state—in jail."

"First offenders get off with a warning."

"Not always." Mitch knew Joan did not fully understand

what a risk she was asking him to take. How could she, when Mitch had never told her about his past? She did not realize the depth of his fear. She did not know how important it was for Mitch never to be picked up by the police.

"Let's tell Tucker about the kid," Joan suggested, "and Tucker can watch for him, too, just like he watches for the guards now. If the kid shows up, Tucker signals us, and we beat it out of there."

Mitch looked dubious. "That platform of Tucker's is a long way up and there are an awful lot of little kids at the fair."

"Not wearing big Batman bandages on their cheeks."

"Please, Mitch?" Alan said. "I want to do my ice-cream trick some more. This is the most fun I've had in my whole life. Please?"

"No," Mitch said. "No more. We're going to sit right here and wait for Tucker."

"Nobody ever keeps their promises," Alan said. He put his head down on the seat and started to cry.

"You can sit here, if you want," Joan said. "Alan and I are going back to the fair. We'll work alone."

Alan's tears instantly vanished.

Joan and Alan got out of the car.

"Don't do this," Mitch said.

"I worked by myself for years, before I met you."

Mitch looked at Joan and Alan, side by side, glaring at him. It was that way too often—Joan and Alan on one side, Mitch alone on the other. He wondered if the three of them would ever seem like a real family.

"All right," Mitch said. "We'll tell Tucker. We can use the same signal we have for fair guards or cops." He got slowly out of the car.

"Lock the doors," Joan said. "You don't know what sort of people go through this parking lot."

Alan laughed.

The three headed back through the main entrance of the fairgrounds, showing the ink stamps on the backs of their hands that allowed them to get in without paying an entrance fee. Their first stop was the commercial exhibit building, where Mitch picked up another free shopping bag. Next they headed for The River of Fear to tell Mitch's brother, Tucker, to watch for a boy with a Batman bandage.

"I want another chocolate marshmallow ice-cream cone," Alan said. "I hardly got to eat any of the last one."

❖ ❖ ❖

AS SOON as the teenagers let go of his arms, Corey headed for the sheep arena. There was no use trying to catch the thief when he had no voice. Corey would find Ellen and she would give him something to write on and he would write down his description of the thief and Ellen would go with him to look for the man. Ellen could be a hero, too, though Corey would still be the main hero because he was the one who saw the man stealing.

When Corey arrived at the sheep arena, three people were walking their sheep in a slow circle. One held a large purple rosette, one held a blue ribbon, and one held a red ribbon. Corey recognized Caitlin's cousin; he was the one with the red ribbon.

Corey stood by the railing and watched the winning sheep parade around the arena for awhile before he began to climb the steps toward where Ellen and Caitlin had sat earlier. Partway up, he realized that Ellen and Caitlin were not there.

Corey looked all around the arena, thinking they had changed their seats, moved lower where they could see the sheep better.

They were gone. He must have just missed them, since he was certain they would have watched Ben show his sheep. Probably they had gone outside to get something to eat. He left the arena to look for Ellen.

Corey walked along a row of food booths, sniffing all the wonderful odors. Cotton candy. Hot dogs. Teriyaki stir-fry. Even though he was too full to eat anything more, it all smelled delicious.

He pressed his nose against the window of the funnel-cake booth. The cook squirted ribbons of batter in a circular motion into a vat of hot oil, going around and around in ever-larger circles, shaping each funnel cake like a miniature braided rug. The oil bubbled around them and the cakes quickly puffed up and turned golden brown. After each funnel cake was fried, the cook lifted it from the oil with a large slotted spoon, shaking the spoon to drain off the excess oil. He put the funnel cake on a paper plate, and sprinkled powdered sugar on it. Maybe, Corey thought, he could squeeze one funnel cake into his over-stuffed stomach.

Corey dug into his pocket and counted his money, dismayed to see how little he had left. How could it be gone so soon? He didn't even have enough to ride on The River of Fear. However, there was exactly enough to buy a funnel cake, and Corey did so, pointing at the cakes and holding up one finger so the cook knew what he wanted.

Tonight, he would ask his parents if they had some chores he could do to earn extra money. Maybe he could wash windows or mow the grass or weed the flower beds. If he could earn some money tonight, he and Nicholas could come back to the fair and ride The River of Fear together. Nicholas was sure to feel better by tomorrow and Corey's voice should be back by then, too. It would be great to ride and scream together.

He took a huge bite of funnel cake, sending a shower of powdered sugar down the front of his shirt. Yum. Chewing happily and making his plans for tomorrow, Corey strolled around the fairgrounds, looking for Ellen. She and Caitlin were not in the sheep barn; they were not on the merry-go-round; they were not in the Arts and Crafts exhibit, where Ellen always liked to go because she said it inspired her to make new things.

Some lumberjacks were putting on a show; Corey applauded as two men in spiked shoes raced to the top of a pole. He watched a man carve totem poles with a chain saw. The saw buzzed and whined as the man fashioned a bear from a cedar log.

When a loudspeaker announced that it was time for the pig races, Corey hurried with the crowd to a fenced area where five piglets waited to dash toward their food.

After the pig races, Corey returned to the sheep barn, intending to ask Ben if he knew where the girls were. Ben, however, was nowhere to be seen.

Corey decided he should call his parents, tell them what had happened, and ask them to come and get him. He hoped he would be able, with his hoarse voice, to make them hear enough to know what he was saying. If he couldn't, they might think it was a prank call and hang up.

He saw a public telephone at the front of one of the exhibit halls. He went there, picked up the receiver, and realized he needed a quarter before he could get a dial tone. He had no quarter. He had no money at all. Phooey. He probably shouldn't have bought that last funnel cake.

Well, he would just walk around and look for Ellen awhile longer. That would be more fun than going home, anyhow, and if he never found her, he could always go to a guard or the information booth and ask them to call his parents.

Corey wandered toward the merry-go-round. He liked the merry-go-round music and wished he had enough money to ride on one of the horses while he waited. He would choose the white horse with the blue and silver saddle.

"Win a genuine stuffed dinosaur! Only seventy-five cents!" When the merry-go-round stopped, Corey heard the man's voice and got angry all over again. If that man wasn't a crook, Corey would not have wasted so much of his money trying to win a dinosaur.

He decided to spy on the bottle booth. Maybe he could discover how the man cheated his customers. He would tell the police and they would come and arrest the man and the mayor would give Corey an award and all the other kids who tried to win a dinosaur and got cheated out of their money would come to the award ceremony and cheer and Corey would get his picture in the newspaper.

Corey sneaked along the narrow alleyway behind the food booths, darting quickly between buildings. When he was near the bottle booth, he crouched behind a large trash bin and peered out.

He wished he could disguise himself, so the bottle-booth man wouldn't recognize him. All the good spies he had read about wore disguises. He looked quickly around; no one could see him behind the trash bin. It was the perfect place to put on a costume, if only he had one.

Since he didn't, he would have to change his appearance as best he could. Corey picked at one corner of the Batman bandage, held it tightly and clenched his teeth. Taking a bandage off was worse than getting hurt in the first place. Silently he counted, *one, two, three*. On *three*, he yanked the Batman bandage from his face, wadded it up, and stuffed it in his pocket. Next he took off his T-shirt, turned it inside out so the zoo logo and the picture of the elephants didn't show, and put it back on. Using both hands, he mussed up his hair. He couldn't think of anything else he could do to change his appearance, so he peeked out and spied on the bottle booth.

As he watched, he heard The River of Fear spiel again. He wondered how it would feel to take the death-defying plunge down Whiplash Waterfall, to enter the Tunnel of Terror, and to meet the monsters of Mutilation Mountain. He would *have* to earn some money and return to the fair.

People kept walking between the trash bin and the bottle booth, making it difficult for Corey to see. He shifted and peeked out the other direction.

The woman and the boy who kept dropping his ice cream sauntered toward him. The child was licking another ice-cream cone.

Some people never learn, thought Corey, and just as he thought it, the boy tripped and fell, sending the ice-cream cone splattering into the dirt at the feet of a couple who were holding hands. The boy instantly began to cry. Corey watched as the couple tried to help the boy up but he only wailed louder.

Corey's mouth fell open in surprise. There was the man with the shopping bag! The thief! Corey stared as the man lifted a wallet out of the tote bag of the woman who was trying to help the boy. The man dropped the wallet into his MADE IN

THE U.S.A. shopping bag, exactly as he had dropped in the other woman's purse, earlier. The couple, their attention focused on the crying child, never noticed him. Neither did any of the people nearby. The kid was having a first-class tantrum over his ice-cream cone.

Corey leaped from behind the trash container. Waving both arms wildly and forcing unintelligible squeaks from his raw throat, he rushed toward the man with the bag.

CHAPTER

◇ 8 ◇

THE BOY stopped crying, pointed at Corey, and yelled, "Mom! Look!"

The helpful couple, who still did not realize they were the victims of a thief, looked at Corey in surprise.

The man with the shopping bag took one look at Corey and said, "That's him," before he whirled around, and ran. He wove in and out between people, elbowing them out of his way and not caring who he bumped into.

Corey rushed after him.

The boy said loudly, "Let's go home, Mom. I didn't want that dumb ice-cream cone, anyway."

The victimized couple looked at each other, shrugged, and walked away.

As Corey dashed past the woman and the boy who kept dropping his ice-cream cones, the woman put her hand on Corey's shoulder, stopping him.

"Is something wrong, little boy?" she asked. "Do you need help?"

Corey pointed toward the man and tried to say, "Thief."

"I'm sorry," the woman said. "I can't understand you. You'll have to speak up."

Corey tried to leave but the woman clung to his shoulder, holding him back. By the time he could push her hand off and dart away from her, the momentary distraction had caused him to lose sight of the man.

Where had he gone? Corey kept moving as he looked frantically for the thief. The man could not disappear into thin air.

◇ ◇ ◇

MITCH'S HEART thudded in his chest. He should never have let Joan talk him into this. He looked around for a trash can, planning to throw in the shopping bag, contents and all. If the kid caught up with him, there would be no evidence.

Instead, he saw a fair security guard sauntering toward him. Mitch's mouth went dry. That fool, Tucker! Not only did he miss the kid, he missed a guard, as well. He glanced upward at the platform where his brother was supposed to be keeping watch, wondering how his own flesh and blood could be so stupid.

The guard kept coming. Mitch couldn't turn back, not with that crazy kid after him. He didn't want to pass the guard, either. Impulsively, he ran toward The River of Fear platform. He would give the bag to Tucker and let him dispose of the wallet.

A flash of white above him made Corey look up. It was the shopping bag. The thief was halfway up the steps to The River of Fear.

Corey charged after him. There was nothing at the top of these steps except The River of Fear platform. The thief would be trapped up there and the man who runs the ride could call for help. Corey climbed as fast as he could, keeping to the right because people who had just been on The River of Fear were coming down. He wished he could still speak, to tell them he was chasing a thief. If they knew, they would want to stay and watch.

As he climbed, he heard the spiel and the roar of Whiplash Waterfall and the terrified screams of the people who were still riding. Too bad Nicholas wasn't with him.

On the platform above Corey, Mitch spoke rapidly to Tucker. "The kid's after me; why didn't you signal?"

"I never saw him," Tucker said.

"I have to get out of here," Mitch said.

"Get on the ride. No one can see you in there."

"How long does it last?"

"Five minutes."

"Just long enough for the kid to get a guard and be waiting when I get off," Mitch said. He glanced nervously over his shoulder.

"You could go down the back stairs," Tucker said, "the ones I use for maintenance."

"Good. Where are they?"

"You can't get to the back stairs until the ride stops."

"I can't wait!" Mitch stormed over to the edge of the platform, looked down, and stormed back. "The kid's coming up."

"Why did you come up here?" Tucker asked. "Why didn't you run into one of the buildings?"

"I didn't think he would see me come up here, but he did. I swear the kid has X-ray eyes."

"Let's put the kid on the ride."

Mitch's face relaxed into smile. "You're a genius, Tucker. It must run in the family. And once he's on it, in the middle somewhere, where he can't be seen or heard, you can stop the ride. Keep him inside for awhile until Joan and I get away from here."

"No problem," Tucker said. "This ride breaks down all the time; no one will think anything of it if I say it needs repair again."

"Get the other people off first. We don't want anyone helping him."

Corey clambered onto the platform. The thief stood on the far side. Corey went straight to the ride operator, mouthing the word, "Help!"

"What's wrong, sonny?" the man said. "Calm down now and tell old Tucker your problem."

To the right, a string of boats emerged from the main, enclosed part of the ride and stopped beside the platform. A group of shrieking, laughing people got off and started down the steps.

"Help," Corey repeated.

"Wait a minute," Tucker said. "I can't hear you."

Corey gripped Tucker's arm until the people were gone. Then he pointed at the man with the shopping bag and tried to say, "Thief." He wondered why the thief just stood there, with his back to Corey, looking down at the fairgrounds. Didn't he realize that Corey had followed him up the steps?

"Come over here, sonny," Tucker said, "where I can hear you better." He stepped closer to where people board the ride.

Corey followed. "Thief," Corey rasped again, as he pointed at the man.

The last customer went down the steps. The thief still looked away from Corey.

Tucker bent so that his face was level with Corey's. "Now then, sonny," he said, "what is it you want to tell me?"

Corey tried again to say, "Thief."

"Thief?" Tucker said. "Is that what you are saying? Thief?"

Corey nodded and pointed at the man's shopping bag.

"He steals things and hides them in the bag?" Tucker said.

Corey's head bobbed up and down vigorously. Someone finally understood him.

"You are a brave boy to chase a thief by yourself," Tucker said.

Corey grinned, glad that someone appreciated his courage.

"Get on with it!" The thief strode toward them across the platform.

Corey stayed close to Tucker.

"This boy claims you've been stealing, Mitch," Tucker said. "It isn't nice to steal things. Didn't your mother teach you anything?"

The two men grinned at each other.

How did he know the thief's name? Corey wondered. Why was the thief smiling? An uneasy feeling spread through Corey's insides. It was odd that the thief had just stood there while Corey talked to Tucker and odd that Tucker called the man by name and odd that both of them were smiling. Too odd.

He should not have followed the thief up here; he should have let that boy's mother help him or he should have found a guard. Corey took a step away from Tucker but Mitch quickly blocked his way.

Tucker turned some knobs on the control panel. The volume on the spiel boomed louder.

The stairs were the only escape route but Mitch stood between Corey and the stairs. Corey looked around him, forced a wide smile onto his face, and waved, pretending that someone had just joined them on the platform.

When Mitch turned to see who Corey was waving at, Corey made a dash for the steps.

As Corey darted past Mitch toward the top of the steps, two strong hands clamped down on his shoulders.

"Hey!" Corey squeaked.

Mitch spun Corey around, lifted him like a rag doll, and dropped him into one of the boats. Even if Corey had been able to make a sound, it happened too fast for him to say anything.

Corey landed with a *thunk* in the bottom of the boat. As he sat up, he saw the thief put his arm on Tucker's shoulder.

"Nice try, kid," Tucker said, "but you can't trick Mitch Lagrange that easily."

They laughed while Tucker pulled a large lever.

The River of Fear ride started. The boat Corey was in sped forward past the left end of the platform and into the enclosed part of the ride. Corey knelt at the bottom of the boat, clutching the sides.

Seconds later, he began his death-defying descent down Whiplash Waterfall.

CHAPTER

◇ 9 ◇

"GRANDPA?" Ellen whispered. "Are you here?"

Tick. Tick. Tick. Ellen had never noticed before that the clock on her bedside table made such a loud noise. She tried to ignore it, concentrating on the pencil and paper in her hands.

"If you can hear me, Grandpa, I need your help. I got a message today and I have to know if it is from you. If it is, could you please send me some sort of sign?"

Tick. Tick. Tick.

Ellen waited, hardly breathing. Surely, if Grandpa could hear her, he would grant her request. He would let her know, somehow, that he was there.

"I love you, Grandpa, and I miss you. We all do. It would help us a lot if you could send me a sign, to let me know you hear me."

The pencil was still.

Ellen sighed, opened her eyes, and looked at the clock. Six-fifteen. She had been trying for nearly half an hour without success. She pushed her chair away from her desk and stood up. Prince, Ellen's dog, woke up, stretched, and came over and sat beside Ellen. He lifted one paw, the way he did when Ellen told him to shake hands.

Absentmindedly, Ellen reached down to shake Prince's paw but as her hand closed around his foot, she stopped. Grandpa had taught Prince that trick. When the rest of the family had despaired of ever teaching Prince anything more than "sit" and "stay," Grandpa had worked with him day after day until Prince finally caught on. Whenever Grandpa came to visit, Prince always ran to him and shook hands.

Was that the sign? Had Grandpa told Prince to shake just now, or had Prince merely held up his paw to get Ellen's attention?

Feeling unsteady, Ellen put one hand on her dresser for support. She immediately pulled back when she realized her hand had inadvertently landed on the silver elephant that Grandpa gave her for Christmas last year.

"His trunk is up," he had told her, "which means he's holding good luck. Good luck for you."

Ellen thought she had never seen anything so exquisite. The lines in the elephant's hide, the tiny tail, the eyes—everything was perfect. She had worn it daily, until the accident. She had not worn it since. Why was her hand drawn to it now?

"Ellen! Dinner's ready." Ellen jumped at the sound of her mother's voice.

My nerves are shot, she realized, as she headed toward the kitchen, with Prince at her heels.

"I certainly didn't think Mrs. Warren would keep Corey and Nicholas at the fair this late," Mrs. Streater said, as she dished up salad. "They've been gone since nine this morning."

"You know how boys are," Mr. Streater said. "They probably begged to go on every ride."

"When I saw them, they looked like they were having a great time," Ellen said. "They didn't even stay to watch the sheep show."

"Do you know what Corey told me last night?" Mr. Streater said. "He said the reason he wanted to go on the rides was so he could scream a lot."

"I warned him about that, with his bad throat," Mrs. Streater said, "but I don't think he was listening. He was going on about some gruesome ride he plans to invent."

Ellen rolled her eyes while Mr. Streater chuckled.

"I thought they would be home in time for dinner," Mrs. Streater said.

"Corey will not be hungry after a day at the fair," said Mr. Streater. "Remember how much he ate last time?"

"When I saw him," Ellen said, "he had a big plate of curly fries."

"Julia Warren doesn't usually let Nicholas eat a lot of fatty food," Mrs. Streater said. "I hope she didn't let those boys go off on their own."

"You worry too much," said Mr. Streater. "Enjoy the quiet while you can; Corey will be home soon enough and then we'll have to hear every detail of his day at the fair. Twice."

"Mrs. Warren was with them in the sheep arena," Ellen said.

"Good."

Although Ellen tried to reassure her mother, it increased her own nervousness to listen to her mother's worries. The later it got with no sign of Corey, the more Ellen wondered if she should tell her parents about the message.

What if Corey wasn't home yet because he was in terrible trouble?

"Have some lasagna, Ellen," Mrs. Streater said. "It's Father's veggie recipe."

Ellen took the pan her mother handed her. Veggie lasagna. Grandpa's favorite meal—the only recipe that he personally ever prepared.

Ellen chewed the noodles, tomato sauce, cheese, and spinach. Was *this* a sign from Grandpa? Mom had not made veggie lasagna in months. Why did she choose tonight?

"I was in the mood to cook this morning," Mrs. Streater said, "so I made a double recipe and froze some."

This morning. It can't be a sign from Grandpa, Ellen thought. The lasagna was made this morning, before I got the message, before I asked for a sign. I'm getting crazy, thinking about this.

She tried to eat but nothing tasted good. "May I be excused?" she said and, when her mother nodded, she left the table and went back to her bedroom. She wandered aimlessly around for awhile, looked out the window, and finally picked up a magazine. She glanced at the cover and realized it was the magazine that Grandpa had bought a subscription to, as a treat when Ellen got all As on her report card. She put it down, refusing to let herself think that the magazine was a sign telling her that Grandpa was here.

She took the message out of her pocket and read it again. *It is for you to know that the smaller one faces great danger. He will pay for his mistake. It is for you to know that the paths of destiny can be changed and the smaller one will need your help to change his. You will know when it is time. Do not ignore this warning.*

Maybe, instead of trying to contact Grandpa, she should try to contact any of the spirits, just as The Great Sybil had the first time. Maybe the message was from Ellen's guardian angel. Or maybe it was from some other spirit.

Once again, Ellen picked up a piece of paper and pen. She sat at her desk, with the window shade down and the lights off. She closed her eyes, breathed deeply several times, and whispered, "Loving spirits, do you have a message for me? I come to you in love and friendship, asking for help to protect my brother."

She waited a few moments and then spoke again. "If Corey will need my help, spirits, please send another message and tell me when."

The pen jerked into action, rubbing the paper violently. It lasted barely two seconds. By the time Ellen could react, it was over.

She opened her eyes. The paper held a single word, printed in large capital letters that slanted to the left: URGENT.

The first message had said, "You will know when it is time." The second message seemed to say, the time is now.

The back of Ellen's neck prickled. It was no longer important to her who the messages might be from. What mattered was that Corey needed help, and he needed it now.

Trying to act calm, Ellen returned to her parents and said, "Something strange happened and I want to tell you about it."

Mr. and Mrs. Streater, alerted by the tone of Ellen's voice that this was no ordinary discussion, stopped what they were doing and paid close attention.

Ellen started at the beginning, and told every detail of her time with The Great Sybil. When she got to the part where

The Great Sybil asked if she had recently lost a loved one, Mrs. Streater said, "Oh, Ellen."

Mr. Streater said, "What hogwash! I'm surprised you would take such nonsense seriously."

"I thought the message might be from Grandpa," Ellen said, "so when I got home, I tried talking to him. I asked him to let me know if he was sending a message. I thought, if Grandpa's spirit is here, he could give me some sign."

Mr. Streater stood up and began pacing back and forth while Ellen continued.

"As soon as I asked for a sign," Ellen said, "Prince came over and put up his paw to shake hands. Grandpa taught him that trick. I didn't say, 'shake,' or give Prince any signal; he just did it on his own."

"Now, Ellen . . ." Mr. Streater began but Ellen continued to talk.

"Then I came downstairs and we had veggie lasagna for dinner, Grandpa's recipe. And when I looked around for something to read, I picked up the *Earth Watch* magazine that Grandpa gave me a subscription to and it seems like those could all be signs that Grandpa sent the messages." She didn't mention the elephant. It was the last gift Grandpa gave her and perhaps the most important sign of all but she didn't want to talk about it.

"Those were not signs from Grandpa," Mr. Streater said firmly. "They are only proof that a person lives on in the memory of his loved ones because of what that person did when he was alive. Grandpa will always be a part of your life and you'll think of him every time Prince shakes hands or you eat veggie lasagna or read your magazine or go to the zoo or do any number of other things that you and Grandpa did together." He put his hands on Ellen's shoulders and looked directly into her eyes. "They are memories," he said, "Not supernatural signs."

"But what about the messages?" Ellen said. "The first one might have been some trick that The Great Sybil did but the second one came when I was alone in my room."

"What second one?" Mr. Streater said.

"After dinner, I tried to contact the spirits, the way The Great Sybil did. I was worried about Corey and I asked the spirits to let me know if Corey needs help."

"And?" Mr. Streater said.

"And it happened again. The pencil moved by itself. It wrote, URGENT."

She held out the piece of paper and Mr. Streater looked at it. As he slowly sat down, he said, "I don't know what is going on here, but I don't like it one bit."

The telephone rang and Mrs. Streater answered.

"Hello?" she said. "He isn't here. Is this Nicholas? Where are you? Isn't Corey with you? Let me speak to your mother, please."

As Ellen listened to her mother's side of the conversation, her stomach began to turn flip-flops.

After she hung up, Mrs. Streater said, "Nicholas got sick and Julia brought him home. Corey stayed at the fair."

"What?" Mr. Streater jumped to his feet. "She left Corey there by himself?"

Mrs. Streater's voice, when she answered, sounded brittle, as if it would shatter into tiny pieces at any moment. "She thought Corey was with Ellen. She left him where they were showing the sheep and she said she knew you saw him, Ellen, and Corey promised to stay with you."

"I *did* see him," Ellen said. "But I saw Mrs. Warren and Nicholas, too. I didn't know they were going to leave without Corey."

"No one is blaming you. It was a misunderstanding."

"How long ago did they leave him?" Mr. Streater asked.

Mrs. Streater leaned against the table, as if she was afraid she would fall over without support. "Julia said she and Nicholas have been home since three-thirty."

Minutes later, Mr. and Mrs. Streater and Ellen were in their car, driving toward the fairgrounds.

Silently, Ellen urged her father to drive faster. *Hurry*, Ellen thought. *Please hurry! Corey is in terrible danger.*

CHAPTER
⬥ 10 ⬥

COREY GRIPPED the side of the boat, certain he was going to be flung out as the boat sped down the waterfall.

The boat had a seat, with a safety belt, and a metal bar that pulled down across the lap of someone who was seated properly. But the men had shoved Corey into the boat and started the ride before Corey could use the safety devices. He stayed on the floor, clung to the side of the boat, and tried to keep his balance as the boat rushed forward.

After the boat plunged over the crest of the waterfall, it twisted around curves, jerked upward, and then dropped straight down, as if a trapdoor had opened underneath it. Corey's knees left the floor and slammed back down. Corey had thought the roller coaster was exciting; this made the roller coaster seem like one of the kiddieland rides.

The boat zoomed around a curve and then slowed as it entered the blackness of the Tunnel of Terror. Corey blinked, trying to adjust his eyes to the dark. A huge hairy hand, holding a dagger, appeared just ahead. As the boat approached, the dagger, dripping blood, plunged toward Corey. Corey ducked, his heart drumming rapidly.

A cold wind blasted him from the right; when he looked, he saw a scarred, one-eyed face and heard a horrible laugh.

It's all fake, Corey told himself. It's just sound effects and tricks, like in the Historical Society's haunted house that he and Ellen helped in last Halloween.

A large wolf-like animal rushed toward him, foaming at the mouth. Just inches from Corey's boat, the wolf ducked down and then, as the boat passed, it leaped up again, snapping its huge jaws at Corey.

Corey leaned away from it, only to feel something slimy on the back of his neck. He gasped and twisted around. Wet seaweed dangled from above.

A sea serpent slithered partway out of the water; its claws reached toward Corey, trying to grab him and pull him into the water. The boat began to rock, throwing Corey violently from side to side.

Tears spilled down Corey's cheeks. Even if the sea serpent *was* fake, it was the creepiest thing he had ever seen. And maybe it was real. He no longer knew what to think or believe. He had thought the man who ran The River of Fear ride would help him and instead he was a crook, too, and maybe they were never going to stop the ride and let Corey get off. What if that was how they planned to keep Corey from talking to a guard? Maybe Corey was going to keep going around and around on the ride, diving down Whiplash Waterfall and through the Tunnel of Terror for the rest of the night.

And, he knew, there was more ahead. He knew, from listening to The River of Fear spiel, that if he made it out of the Tunnel of Terror alive, he still had to face the monsters of Mutilation Mountain.

The sea serpent's claws came closer. More wet, slimy seaweed dropped from the ceiling and brushed against Corey's face. No matter which way he turned his head, fingers of seaweed reached for him. Corey smelled a dank, moldy odor. He screamed his silent scream, knowing he wasn't making any sound, feeling the hurt in his throat, but unable to stop himself.

The boat bounced upward, as if the monster were underneath it. The serpent's face emerged ahead of the boat now, its evil eyes gleaming red, and Corey was positive the boat and the serpent were going to collide. The serpent opened its huge jaws, revealing sharp fangs. The boat moved closer.

When the boat was inches from the serpent's open mouth, the boat stopped.

The dim light went out; the serpent's eyes ceased to glow. Corey was surrounded by total blackness.

All sound effects ended when the boat quit moving. Corey trembled in the bottom of the boat, waiting to see what would happen next.

Silence.

Blackness.

For a few moments, he thought this was just part of the ride and that, after a moment of stillness, something loud and ferocious and terrible would jump out at him. He gritted his teeth and braced himself but when the minutes stretched on and nothing happened, Corey realized that the ride had stopped.

Had the man stopped it on purpose or was it broken again? Whatever the reason, it was no longer running.

Corey was stuck in the middle of the Tunnel of Terror.

◇ ◇ ◇

"NO," the woman in the fair office said, as she looked at the picture of Corey that Mrs. Streater had in her wallet. "He has not come to the office for help. I've been here since noon. Are you sure he didn't go home with a friend?"

"Positive," Mr. Streater said.

"Did you have a meeting place selected, in case you became separated?"

"We didn't bring him," Mrs. Streater said. "He came with someone else."

"The merry-go-round," Ellen said. "Last year, when we came to the fair, we agreed to meet at the merry-go-round, if we got separated. Maybe Corey is waiting for us there."

"I suggest you look there," the woman said. "Meanwhile, I'll alert the security guards to watch for him. What is he wearing?"

Mrs. Streater started to describe Corey's clothing. Ellen added, "He has a big Batman bandage on his cheek."

"I'll have the guards look for him," the woman said.

Mr. and Mrs. Streater and Ellen hurried to the merry-go-round. Corey was not there.

"Let's check all of the most likely places, before we panic," Mr. Streater said. "You know how Corey is. If he's having fun, he probably hasn't even realized what time it is. No doubt he is wandering around, making up some fantastic tale about carousel horses that fly or pretending he's won first place in every competition and will have his picture in the newspaper.

Ellen, you look in the sheep barn. Maybe Corey is hanging around there, watching Caitlin's cousin."

"I'll check out the rows of food stands," Mrs. Streater said. "He always wants to eat everything they sell."

"I'll do the midway rides," Mr. Streater said. "Meet back here as soon as you can."

Corey was not in the sheep barn. Ellen's panic increased. If I ever needed help from a guardian angel, Ellen thought, now is the time. And any spirits who cared to guide her to Corey would be welcome, too.

Ellen rushed out of the sheep barn and ran toward The Great Sybil's trailer. The small ticket booth was empty. A sign on The Great Sybil's door said, CLOSED FOR DINNER. BACK IN 10 MINUTES.

Ellen knocked on the door. When there was no response, she pounded as hard as she could. "Sybil!" she called. "It's Ellen Streater. I need your help."

The door opened an inch. The Great Sybil peeked out.

"My brother didn't come home," Ellen said. "We think he's lost at the fair, or else something has happened to him."

The Great Sybil opened the door and motioned for Ellen to enter. She sat on one of the chairs and Ellen sat on the other.

"I tried the automatic writing at home, by myself," Ellen said. "I got another message. It said: URGENT."

"Oh, my," said The Great Sybil. "The smaller one needs your help right now."

"The trouble is, I don't know how to help him. I don't know where he is or what has happened."

"Let us begin," said The Great Sybil, as she dimmed the lights.

"I don't have anything to write with."

The Great Sybil opened a drawer on her side of the table and removed a yellow legal tablet and a pencil.

Ellen held them in front of her and forced herself to breathe deeply, trying to calm her jangling nerves.

"We beg for your help, loving spirits," said The Great Sybil, without any preliminaries. "Ellen needs guidance. Please enlighten her. Let her know where her brother is."

Silently, Ellen added her own plea. *I know Corey is in danger. Please help me, spirits. Please help me find him before it's too late.*

Tears formed behind Ellen's closed eyelids and she squeezed her eyes tightly shut.

"We await your message," said The Great Sybil.

"Please hurry," whispered Ellen. It was hard for her to keep her mind focused on the spirits. Her thoughts kept darting back to Corey and the various possibilities of where he might be. Should she be out searching for him instead of sitting here, hoping for a message that might never come?

"We await your message," The Great Sybil said softly.

Ellen wondered how the woman could be so calm. Why didn't she simply yell, "Hey, spirits! We need help fast!" If the angels or spirits or whomever she was talking to were as wise and loving as The Great Sybil said, they would understand the need to hurry.

"Please enlighten us," The Great Sybil droned.

Ellen opened her eyes. She couldn't waste any more time. "Sybil," she said.

The Great Sybil's eyes remained closed. Her hands were clasped tightly together as she silently beseeched the spirits for help.

As Ellen stared at the fortune-teller, the pencil leaped into motion. It jerked quickly across the paper, writing frantically, as if her hand were the mechanical hand of a robot and, once programmed, there was no way to stop it.

This time, of course, Ellen didn't try to stop it. If the message would help her find Corey, it didn't matter how she got it. The spirits could make her stand on her head and write with her toes, for all she cared, as long as Corey was safe.

The writing stopped. The pencil dropped from Ellen's hand. As soon as The Great Sybil turned the lights up, Ellen read the message aloud.

It was the same back-slanted handwriting as before. This time it said, *It is for you to know that there is darkness in the tunnel. The little one sees not. The sign is untrue. Go inside the darkness.*

"The little one sees not!" Ellen said. "That sounds like Corey is blind." The tears that she had been trying to hold back now trickled down her cheeks. "Why can't the spirits talk in plain language?" she asked. "This sounds like they know where Corey is, so why can't they just come out and tell us, instead of making it into a riddle?"

"You must remember," The Great Sybil said, "that the spirits are no longer of this world. It may be extremely difficult for them to send any message at all in a language that we can understand."

"It says the sign is untrue," Ellen said.

"That puzzles me. What sign? Perhaps it means the other messages." The Great Sybil looked perplexed as she studied the piece of paper, shaking her head.

"I had some signs; I thought they proved the message was from Grandpa. This must mean they weren't signs from Grandpa at all; they were just memories, like my dad said."

"Do not sound sad to have memories," The Great Sybil said. "Happy memories are treasures to be cherished. If you remember good times with your grandfather, you can be with him in your mind whenever you wish. That is better than waiting for a sign, over which you have no control."

Ellen stood up. "I'm going to find my parents," she said. "If they haven't found Corey yet, I'll tell them about this new message. Maybe they can get more meaning out of it than we can."

"I will come with you," The Great Sybil said. "They will have questions for me."

Ellen nodded. "Thank you."

The Great Sybil locked the trailer when they left. She and Ellen hurried together across the fairgrounds, toward the merry-go-round. As they approached The River of Fear ride, Ellen stopped.

"Corey wanted to go on The River of Fear," she said, "and it has a tunnel. There was an article about it in the paper and Corey kept talking about the Tunnel of Terror and how he couldn't wait to see what was in it."

"The ride is out of order," The Great Sybil said, pointing to the CLOSED sign which hung at the bottom of the steps to the platform. "They've had trouble with it all week."

Ellen looked at the darkened River of Fear. The loudspeaker that had boomed the spiel across the midway earlier, when she and Caitlin walked past, was silent.

"Maybe he was on it when it broke," Ellen said. "Maybe he got hurt."

"There's a first-aid building on the fairgrounds," The Great Sybil said. "Let's go there."

They walked away from The River of Fear.

CHAPTER

· 11 ·

TUCKER KICKED The River of Fear control box. He did not like this plan. He did not like it one bit. It was easy for Mitch to tell him to stop the ride when the kid was inside the tunnel.

"Leave him in there until the fair closes," Mitch had said. "By the time you let him out, it won't matter how many cops he talks to. We'll be long gone."

"What about me?" Tucker said. "When he comes out, the kid will say I let you push him into the boat and the cops will start asking questions."

"Just say the ride malfunctioned. You lunged for the Off switch and I accidentally knocked the kid into the boat. Nobody can prove otherwise. All you have to do is act concerned and make a fuss over him. It'll be no problem. You'll end up looking like a hero for fixing the ride and rescuing the kid."

Tucker drank his coffee and looked at his watch. No problem. Ha. It was easy for Mitch to say, "No problem." He wasn't the one who would have to answer questions from the fair's security guards and the kid's parents and probably the cops and who knows how many others. Mitch and Joan would be off selling the loot and Tucker would be left to cover their tracks for them. He wasn't sure twenty percent of the profits was worth it. He suspected he wouldn't get the full twenty percent, either. He and Mitch might be brothers but there had never been a strong bond between them. Mitch had made that clear enough, when he refused to put up the bail last year when Tucker asked.

Tucker poured another half cup of coffee from his Thermos, sipping it sullenly. The kid was trouble. If he was smart enough to figure out Mitch and Joan's method of operation, he was smart enough to know that he was not knocked into the boat accidentally.

What if the kid said that Tucker threw him in the boat? What if his parents called the cops? What if the cops decided to run a check on Tucker and found out he was wanted in Oklahoma on that car insurance scam? What, then? Why should he risk going to jail while Mitch and Joan and that toady little Alan got off scot-free?

No! Tucker slammed his cup down on the control box so hard that coffee sloshed over the rim. No way was he going to take a chance on getting arrested again. He should never have tried to help Mitch in the first place but, now that he had, the only choice was to get rid of the kid.

He would turn the ride back on, right now, wait until the kid's boat came out, and let the kid get off.

He wouldn't say a word. He wouldn't pretend it had been an accident. He wouldn't lie and say the ride had malfunctioned.

He would help the kid out of the boat—and then the kid

would "accidentally" stumble and fall off the platform. The kid was short enough to go under the railing.

Tucker looked over the edge of the platform. There was no way a little kid could survive a fall from that height. It would be a horrible but completely believable accident. Lots of people stagger with dizziness when they get off The River of Fear ride; no one would doubt that the kid did, too.

Tucker himself would call for help. He would cry and go to pieces and tell how he tried to catch the kid before he went over the side. Tucker would give such a convincing performance that even the kid's parents would end up feeling sorry for him. And the kid would never tell them anything. Not ever again.

◆　◆　◆

COREY huddled in the bottom of the boat, waiting to see if it would start moving again. After a few moments, he sat up, keeping his hands in front of his face to protect himself from the slimy fake seaweed that now hung limply all around him.

With the eerie music and background noise silenced, and the boat standing still, it was easier to believe that it was only a ride and none of the evil creatures were real. Corey's courage returned.

He could think of two reasons why the ride had suddenly stopped: either it was broken again or else the man had deliberately stopped it while Corey was inside. The second explanation seemed most logical, since the man had forced Corey into the boat and pulled the switch before Corey could get out again.

The man wanted to get rid of me, Corey thought. The man

who ran The River of Fear ride was somehow connected with the thief. They threw me in here to keep me from telling the guards. Probably they plan to wait until the fair closes before they start the ride and let me off. By then, the thief would have stolen a million more wallets and purses and would be safely away from the fairgrounds.

I'll fool them, Corey thought. They think I'll just sit here in this boat and wait for the ride to start again. They think I'm a scaredy-cat baby who's afraid to do anything but wait. Well, I'm *not*! I'll get out and walk back through the Tunnel of Terror and climb out of The River of Fear ride and run past the man, down the steps, and call the police and tell them everything. They'll catch the thief and the ride operator and put them both in jail.

Corey put one hand over the side of the boat, easing his arm into the water. He leaned over, feeling for the bottom. It was concrete, and covered with algae but, as he had hoped, the water was only about eighteen inches deep. He could easily stand up in it.

Corey swung his legs over the side and stood up. The fake seaweed slapped at his cheeks. Water filled his shoes. Holding onto the side of the boat with one hand, he brushed at the seaweed with the other.

Since he wasn't sure how long the Tunnel of Terror was, he decided to walk back the way he had come. Gingerly, he took a step, holding one hand in front of him to feel what might be there. Corey's shoe slipped on the algae and as he tried to regain his balance, his foot splashed water, soaking his shirt. It was not going to be easy to walk.

He slid his feet forward, as if he were skiing, keeping one hand on the boat and one hand outstretched in front of his face. The tunnel was narrow, with barely enough room for him to move.

Slide, slide, slide. Three more steps. He passed the back of the boat and groped for the next boat in the line. Slide, slide. His left hand found a boat just as his right hand felt wet fur. Corey jerked his right hand back and then made himself reach out again. It must be the fake wolf. Corey inched closer, moving his hand across the wolf's body.

The animal blocked his way. He would have to climb over it, in order to continue, or else get in the boat beside him, crawl past the wolf, and then get back in the water. Corey put both hands on the wolf's huge back, and tried to pull himself up but his wet hands slipped on the fur and he couldn't get a good grip.

As he started to climb into the boat, the ride started up again.

The dim lights came on. Shrieks and screams filled the air. The wolf growled and lunged.

The boat zoomed forward, knocking Corey off balance. The wolf thrust its open jaws toward Corey, and Corey grabbed for the beast, to steady himself. His feet slid out from under him on the slippery wet floor and he fell backward, knocking his head against the side of the boat.

The last thing he saw before he lost consciousness was the wolf's jaws snapping closer and closer. Corey instinctively put an arm up, to protect his face. Then he closed his eyes and slithered downward toward the cold, black water.

◇　◇　◇

MR. AND Mrs. Streater returned to the fair office. The head of the security department told them an urgent message had been sent to all the security guards. One of them said he had talked to a small boy with a Batman bandage on his face when he responded to a report of a purse theft. According to his records, that had been at one P.M.

None of the guards had noticed Corey since then.

"It has been hectic all day," the woman in the office said. "We've had more thefts reported at the fair today than in all of the previous years combined. Today has been terrible! The security guards have been so busy that we called in extra help from the volunteer fire fighters."

"Something has happened to him," Mrs. Streater said. "I just know it."

"It's time to call the police," Mr. Streater said. "For all we know, Corey isn't on the fairgrounds any longer. He may have been kidnapped."

◈ ◈ ◈

AS ELLEN and The Great Sybil hurried toward the first-aid office, Ellen kept pondering the latest message. *The sign is untrue.* It sounded as if there had been only one sign, but she had thought there were several signs from Grandpa. Why didn't the message say, *The signs are untrue.*

Ellen stopped walking. "Sybil," she said, "what if that message meant a real sign? What if it meant an ordinary sign, with lettering, instead of a signal?"

"That's possible." The Great Sybil waved a hand in an arc, pointing at the booths and displays. "There are signs all around us."

"I wonder about the CLOSED sign," Ellen said slowly, "on The River of Fear. I keep thinking of that ride because of the word tunnel in the message. I just feel it's important."

"You should trust your feelings," The Great Sybil said.

"I'm going to go back there and talk to the man who operates the ride," Ellen said. "Maybe he knows something about Corey."

The Great Sybil nodded. "I'll inquire at the first-aid office," she said, "and then I'll return and meet you at The River of Fear."

Ellen turned and ran. The message mentioned a sign and a tunnel. The River of Fear ride had both. Maybe the ride had broken, as The Great Sybil thought, but instead of getting hurt, Corey was trapped inside. That would explain the part about darkness and not being able to see.

She knew that by now her parents were probably waiting for her at the merry-go-round, but it was important to talk to the man who ran The River of Fear ride as quickly as possible. He might not realize Corey was trapped. Probably all Ellen needed to do was tell the man her suspicions and he would help her find Corey. Mom and Dad would forgive her for taking so long when they learned that she had rescued her brother.

Ellen reached the CLOSED sign, stepped over the rope, and started up the wooden steps of The River of Fear. The lights on the ride blinked brightly and the spiel again boomed its message across the fairgrounds. The ride must be working again, although there were no other people on the steps. Ellen thought it was odd that the operator of the ride had forgotten to remove the CLOSED sign.

Above her on the platform, she saw the man who ran the ride. Hoping that he would be able to help her find Corey, Ellen climbed faster.

When she was almost to the top, the man saw her coming. "Go back down," he yelled. "This ride is closed."

Ellen continued to climb the steps.

The man met her at the top step. "Can't you read?" he said. "The ride is closed." He kept looking over his shoulder at the ride, as if expecting something to happen.

"I have to talk to you," Ellen said, "about my brother. I think he was on your ride when it broke down. I think he might still be in one of the boats."

The man's expression changed. Instead of looking annoyed at Ellen for ignoring his sign, he now appeared angry.

"Get out of here!" he yelled. "There wasn't any little kid on this ride."

He seemed furious with her. Ellen turned and started back down the steps. She had gone only two steps when she realized what the man had said. How did he know that her brother was a little kid? Ellen's brother might be a teenager or even an adult. Ellen had not mentioned Corey's age, yet the man instantly claimed there was no little kid on the ride.

Corey is, or was, on that ride, Ellen thought. Something happened to him, and the man knows it.

She went back to the top of the platform.

"My brother was on the ride when it broke," she said, "and I need to find him. Now."

The man turned and pulled a large lever. The River of Fear ride stopped. The sudden silence seemed ominous after the noise and lights.

"I told you to get off this platform," the man said. "If you don't leave right now, I will have you arrested for trespassing on private property."

"Where is Corey?"

"I already told you, I don't know anything about any little kid. When the ride broke, there were no people on it. Nobody. I realized in advance that there was a mechanical problem and I got everyone off safely."

"Corey's small. Maybe you missed him." Ellen peered around the man. The ride had stopped with one of the boats partially out of the opening through which they came at the end of the ride. "Maybe he's still in one of the boats. Why don't you start the ride again and let all of the boats come out?"

"No."

Ellen glared at the man. "Why not?" she demanded.

"I don't need to explain anything to you, girlie," he said, "but if you must know, I'm fixing a switch that isn't working right. It's probably going to take me the rest of the night so if you want to look in any of these boats, I suggest you come back tomorrow."

URGENT. The word flashed into Ellen's mind again. Urgent meant right now, not tomorrow. She wasn't sure what the man was trying to hide from her but she knew instinctively that he was not telling her the truth. She couldn't leave; not until she found Corey.

She lunged past the man and pushed the lever back up, starting The River of Fear ride again. If he wouldn't let the boats come out, she would do it herself.

The man grasped her shoulders, pulling her away from the control box. Ellen struggled briefly but quickly realized he was too strong for her. She quit fighting and said, "All right. I'll go. But I'll be back with my parents, and the police."

A look of fear flashed across the man's face and his fingers dug into her arms. "You should have left when I told you," he said. "Now you'll have to leave the hard way."

He shoved Ellen toward the side of the platform.

"Help!"

Ellen shouted as loudly as she could but with the spiel booming, she knew her voice would not be heard by anyone in the midway far below.

CHAPTER

◇ 12 ◇

THE Great Sybil was nearly to the first-aid office when she heard the voice inside her mind. "Help," it said. "Ellen needs help."

The Great Sybil stopped, feeling the gooseflesh rise on her arms, just as it used to do when she received her messages.

It had been so long, so terribly long, since she'd had a genuine message, that she was almost afraid to believe it was true.

Yet, she recognized the feeling instantly—the intuitive certain knowledge that what she was experiencing was a message from the spirits. The sensation was never there when she pretended to communicate. For all the years that she had postured and faked and bluffed, she had never once had this feeling of truth.

A thrill of gratitude ran through The Great Sybil. Her talent was back. She turned around immediately and raced toward The River of Fear.

◇ ◇ ◇

THE MAN pushed Ellen again, until her back was tight against the railing that surrounded the platform. Holding her arms against the railing, he kicked at her ankles, trying to knock her feet out from under her.

Ellen bent her head sideways and bit the man on the wrist, sinking her teeth in as far as she could. He gave a surprised cry of pain but did not let go of her.

As he kicked again at her ankles, Ellen raised her leg and aimed her knee at the man's groin.

He was too fast for her. He swore and jumped back, so that her knee barely touched his thigh. In doing so, he let go of Ellen's arms. She dodged his outstretched hand long enough to look at the line of boats which had now emerged at the end of the ride. They were empty.

The man's eyes followed her gaze and then, instead of grabbing for Ellen again, he stood and stared at the empty boats. Looking surprised, he pushed the lever to Off. This time, Ellen didn't try to stop him. She could see into all of the boats; Corey was not there.

"Are you satisfied now?" the man said. "I told you your brother was not on this ride. Now you can see for yourself. All the boats are here and there's no kid in any of them." He sounded relieved.

Ellen backed away from him, toward the steps. "You tried to kill me," she whispered.

"What?" The man laughed, as if that was the most outrageous statement ever made. "All I did was try to keep you from pulling the lever that operates the ride when I was still working on the switch. You could have been electrocuted."

Ellen watched him warily, fearful that he would grab her again but the man acted as if their struggle had never happened. "You tried to push me over the side," she said.

"Your imagination is working overtime, girlie," he replied. "First you claim your brother is trapped on my ride and then you think I'm trying to kill you. You'd better quit watching so much TV and get yourself a real life."

Ellen glared at him. It was not, she knew, her imagination. The man had tried to push her over the edge of the platform, though she had no proof, no witnesses. The question was, why? Corey was *not* in one of the boats, as she had thought. The man apparently had nothing to hide, so it did not make sense for him to try to get rid of her.

Unless, she thought, he was just as surprised as Ellen when the boats were empty. Maybe he wanted Ellen gone because he didn't want her to be there when Corey came riding out in one of the boats. When Corey didn't come, the man no longer cared if Ellen saw the boats emerge.

The possibilities swished around in Ellen's mind like clothes in a washing machine but it was hard to think logically when she stood within six feet of someone who had just tried to kill her.

The man's change of attitude when he saw the empty boats could mean only one thing: he, too, had expected Corey to be in one of them. Since he wasn't, it meant Corey was still inside the ride.

Go into the darkness, the message said. *The smaller one sees not.*

Ellen said, "I want to go in the Tunnel of Terror."

"Sorry. The ride is closed until tomorrow."

"I don't want to go on the ride. I want to walk inside the tunnel. There must be a way to get in there, to fix anything that breaks."

"You don't give up easy, do you, girlie?"

Ellen backed away from him. She didn't want to make him angry again. Despite his denials, Ellen knew he had tried to push her off the platform. It wouldn't help Corey to have Ellen crumpled in a heap at the bottom of the platform while this creep pretended it was an accident.

"I'm going," Ellen said. Without waiting for a response, she turned and began to run down the wooden steps. She had gone less than halfway down when she saw The Great Sybil step over the CLOSED sign and start up the steps toward Ellen.

"Are you all right?" Sybil called.

Two against one, thought Ellen. With Sybil to help me, I'll get inside the tunnel.

"No! Corey's somewhere in the tunnel and the man on the platform tried to push me off."

Sybil stopped climbing as she listened.

"Hurry!" Ellen cried.

Ellen went back up the steps two at a time, with The Great Sybil on her heels. When they reached the top, they stopped. Ellen looked around, astonished.

The platform was empty.

"He must have gone in the tunnel himself," Ellen said. "He's gone after Corey." Quickly, Ellen told her what had happened.

"I have not trusted Tucker Garrenger from the first day I met him," The Great Sybil said. "When I look at Tucker, I see a black aura and I always sense feelings of guilt."

"We need to go in the tunnel after him," Ellen said. "He tried to push me off the platform; he might try to kill Corey, too."

"We must get help," The Great Sybil said. "This is not a task for us; we need the police. Hurry." She rushed back down the steps.

Ellen hesitated, knowing it would be sensible to follow The Great Sybil and then return with police or guards. But how long would that take? Five minutes? Ten? Too long. She couldn't leave Corey at the mercy of the evil Tucker all that time. She would go after Corey herself.

◆ ◆ ◆

OPPOSITE the platform, on the far side of the boats, a maintenance door led to a set of stairs on the back side of the ride. The painted face of the door was part of the huge picture of monsters that served as a sign for the ride.

Tucker stood behind the maintenance door, with the door slightly ajar. The girl was talking to The Great Sybil. Tucker frowned. How was the fortune-teller involved in this? Was she the girl's friend?

The idea of someone being able to see into the future or talk with spirits gave Tucker the creeps. Now, as he saw Sybil hurry away while the girl stayed on the platform, those psychic abilities alarmed him.

What if the girl had told The Great Sybil how Tucker tried to push her off the platform? For all he knew, Sybil could see into the past, as well as the future. She was probably on her way to get the cops; maybe she would tell them that Tucker was wanted in Oklahoma.

He knew the girl was going to go inside the ride to find her brother and by the time she came out with him, Sybil would be back here with the cops.

I can't stay at the fair, Tucker realized. The girl will accuse me of trying to push her off the platform and the boy will say Mitch and I threw him in the boat and I'll never be able to explain my way out of it. They'll run an ID check and I'll be slapped in jail. I'll have to leave with Mitch and Joan. They can drive me to Portland and I'll find another job there.

Tucker ran down the steps on the back side of The River of Fear and headed toward the parking lot. He hated to leave without collecting his pay from the fair but he'd have his share of the profits from Joan and Mitch. That would be enough to get him by for a few days.

Tucker ran up and down the rows of cars in the parking lot, his panic increasing until he spotted the Mercedes. The motor was running; Mitch was waiting for a chance to pull into the line of cars leaving the fairgrounds.

Tucker ran to the car and pounded on the door. "I'm going with you," he said. "We have to get out of here, fast."

"What happened?" Mitch said, as he reached behind him and unlocked the back door.

"The kid's big sister showed up and now she's gone off with a fortune-teller to tell the cops about us."

"Big sister?" Mitch said. "Fortune-teller?"

Tucker got in next to Alan and told them what had happened.

"You really botched it this time, Tucker," Joan snapped. "Why didn't you warn us that the boy was there? If you had done your job, none of this would have happened."

"How could I warn you?" Tucker said. "You told me to watch for a kid with a Batman bandage on his face, wearing a T-shirt with elephants on it. That kid didn't have either one."

Joan sniffed. "You never got anything right in your life," she said. She looked nervously around the parking lot, checking to be sure no one had followed Tucker.

"That boy can identify me," Mitch said slowly. "You told him my name." He sounded astonished, as if he could not believe his own words. He also sounded terrified.

"It will take them awhile to find the boy," Tucker said. "We can still get away, if we hurry."

"What do you mean, it will take awhile to find him?" Mitch said. "Isn't he with his sister? I thought you said she came to get him."

"She did but when the boats came out, they were empty. The little boy must have fallen out of the boat. No telling if he's alive or not."

"And the girl?"

"She went inside the ride to look for him."

"If the girl is inside the ride, looking for her brother," Mitch said, "maybe we can get to her before she talks to anyone." He pulled into a parking space and turned off the engine.

"What are you suggesting?" Joan said.

"It would look like they both fell off during the ride," Mitch said slowly. "A terrible accident."

"Mitch!" Joan said. "You can't kill those children just to avoid a pickpocket charge."

"It isn't the pickpocket charge he's worried about," Tucker said. "It's the other."

Joan's eyes narrowed to thin slits. "What other?" she said.

"You talk too much, Tucker," Mitch said.

"What other?" Joan repeated. "The charge against Tucker in Oklahoma?"

"Hurry," Mitch said, as he got out of the car. "We have to keep those kids from going to the cops."

"There are other ways to do that," Joan said, "besides murder."

"I know what I'm doing," Mitch said coldly, "and if you had not insisted on working the fair, it wouldn't be necessary."

"Can I go with you?" Alan said.

"May I go with you?" corrected Joan. "No, you may not. You stay in the car and if anyone asks you where your parents are, you say we're coming right back. Is that clear?" She opened the glove compartment and removed a flashlight.

Leaving Alan to pout on the back seat of the car, Joan and Mitch strode toward The River of Fear ride, with Joan insisting Mitch was making a mistake and Mitch ignoring her.

Tucker followed, glaring at their backs. Why didn't they ask him what he thought? Mitch and Joan always made him feel like a bumbling six year old with no brain.

CHAPTER
· 13 ·

ELLEN WAS glad The Great Sybil was going for help; she had no doubt that it was needed. She was just as certain that she could not wait for it to arrive before she went after her brother.

Tucker's tool kit sat on the platform, next to the control box. Ellen opened it and removed a hammer. She wasn't eager to fight with anyone but if she needed to do so, she would have a weapon. Gripping it tightly in one hand, she stepped into the water of The River of Fear ride. She walked past the row of boats and into the enclosed ride where the boats immediately went over the edge of Whiplash Waterfall. Even with the ride turned off, she didn't see any way to go down the waterfall on foot. It was too steep and too slippery.

She returned to the boarding platform and then climbed into one of the boats and out the other side. To her left, she saw the outline of a door in the painted picture of monsters. She opened it and stepped through to the back side of the ride, the part the public never saw. As she had hoped, there was another set of steps. They were more like scaffolding than an actual stairway. There were also two landings, with doors that opened into the ride. Apparently, this was how maintenance was done.

She did not see the ride operator. Had he gone into the ride or had he run down these back stairs and left the area altogether? Maybe he had decided to make his escape before Ellen could go to the police.

Quickly, Ellen climbed down the scaffolding to the first door, which was less than a third of the way down. It probably opened to the middle of the waterfall part of the ride. Since the message specified the tunnel, Ellen continued down the steps to the lower door.

Putting her hand on the knob, she turned it as quietly as she could and pushed the door open. A dank, rotten odor drifted out of the darkness. Ellen put her hand over her nose and mouth, not wanting to inhale it. What was she getting into, anyway? Maybe she should wait for The Great Sybil to return with help.

Ellen peered into the blackness, blinking to adjust her eyes. Was Corey somewhere in that foul-smelling hole, in need of help?

She stood still, listening. If the man was in here, she thought she would be able to hear movement. She heard nothing. Quickly, before she could change her mind, she stepped inside, onto a walkway that extended into the ride. Noiselessly, she closed the door behind her so that if the man was still outside, he would not realize where she was.

It was completely dark and silent. Too silent. If Corey was trapped inside this tunnel, surely he would be calling for help. Unless, she thought, he's unable to.

The odor was worse with the door closed. Ellen kept one

hand over her face. The other hand, which held the hammer, she extended out in front of her. She took a step forward.

She wanted to call out for Corey but if Tucker was in here, she didn't want him to know where she was.

She took another step and another—and walked off into air. The walkway had ended. As she flailed her arms, grasping for something to break her fall, she dropped the hammer. She plunged down, landing in cold water that came partway up her leg. The hammer splashed somewhere in front of her.

Ellen stood in the water, feeling behind her for the walkway. It hit her at shoulder height. She bent her knees, testing her legs for injury. Although the fall had scared her half to death, she was not hurt.

If Tucker was in here he would have heard the splash as she fell; he would have no trouble finding her. She listened, turning her head, but still she heard nothing, no indication that anyone else was near.

The concrete floor under the water was slick and she realized that the damp, moldy smell which filled her nostrils originated under the water. It's like walking through the sewers, she thought, and shuddered.

She believed she was in the middle of the ride, where the boats go through the tunnel. If Corey had come into The River of Fear at the beginning and not come out at the end, he had to be somewhere in this darkness.

She moved forward carefully, feeling with one foot before she inched her body forward.

She went a few more feet and bumped smack into a huge, furry beast. Stifling a scream, Ellen stood perfectly still, waiting to see if the beast was real. Her brain told her: of course it is not real, it's only a prop for the ride. Although she believed her brain, she could not keep her heart from pounding wildly as she tentatively put out a hand and felt the creature's coarse fur.

It was a bear or a wolf or some other large wild animal. It did not move at her touch and she told herself again that it was only a fake. She moved her hands along the animal's back, toward its neck. When she reached the head, her fingers touched flesh. Warm, human flesh.

She jerked her hand away and, for one brief instant, swayed dizzily. It would have been a relief to faint. Instead, she clenched her teeth tightly together, took a deep breath, and reached out again. She had touched a human arm. She forced her hands to keep moving. A body lay on its stomach across the animal's enormous head, one hand on the beast's back, the other hand dangling.

The person, Ellen knew, was not part of The River of Fear ride. Fake bodies are not warm.

Like a blind person reading Braille, Ellen moved her fingertips across the body's narrow shoulders. It was a child. Corey? Ellen's breath came faster. There was a lump on the side of the head, as if someone—or something—had struck the person with a heavy object.

"Corey?" she whispered. "Is that you?"

She moved her hands more slowly as she reached for the body's face. It was easier to feel a shirt than bare skin. Her fingers inched carefully across an ear, toward the cheek.

Ellen froze for an instant and then patted the face frantically, feeling as quickly as she could. The Batman bandage was gone, but the scab of Corey's cut still slashed diagonally from cheekbone to chin.

"Corey!" she said. "Wake up!"

There was no reply.

Ellen slid her hand between Corey's chest and the back of the breast, feeling for a heartbeat. Before she knew who the person was, her touch had been tentative; now, her hands pressed firmly against her brother's T-shirt.

Was he breathing? She couldn't find a heartbeat. Remembering how her mother always took her own pulse when she was exercising by feeling the sides of her throat, Ellen quickly put her hands on Corey's neck.

Tears of relief stung Ellen's eyes as life throbbed beneath her fingers. He was alive. He was unconscious but at least he was alive.

She dipped her hands in the cold water and patted it on Corey's neck, slapping him lightly to try to rouse him. He groaned but did not wake up.

Ellen grabbed Corey's limp arms and pulled. "Stand up," she said, but Corey seemed stuffed with cotton. She would have to get him on her back and carry him.

She put her hands under Corey's arms, held tight, and lifted. He slid toward her, across the back of the beast. His feet splashed into the water, touched the bottom, and kept on sliding. Ellen staggered backward in the water, trying to keep her balance.

"Wake up, Corey," she pleaded. She had hoped to maneuver him onto her back and carry him out but in his unconscious state, he seemed to weigh two hundred pounds.

"Ohhh," said Corey.

Keeping her hands clasped tightly around his chest, to keep him from sliding further into the water, she tried to shake him. "Wake up!" she repeated.

Corey groaned again.

She tried to hoist him upward, across her shoulder, but he was too heavy.

I can't carry him, Ellen realized. I'll have to drag him out of here.

Still clutching Corey around the chest, she began to walk backwards through the tunnel. Corey's head hung down, with his chin on his chest; his feet trailed behind him in the water. She wondered how Corey got the lump on his head. Who hit him? How much damage was done?

Suddenly, Ellen remembered reading that an injured person who was unconscious should not be moved until a doctor arrived because there might be a spinal cord injury. It was possible to break the person's neck and cause permanent paralysis. Visions of Corey in a wheelchair flashed across her mind.

What have I done? she wondered. I should have left him where he was and gone for help. Well, it was too late now. She sloshed backwards, dragging the limp Corey with her.

Her arms ached and it was all she could do to hold onto him. Thank goodness the door she had come through was not too far. Her shoe slipped on the algae and she could not put her arms out to regain her balance. She sat down, hard, in the water.

She scrambled quickly to her feet and stood for a moment, with Corey's wet body pressed against her chest, letting the pain in her rear end subside. She was soaked and scared and sorry she had come into the tunnel alone. The man who ran the ride must not have come inside the tunnel looking for Corey, after all. If he had, he surely would have heard her splashing around and talking to Corey.

Well, she told herself, it won't do any good to stand here and cry. I have to get Corey to a doctor.

Mentally, she repeated part of her favorite childhood story: "I think I can, I think I can, I think I can."

She started moving again, toward the walkway by the door. She would not let herself wonder how she was going to get Corey up on the walkway when she reached it.

CHAPTER

• 14 •

WHEN MITCH and Joan, with Tucker on their heels, reached The River of Fear, the midway around it was empty.

"It's almost time for the fair to close," Tucker said.

"Maybe they're still inside," Mitch said. "Both of them."

He went around to the back side of the ride, to the bottom of the maintenance stairs. Joan followed. "I still don't think we should do this," Joan said.

"You're the one who wanted to work the fair."

"I wanted to lift a few wallets. I didn't want to kill any children."

"You don't have to."

Mitch climbed to the lower of the two doors. Joan hesitated and then climbed after him.

"If anyone comes," she told Tucker, "start the spiel."

Tucker did not answer. Why should he stand guard for them while they did this? There wasn't anything in it for him. He would be guilty of helping them and he wasn't sure they would get away with it. One kid falling off the platform was believable; a pair of kids falling off the ride was too unlikely. The cops were sure to be suspicious. And what about the fortune-teller? How much did she know?

A new plan hatched in Tucker's mind. He would wait until Joan and Mitch were way inside the ride. Then he would turn it on, send the boats whizzing through, and make Joan and Mitch fear for their lives.

He would leave Joan and Mitch in the ride and drive the Mercedes away from the fair himself. He would sell the valuables they had stolen, take the cash, and deliver the car to the stripper. That would show Joan and Mitch who was an idiot and who wasn't. If Alan had a fit, well, Tucker could always abandon him on some country road.

Tucker went around to the front of The River of Fear and climbed the steps to the platform. Smiling at his own cleverness, he stood beside the On/Off lever and waited. He wanted to be sure Mitch and Joan were far from the door, deep in the Tunnel of Terror, before he turned the ride on and left.

◈ ◈ ◈

THE Great Sybil burst through the door of the fair office.

"There are two children in danger," she panted.

A security guard, who had been pouring himself a cup of coffee to celebrate the fact that the fair was now closed for the night, put the cup down and snapped to attention. "Where?" he said.

"The River of Fear ride. They need help."

"Who are they?" the guard asked.

"Ellen and Corey Streater. Ellen almost got killed once and now she needs help again."

"Corey?" The guard reached for the two-way radio that hung from his belt. "Corey Streater?"

"That's correct," The Great Sybil said.

"That's the kid who is missing." The guard spoke into the radio. "All security personnel to The River of Fear ride," he said. "Fast. And have the Sheriff set up a roadblock. Check all cars before they leave the fairgrounds."

He ran out the office door; The Great Sybil ran after him. As the last of the fair patrons straggled out the gates, every guard on the grounds rushed toward The River of Fear.

◈ ◈ ◈

MR. AND Mrs. Streater stood next to the merry-go-round, watching as the attendants locked the ride.

"Ellen should have been here by now," Mrs. Streater said. "It doesn't take this long to look in the sheep barn."

Two guards ran past. Mr. and Mrs. Streater looked at each other and, without saying a word, ran after the guards.

◈ ◈ ◈

ELLEN staggered backwards through the slimy water until she reached the walkway. She looked up toward where she thought the door through which she had entered The River of Fear was. It might as well be a mile away, she thought. The edge of the walkway was shoulder high and there was no way she could lift Corey's inert body that far. She stood in the water, her aching arms holding her unconscious brother.

"Help!" she called. "In here! Help!"

To her astonishment, the door above her opened. Although she had hoped someone might hear her, she never dreamed anyone would happen to be close enough the first time she called for help.

"Down here!" Ellen cried. "I'm down here in the water."

A flashlight beamed downward; Ellen shut her eyes and turned her head away from the sudden light.

"It's both of them," said a woman. "The girl and the boy."

"Stay where you are," a man called. "We're coming to get you."

Tears of relief sprang to Ellen's eyes. These people must have been looking for her and Corey, and just happened to be close to the maintenance door when Ellen called out.

Splash! Someone jumped over the edge of the landing, dropping into the water beside Ellen and Corey. The flashlight still shone down from above. Ellen smiled gratefully at her rescuer, a dark-haired man in a dark blue shirt. "Corey's hurt," she said. "You'd better get him out first and come back for me."

The man did not reply.

Ellen's smile faded when she saw the way he looked at her. His eyes seemed cold, like steel marbles. His jaws were clenched and a muscle twitched rhythmically in one cheek as he moved toward her. With horror, Ellen realized he had not come to rescue them.

"Who are you?" she whispered. "What do you want?"

He put his hands on her shoulders, pushing her backwards. Ellen twisted, trying to get away.

She couldn't hold Corey up out of the water and fight off an attacker at the same time. If she let go of Corey and tried to escape, Corey would surely drown. If she didn't drop Corey, they were both going to drown.

Ellen screamed.

Whoever was holding the flashlight quickly shut the door.

◈ ◈ ◈

THE Great Sybil and the guard ran toward The River of Fear as other guards and police officers converged from all directions.

"The ride is closed," the guard said. "There's no one there."

"Go inside," The Great Sybil said. "They're in the tunnel."

"Are you sure?" said a second guard.

"We've looked everywhere for that boy," said a third guard. "We may as well check inside The River of Fear ride, too."

"Hurry!" Sybil implored.

As the guard ran toward the wooden steps to the platform, Tucker stood at the top, waiting for Joan and Mitch to get deep in the ride and dreaming about what he would do with his unexpected windfall. Intent on his plan to get even, he did not notice the guards hurrying toward him. He smiled, pulled the lever, and started the ride.

Inside the ride, the dim lights came on and the sound effects boomed into the darkness. Ellen stared at her attacker's face as she struggled to get away from him. The unexpected noise of the ride starting caused him to loosen his grip temporarily but, burdened as she was with Corey's limp body, Ellen could not move quickly enough to take advantage of the man's distraction.

Now he shoved Ellen again, trying to push her under the water. She staggered backwards, desperately trying to keep her balance.

Behind him, Ellen saw a boat enter the tunnel and come toward them.

The man yelled, "Joan! Tell Tucker to turn this thing off! What's he trying to do, kill us all?"

"Maybe he's trying to warn us that someone is coming."

The flashlight went off.

With the man momentarily inattentive, Ellen thought: This is my chance. As soon as the boat was close enough, she heaved Corey upward with all her might and dropped him over the side, into the bottom of the boat. She hoped she was not making Corey's injuries worse by dumping him into the boat that way but the alternative, drowning, was even worse.

The next boat approached; Ellen grabbed hold and swung one leg over the side. As her second foot came out of the water, the man's arms went around her waist and pulled with such force that Ellen was yanked backwards away from the boat.

"The boy's gone!" Mitch said. "He's in one of the boats."

Ellen kicked furiously and, twisting out of his grasp, dropped to her hands and knees on the slimy bottom.

"Joan! Get down here and help me," Mitch said. "She's slippery as a bar of soap."

As he grabbed for her, Ellen ducked away from him and crawled under the walkway.

Joan tiptoed out the door. Instead of telling Tucker to turn the ride off, she hurried down the back steps, and ran toward the car. Mitch was going to drown that girl just to keep the cops away from Tucker. And if she stayed here, she'd be an accomplice.

Picking a few pockets had been fun, and stealing cars and parting them out was lucrative. But Joan drew the line at murder. Especially a kid. She had never seen Mitch act this way. He liked kids. He'd always been good to Alan. That's one reason Joan had married him; she knew Alan needed a man in his life. But Alan did not need a man who was wanted for murder.

When Joan didn't answer him, Mitch dropped to his knees in the filthy water and began reaching under the platform.

"I know you're under there," he said.

CHAPTER

◈ 15 ◈

TUCKER KEPT his hand on the lever for a few seconds after he pulled it, imagining the scene inside the ride. As he turned to leave, Joan dashed from behind The River of Fear and started across the midway. Tucker stared down at her, confused. Where was she going? Where was Mitch? Why didn't she signal to Tucker?

The two of them were cutting him out! The thought hit him like a snowball striking the back of his neck, sending shivers of shock down his spine. It was the only logical explanation why Joan would run away like that. Mitch must be ahead of her. Joan and Mitch did the dirty work and then, instead of coming up the platform for Tucker, they beat it back to their fancy-dancy Mercedes and left Tucker to take the rap.

Well, he would not let them get away with it. The fact that *he* had planned to cut *them* out did not lessen Tucker's outrage as he rushed down the steps, arriving at the bottom just as three patrol cars pulled up. Two officers got out of each car.

For a moment, Tucker stood frozen with fright. Then he said, "The ride has malfunctioned. It won't stop until I go to the main electrical center and trip the fuse." To his vast relief, the officers did not detain him.

Tucker broke into a trot, headed for the parking lot and the Mercedes. He had to get there before Mitch and Joan drove off.

They tricked me, Tucker thought bitterly, as he ran. They got me to stand guard and then they left me to face the cops alone.

An ambulance sped past, its red lights whirling.

Each time his feet hit the pavement, Tucker grew more furious. His own brother had cut him out.

At the far end of the parking lot, a line of cars waited to exit. There, almost at the end of the line, was the Mercedes, with Joan behind the wheel. Tucker pounded on the locked door until Joan rolled down her window.

"Let me in," Tucker said.

"What do you want?"

"I'm going with you. I want my cut." He reached through Joan's open window, unlocked the back door, and climbed into the back seat. Then he saw that Alan sat in front with Joan and the back seat was empty.

"Where's Mitch?" he asked.

"He's meeting us later," Joan said.

Tucker stared at the back of Joan's head. "You left him, didn't you?" he said, unable to keep the amazement out of his voice. "You left your own husband to take the rap."

"Shut up, Tucker. There won't be any cuts for any of us if we don't get out of here soon. This traffic is terrible."

"What if the cops find him?"

"Mitch can talk his way out of anything. He'll catch up to us in Portland."

"You can't let the cops take Mitch in," Tucker said. "What if they fingerprint him?"

"What if they do? Mitch doesn't have a record."

"He never told you?"

Joan swiveled around so she could see Tucker's face. "Told me what?"

"Nothing," Tucker said. "Forget I said that."

"Told me *what*?"

Tucker wiped the perspiration off his brow and looked out the window. "I thought you knew," he said. "I just assumed Mitch had told you."

"Tucker!" Her voice hissed, like a poisonous snake. "If you don't tell me, right now, what you are talking about, I will turn you in to the cops."

Tucker pointed at the back of Alan's head.

"Alan," Joan said, "get out and go see if you can figure out why traffic isn't moving."

"I want to hear about Mitch."

"Go!"

Alan opened the car door and walked off.

"Ten years ago," Tucker said, "Mitch was convicted of armed robbery and assault. After the trial, while he was being transferred from the county jail to a state prison, he escaped; he got away from two guards and was never caught. He lost thirty pounds, had plastic surgery on his nose, cut his hair short, and changed his name."

"His name?" Joan said. "Mitch Lagrange is not his real name?"

"No. His real name is Michael Garrenger."

"I married someone called Mitch Lagrange."

Tucker was sorry he had spilled his brother's secret but it was almost worth it to hear the shock in Joan's voice.

Alan rushed back to the car. "You know why we're going so slow?" he said. "It's because there are cops up ahead, and they're checking every car."

◇　◇　◇

ELLEN heard splashing as the man moved beside the edge of the walkway. She couldn't see his face but she sensed that he was peering under the walkway every few feet, trying to see where she was.

The thick algae squished up between her fingers as she crawled through the water. The foul smell was worse under the walkway, where the water was more stagnant. She wondered if the smell was part of the scary effect of The River of Fear or merely the result of poor maintenance.

This water is probably full of germs, she thought, and gagged at the idea of crawling on her hands and knees through zillions of wriggling creatures, all carrying terrible diseases.

She heard another row of empty boats enter the tunnel. They moved quickly, so there was no time to form a plan or consider where the man was standing. As the boats went past, Ellen sprang out from under the walkway, grabbed the side of a boat and jumped headfirst into the bottom of the boat.

She almost made it. She landed in the bottom of the boat but couldn't get her legs tucked in fast enough. The man grasped her ankles and tugged. Ellen kicked, trying to free herself. The man ran along beside the moving boat, yanking on her legs.

Ellen grabbed the safety bar but her hands were slippery

from crawling around in the algae and when the man tugged harder, she was unable to keep her grip. He pulled her up and over the edge. Although she tried desperately to cling to the side of the boat, it slid away from her outstretched fingers.

The man held fast to her ankles and Ellen fell face downward into the water. Immediately, she felt a foot on her shoulders, holding her under.

CHAPTER

◆ 16 ◆

ELLEN TWISTED and kicked. The foot moved off her shoulders but now the man's hands pressed hard on the back of her head. Ellen felt as if her lungs would burst like popped balloons if she didn't get some air soon.

Help! she screamed in her mind. Grandpa! Guardian Angel! Spirits! Anyone! Help me!

But even as she pleaded, Ellen knew that she would have to help herself.

Empty boats streaked past beside her, so close, yet so unreachable.

Frantically, Ellen scooped a fistful of algae from the bottom and flung it over her shoulder at the man. He was leaning over her, holding her head down. The foul-smelling algae hit him in both eyes, temporarily blinding him.

Cursing, he let go of Ellen in order to wipe the algae from his face. She scrambled to her feet, gulped air, and dove into the last boat in the row.

As she rode away from him, she heard him yell, "Joan! Where are you? Turn on the light!"

A short distance ahead, the wolf lunged low toward the side of the boat, then raised its head as the boat passed, snapping its huge jaws.

Ellen realized that when Corey had been knocked unconscious, the wolf's head must have come along just at the right moment to lift Corey and raise his limp body up, keeping him out of the water. When the ride stopped, Corey still lay on the wolf's head. If the wolf had not been there, Corey would surely have drowned in the foul water.

Her boat passed the enormous beast. Instead of being scared of the vicious-looking creature, Ellen felt like hugging it.

She continued on through the Tunnel of Terror and past all the horrible monsters of Mutilation Mountain. Under ordinary circumstances, she would have been scared silly by the Dracula, werewolf, and other horrid creatures. This time, she barely noticed them. She was too shaken by her encounters with real danger to be frightened by anything fake.

After what seemed like an hour, she emerged at the top of The River of Fear platform. It was crowded with people.

"There she is! Ellen's here!"

Ellen recognized The Great Sybil's voice.

Below, the red lights of an ambulance flashed around and around near the bottom of the steps.

A police officer and The Great Sybil helped Ellen climb out of the boat. The officer turned the ride off.

"Corey's in one of the other boats," Ellen said. "He's unconscious."

"We already found him," the officer said. "A paramedic is

examining him now." He called over the side of the platform. "Mrs. Streater! Mr. Streater! Your daughter is safe!"

Below her, Ellen saw her parents standing next to two men in white jackets. Corey lay on a stretcher beside them.

Her parents waved at her and then bent over Corey again.

"What happened?" The Great Sybil said.

"A man inside The River of Fear tried to kill me," Ellen said. She started to shake. Her teeth chattered as if it were a freezing December night instead of a balmy August evening.

"Here." The Great Sybil removed the fringed shawl that she had on and wrapped it around Ellen's shoulders.

"I'm not really cold," Ellen said. "I don't know why I'm shivering."

"Nervous reaction," said the police officer. "Who tried to kill you? How?"

The officer raised his eyebrows but listened intently as Ellen told exactly what had happened inside The River of Fear ride. Partway through her story, he directed two other officers to look for suspects on the maintenance stairway on the back side of the ride.

"It was Tucker Garrenger," The Great Sybil said. "He's the only one who would know to go inside the ride." She frowned. "I can't think who the woman would be, though."

"Who is Tucker Garrenger?" the officer said.

"He's been running this ride," The Great Sybil said, "and I haven't trusted him from the very first."

"The man inside wasn't the man who was running the ride," Ellen said. "The man who tried to drown me wasn't the same man who tried to push me off the platform."

"*Two* men tried to kill you?" the officer said.

Ellen nodded. She didn't blame the officer for looking dubious; she could hardly believe it herself.

"The man in the water," Ellen said, "was average height and build and he had thick, dark hair. And evil eyes." She shivered harder, remembering how the man had looked at her. "And he kept talking to someone named Joan."

The siren on the ambulance bleeped. Ellen jumped at the sudden sound and then quickly looked down. The medics were sliding the stretcher bearing Corey into the ambulance.

Corey lay still as stone. Mrs. Streater climbed in the back of the ambulance and knelt beside Corey. Mr. Streater looked up, waved at Ellen, and pointed to the ambulance before he, too, climbed in.

Ellen waved back. Her parents were going to accompany Corey to the hospital. It must be serious, for both of them to go, leaving her here. Even though they could see that she was unharmed and did not need their assistance, it was unlike her parents to take off like that without explaining to her first.

And what about the Streaters' car? Dad must be in a terrific hurry to get to that hospital, if he was leaving his car at the fairgrounds, to be retrieved later.

Ellen knew that the police officers or The Great Sybil would be sure that Ellen got safely home. Maybe Dad had arranged for the police to drive Ellen to the hospital when they finished questioning her. Even so, she trembled harder as she watched both of her parents and her brother leave the fairgrounds in an ambulance, its siren wailing and its red lights flashing. Surrounded by people, Ellen felt completely alone.

CHAPTER

◆ 17 ◆

MITCH SPAT into the water and wiped more algae from his face. "They got away," he muttered. "Both of them."

The only sound was the splash of the boats in the distance and the noises of the scenes in the tunnel.

Mitch sloshed through the foul-smelling water toward the landing. Joan had said maybe someone was coming. She must have slipped outside to watch and listen. Or maybe she had gone back up the steps to tell that idiot Tucker to turn the ride off. Mitch could not imagine what had possessed Tucker to turn the thing on in the first place. Tucker knew Mitch and Joan were inside; what was he thinking?

Furious, Mitch hoisted himself onto the landing and pushed open the door. "Joan?" he whispered.

Where was she?

He heard voices now, excited voices. A loud babble came from the front side of The River of Fear. He had to get out of there before the girl talked to anyone.

"Joan?"

If she had climbed up to tell Tucker to turn the ride off, she would be on the front side of the ride by now. Surely, if the voices were guards or cops, Joan would hightail it back to warn him. Unless she couldn't. Maybe Joan had no choice but to talk to them, too. She'd figure out some lie, some way to throw them off the track until Mitch got away. He just hoped that idiot, Tucker, kept his mouth shut and let Joan do the talking.

Silently, keeping as close to the back side of the ride as he could, Mitch glided down the maintenance steps. When his feet were on solid ground, he looked around carefully, still hoping to find Joan waiting for him. He didn't like going to the car without her. He decided to wait a few minutes, just in case she returned.

There were more voices now and lights shone over the top of The River of Fear. Mitch chewed on his lip and wished he could light up a cigarette.

A siren shrieked. Mitch jumped at the sudden, close sound. Sirens, any kind of sirens, were bad news. He could wait no longer. Joan had probably gone back to the car and was waiting for him there.

Mitch hurried through the darkness, away from the back of The River of Fear. His mind raced ahead to what he would do if Joan was *not* waiting in the car. Should he take Alan and leave, trusting Joan would contact him through their man in Portland? Or maybe her mother. Joan could always go to her mother's place, knowing Mitch would eventually come for her there.

He concentrated so hard on his own thoughts that he did not hear the footsteps behind him. When the police officer spoke, Mitch tried to run but by then it was too late. A second officer quickly cut him off.

"We'd like to talk to you," one officer said.

Mitch silently cursed himself for hanging around so long, waiting for Joan.

"How did you get so wet?" the older officer, Sergeant Hall, said. "Your clothes are soaked, clear to your waist."

"Some kid spilled his Coke on me. I tried to wash it out in the rest room."

"Sure."

Mitch said, "I'm a hard working, law-abiding citizen and if you don't have anything better to do than harass me, I suggest you let me be on my way before I file suit for unlawful arrest."

The two officers exchanged a glance. "Something doesn't add up," Sergeant Hall said. "Why would he try to kill some girl he doesn't know? What is he hiding?"

"I'm not hiding anything," Mitch said, "and I certainly did not try to kill anyone."

"I want a fingerprint check," Sergeant Hall said.

"I want a lawyer," Mitch replied.

The younger officer began to read Mitch his rights.

◈ ◈ ◈

ELLEN RODE in the back seat of the police car, with Sybil beside her. She felt disconnected from reality, as if she were watching herself in a home video. People in the cars they passed peered curiously in the window at her, no doubt wondering what crime she had committed. If Ellen had not been so worried about Corey, she would have enjoyed the adventure.

The police car pulled into the hospital's emergency entrance and dropped Ellen and Sybil off. The admitting clerk gave them directions to a family waiting area. When they got there, it was empty. Ellen paced nervously until, a few minutes later, Mrs. Streater came in. She hugged Ellen and said, "They're X-raying Corey now. He's still unconscious."

Ellen introduced The Great Sybil to her mother.

"I'm going in to stay with Corey," Mrs. Streater said. "I'll come back as soon as I know anything."

A nurse stopped to tell them there was free coffee, tea, or cocoa in the small kitchen adjoining the waiting area. After Ellen got a cup of cocoa and The Great Sybil fixed some tea, they returned to the waiting room.

"I've finally quit shaking," Ellen said.

"You had a terrible scare."

"If you had not helped me get the last message about the sign and the tunnel," Ellen said, "we would not have found Corey in time. How can I ever thank you?"

"You already have. Because of you, my psychic gifts have been returned to me."

"Me?" Ellen said. "What did I do?"

"You made me care enough to try to help with no thought of benefit for myself." She told Ellen how she received the word *help* as a message.

"Who sent it?" Ellen asked.

The Great Sybil smiled and shrugged. "Maybe the same spirit who sent your messages."

"I wish I knew who that was," Ellen said. "Without the messages, we would never have thought to look for Corey in The River of Fear. Who helped us?"

"Who helped us? Your grandfather? God? A guardian angel? Who knows?" The Great Sybil sipped her tea and gazed out the window. "Some questions have no answers," she said. "They only have possibilities."

"I'd like to believe my messages were from Grandpa," Ellen said, "but since there's no way to prove it, I'm not going to try to get any more messages. I have my memories of Grandpa and that is enough."

"You are wise, just as your name implies."

Mr. Streater hurried into the waiting room. "Corey's awake," he said. "He woke up as he was leaving the X-ray room."

Feeling giddy with relief, Ellen hugged her father. Then, for good measure, she hugged The Great Sybil, too.

"There's something wrong with his voice," Mr. Streater said, "but the doctors don't think it's related to the bump on his head. They're getting Corey settled in a room now; you can see him in a few minutes."

The Great Sybil said she would stay in the waiting room but Ellen insisted that she go in to see Corey, too. "If it weren't for you," she said, "Corey might not be alive."

They found Corey lying in bed, sucking on lemon throat lozenges.

"He has a concussion," Mrs. Streater said, "but the doctors think there will be no lasting problems."

"What about his voice?" Ellen asked.

"He screamed too much at the fair," Mrs. Streater said.

Laughter bubbled out of Ellen as she looked at Corey.

The police officer who had driven Ellen and The Great Sybil to the hospital came into Corey's room. "I thought you would like to know that Tucker Garrenger was picked up when he tried to leave the fairgrounds with a woman driving a stolen

Mercedes. It turns out he was wanted in Oklahoma on an insurance fraud charge."

"I'm not surprised," The Great Sybil said. "He had guilt written all over him."

"We suspect the woman, Joan Lagrange, and her husband are responsible for a string of car thefts in recent weeks, both in Seattle and Vancouver, British Columbia."

"What about the man who tried to drown me?" Ellen asked.

"That was Joan's husband, Mitch. We caught him behind The River of Fear ride. His real name is Michael Garrenger; he's Tucker's brother. When we put his fingerprints into the system, we learned the F.B.I. has been looking for him for years."

"I knew it!" rasped Corey. "I told the guard that the man with the shopping bag was wanted by the F.B.I. I bet that woman whose purse he took was really a movie actress in disguise, too."

"Hush, Corey," Mrs. Streater said. "Save your voice."

"So they tried to kill Ellen to avoid being questioned by the police," The Great Sybil said.

"What about the things they stole?" Corey said. "The purse and the wallets?" The throat lozenges were helping; he could actually be understood.

"It was all in the trunk of the car," the officer said. "We found cameras, purses, even a cellular telephone. There were shopping bags full of stolen goods."

"White shopping bags," squeaked Corey triumphantly, "with blue and red lettering on the side, just like I said." He coughed and put another lozenge in his mouth.

"Joan's nine-year-old son helped them pick pockets," the officer said. "He dropped his ice cream, to distract the victims."

The officer shook his head sadly. "He'll go into a foster home now. I hope it isn't too late to straighten him out."

A doctor came in to check Corey.

"When can I go home?" Corey asked.

"It's a little early to say," the doctor said. "Probably a day or two."

"I have to leave tomorrow morning," Corey said, "while the fair is still on."

"Surely you don't want to go back to the fair, after all that happened," The Great Sybil said.

"I have to spy on the bottle-booth man," Corey said. "He is cheating."

"This family," said Mrs. Streater, "will be the death of me."

"You've done quite enough spying," said Mr. Streater. "You'll have to wait until next year to go to the fair again."

"Will you be back next year?" Ellen asked The Great Sybil.

The Great Sybil shook her head. "The Great Sybil is retiring. From now on, I'm just plain Sybil."

"No more contacting the spirits?" Ellen asked.

"No. At least, not for money."

"Next year," whispered Corey, "I'm going to ride The River of Fear before I ride the roller coaster, so I can be sure to scream loud."

"Next year," said Mrs. Streater firmly, "you are going to the fair with us and we are staying far away from The River of Fear."

"But I never got to see the monsters of Mutilation Mountain," Corey said.

"They were stupid," said Ellen. "Just a bunch of werewolves and Dracula look-alikes."

"*You* went on The River of Fear?" In his astonishment,

Corey started to sit up, then groaned and lay back down again.

"I didn't have much choice," Ellen said.

"Were you scared?"

Ellen thought about the fake monsters and started to say, *no*. Then she remembered the face of Mitch Lagrange as he shoved her backwards into the dark water.

"I was scared," she said. "I was absolutely terrified."

Corey smiled happily. "I can hardly wait for next year," he said.

EPILOGUE

THE HALL clock chimed once.

One o'clock in the morning. Ellen was astonished to realize she had whispered into the darkness for a whole hour. In all that time, she had never had any reason to think that Grandpa's spirit heard her, yet she felt serene for the first time since the day of the accident.

"Thanks for listening, Grandpa," Ellen said. "I miss you and love you. I always will."

She opened her hand, feeling in the dark for the ends of the silver chain. Holding one end in each hand, she reached behind her neck and fastened the clasp.

She slid back into bed, letting the silver elephant remain on the outside of her nightgown.

Her anger that Grandpa had been cruelly snatched away, his life snuffed out like a heel grinding a match, was gone. In its place was the belief that Grandpa had merely crossed an invisible line into a new state of being.

Ellen could not begin to imagine where he was or how he looked. Oddly, it didn't matter. As Sybil said, some questions don't have answers. They only have possibilities.